RUN,
ODDS,
RUN

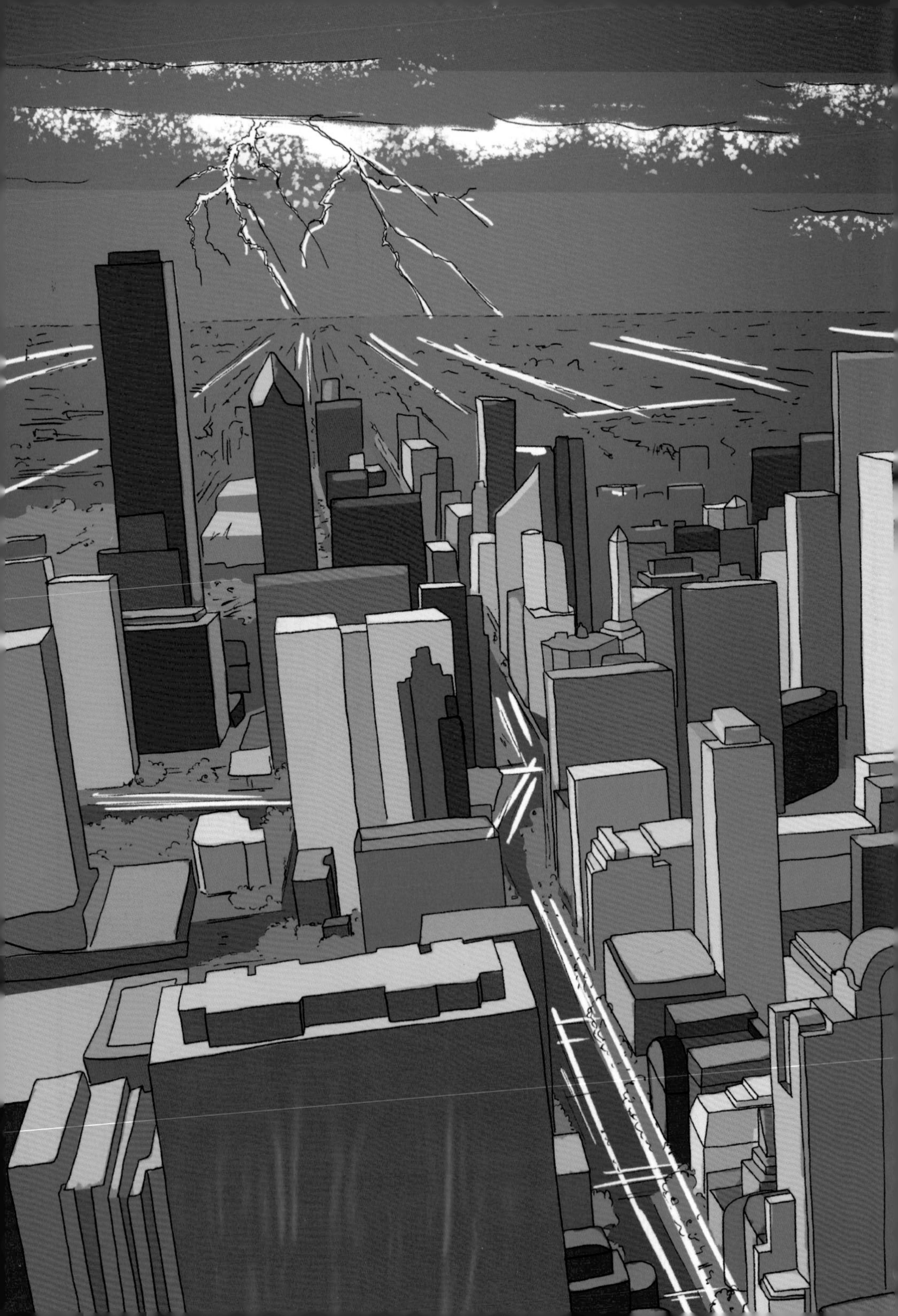

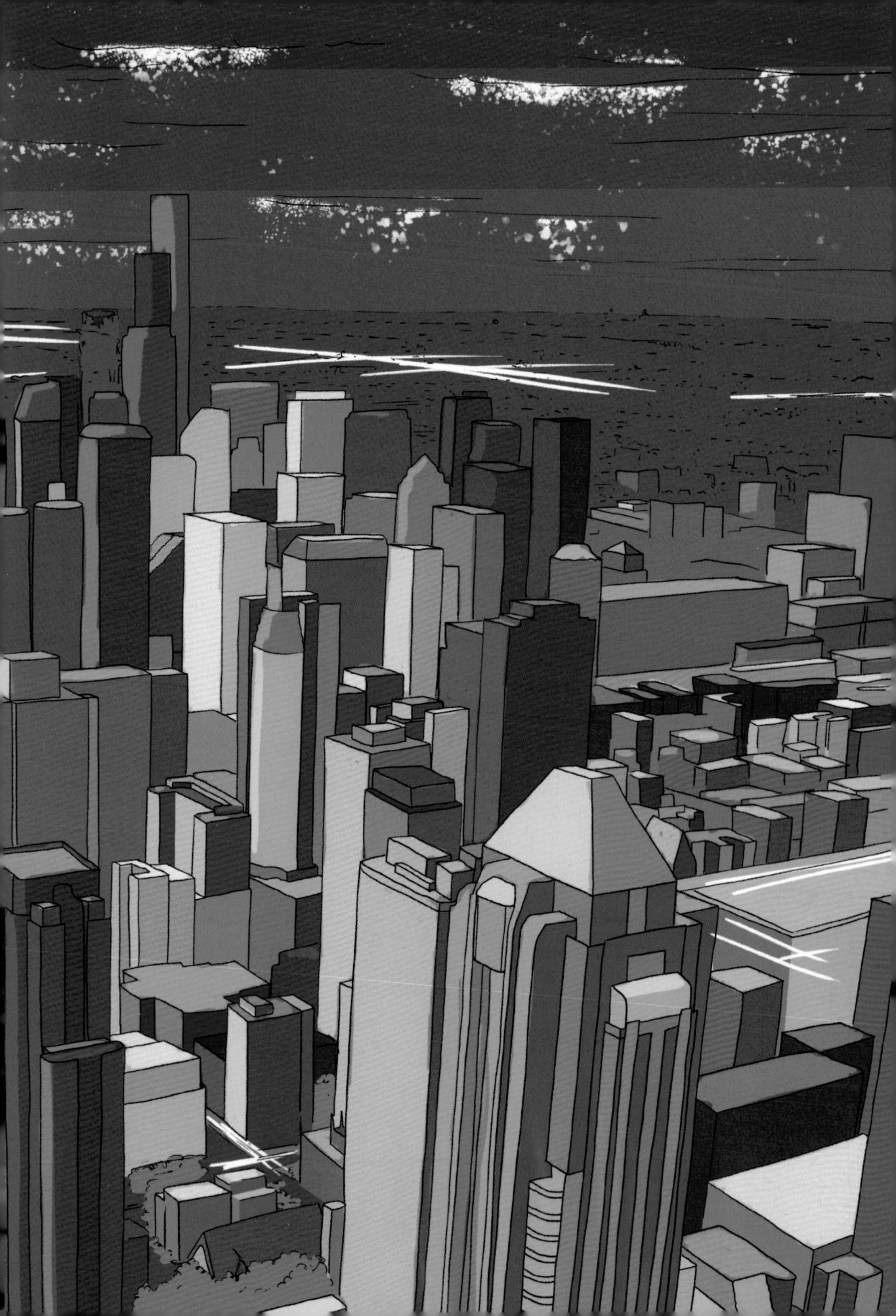

The Odds: Run, Odds, Run

Interior art colorized by Walter Carzon Studio

For information address HarperCollins Children's Books, a division of HarperCollins Publishers, 195 Broadway, New York, NY 10007.
www.harperalley.com
Library of Congress Control Number: 2022941987
ISBN 978-0-06-306898-8 — ISBN 978-0-06-306897-1 (pbk.)
22 23 24 25 26 RTLO 10 9 8 7 6 5 4 3 2 1
❖
Originally published in Australia by McPherson's Printing Group

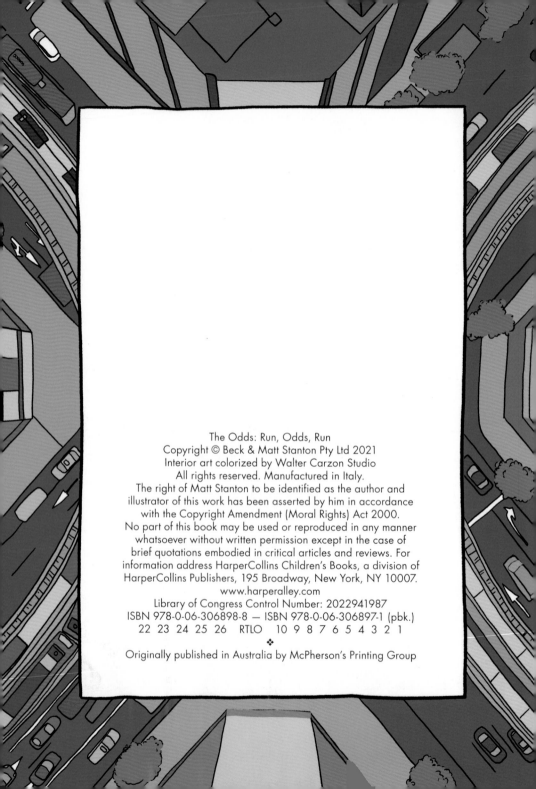

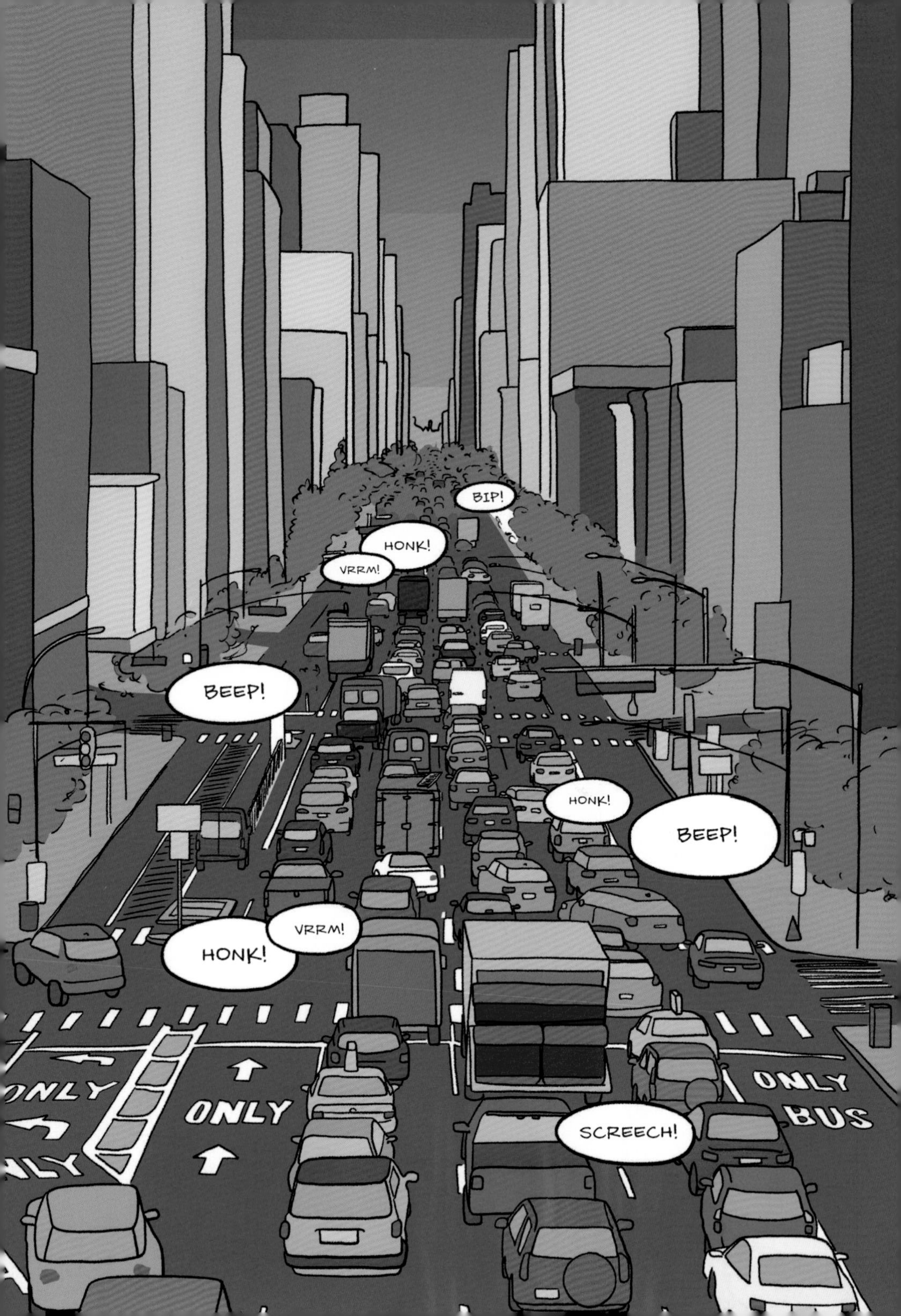
BIP!
HONK!
VRRM!
BEEP!
HONK!
BEEP!
VRRM!
HONK!
SCREECH!
ONLY
ONLY
BUS

For Bonnie, Boston, Miller, and Sully

You are even more extraordinary than I imagined.

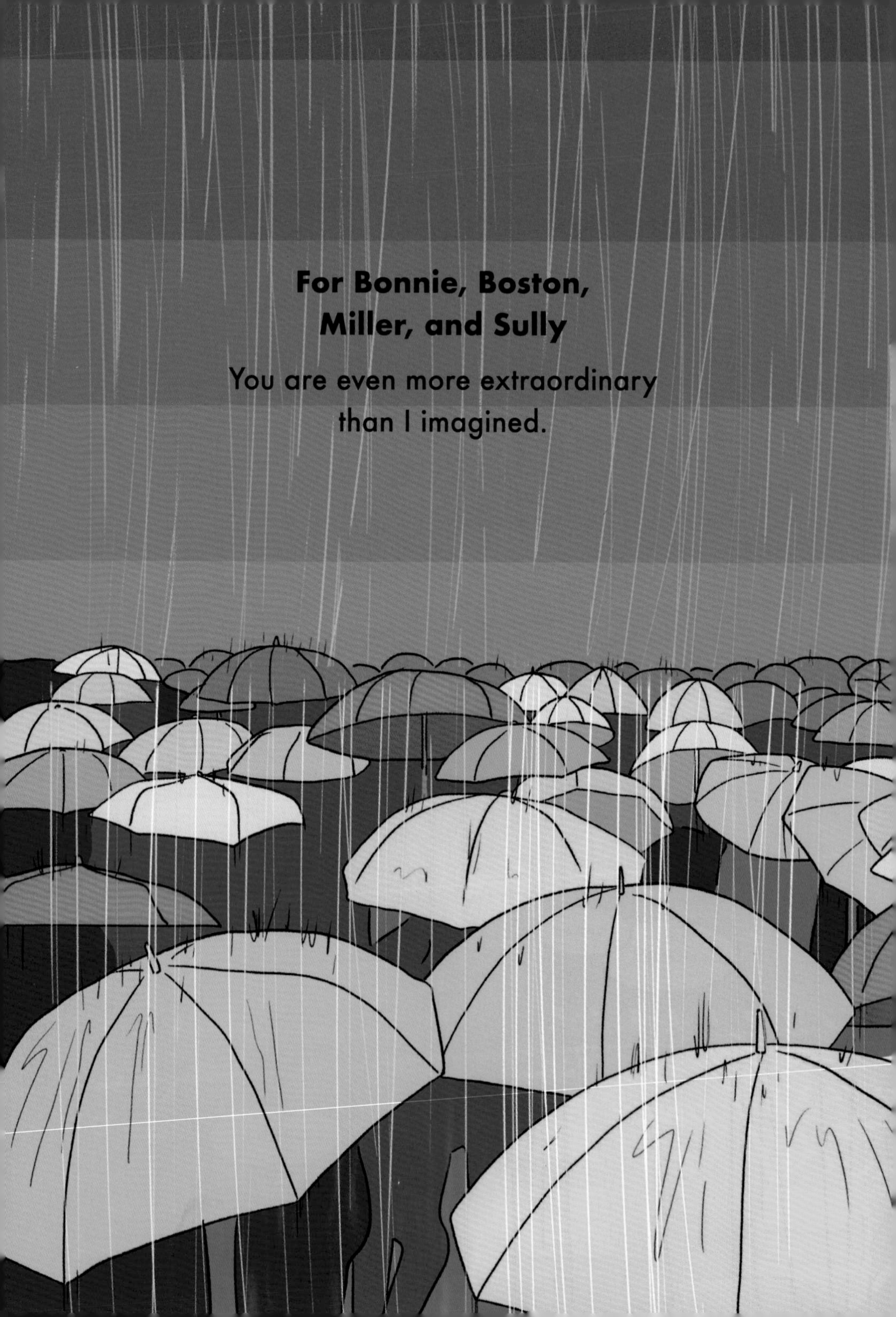

THE ODDS
RUN, ODDS, RUN

words and pictures by

Matt Stanton

HARPER alley
An Imprint of HarperCollinsPublishers

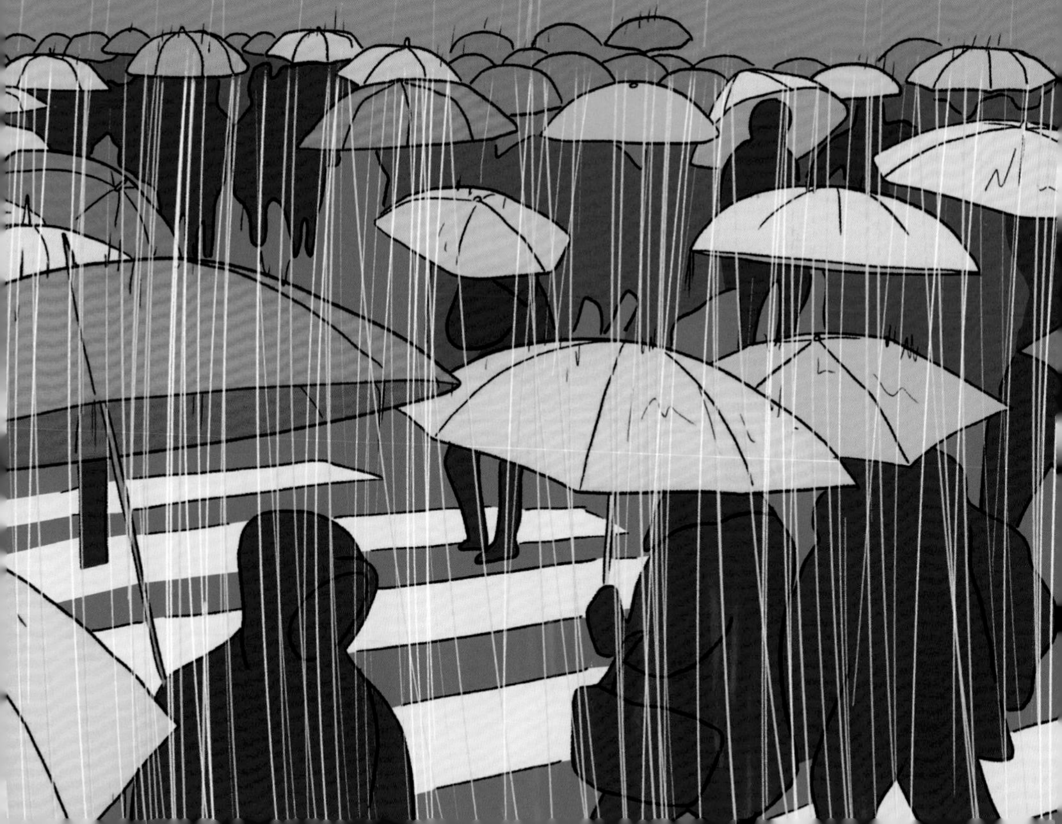

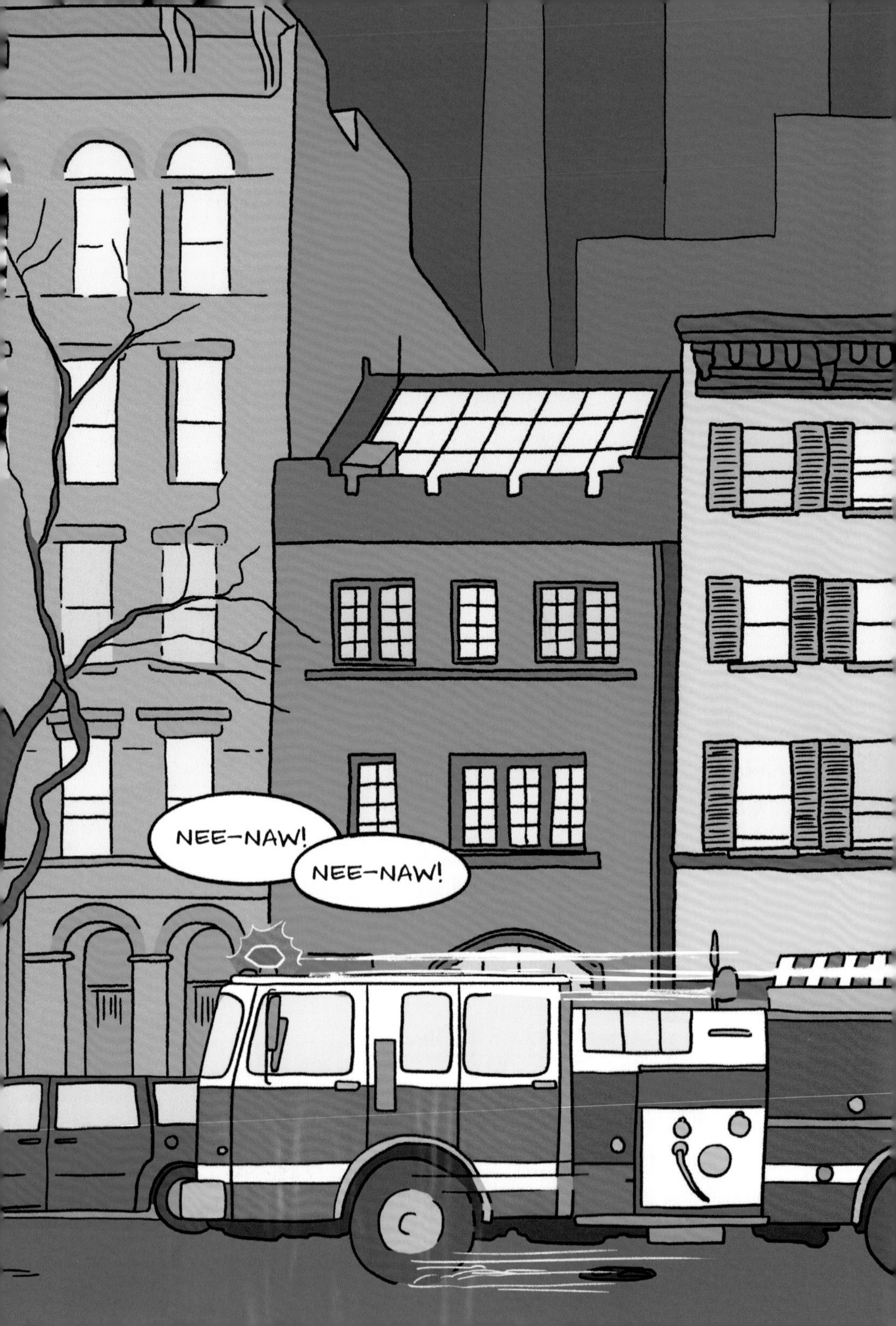
NEE-NAW!
NEE-NAW!

CHAPTER ONE
The Odds are a problem

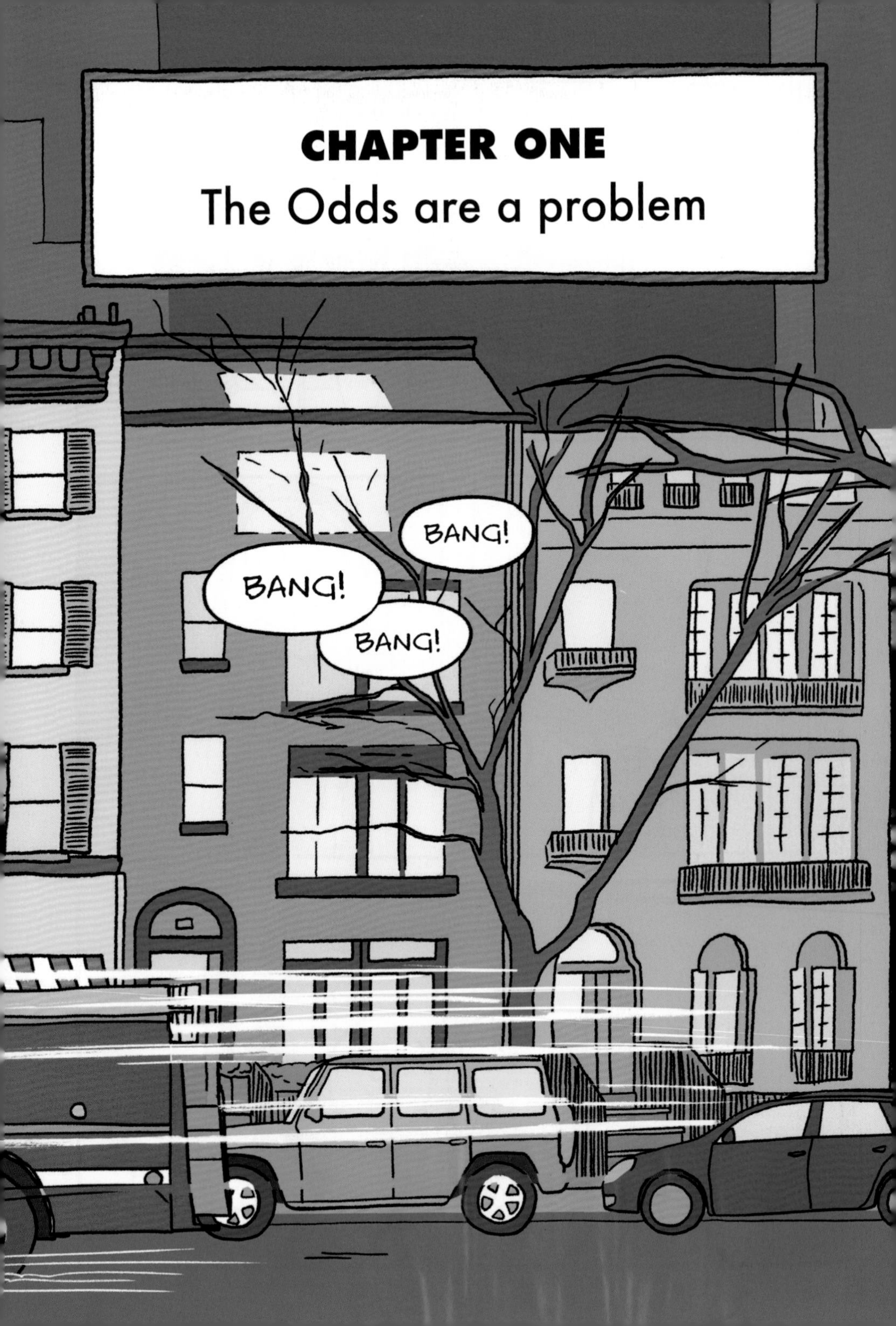
BANG!
BANG!
BANG!

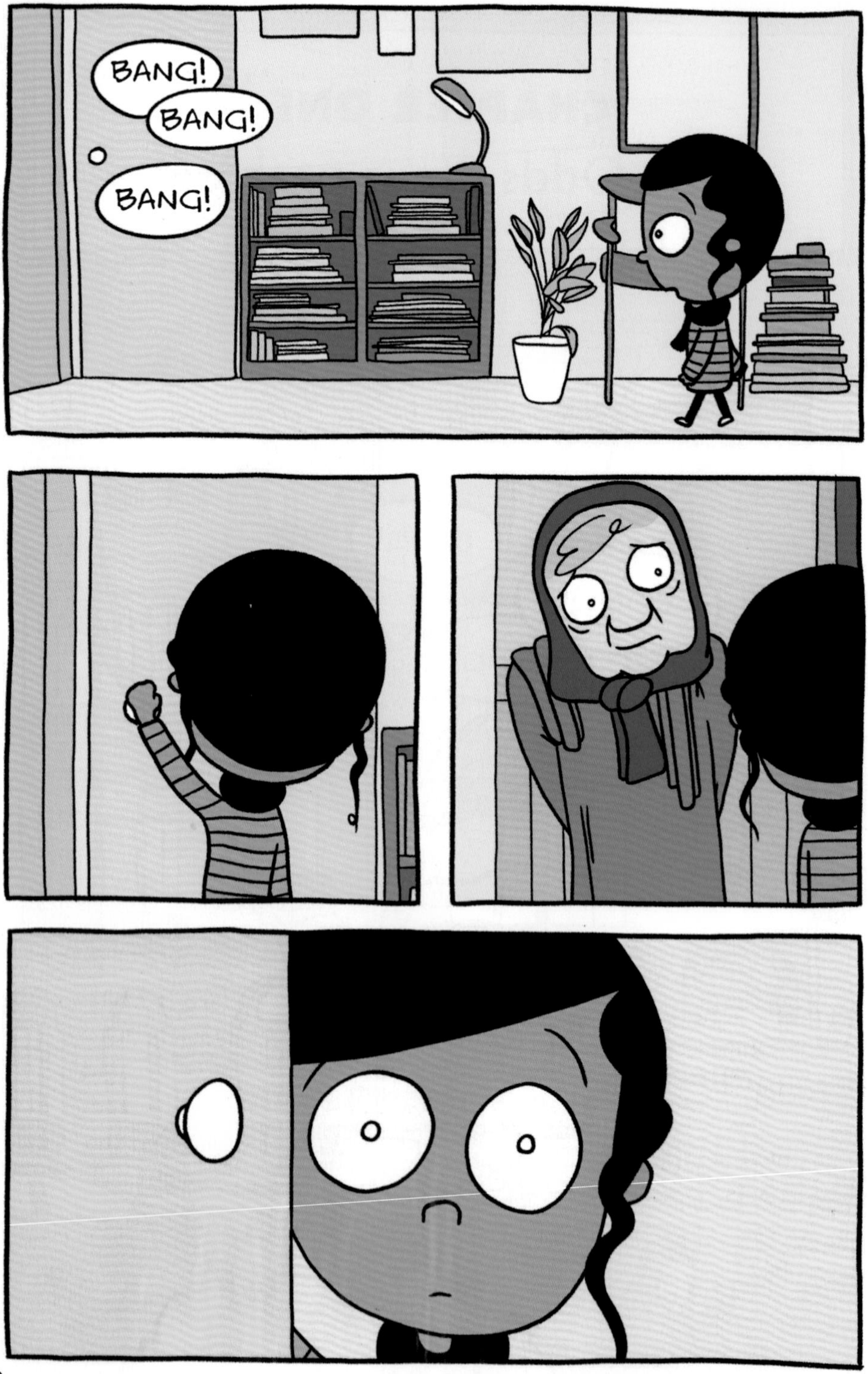
BANG!
BANG!
BANG!

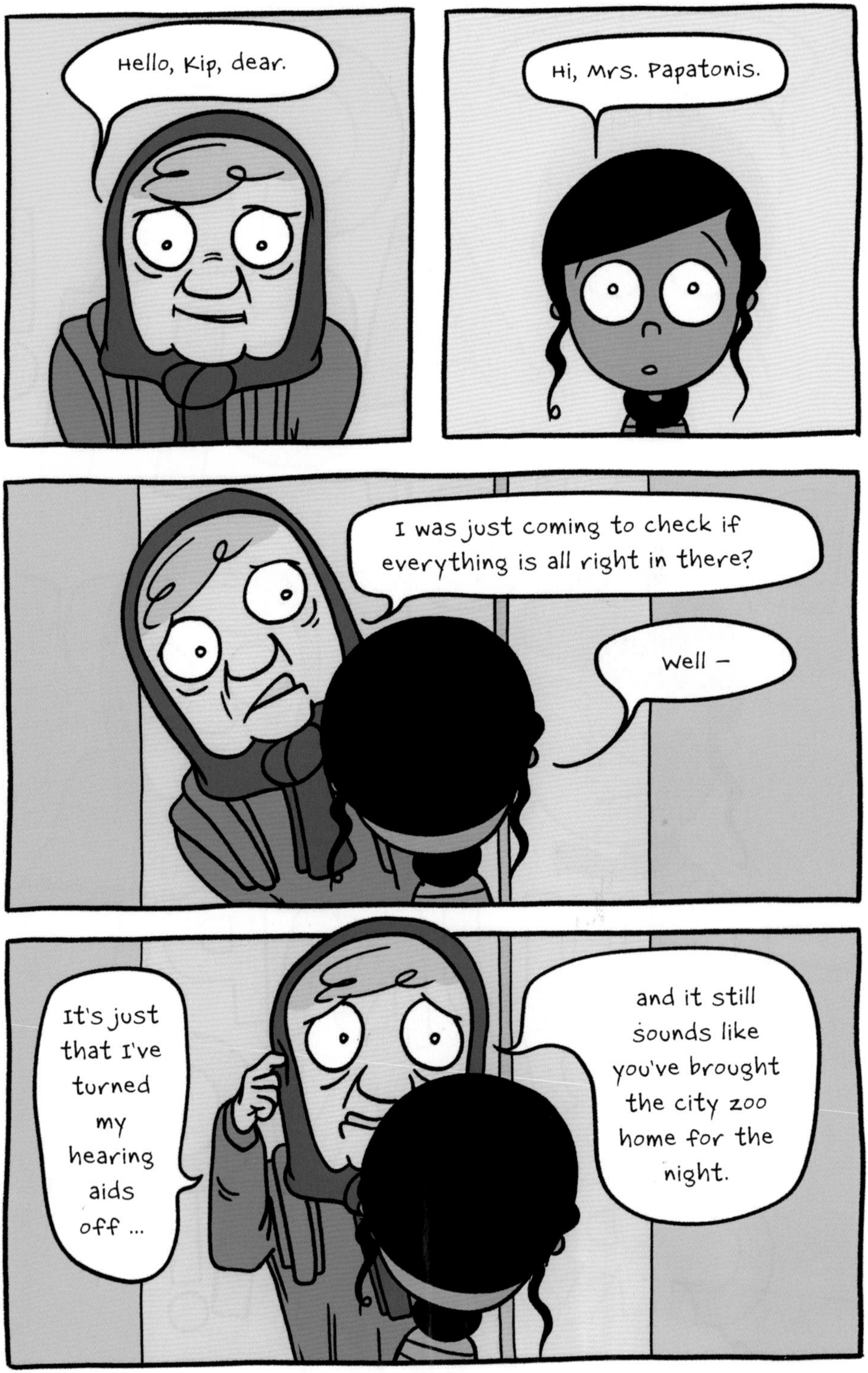
Hello, Kip, dear.
Hi, Mrs. Papatonis.
I was just coming to check if everything is all right in there?
Well –
It's just that I've turned my hearing aids off ...
and it still sounds like you've brought the city zoo home for the night.

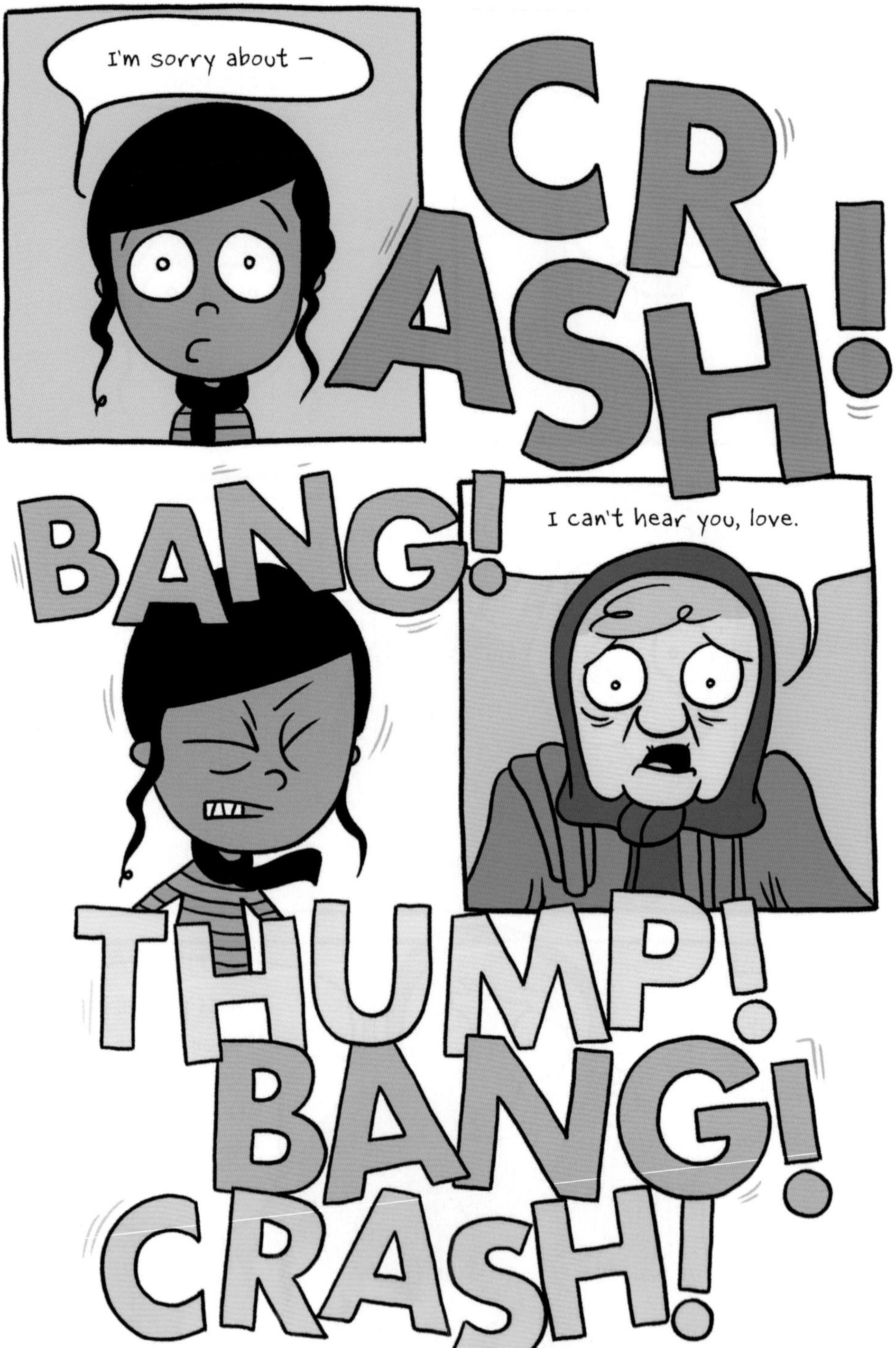
I'm sorry about –
CRASH!
BANG!
I can't hear you, love.
THUMP!
BANG!
CRASH!

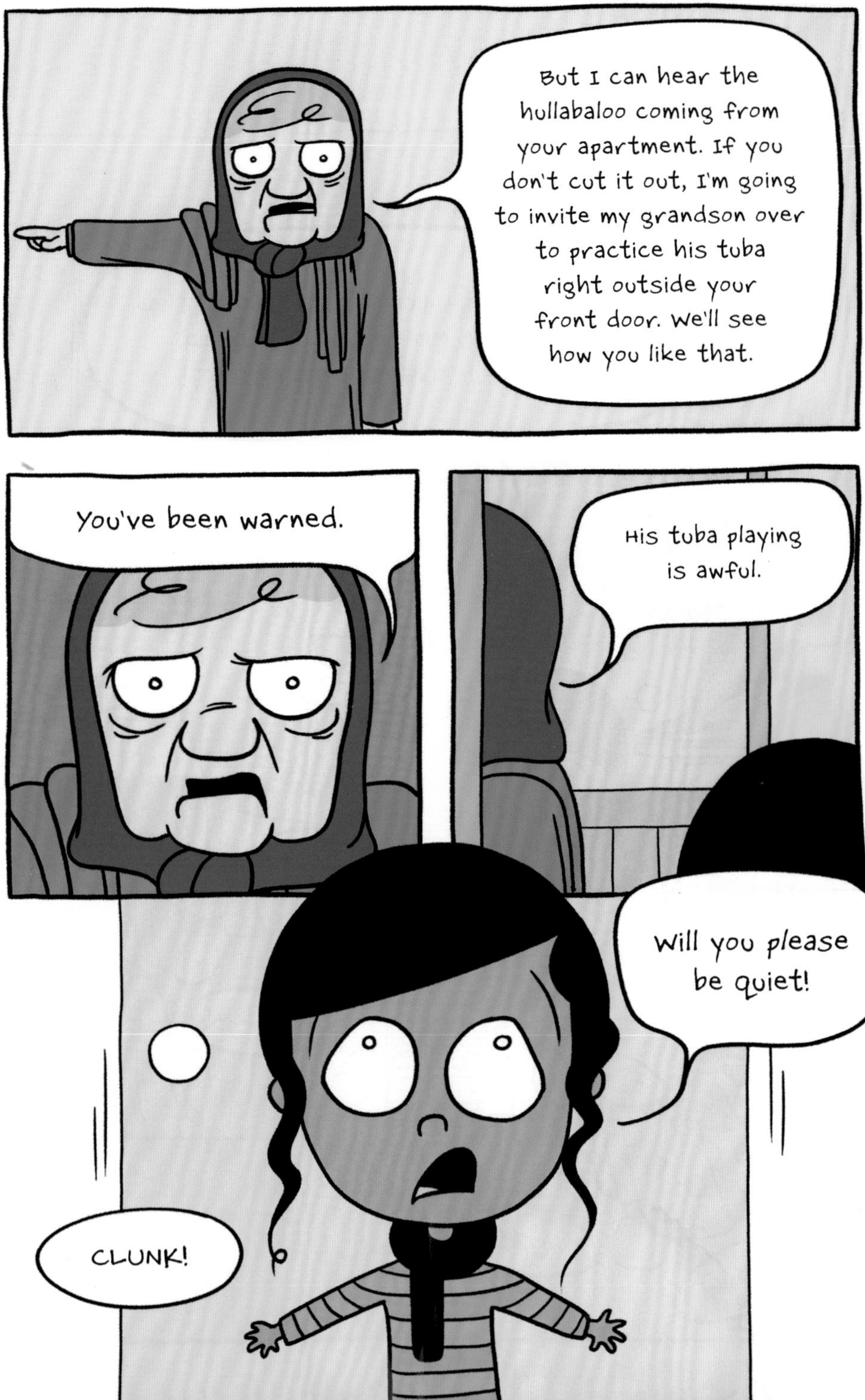
But I can hear the hullabaloo coming from your apartment. If you don't cut it out, I'm going to invite my grandson over to practice his tuba right outside your front door. We'll see how you like that.
You've been warned.
His tuba playing is awful.
Will you *please* be quiet!
CLUNK!

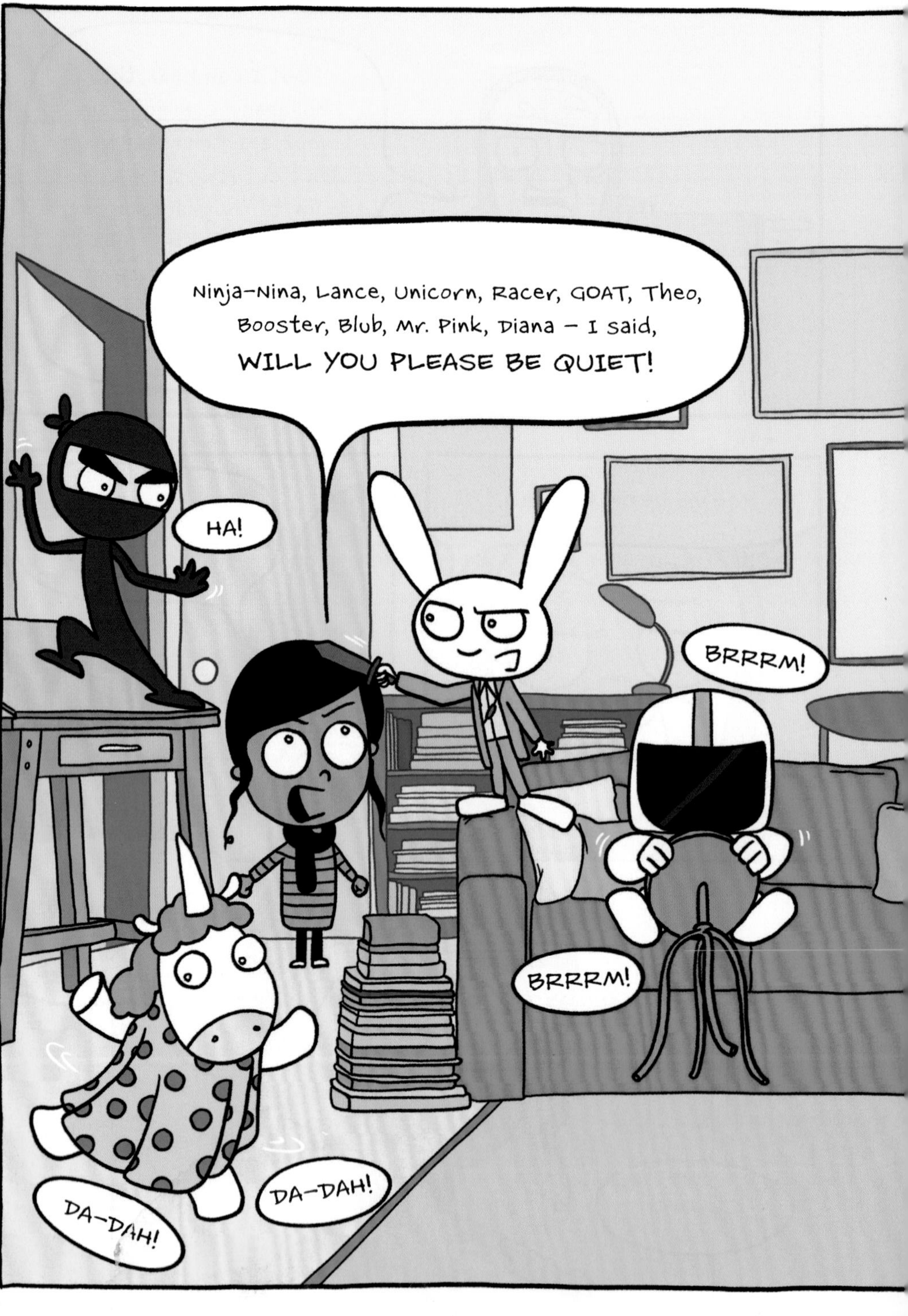
Ninja-Nina, Lance, Unicorn, Racer, GOAT, Theo, Booster, Blub, Mr. Pink, Diana – I said, WILL YOU PLEASE BE QUIET!
HA!
BRRRM!
BRRRM!
DA-DAH!
DA-DAH!

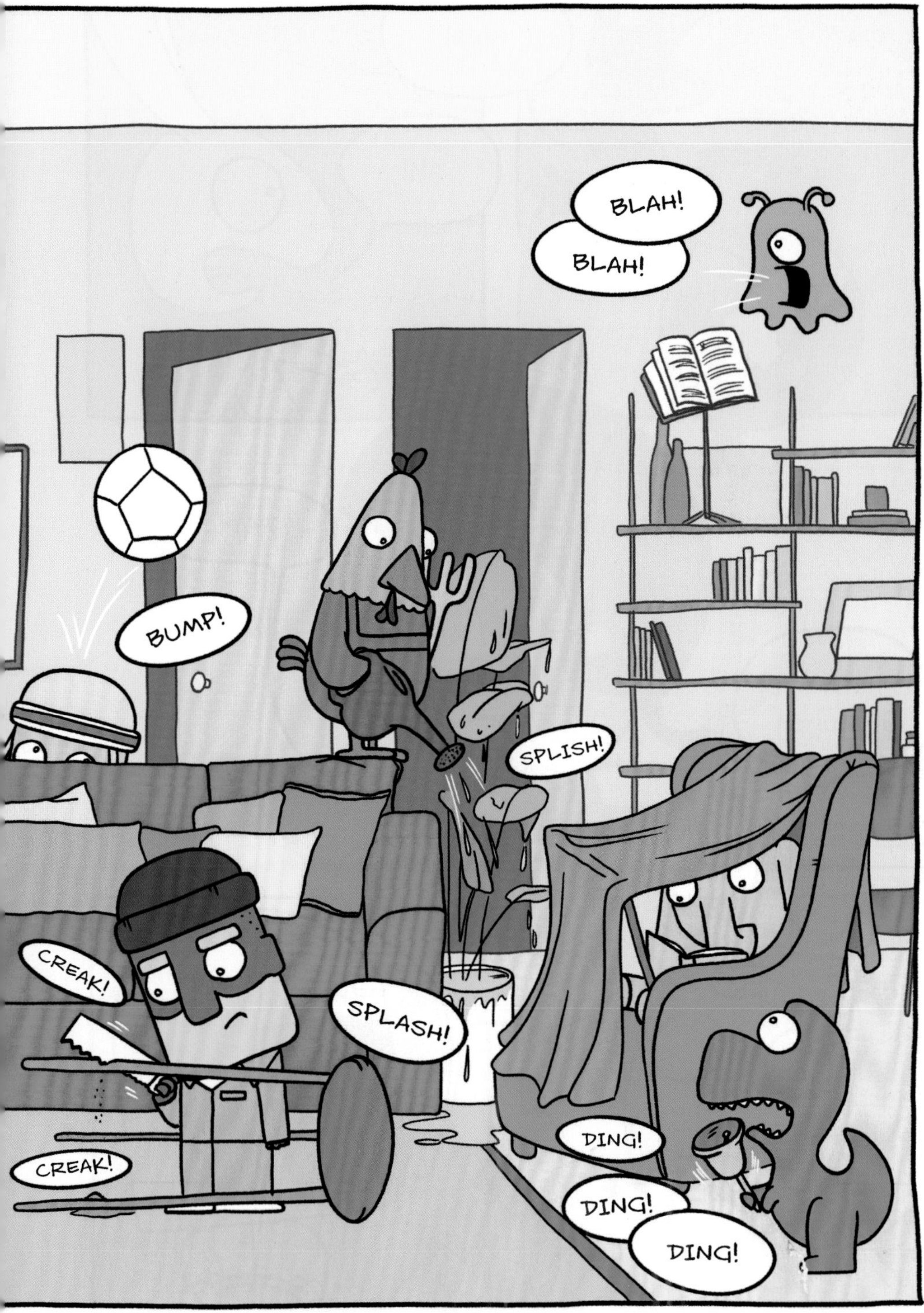
BLAH!
BLAH!
BUMP!
SPLISH!
CREAK!
SPLASH!
CREAK!
DING!
DING!
DING!

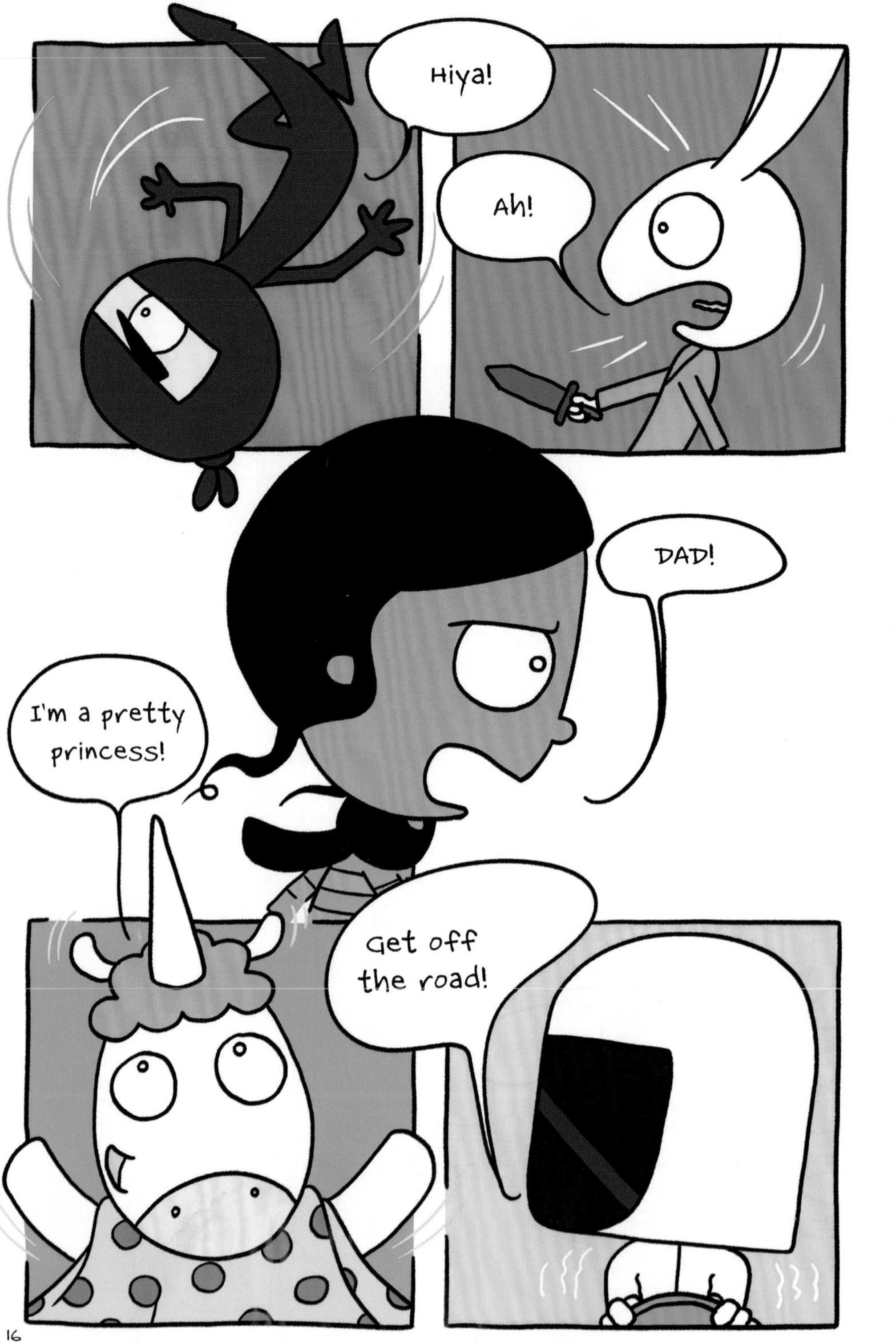
Hiya!
Ah!
DAD!
I'm a pretty princess!
Get off the road!

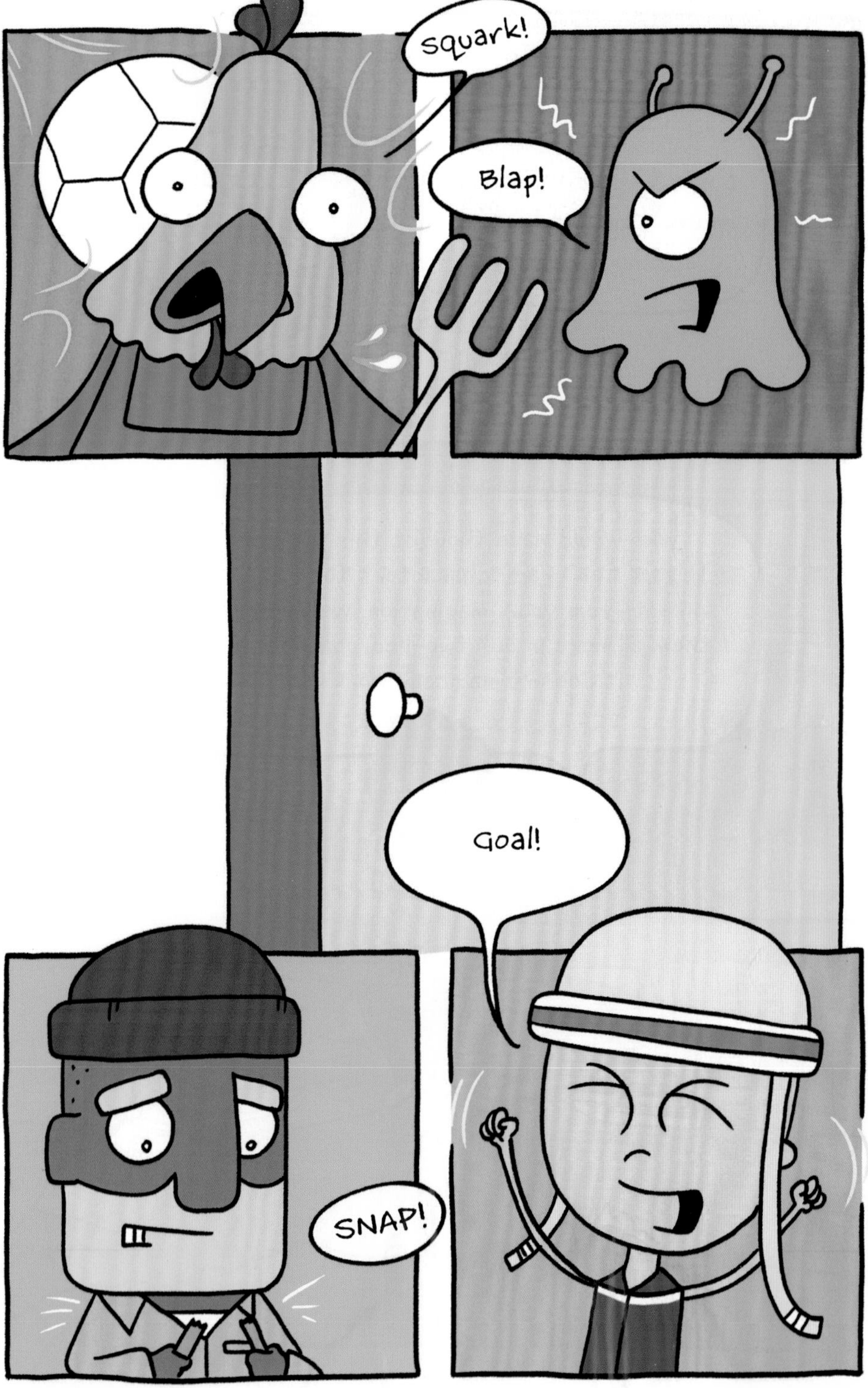
Squark!
Blap!
Goal!
SNAP!

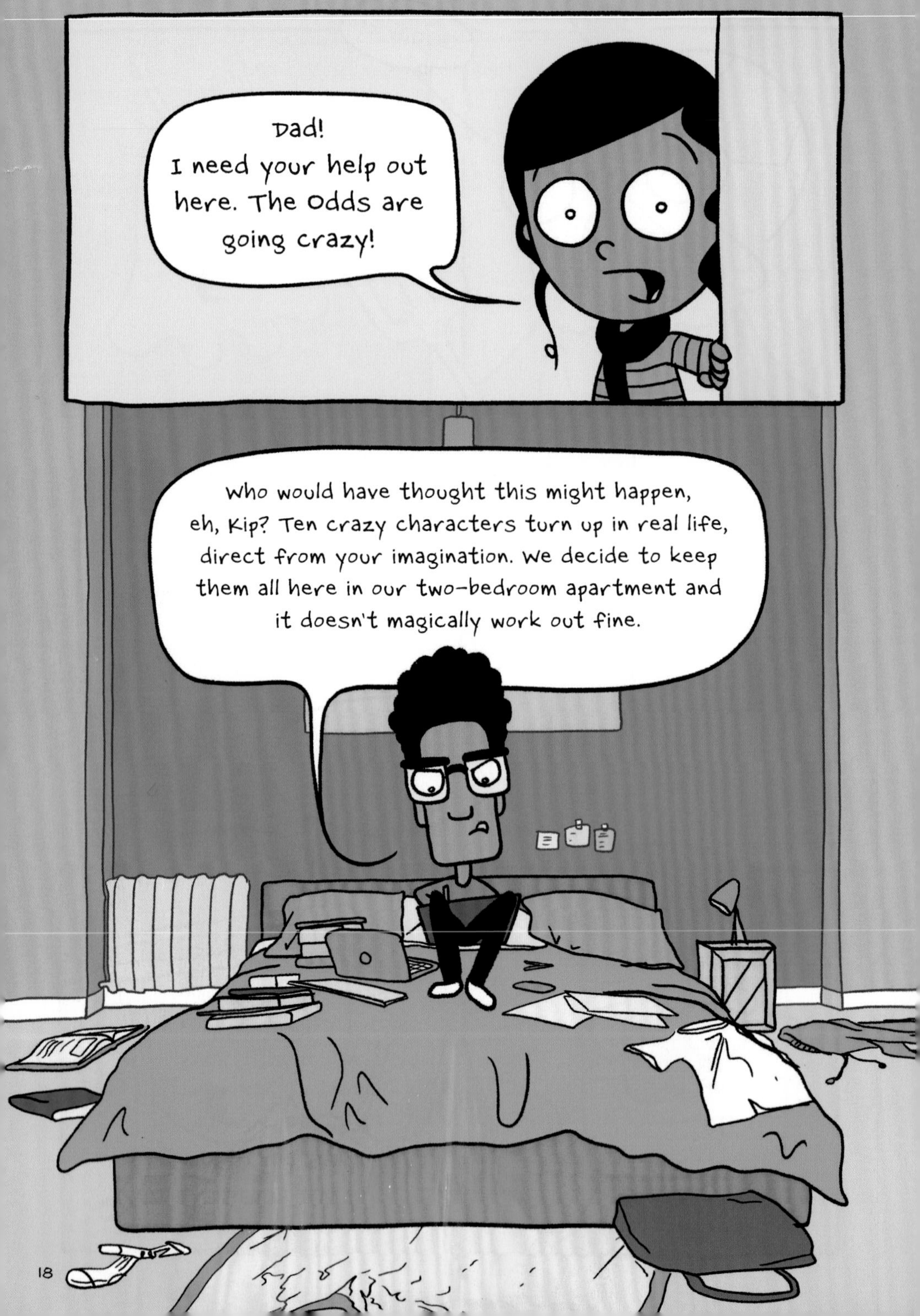
Dad! I need your help out here. The Odds are going crazy!
Who would have thought this might happen, eh, Kip? Ten crazy characters turn up in real life, direct from your imagination. We decide to keep them all here in our two-bedroom apartment and it doesn't magically work out fine.

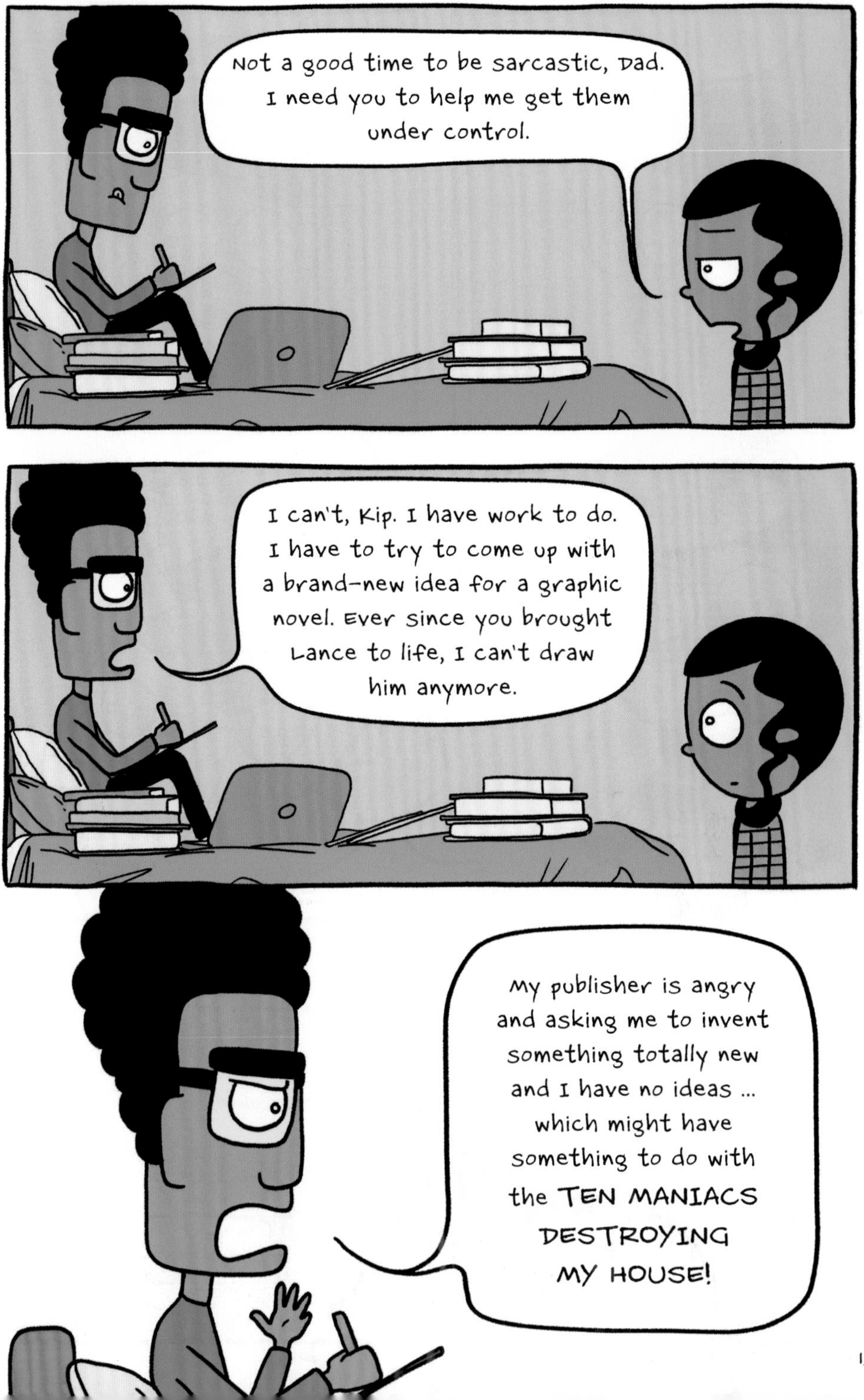

Not a good time to be sarcastic, Dad. I need you to help me get them under control.
I can't, Kip. I have work to do. I have to try to come up with a brand-new idea for a graphic novel. Ever since you brought Lance to life, I can't draw him anymore.
My publisher is angry and asking me to invent something totally new and I have no ideas ... which might have something to do with the TEN MANIACS DESTROYING MY HOUSE!

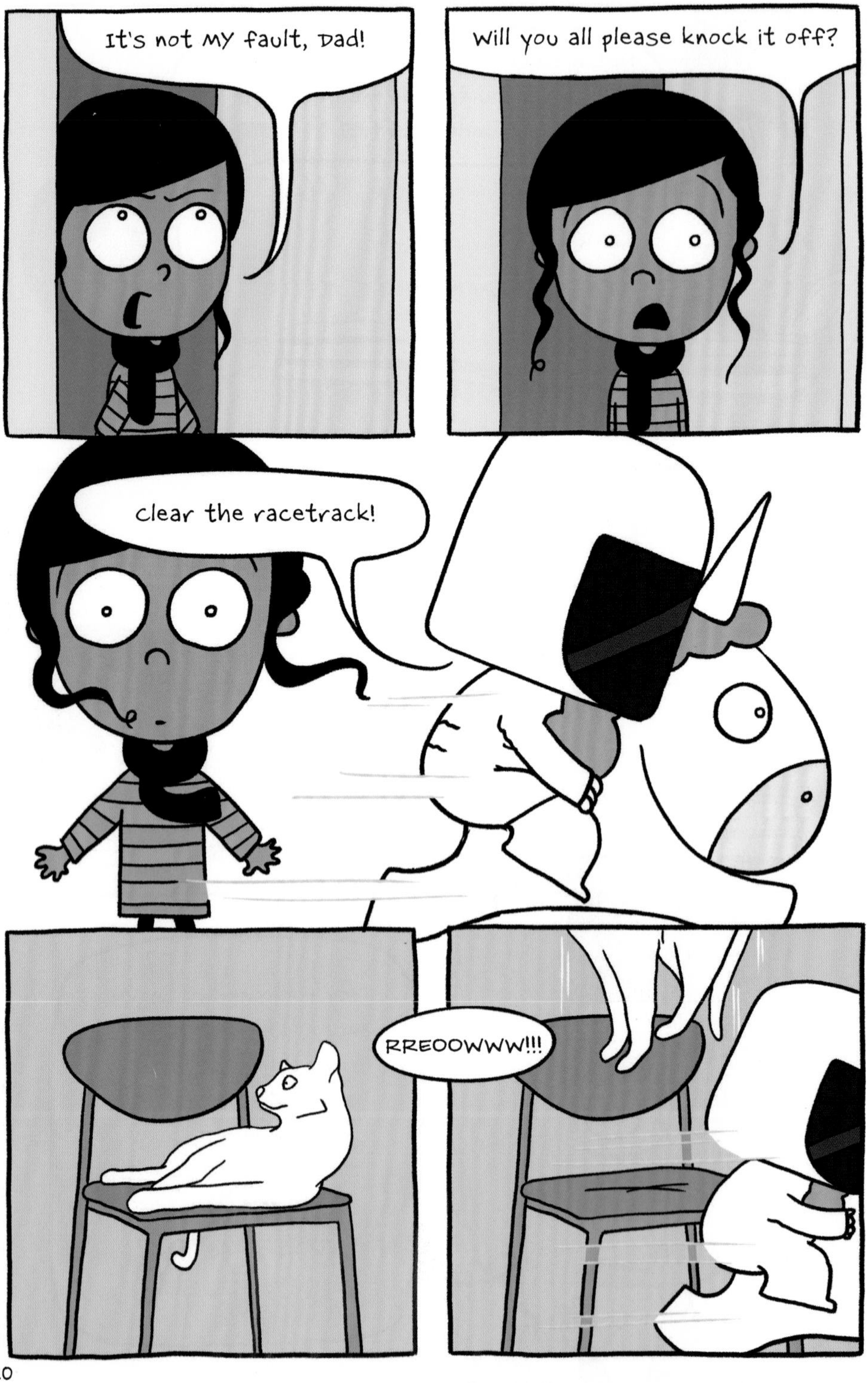
It's not my fault, Dad!
Will you all please knock it off?
Clear the racetrack!
RREOOWWW!!!

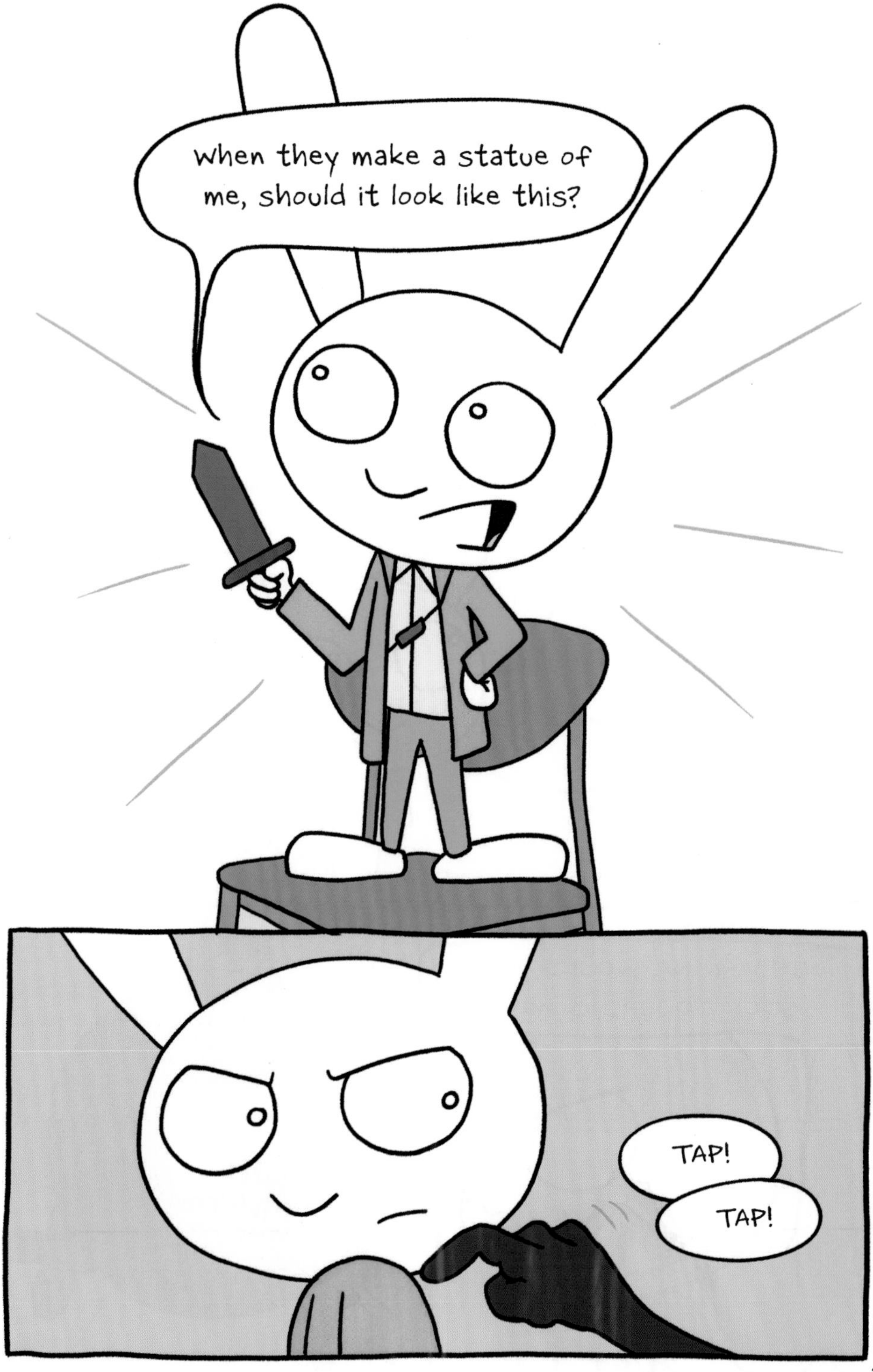
When they make a statue of me, should it look like this?
TAP!
TAP!

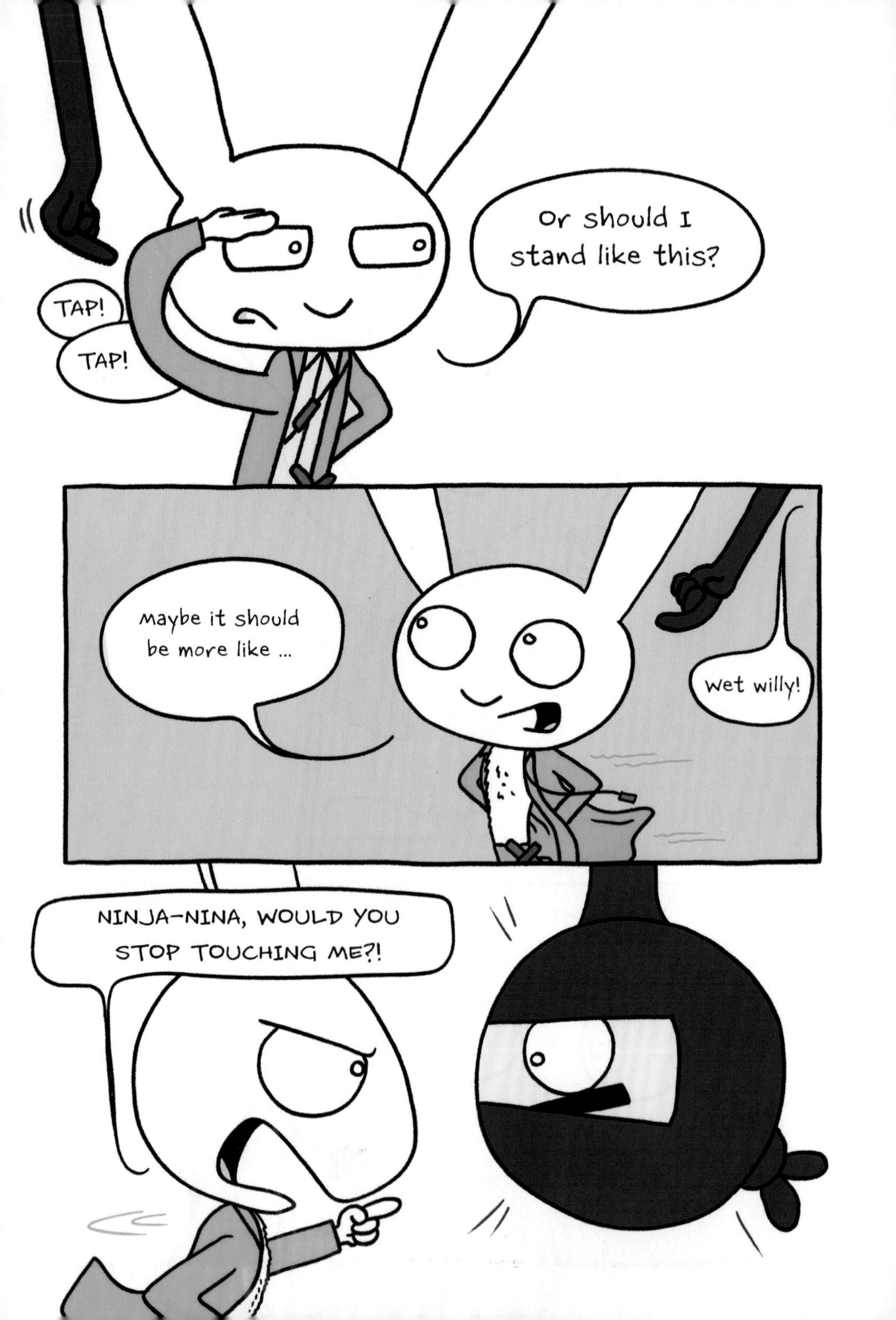

TAP!
TAP!
Or should I stand like this?
maybe it should be more like ...
wet willy!
NINJA-NINA, WOULD YOU STOP TOUCHING ME?!

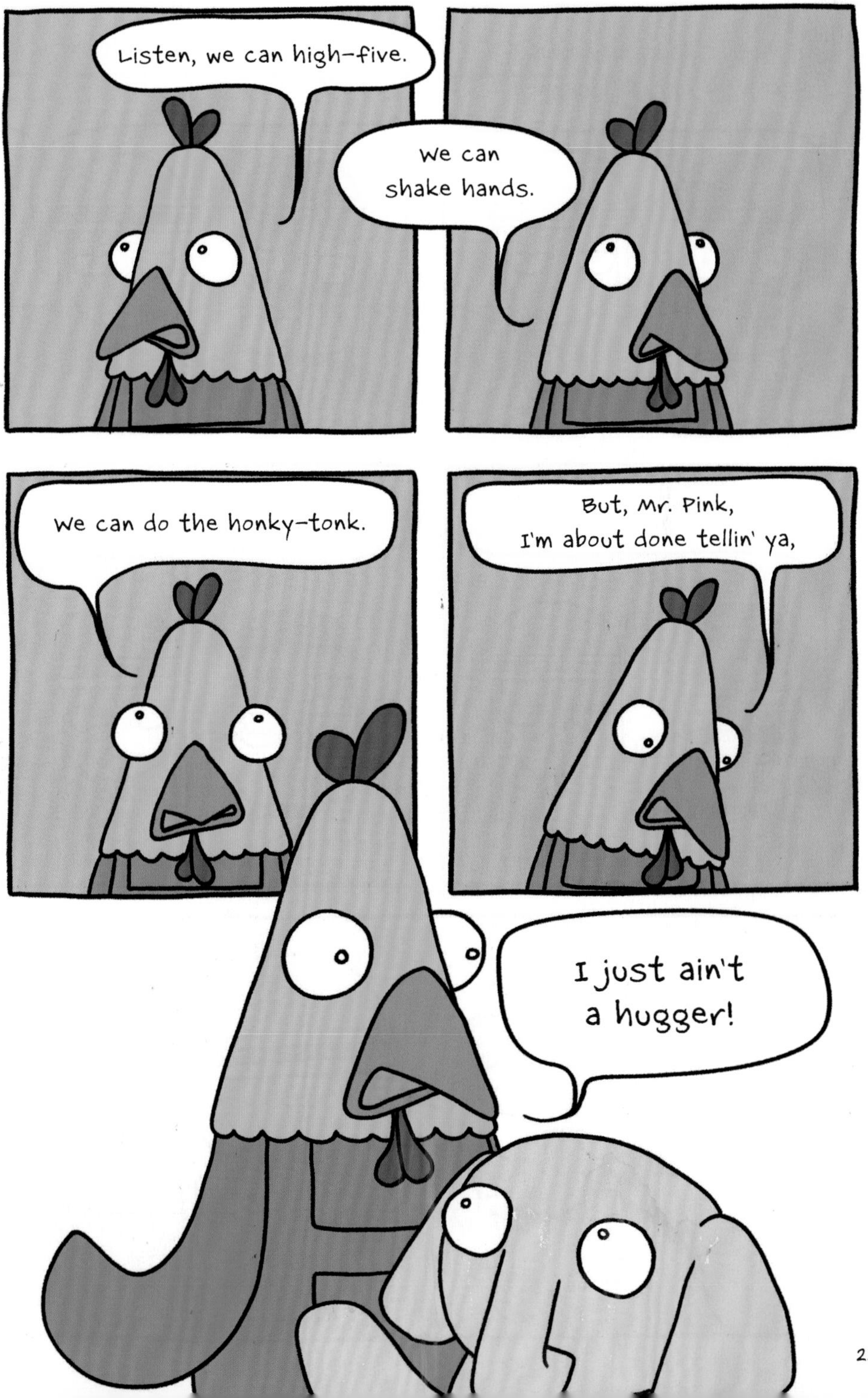
Listen, we can high-five.
we can shake hands.
we can do the honky-tonk.
But, Mr. Pink, I'm about done tellin' ya,
I just ain't a hugger!

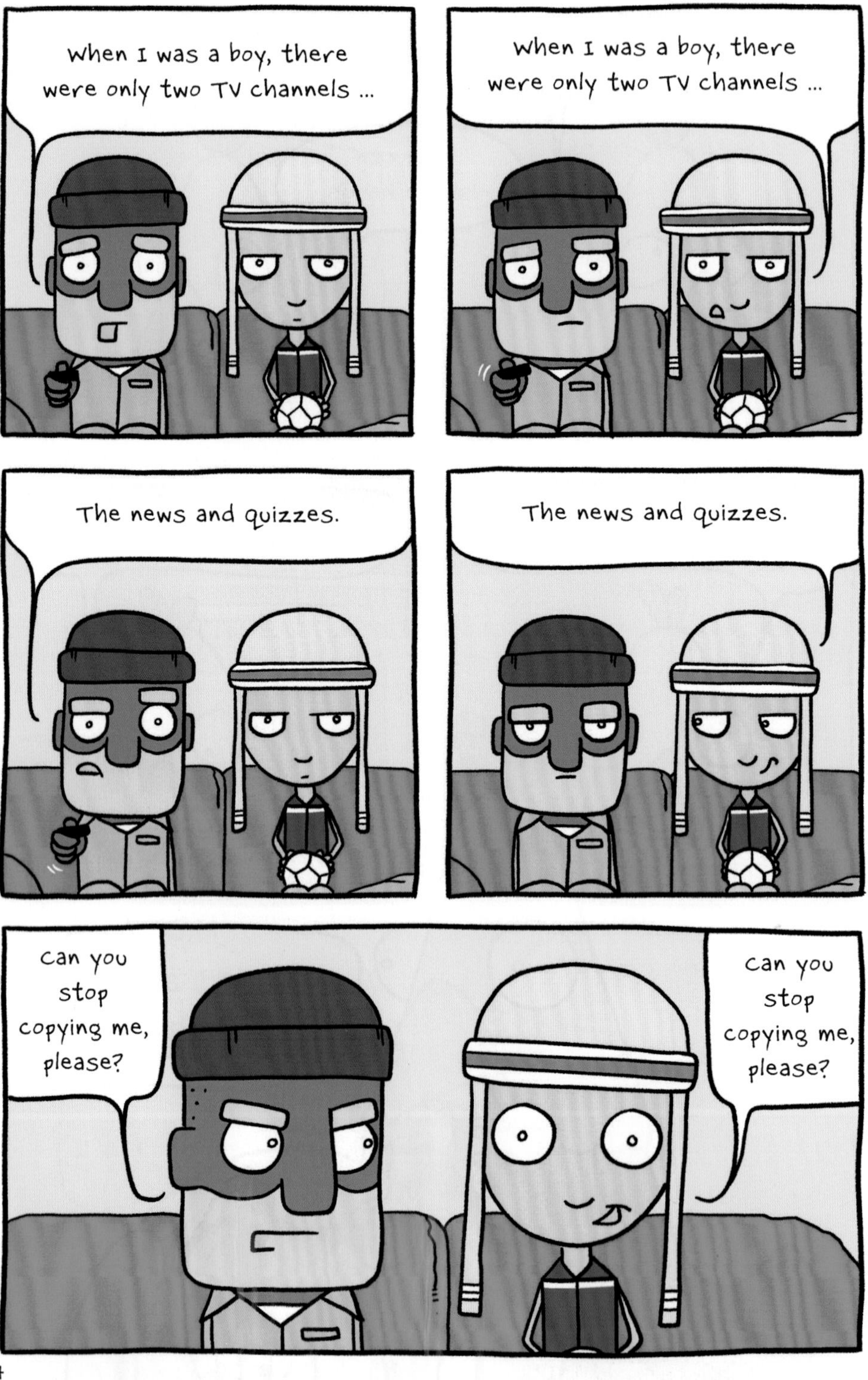
When I was a boy, there were only two TV channels ...
When I was a boy, there were only two TV channels ...
The news and quizzes.
The news and quizzes.
Can you stop copying me, please?
Can you stop copying me, please?

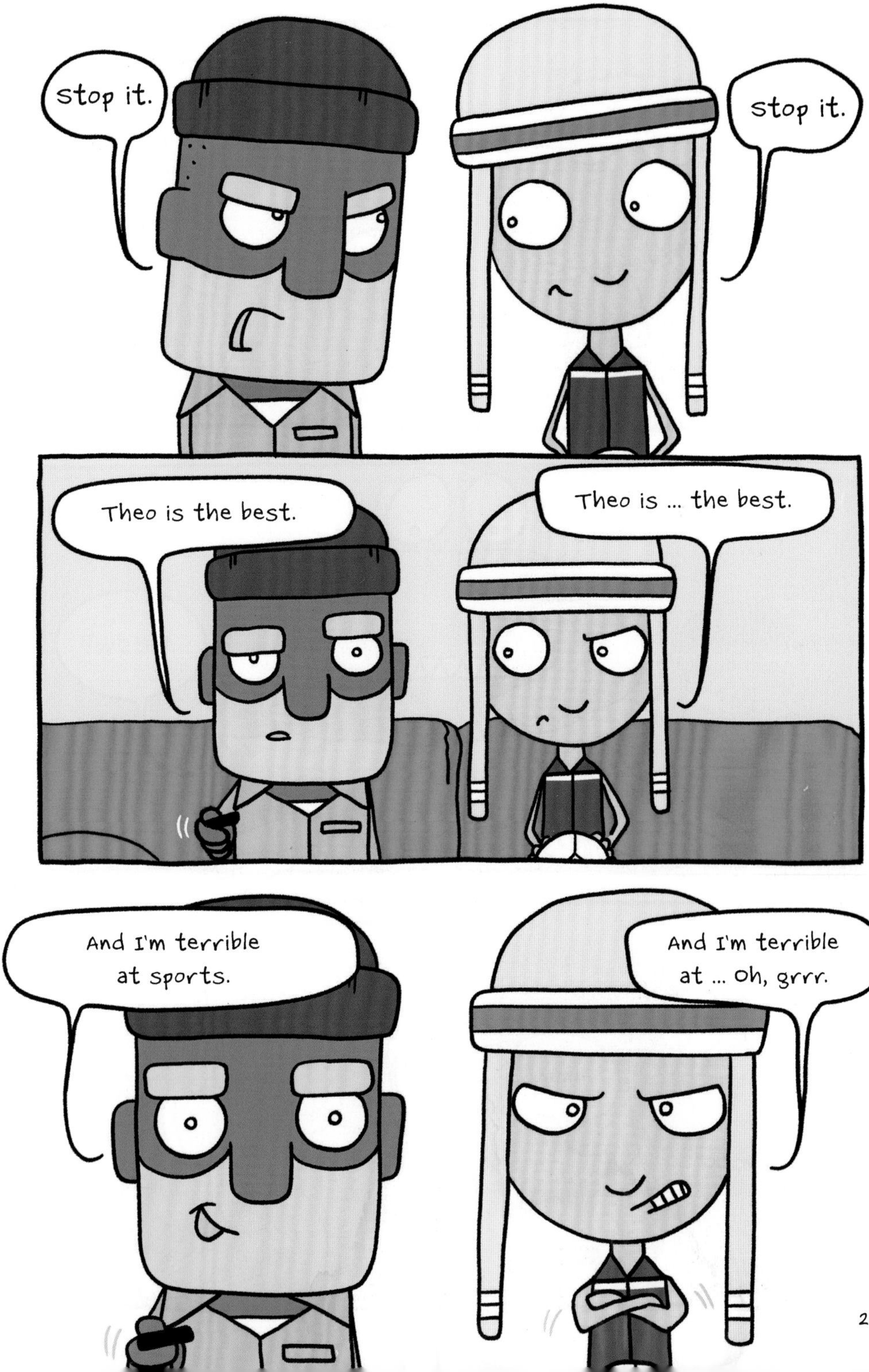
Stop it.
Stop it.
Theo is the best.
Theo is ... the best.
And I'm terrible at sports.
And I'm terrible at ... Oh, grrr.

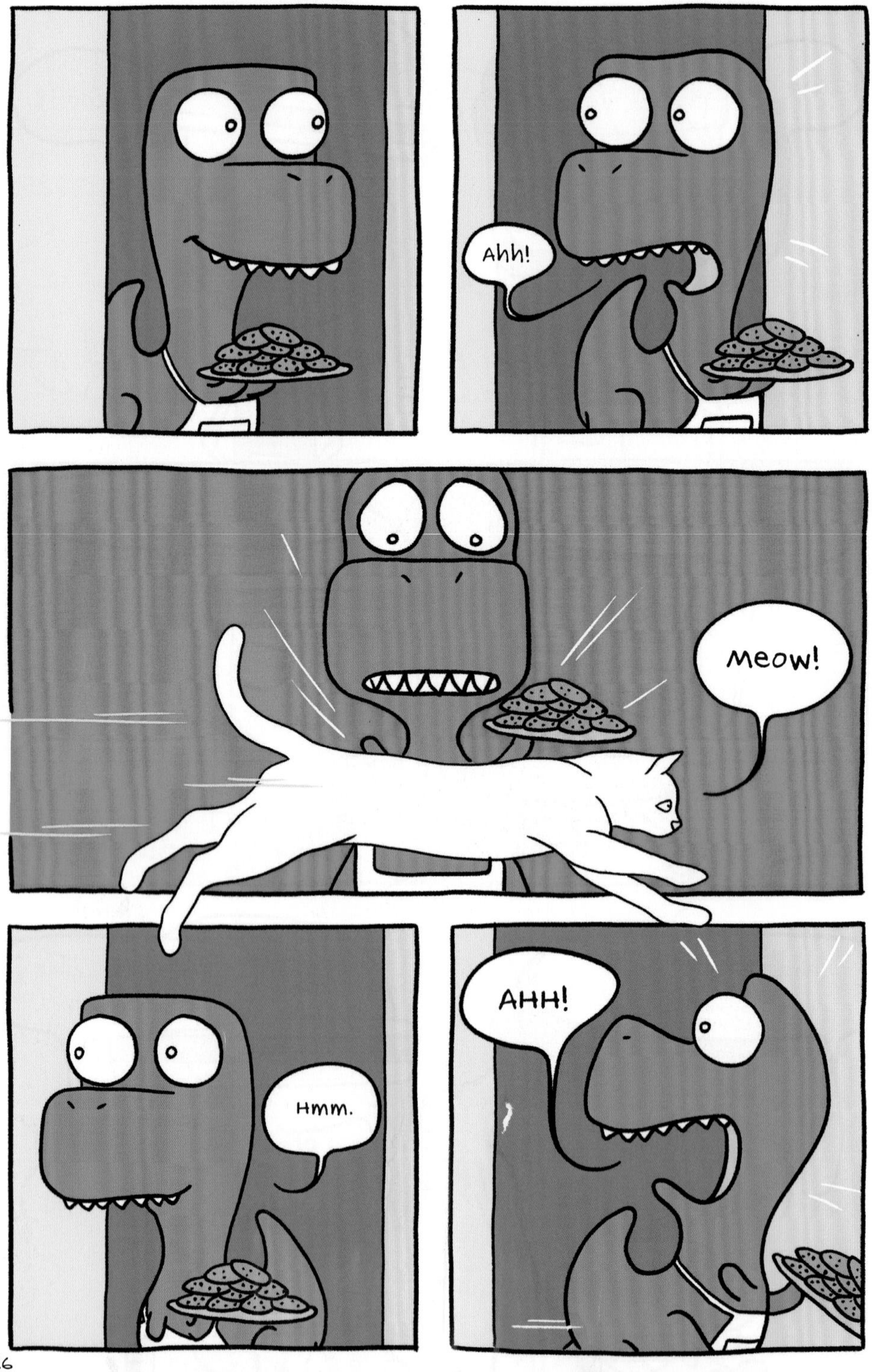
Ahh!
MEOW!
Hmm.
AHH!

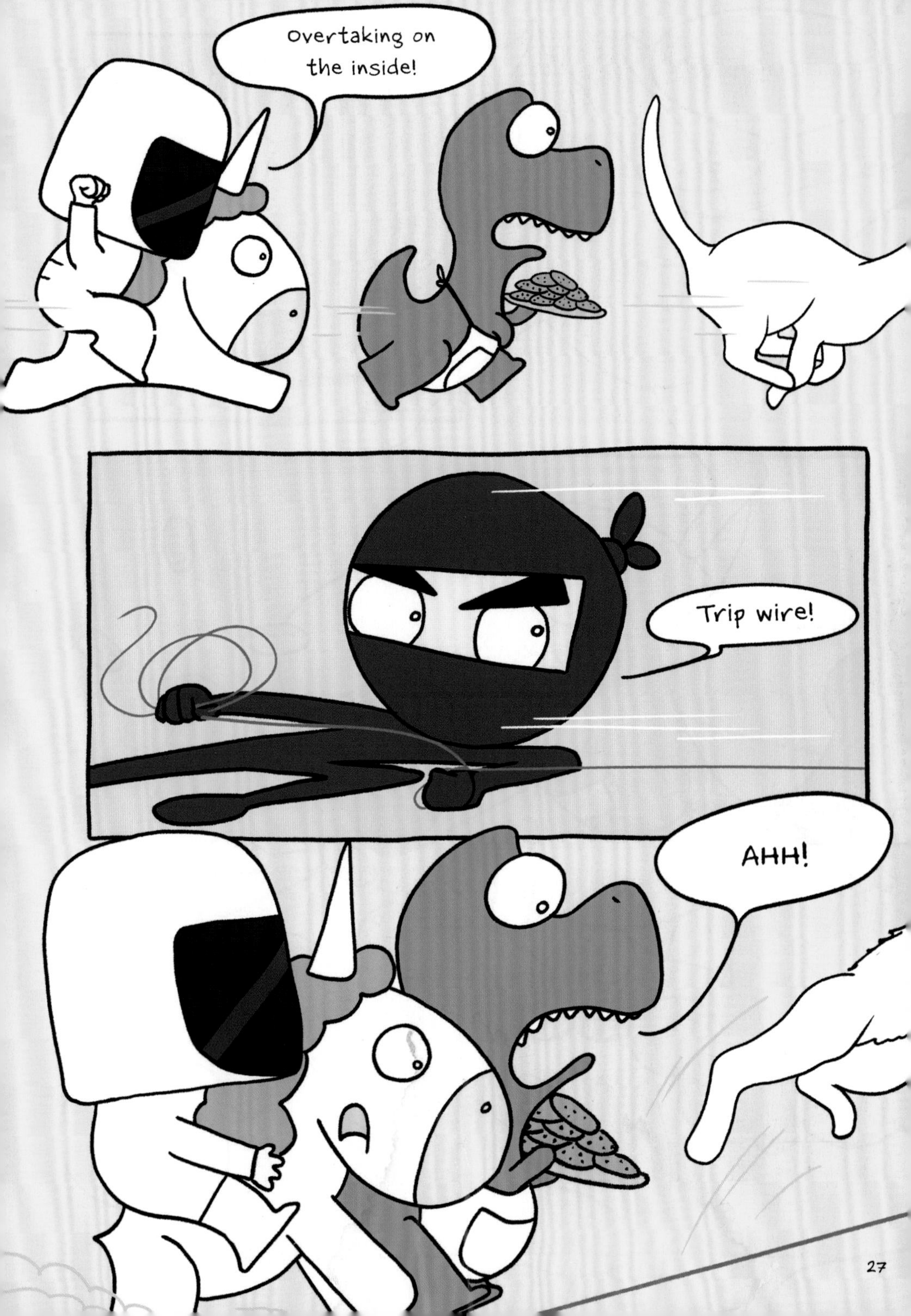
Overtaking on the inside!
Trip wire!
AHH!

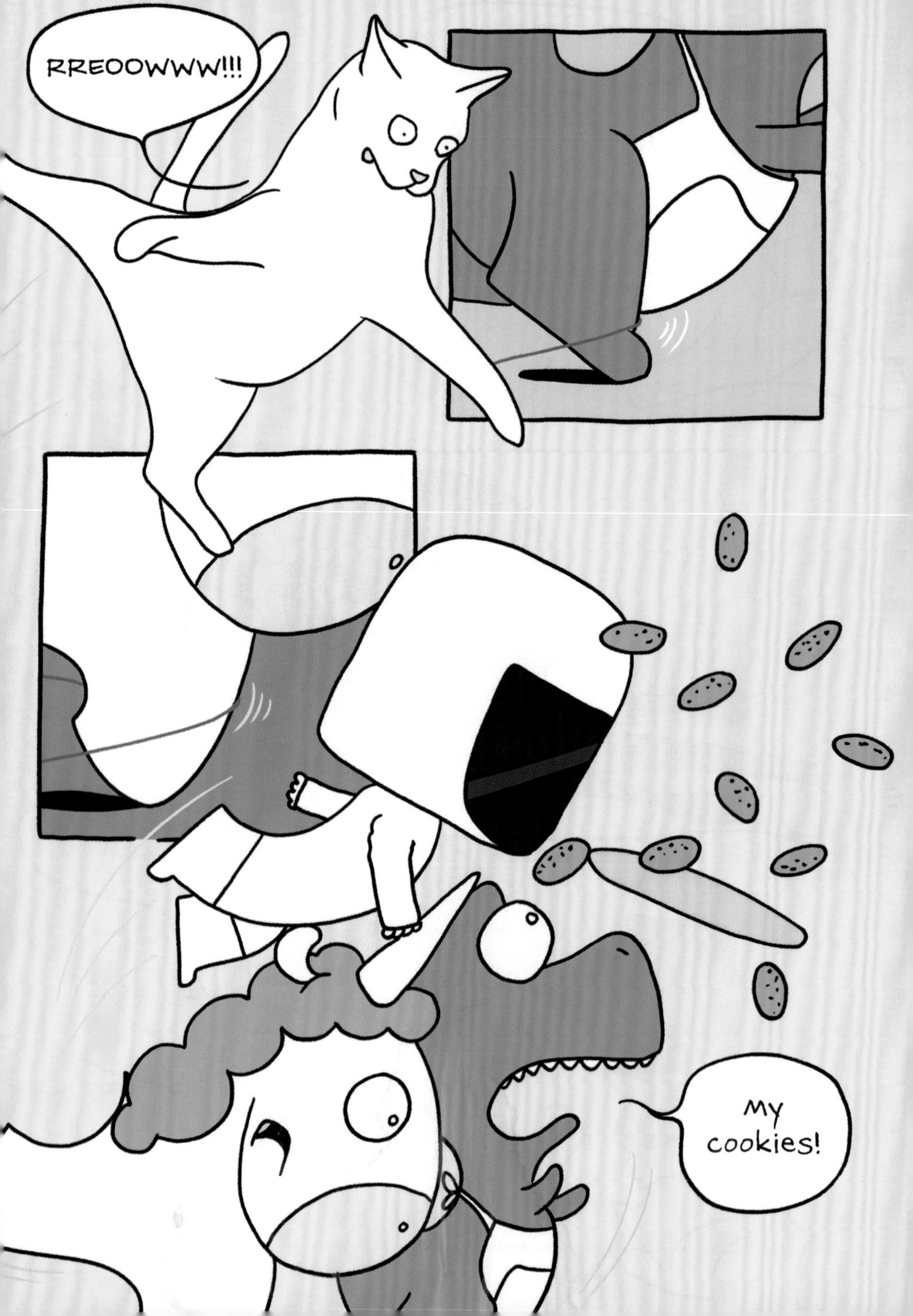
RREOOWWW!!!
My cookies!

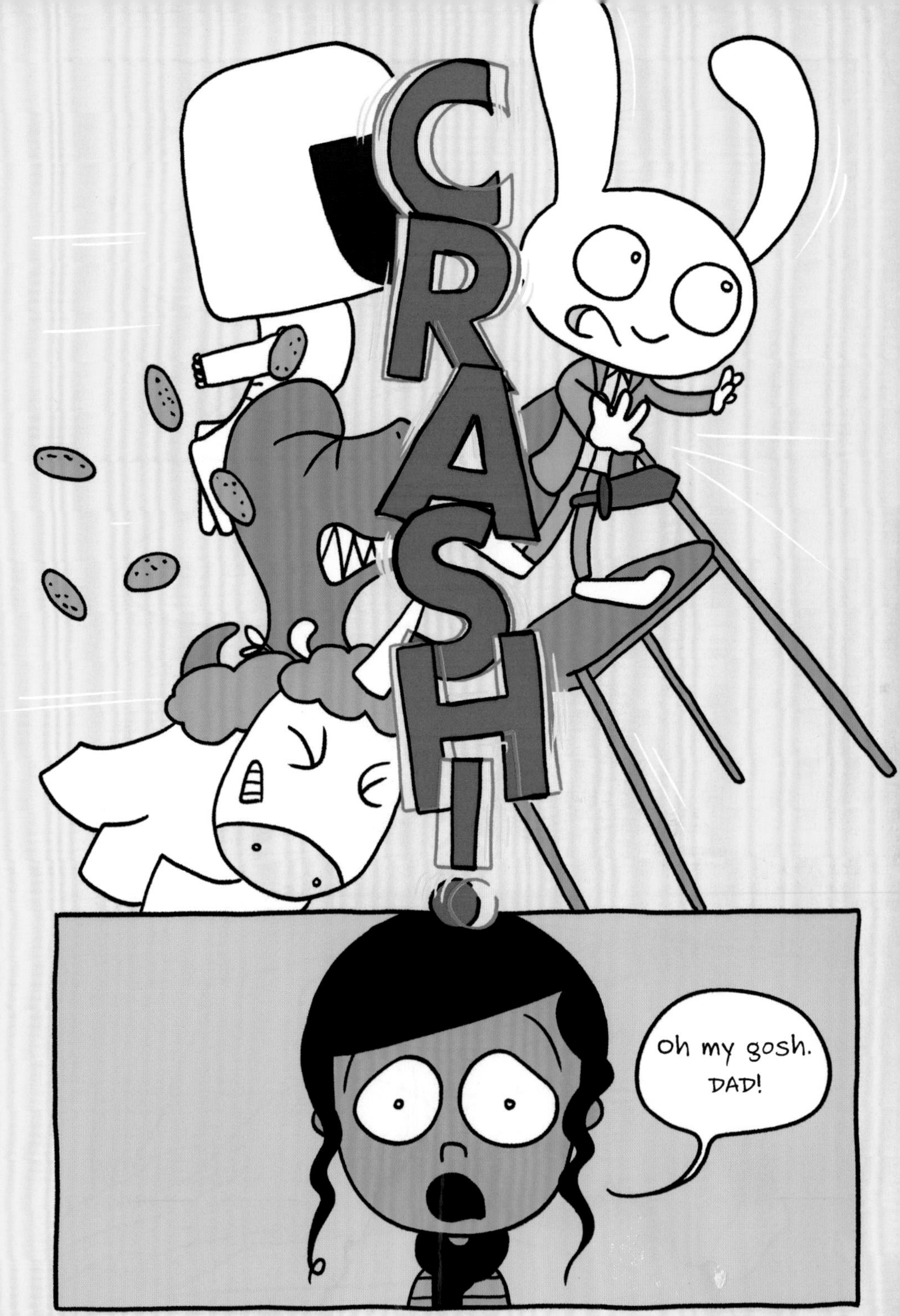
CRASH!
Oh my gosh.
DAD!

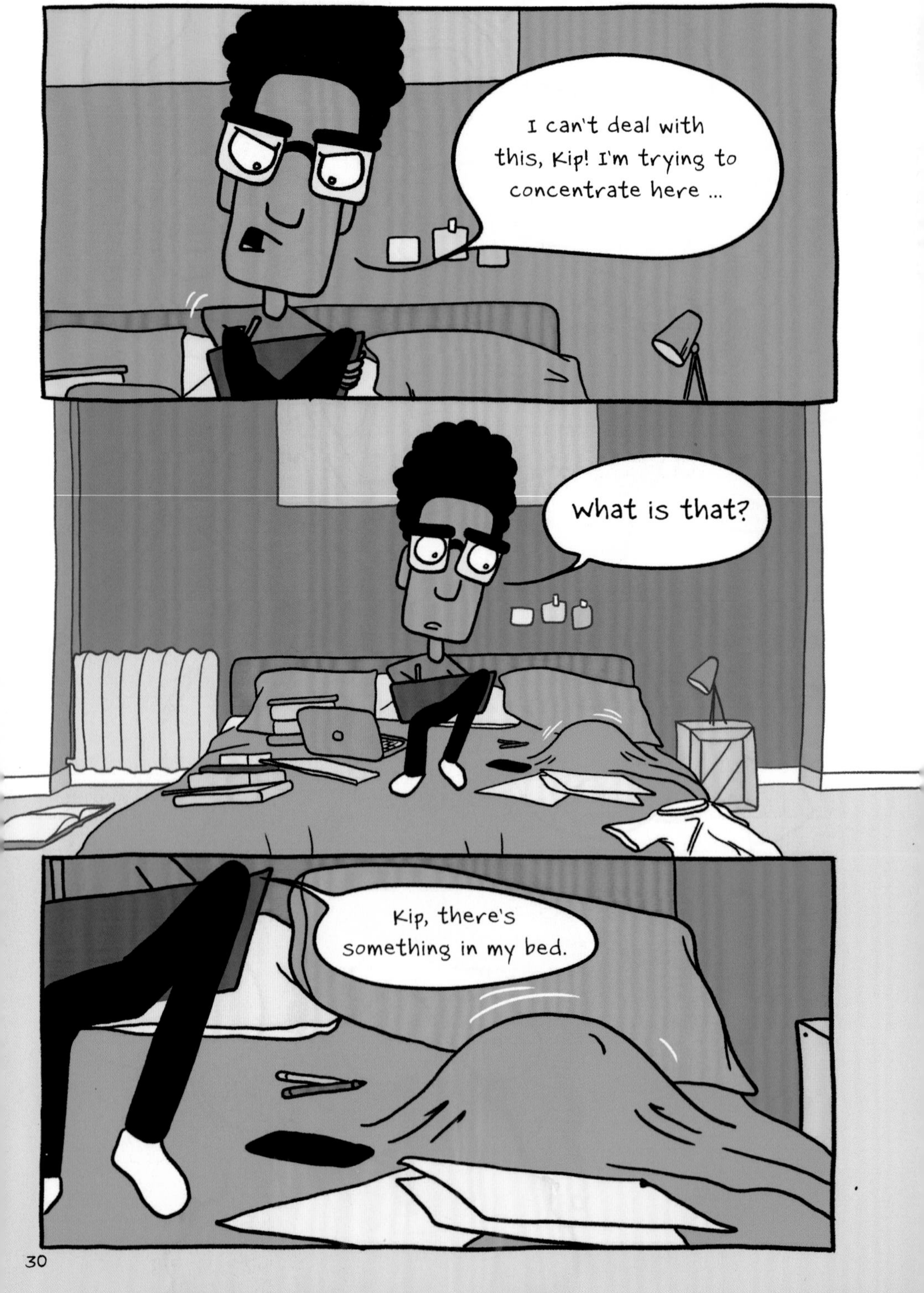
I can't deal with this, Kip! I'm trying to concentrate here ...
what is that?
Kip, there's something in my bed.

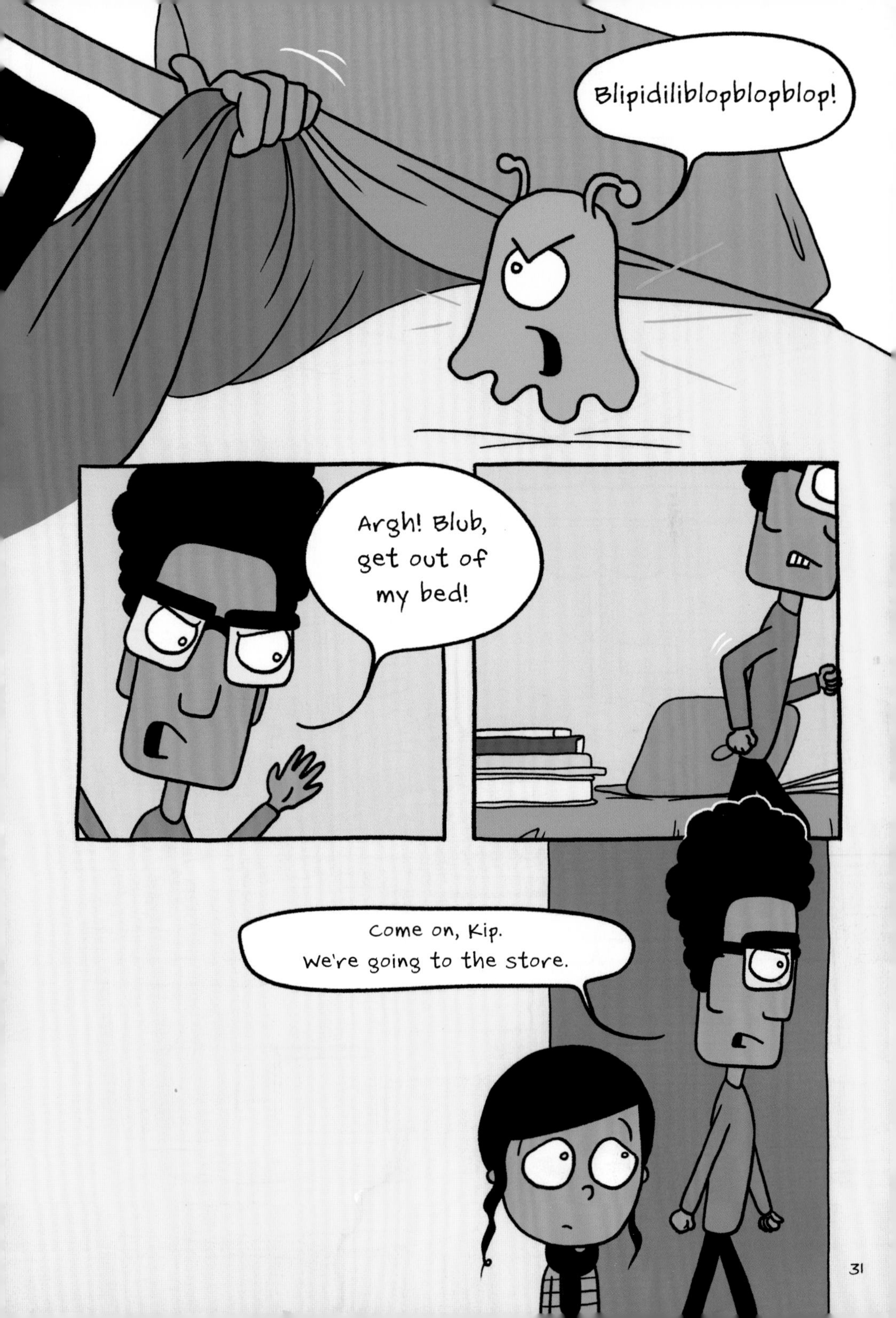
Blipidiliblopblopblop!
Argh! Blub, get out of my bed!
Come on, Kip. We're going to the store.

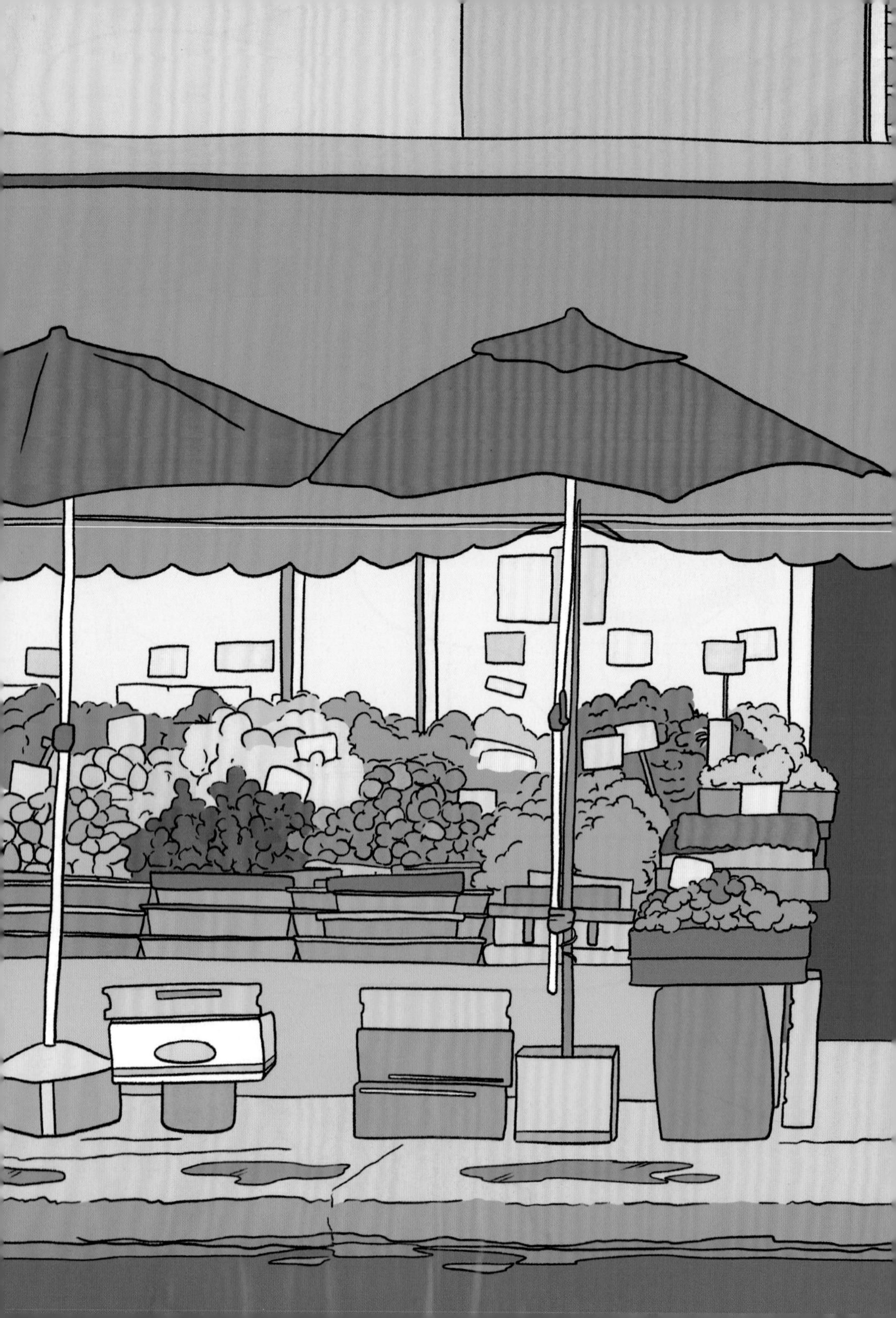

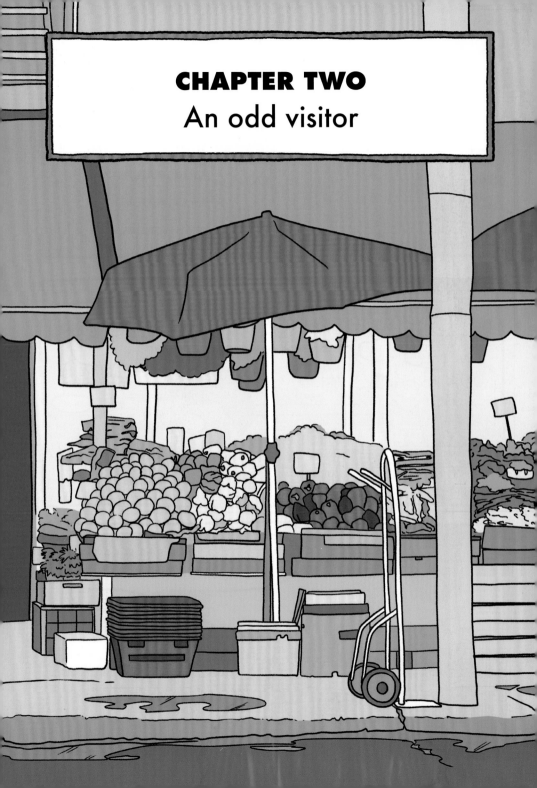

CHAPTER TWO
An odd visitor

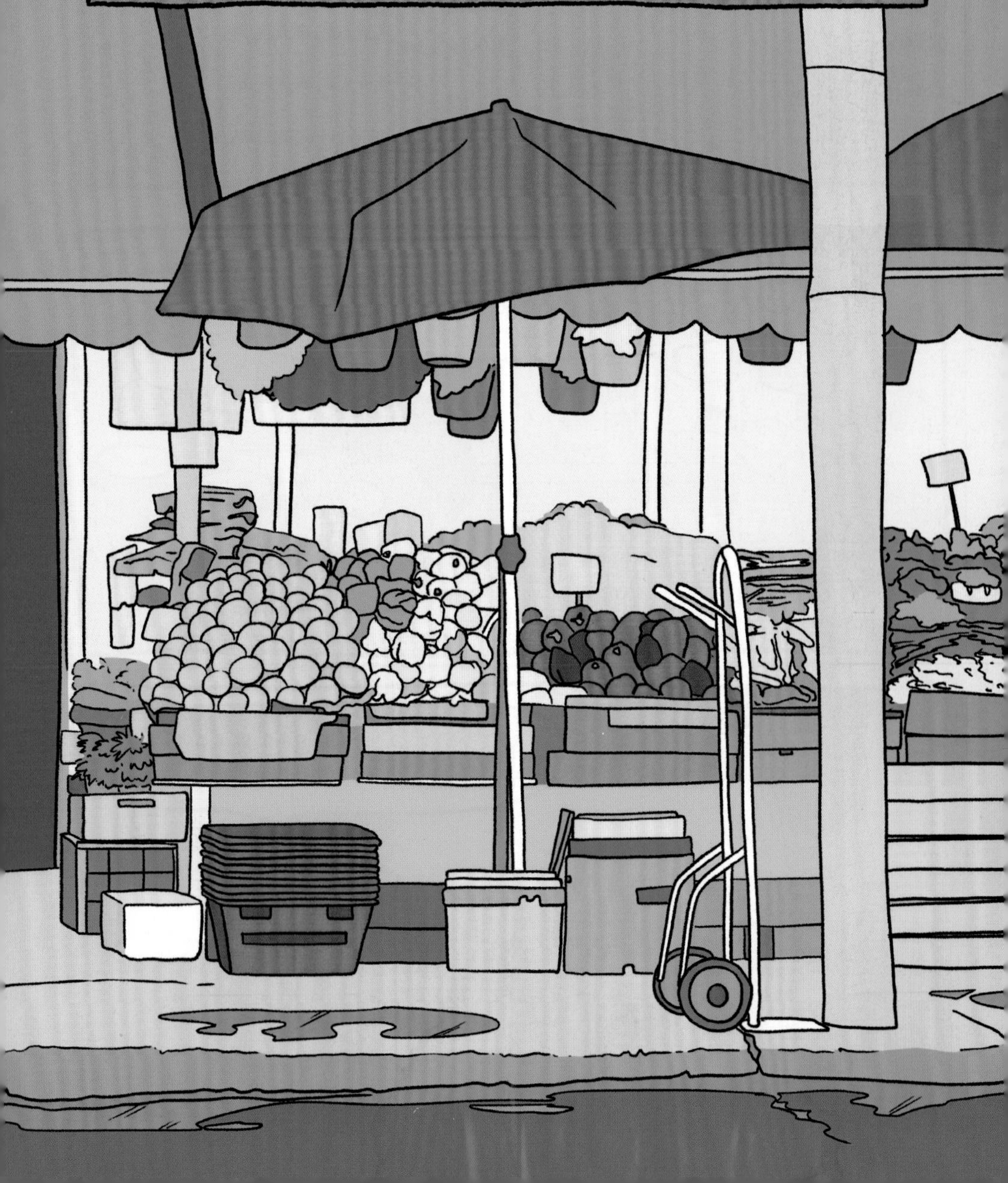

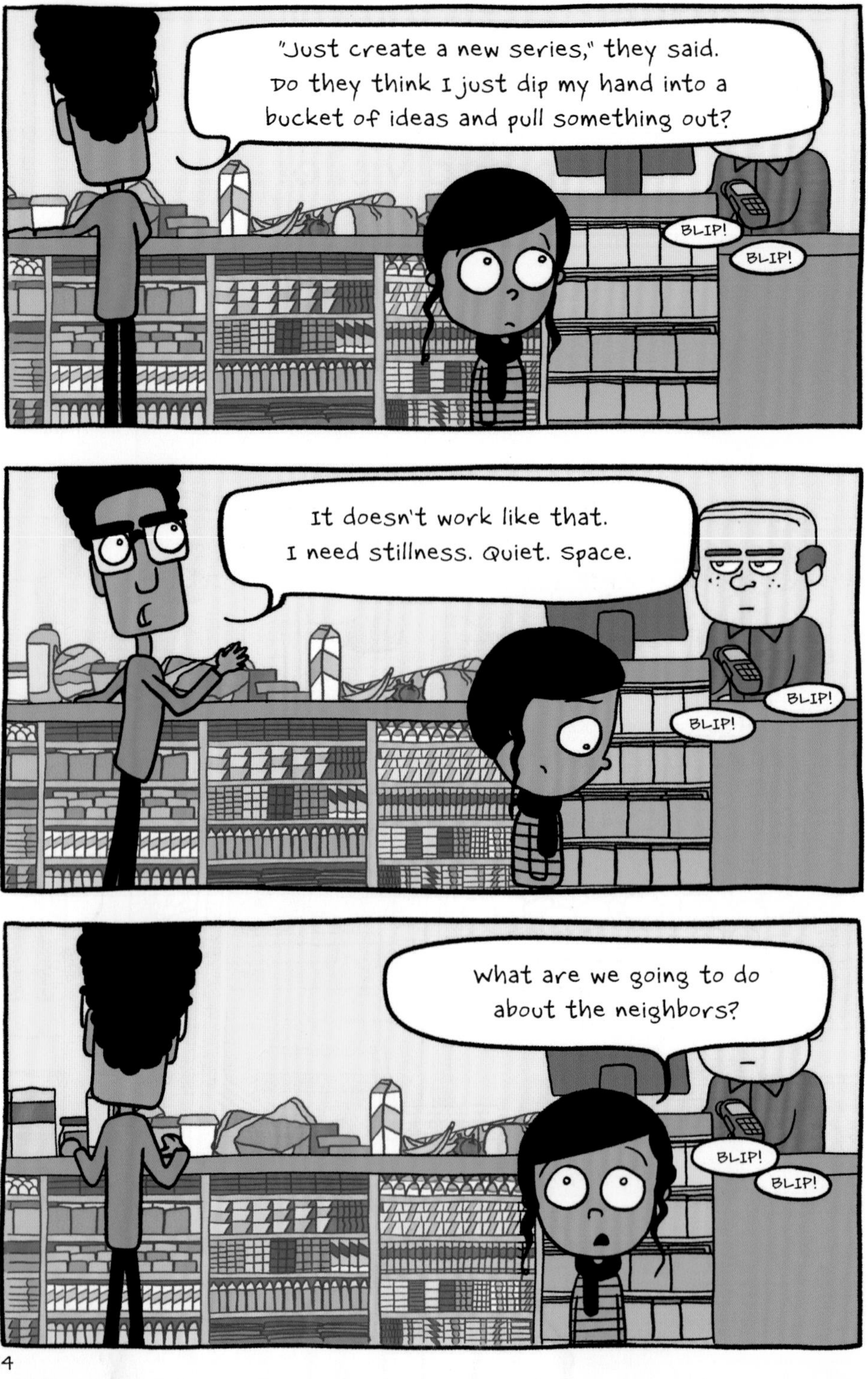
"Just create a new series," they said. Do they think I just dip my hand into a bucket of ideas and pull something out?
BLIP!
BLIP!
It doesn't work like that. I need stillness. Quiet. Space.
BLIP!
BLIP!
What are we going to do about the neighbors?
BLIP!
BLIP!

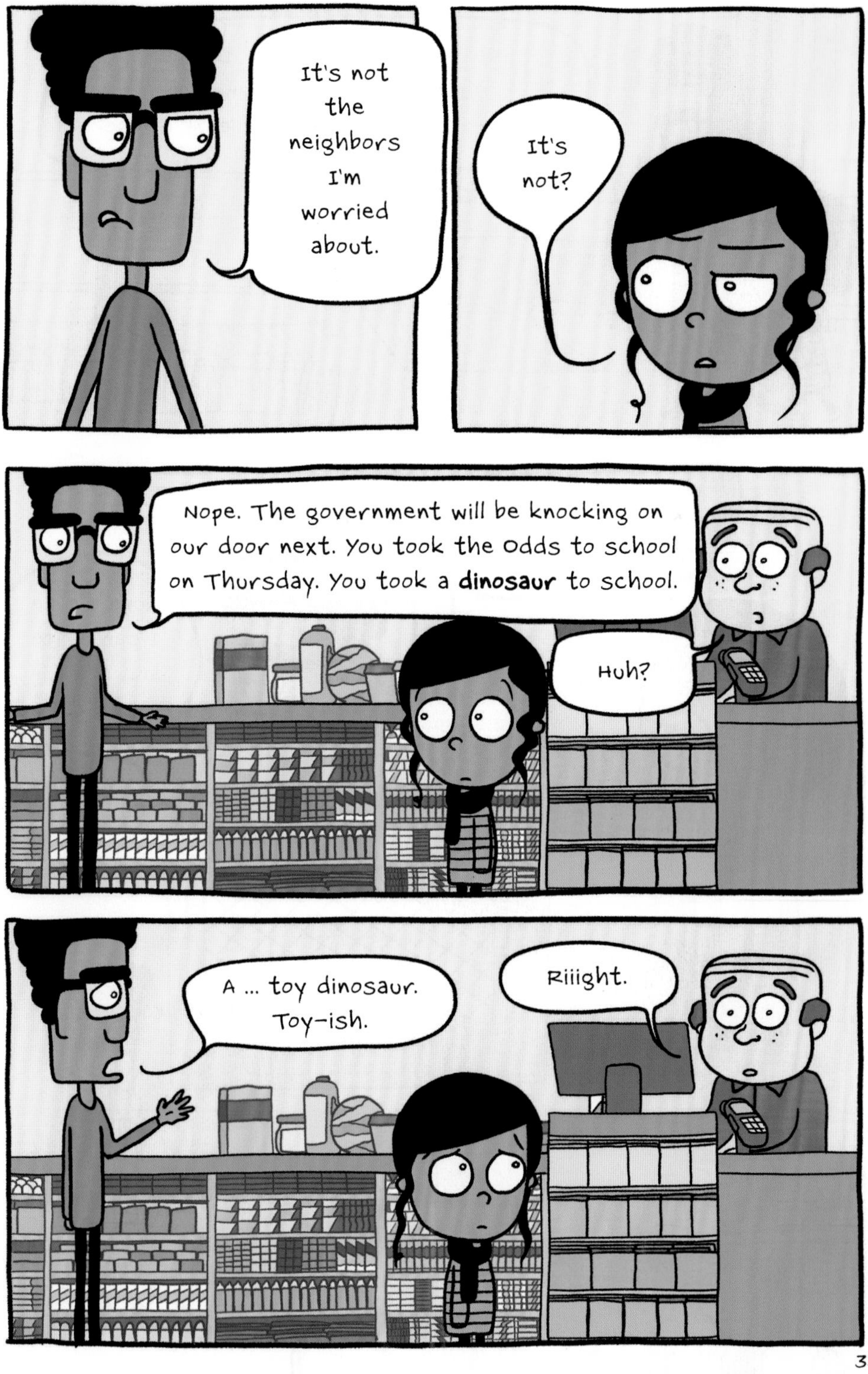
It's not the neighbors I'm worried about.
It's not?
Nope. The government will be knocking on our door next. You took the Odds to school on Thursday. You took a **dinosaur** to school.
Huh?
A ... toy dinosaur. Toy-ish.
Riiight.

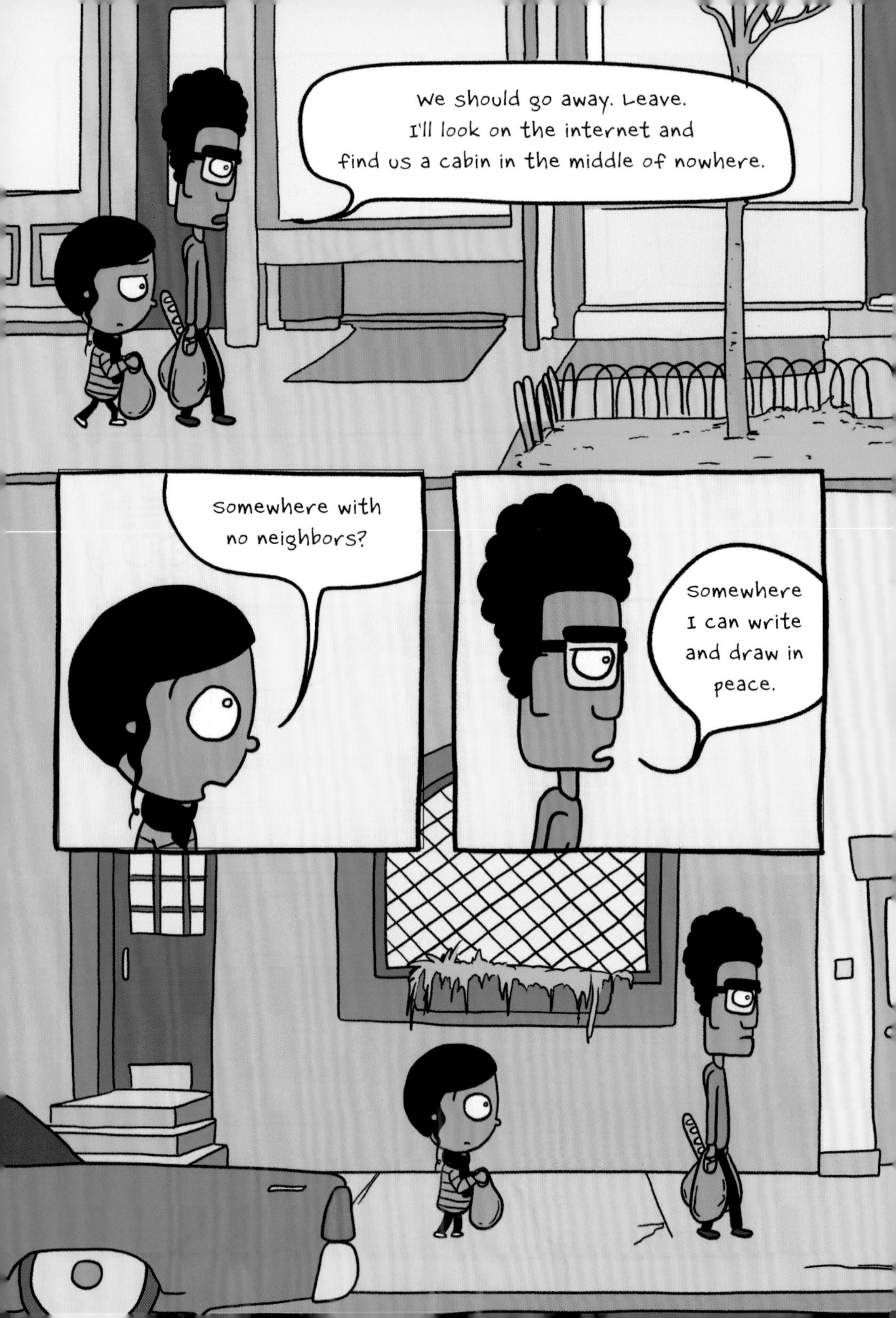
We should go away. Leave. I'll look on the internet and find us a cabin in the middle of nowhere.
Somewhere with no neighbors?
Somewhere I can write and draw in peace.

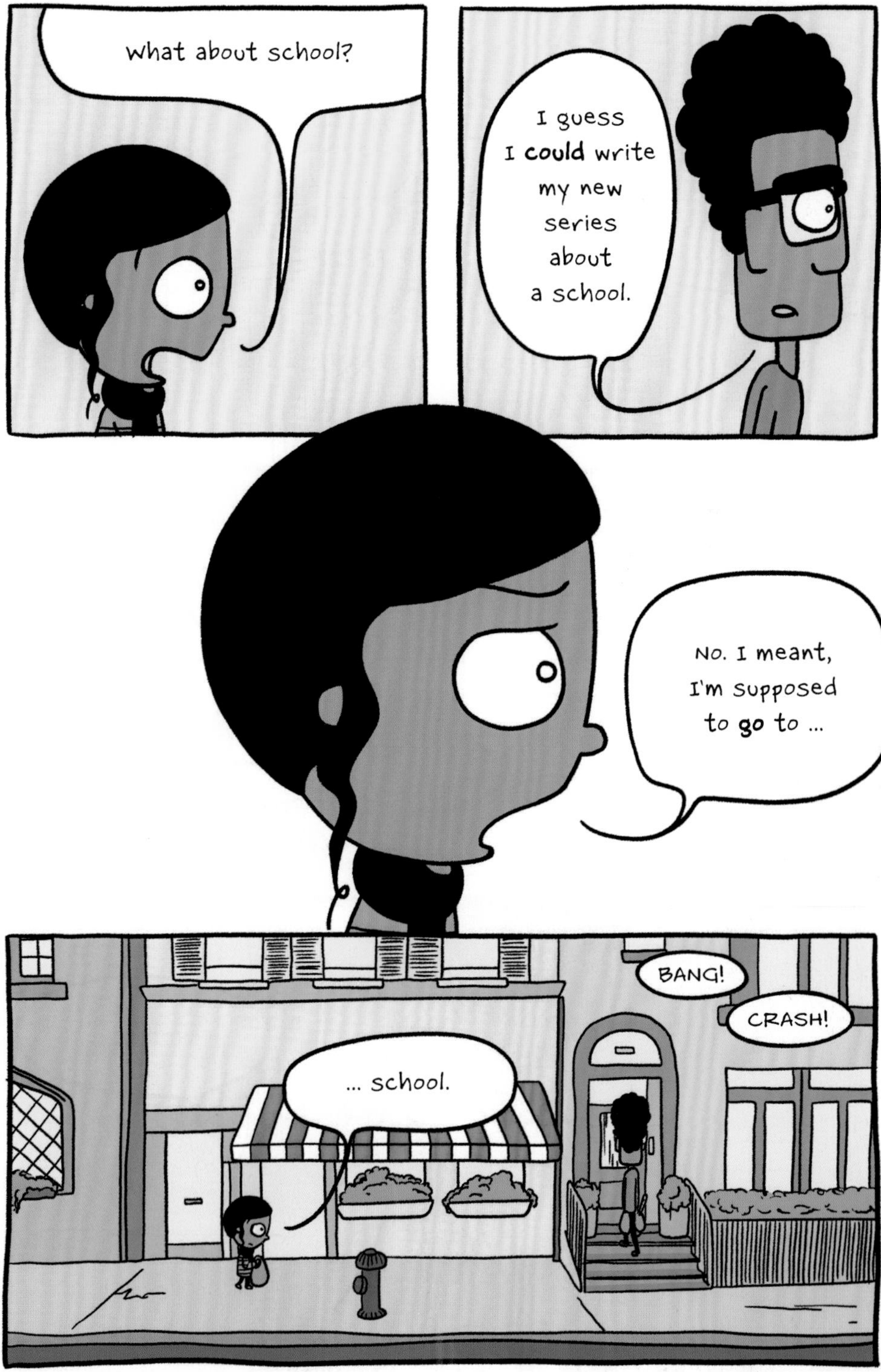

what about school?
I guess I **could** write my new series about a school.
No. I meant, I'm supposed to **go** to ...
BANG!
CRASH!
... school.

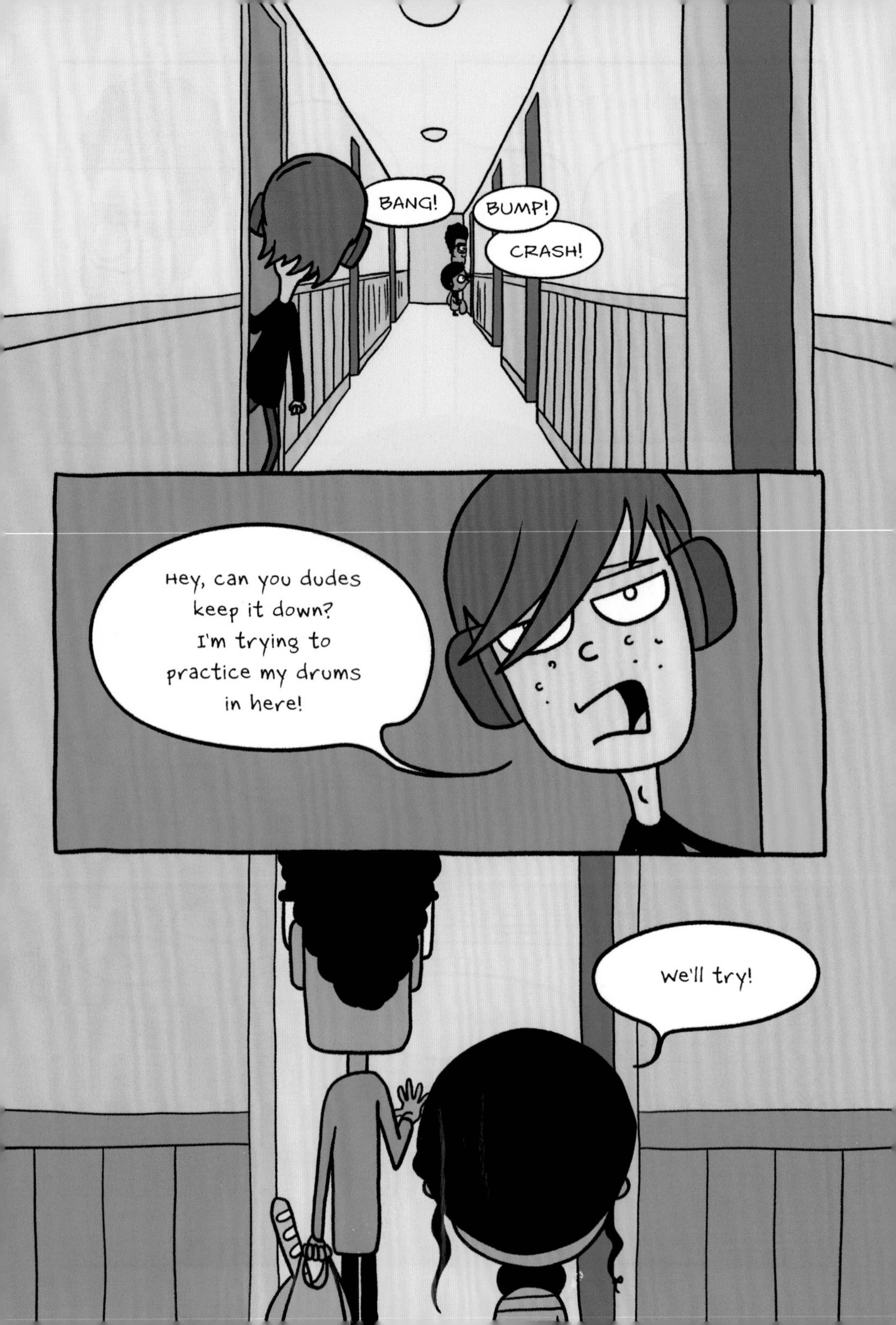
BANG!
BUMP!
CRASH!
Hey, can you dudes keep it down? I'm trying to practice my drums in here!
We'll try!

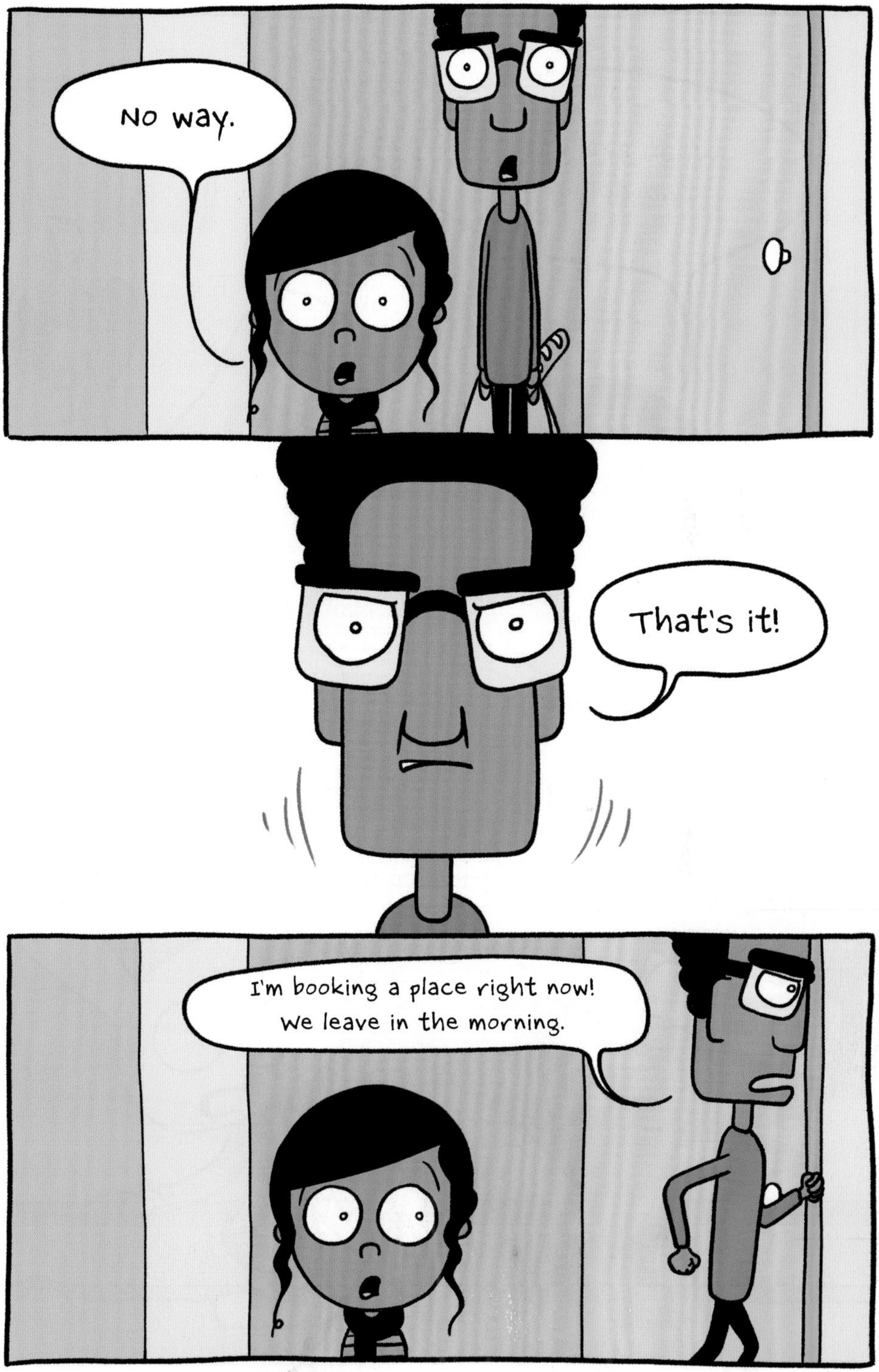
No way.
That's it!
I'm booking a place right now! We leave in the morning.

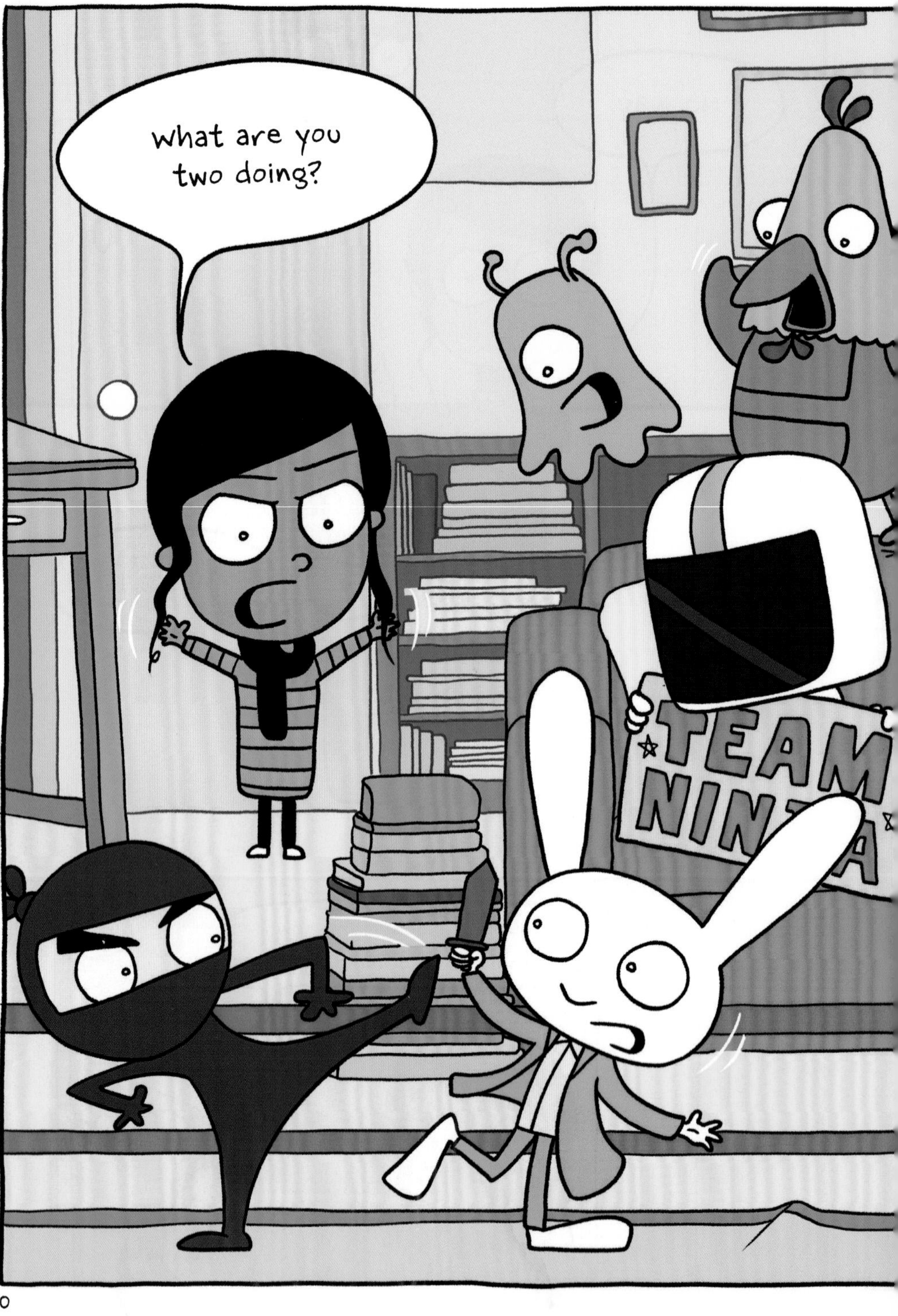
what are you two doing?
TEAM NIN

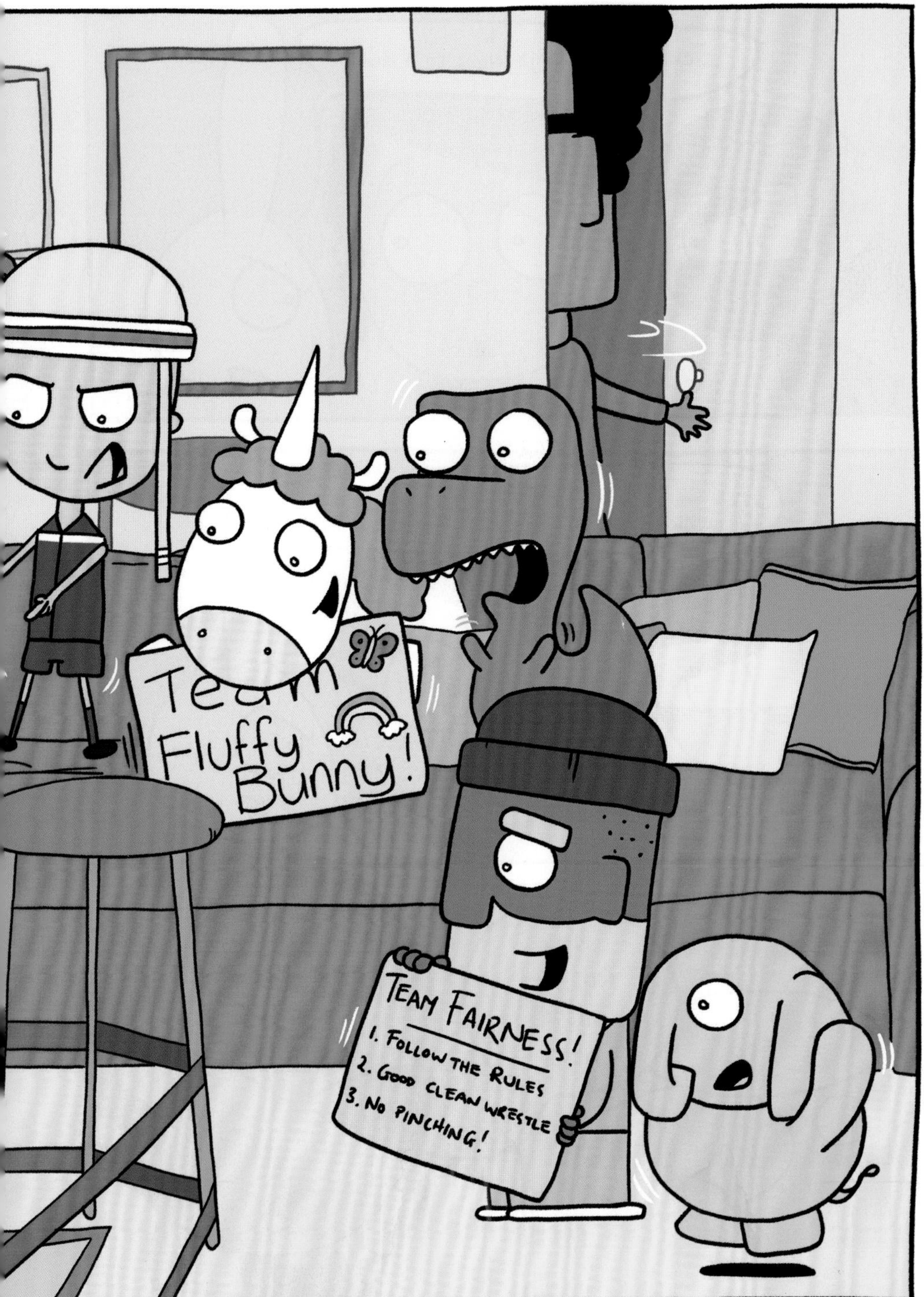
Team Fluffy Bunny!
TEAM FAIRNESS!
1. FOLLOW THE RULES
2. GOOD CLEAN WRESTLE
3. NO PINCHING!

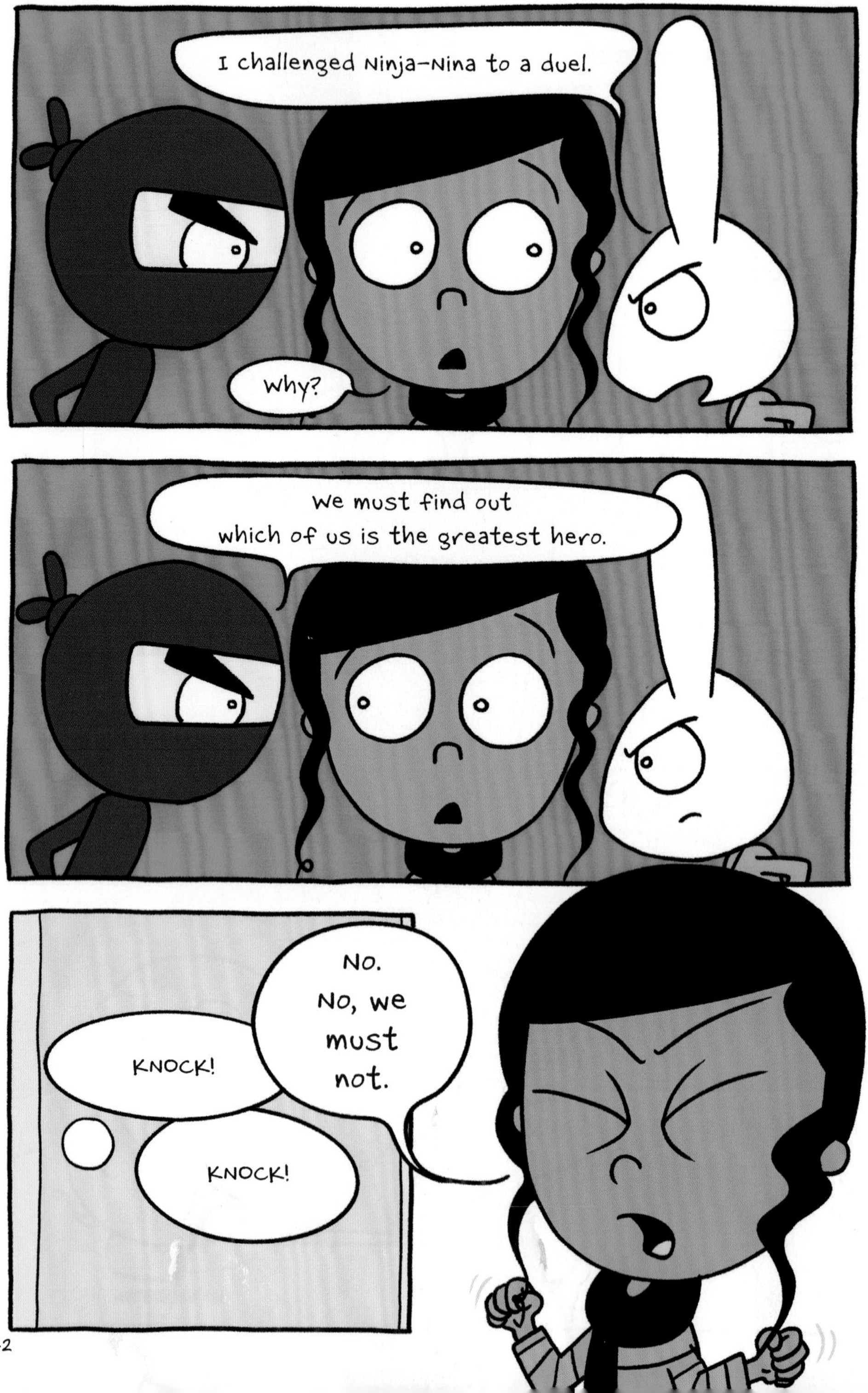
I challenged Ninja-Nina to a duel.
Why?
We must find out which of us is the greatest hero.
KNOCK!
KNOCK!
No. No, we must not.

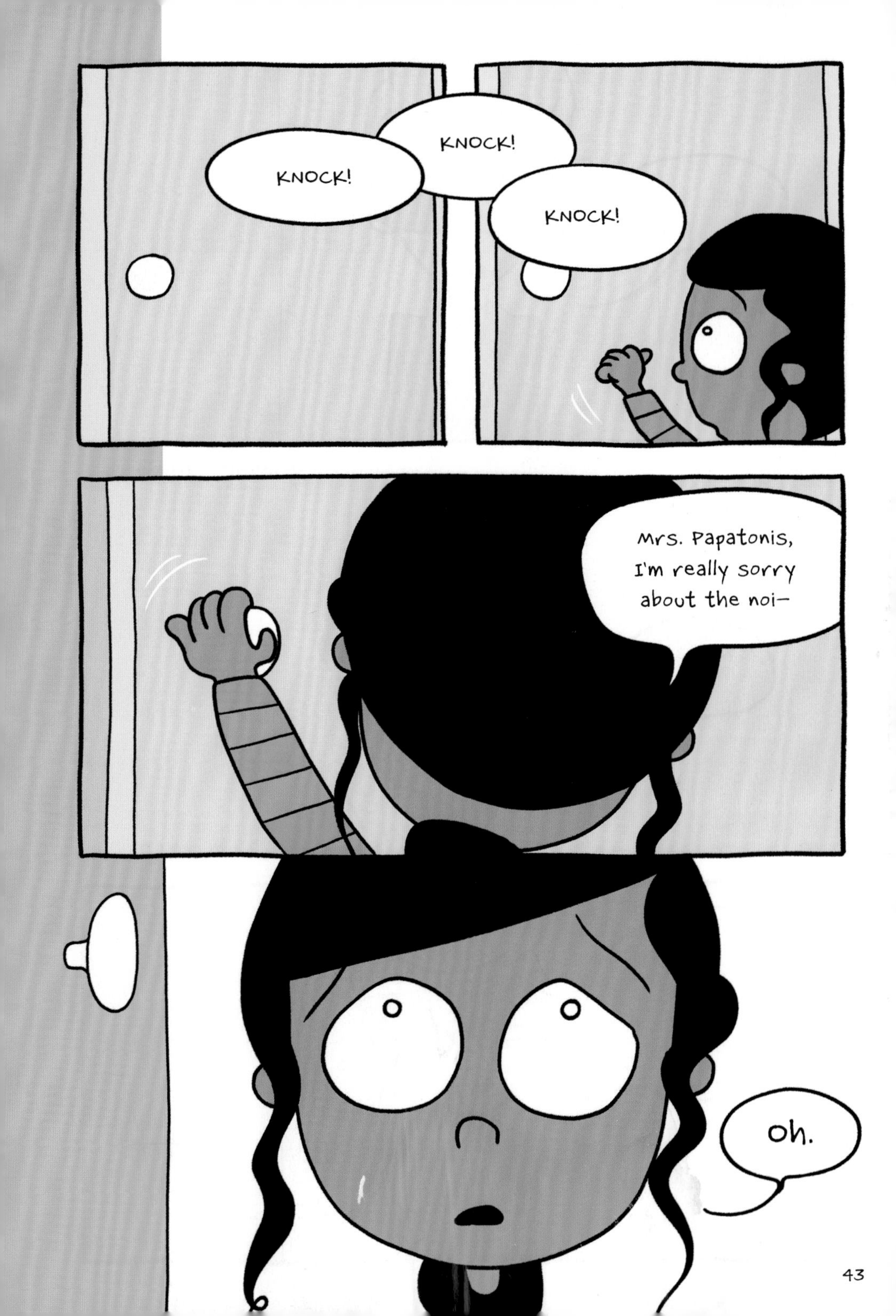
KNOCK!
KNOCK!
KNOCK!
Mrs. Papatonis, I'm really sorry about the noi–
Oh.

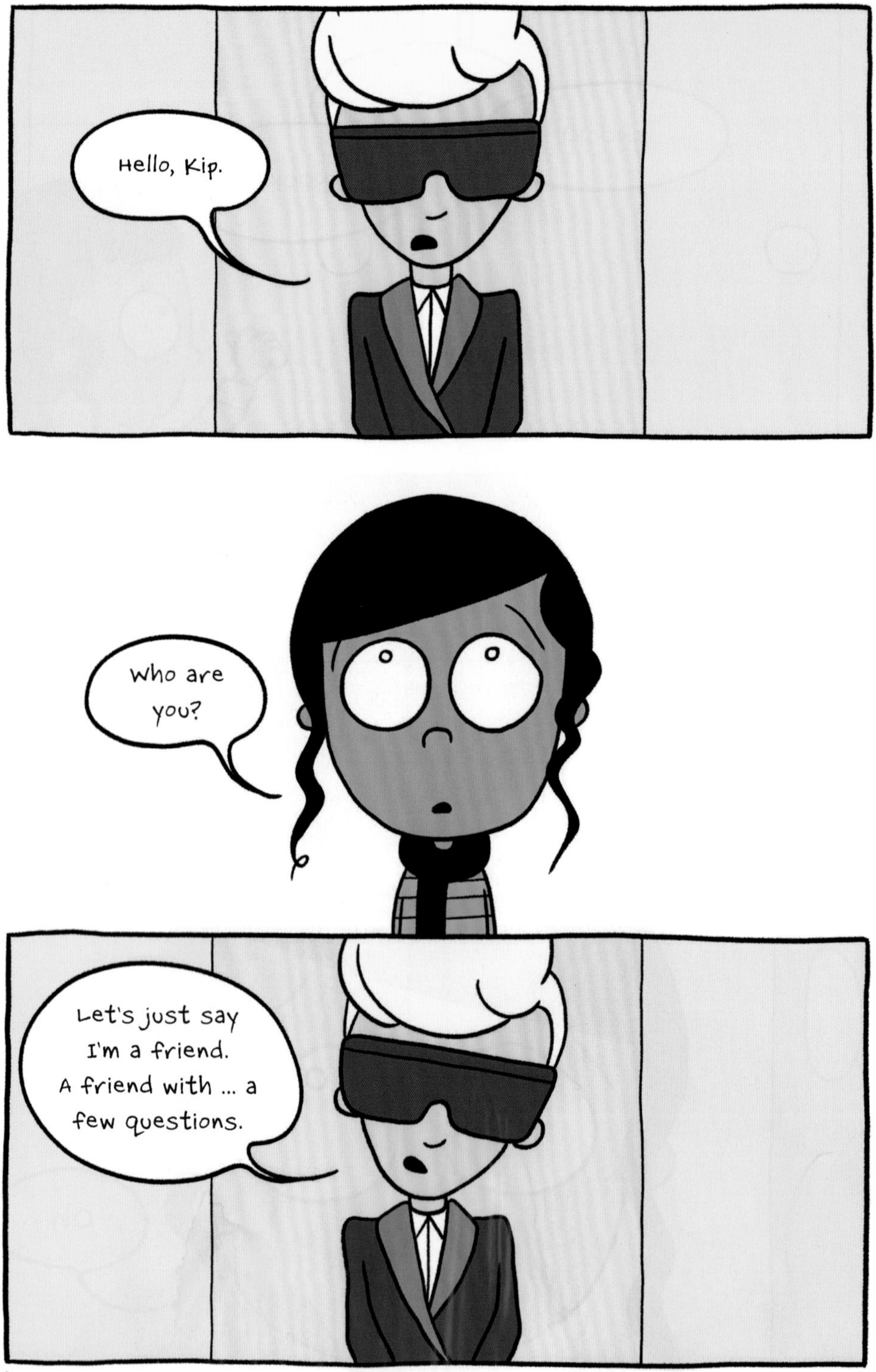
Hello, Kip.
Who are you?
Let's just say I'm a friend. A friend with ... a few questions.

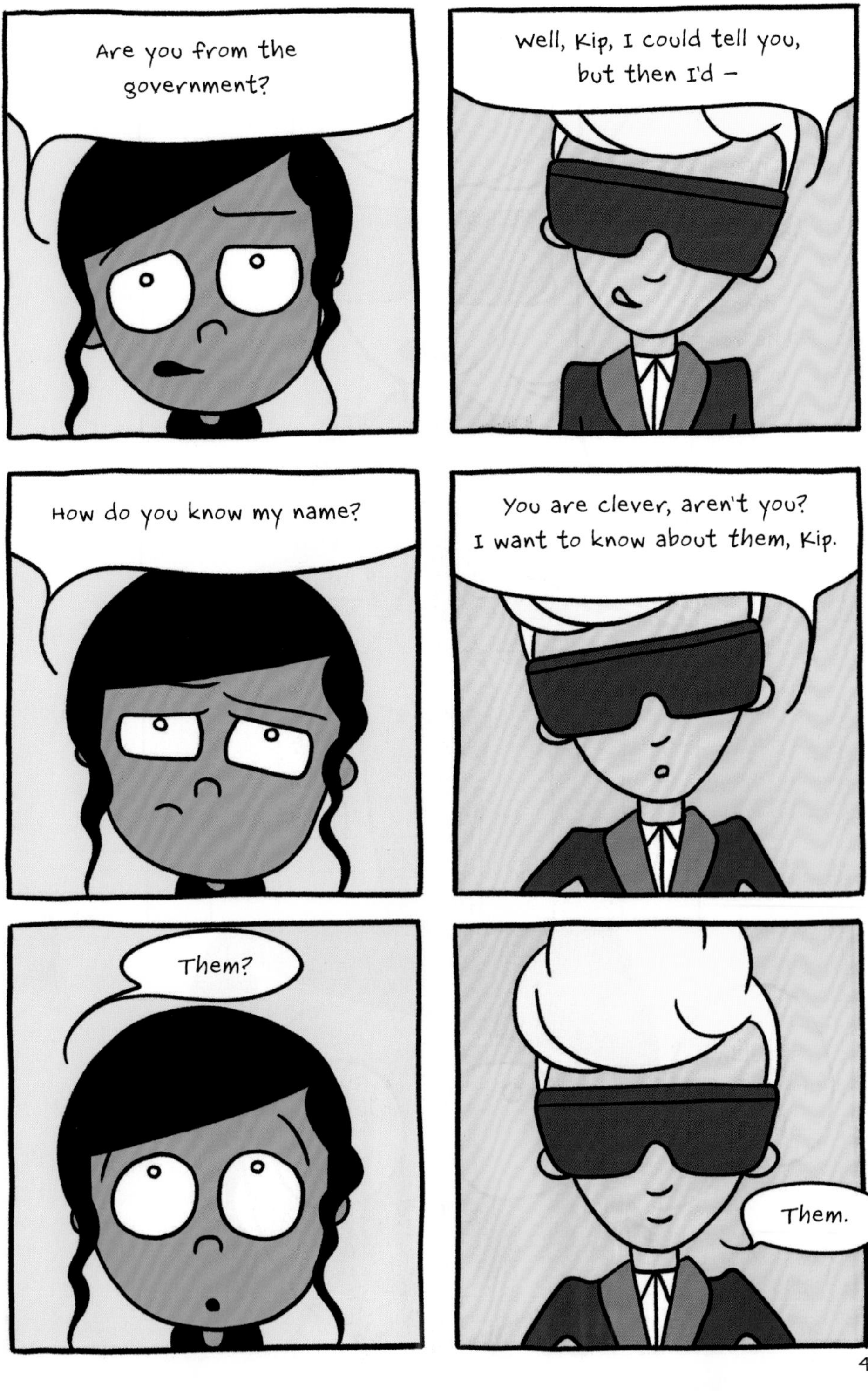
Are you from the government?
Well, Kip, I could tell you, but then I'd –
How do you know my name?
You are clever, aren't you? I want to know about them, Kip.
Them?
Them.

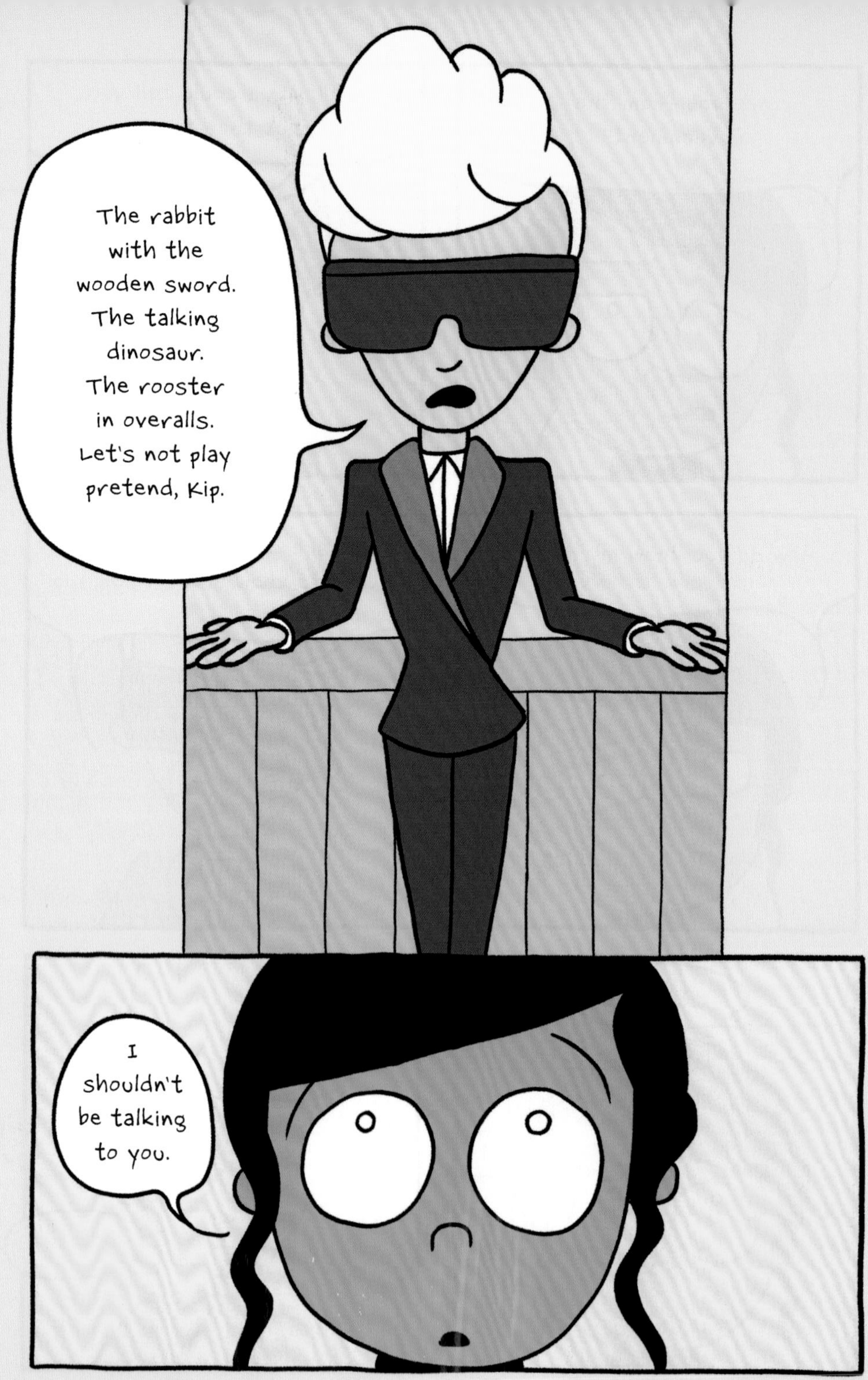
The rabbit with the wooden sword. The talking dinosaur. The rooster in overalls. Let's not play pretend, Kip.
I shouldn't be talking to you.

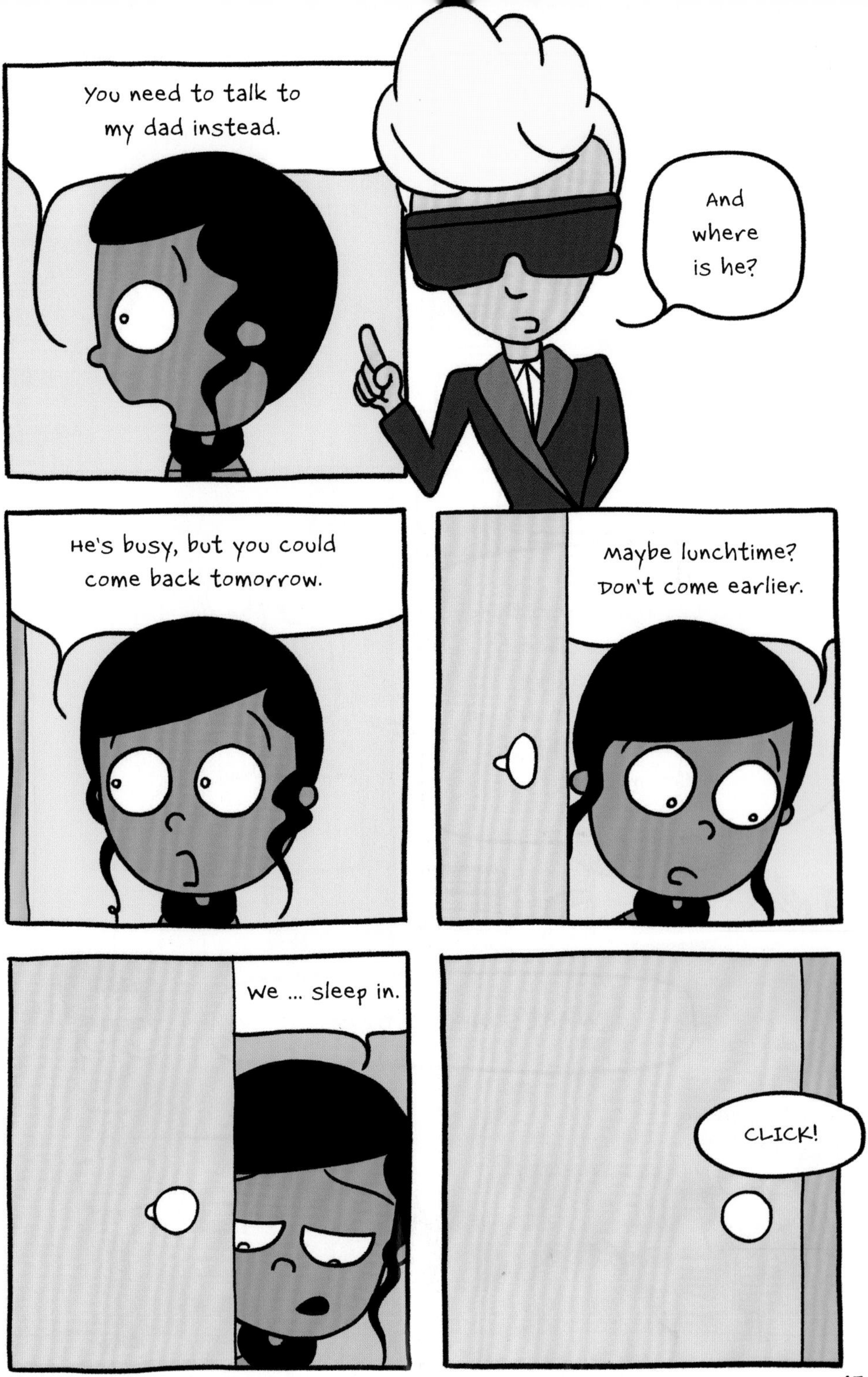
You need to talk to my dad instead.
And where is he?
He's busy, but you could come back tomorrow.
Maybe lunchtime? Don't come earlier.
We ... sleep in.
CLICK!

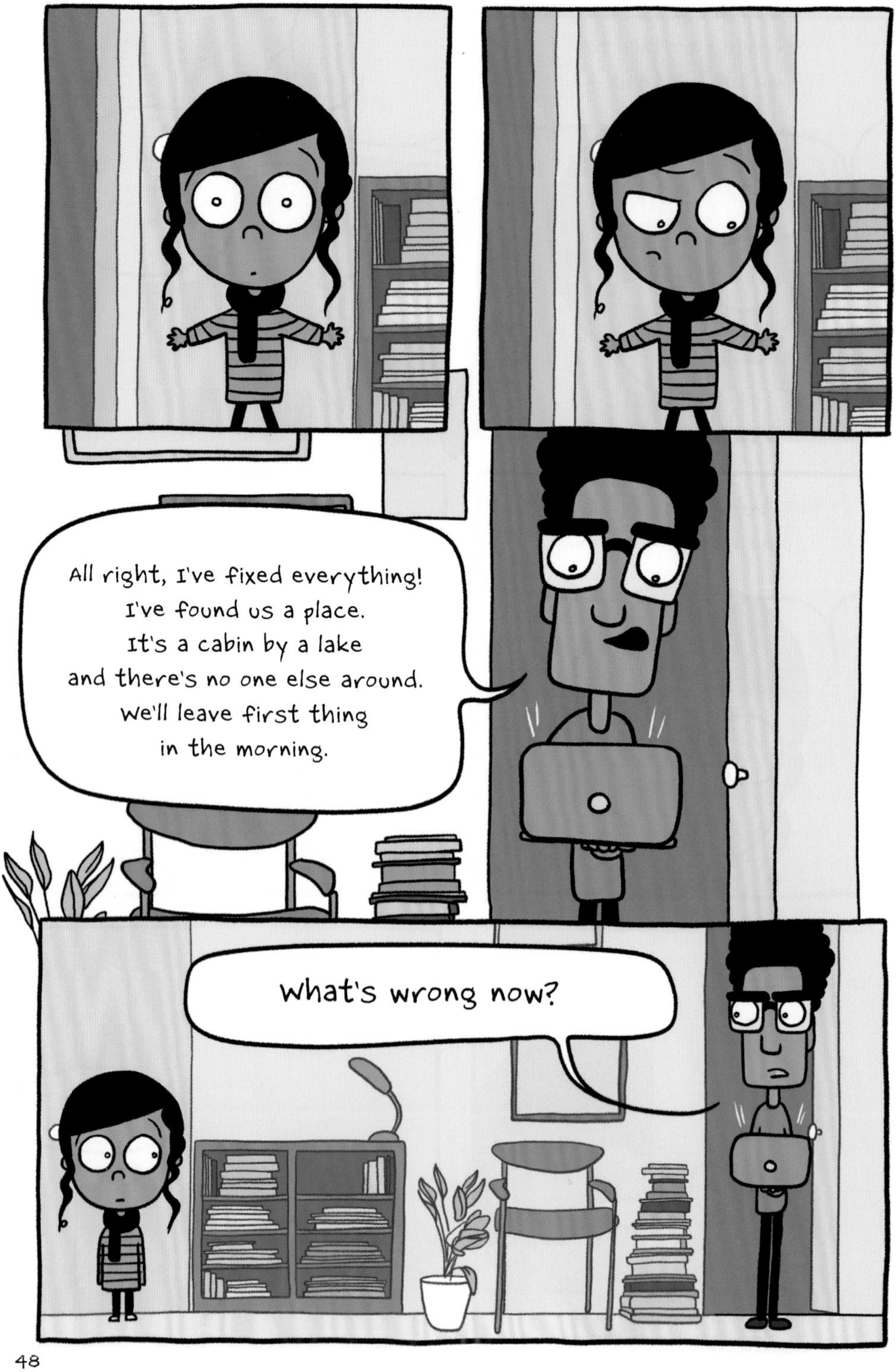
All right, I've fixed everything! I've found us a place. It's a cabin by a lake and there's no one else around. We'll leave first thing in the morning.
What's wrong now?

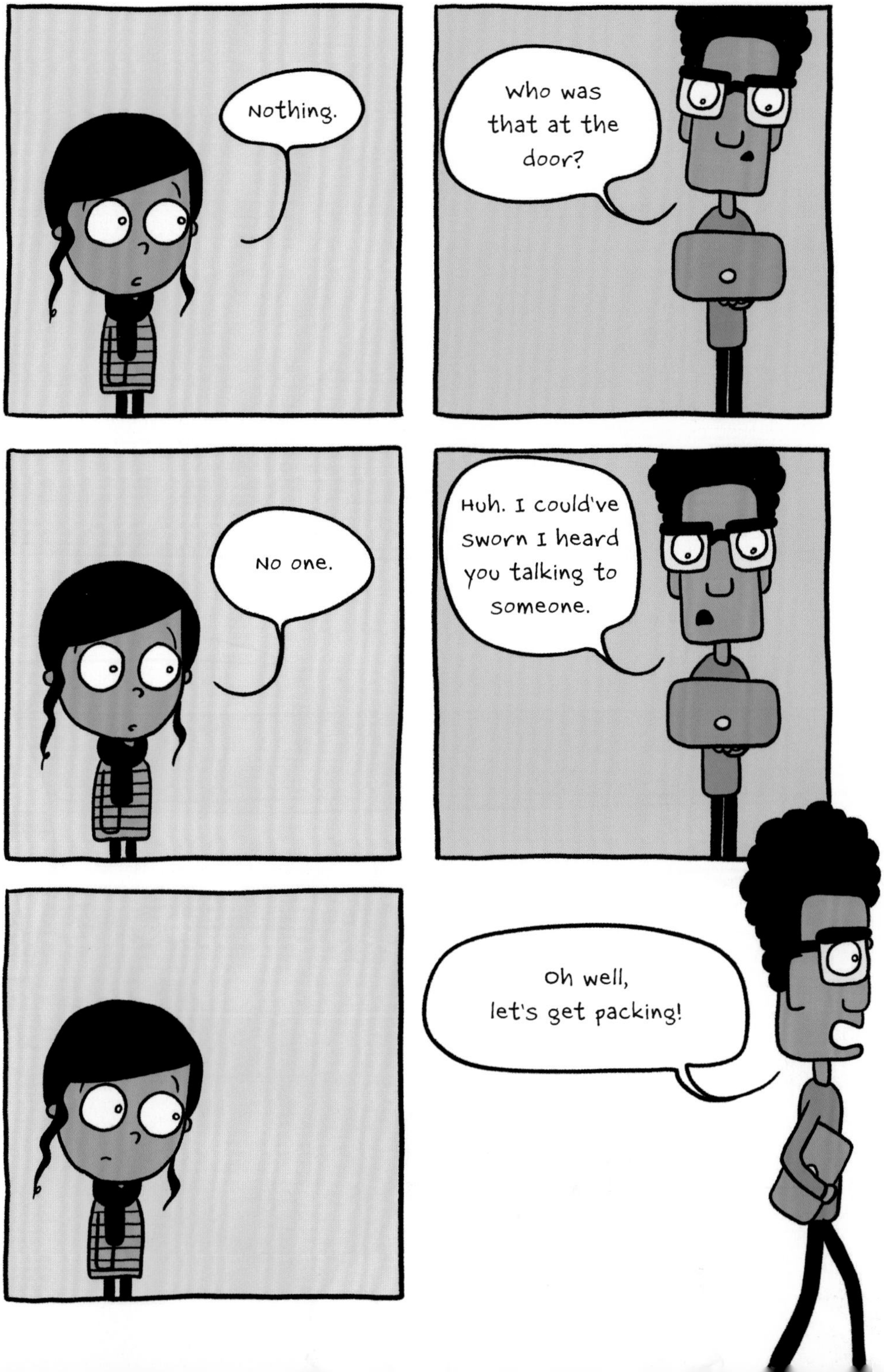
Nothing.
Who was that at the door?
No one.
Huh. I could've sworn I heard you talking to someone.
Oh well, let's get packing!

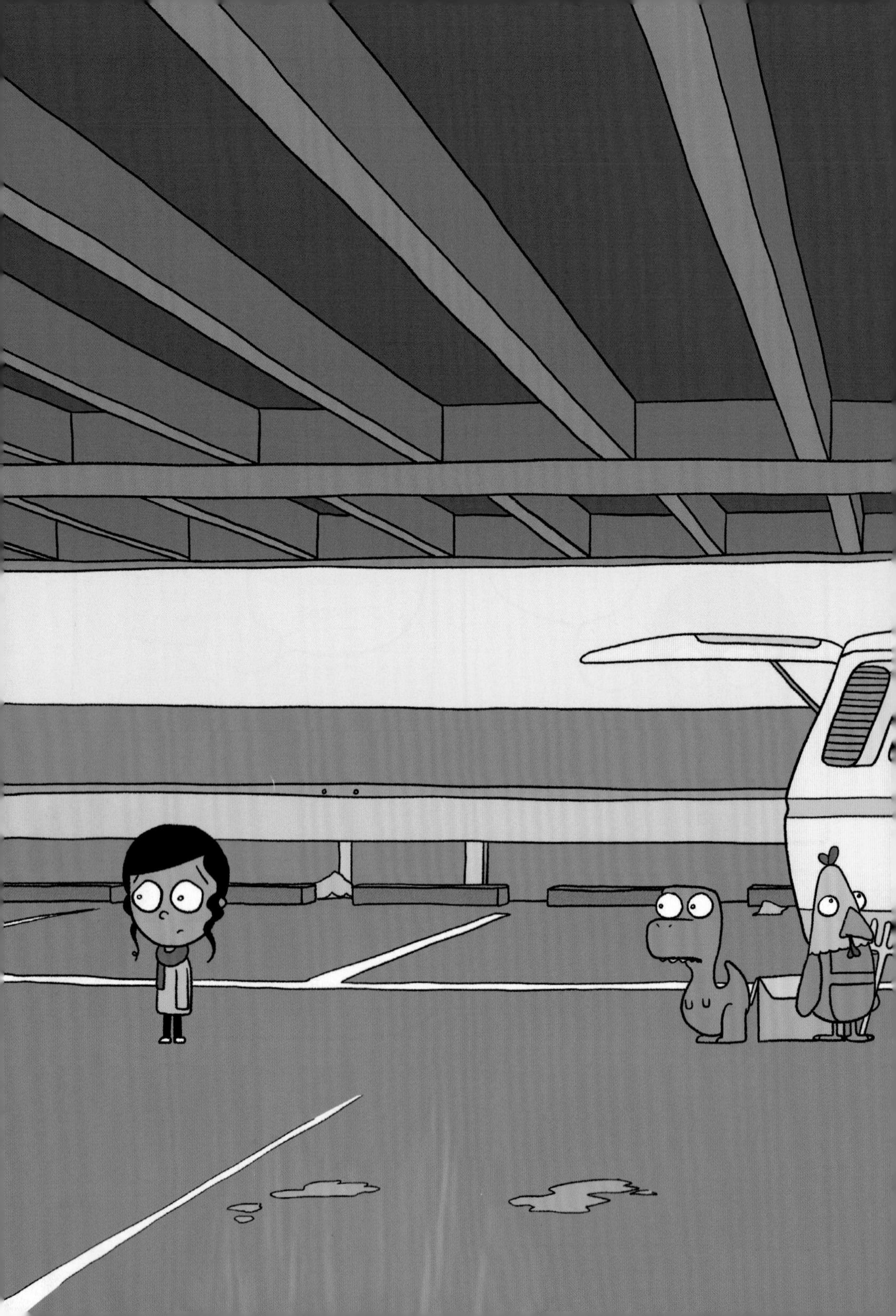

CHAPTER THREE
Odds on the run

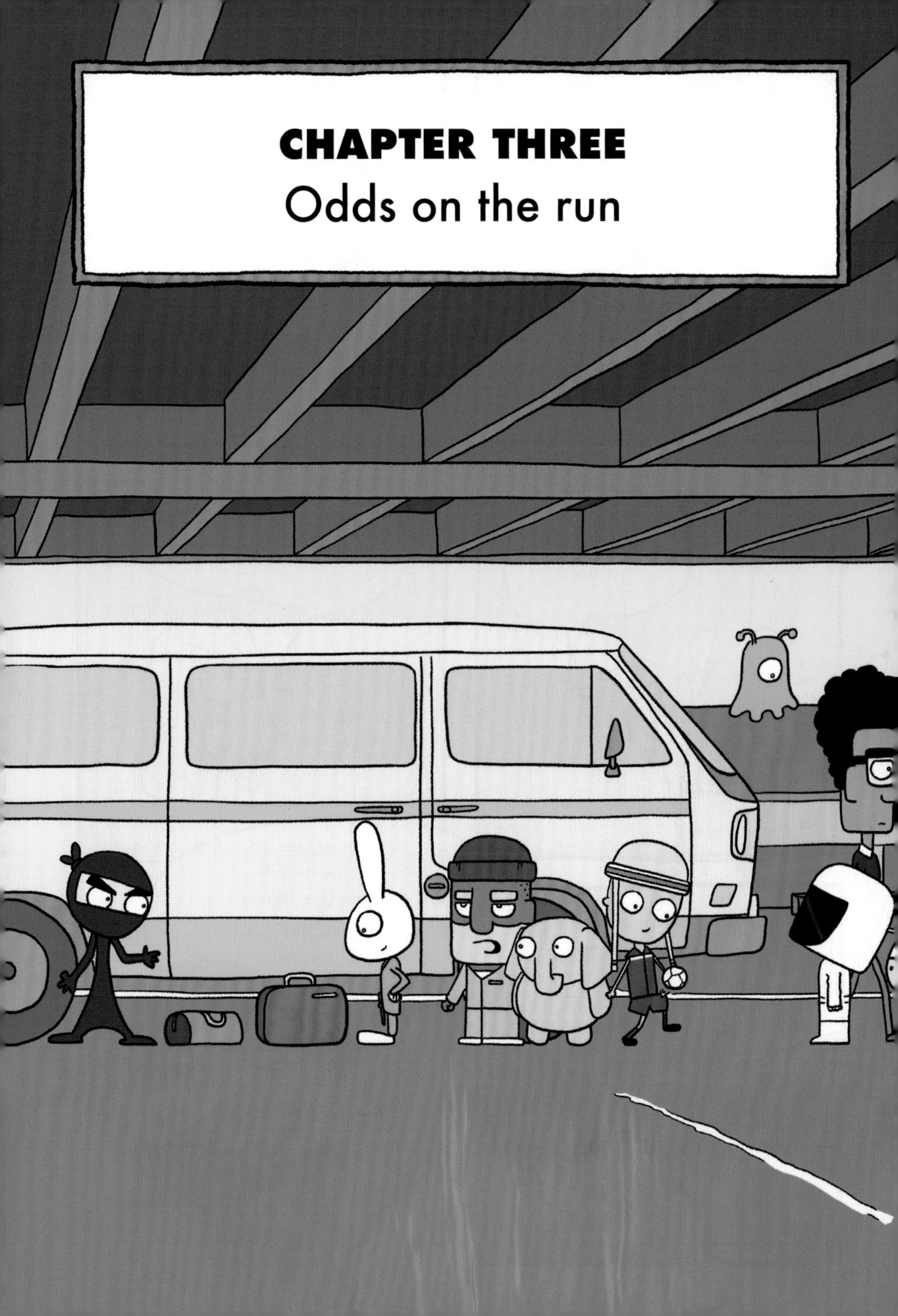

As we embark upon this epic quest together,

I want to thank you all for the honor of making me your leader.

say what now?

Blipblop!

Did I sleep through an election again?

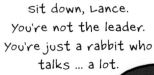

Sit down, Lance. You're not the leader. You're just a rabbit who talks ... a lot.

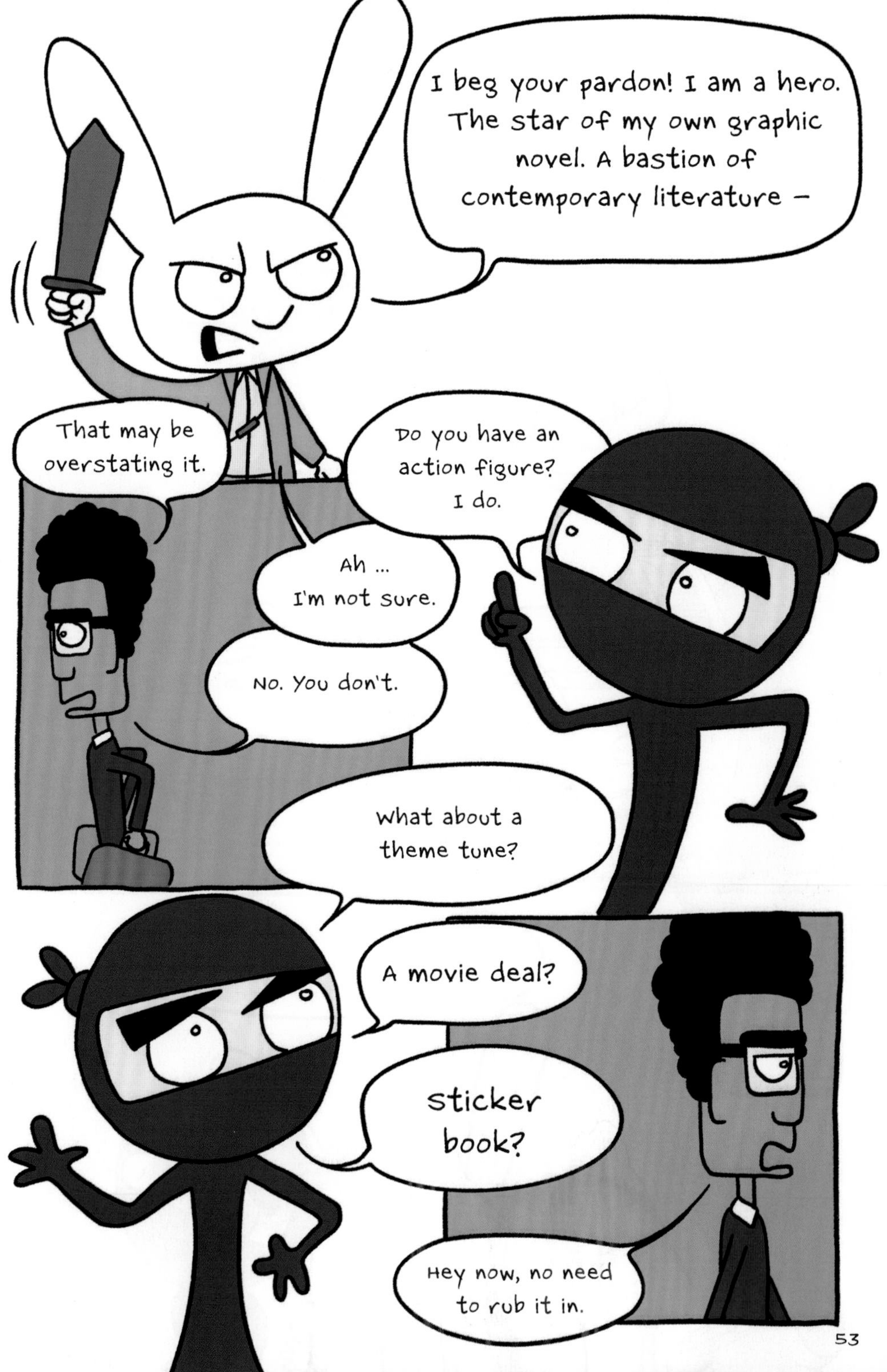
I beg your pardon! I am a hero. The star of my own graphic novel. A bastion of contemporary literature –
That may be overstating it.
Do you have an action figure? I do.
Ah ... I'm not sure.
No. You don't.
What about a theme tune?
A movie deal?
Sticker book?
Hey now, no need to rub it in.

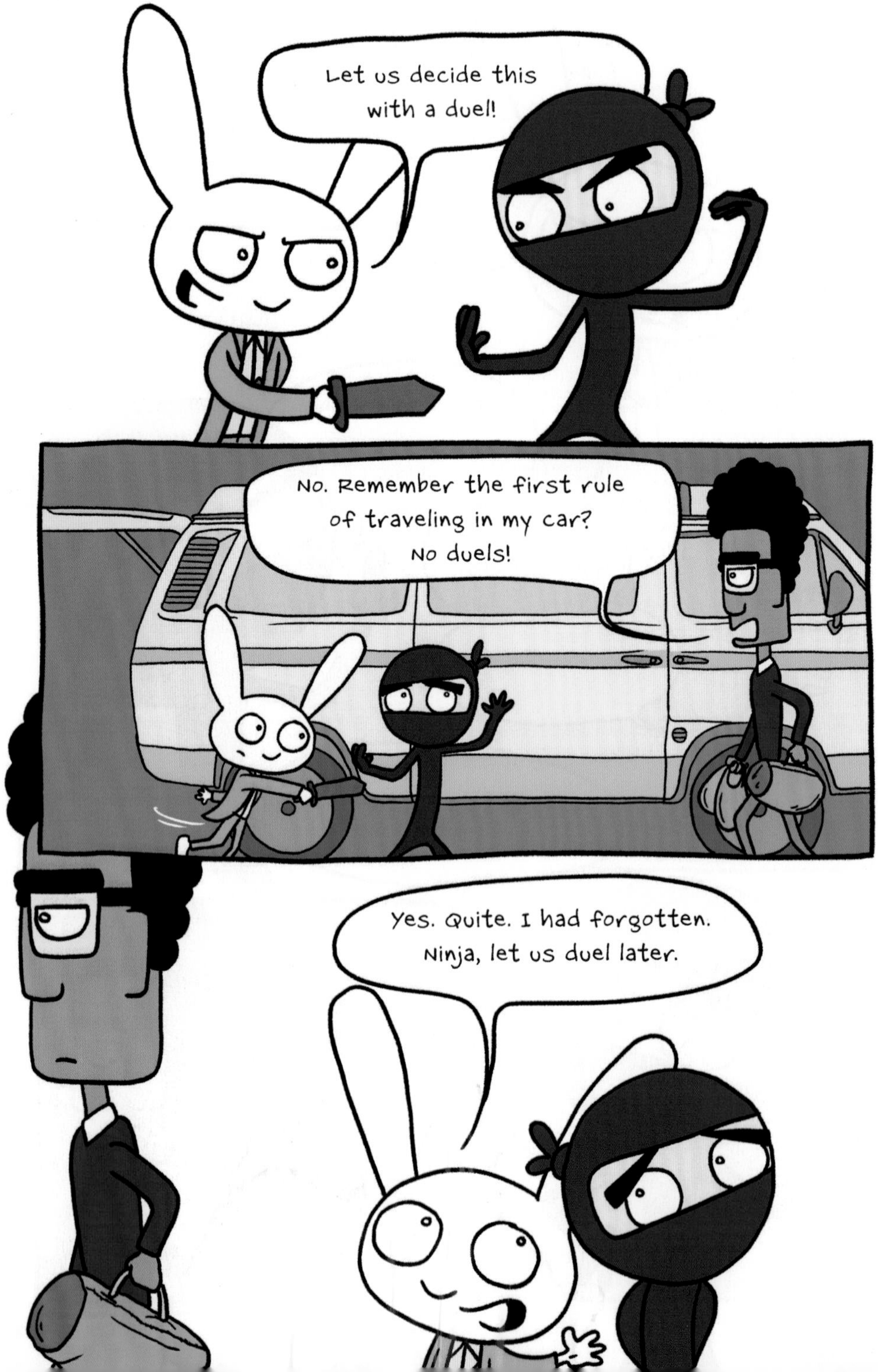
Let us decide this with a duel!
No. Remember the first rule of traveling in my car? No duels!
Yes. Quite. I had forgotten. Ninja, let us duel later.

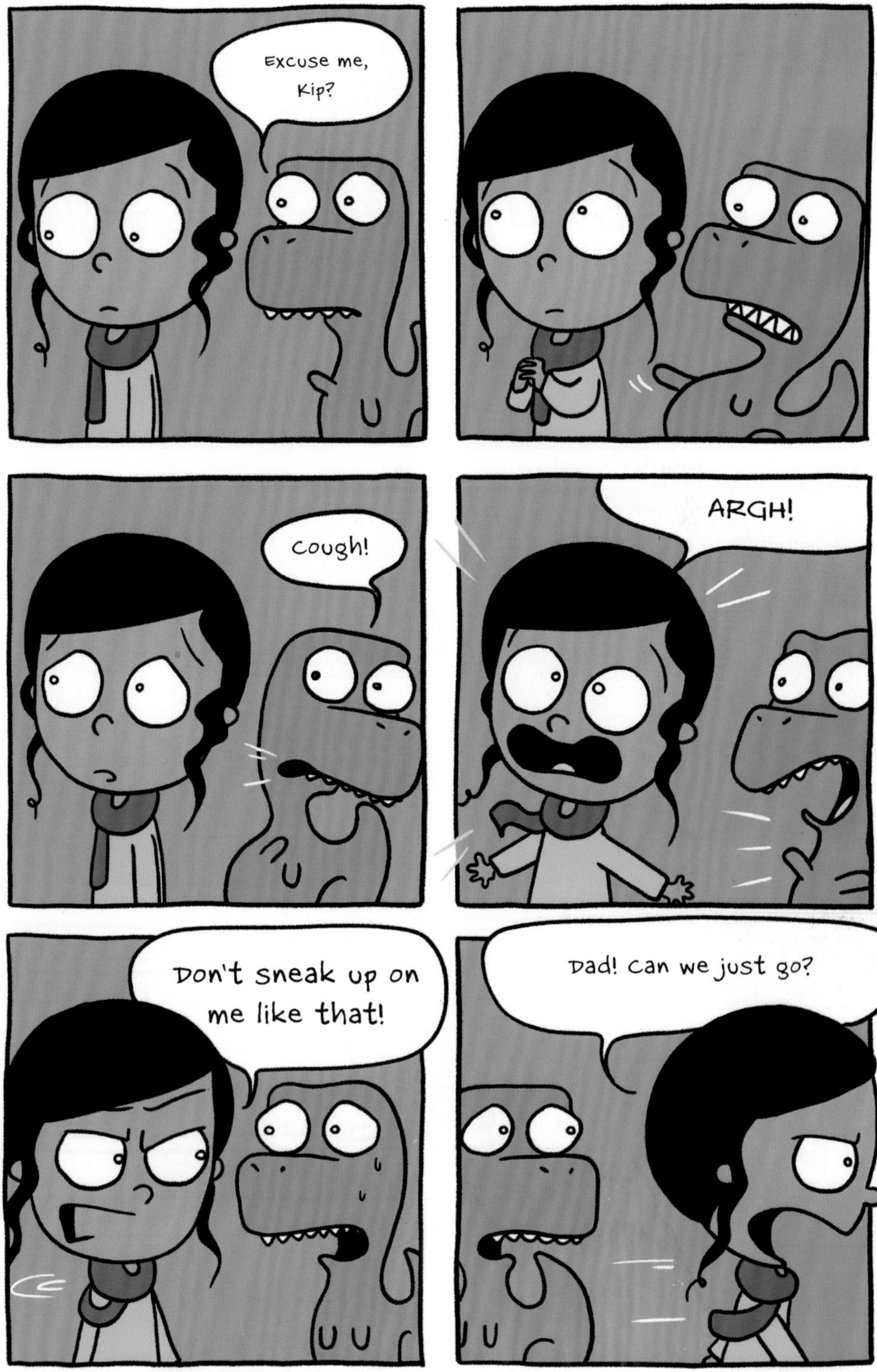
Excuse me, Kip?
Cough!
ARGH!
Don't sneak up on me like that!
Dad! Can we just go?

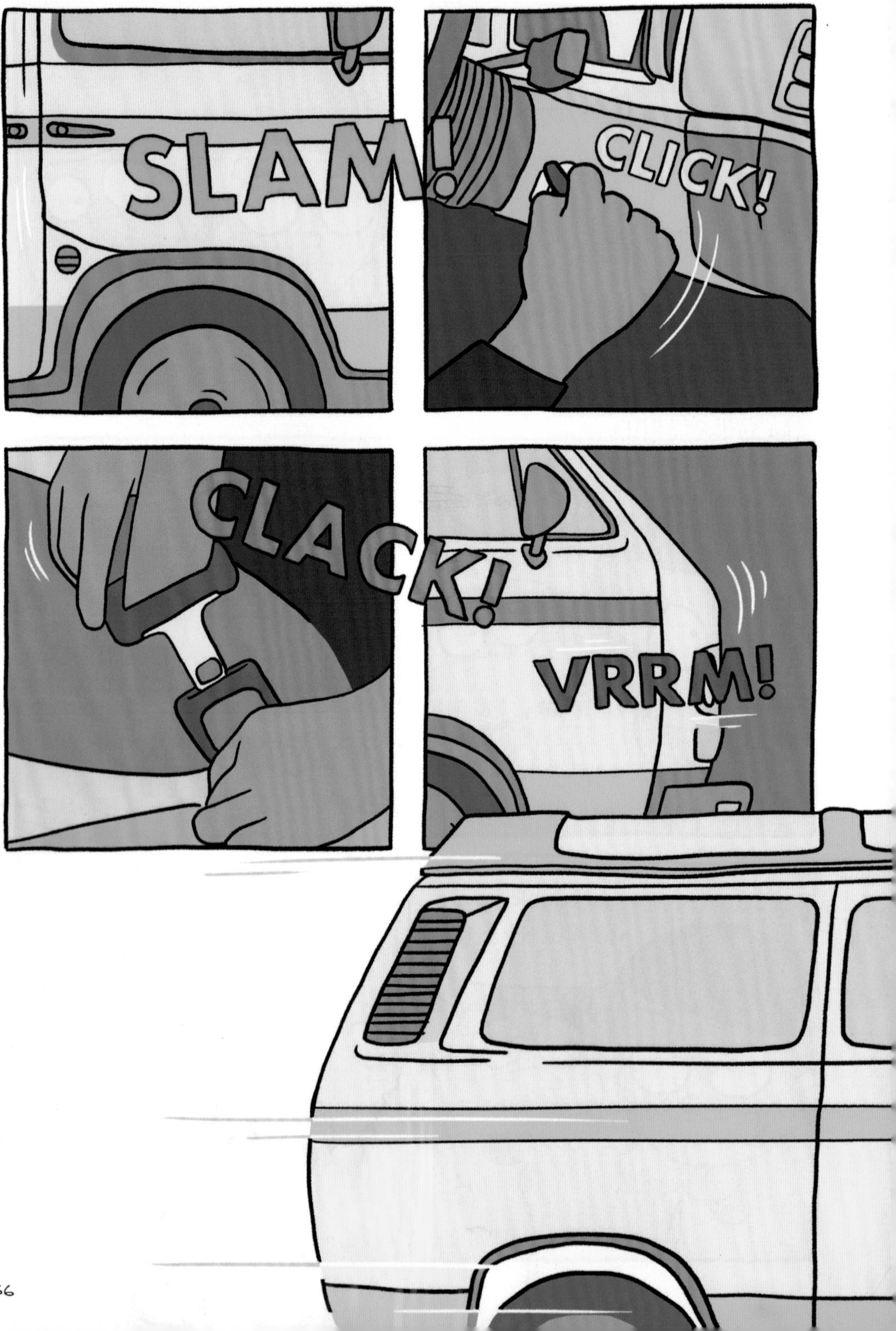
SLAM!
CLICK!
CLACK!
VRRM!

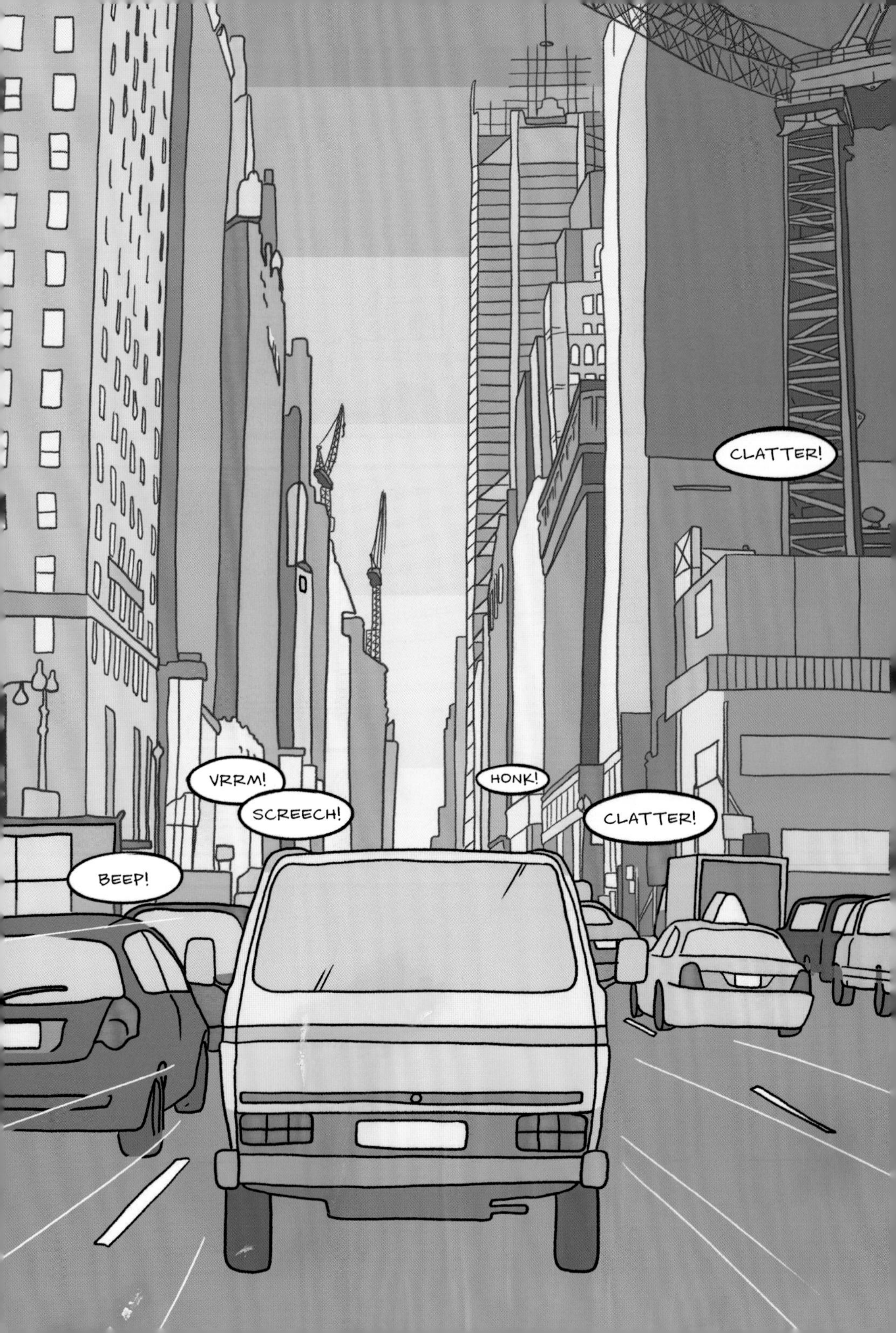
CLATTER!
VRRM!
SCREECH!
HONK!
CLATTER!
BEEP!

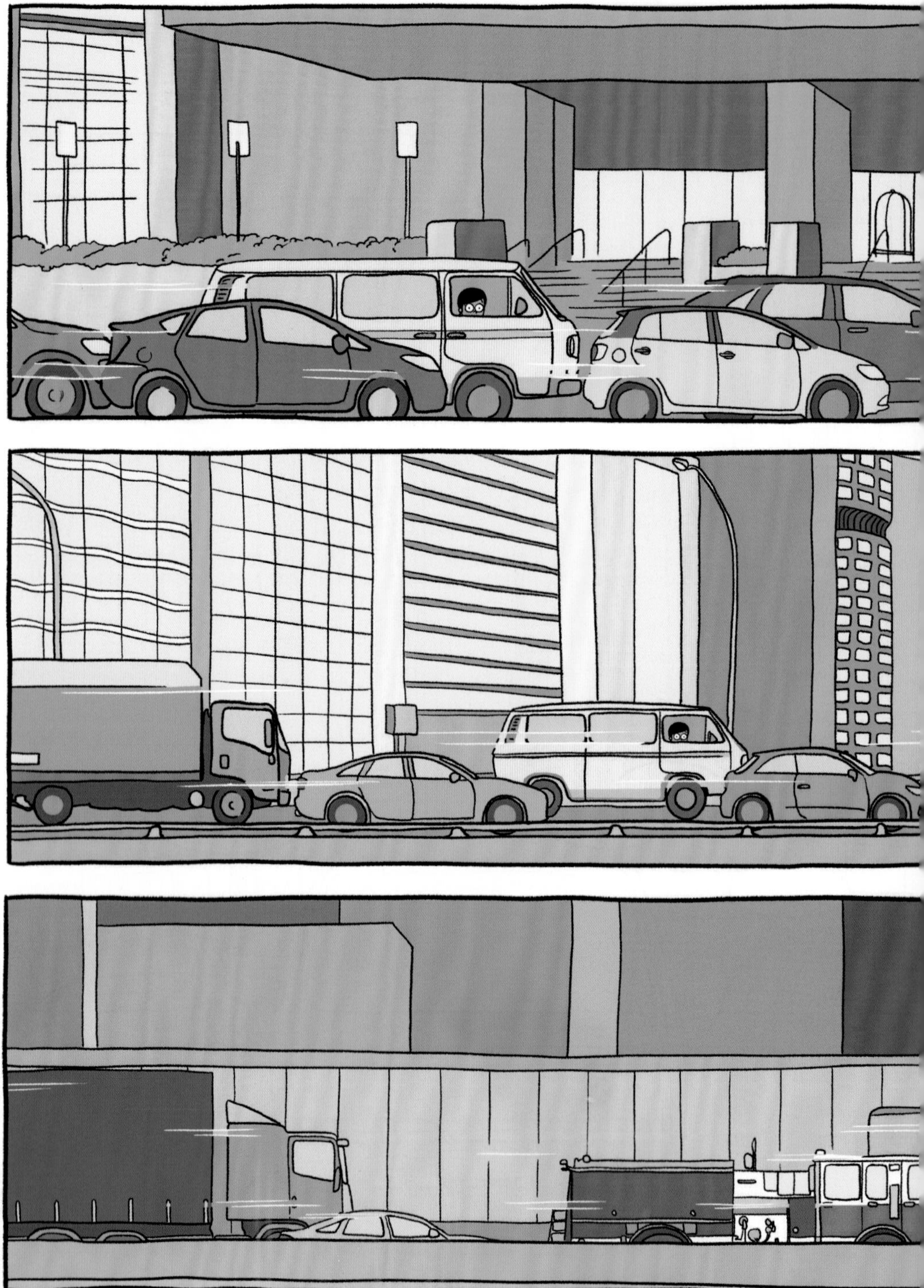

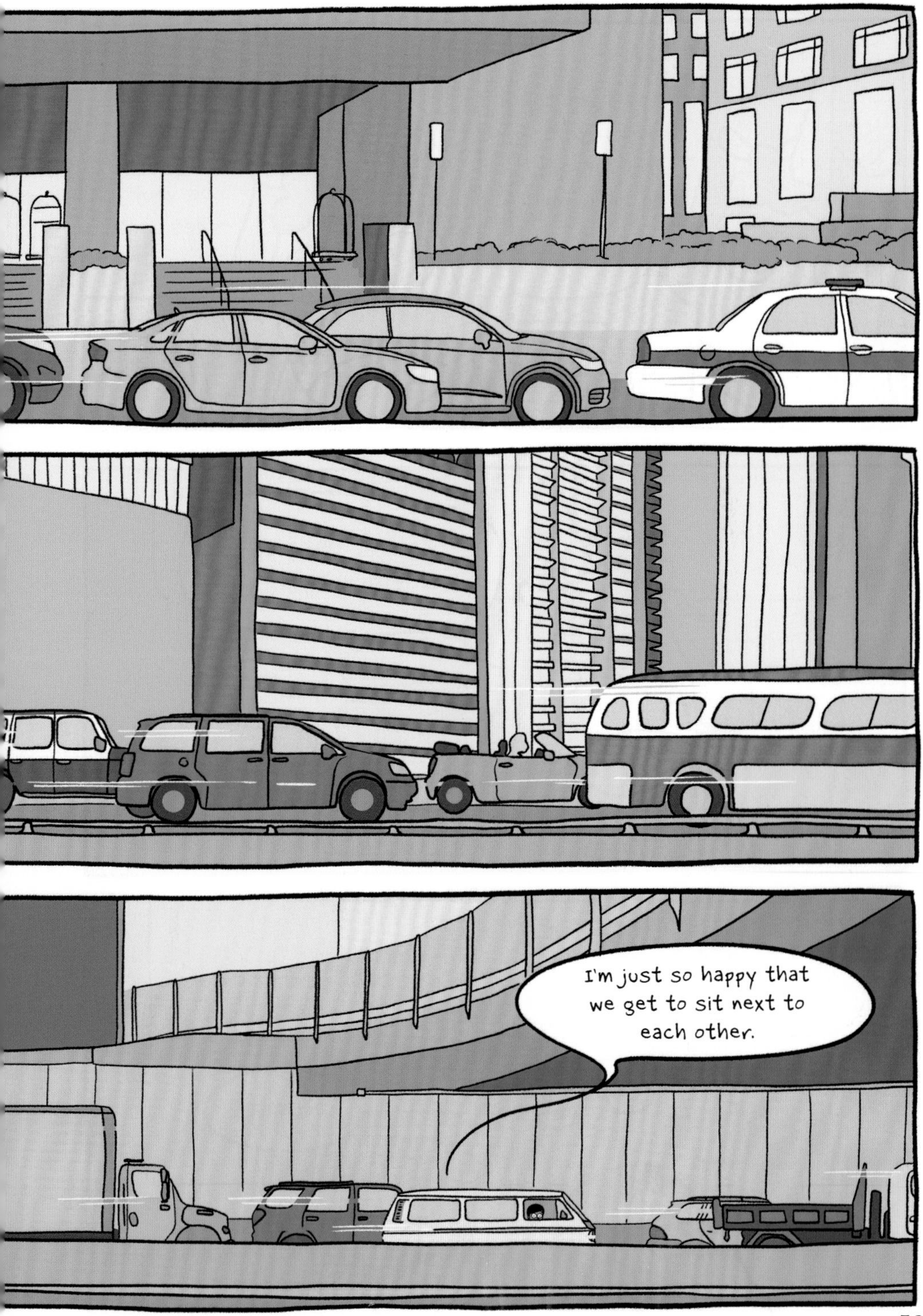
I'm just so happy that we get to sit next to each other.

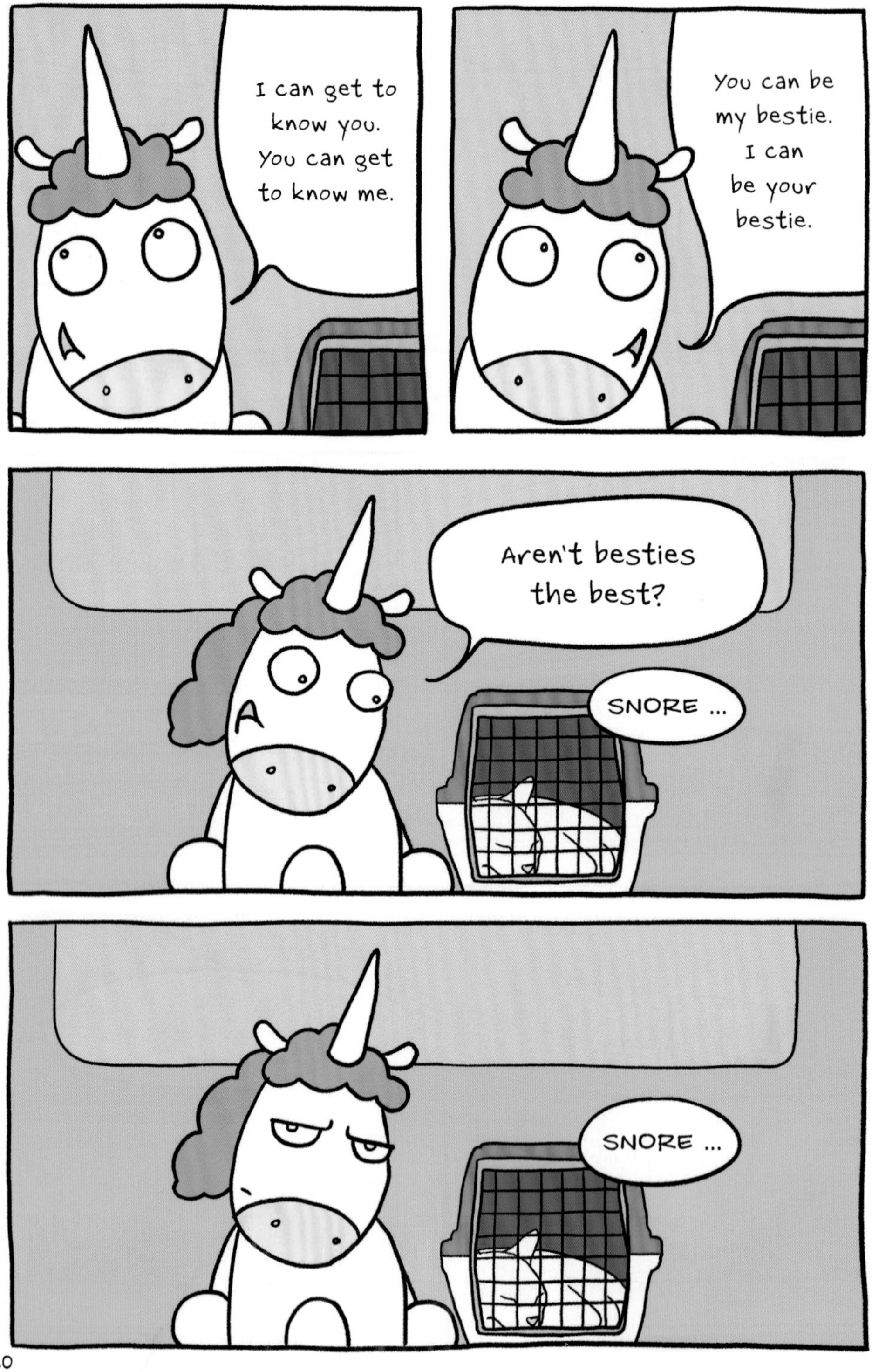
I can get to know you. You can get to know me.
You can be my bestie. I can be your bestie.
Aren't besties the best?
SNORE ...
SNORE ...

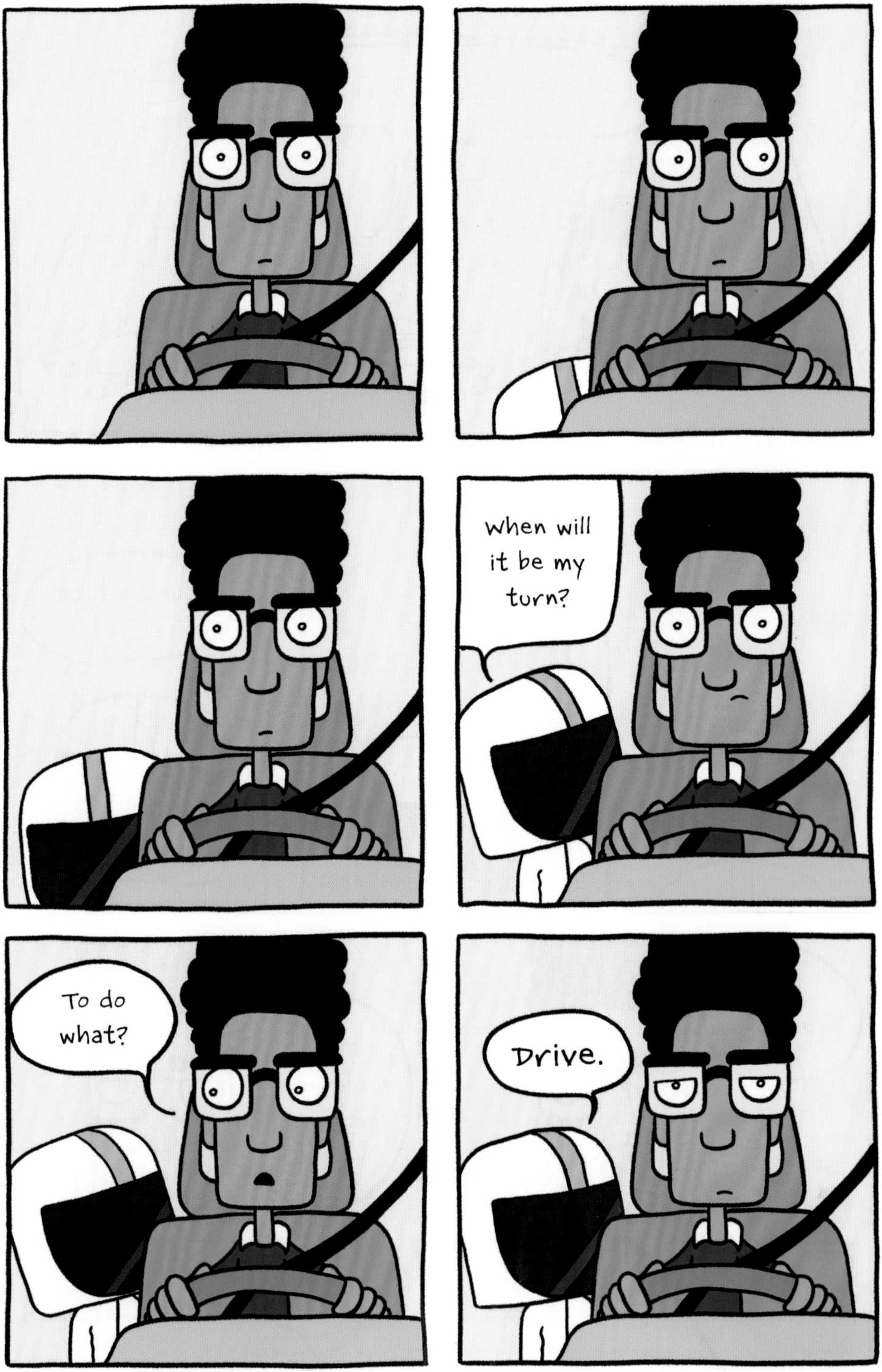
When will it be my turn?
To do what?
Drive.

Never. Sit down, Racer.
Just a **little** drive?
SIT DOWN!
This could be a long trip, Kippo.

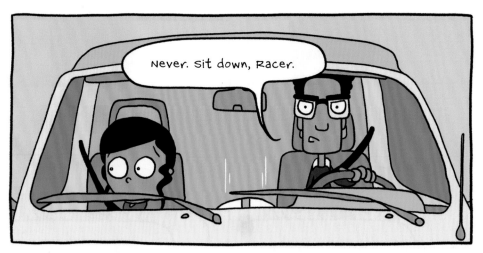

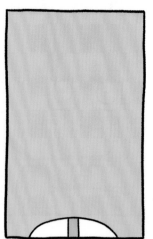

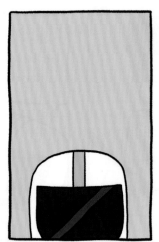

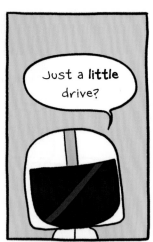

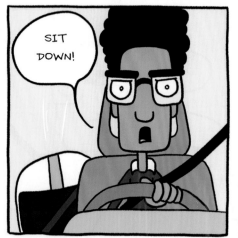

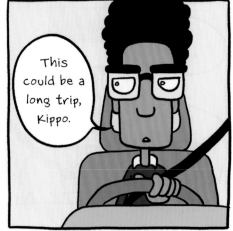

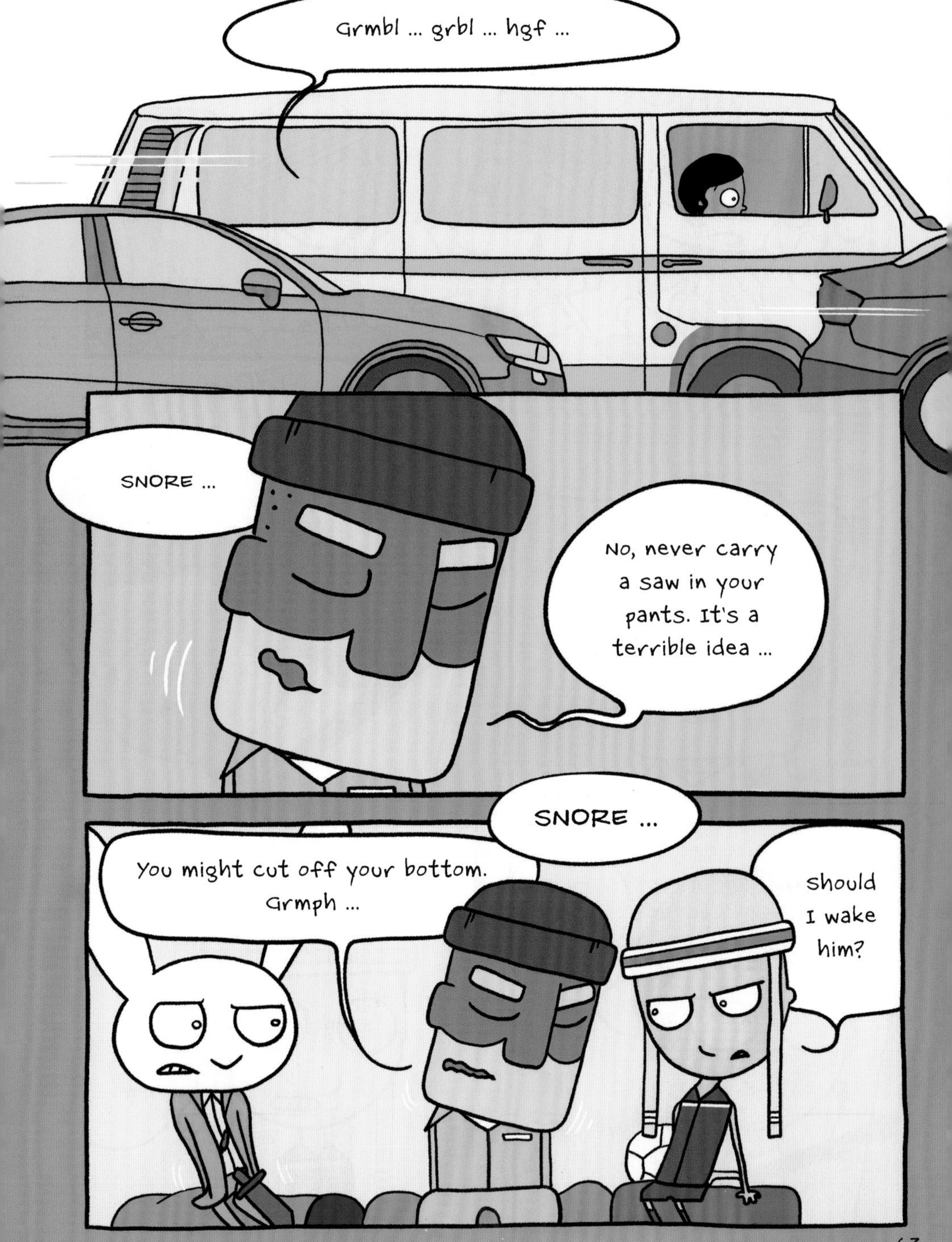
Grmbl ... grbl ... hgf ...
SNORE ...
No, never carry a saw in your pants. It's a terrible idea ...
SNORE ...
You might cut off your bottom. Grmph ...
Should I wake him?

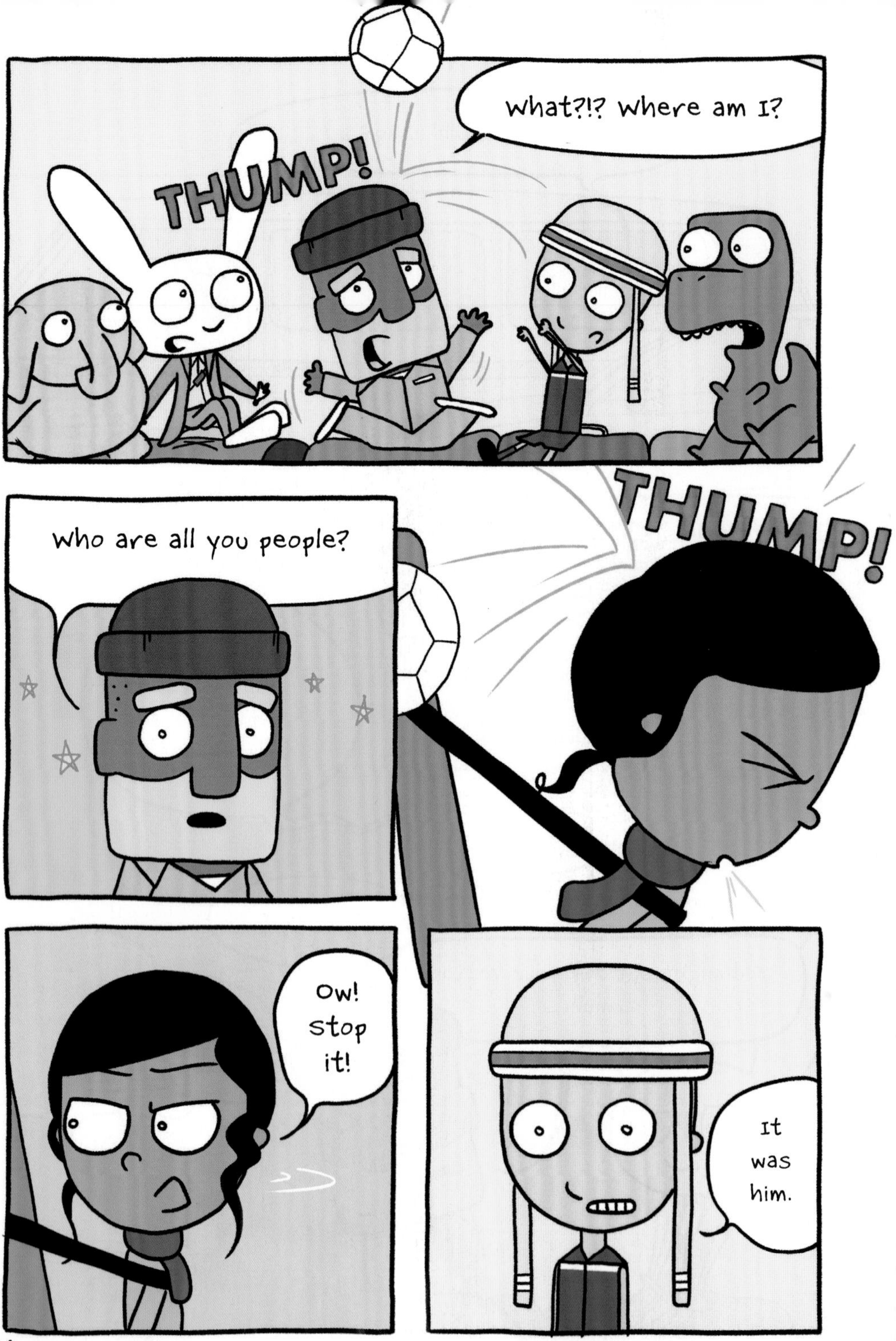
What?!? Where am I?
THUMP!
Who are all you people?
THUMP!
Ow! Stop it!
It was him.

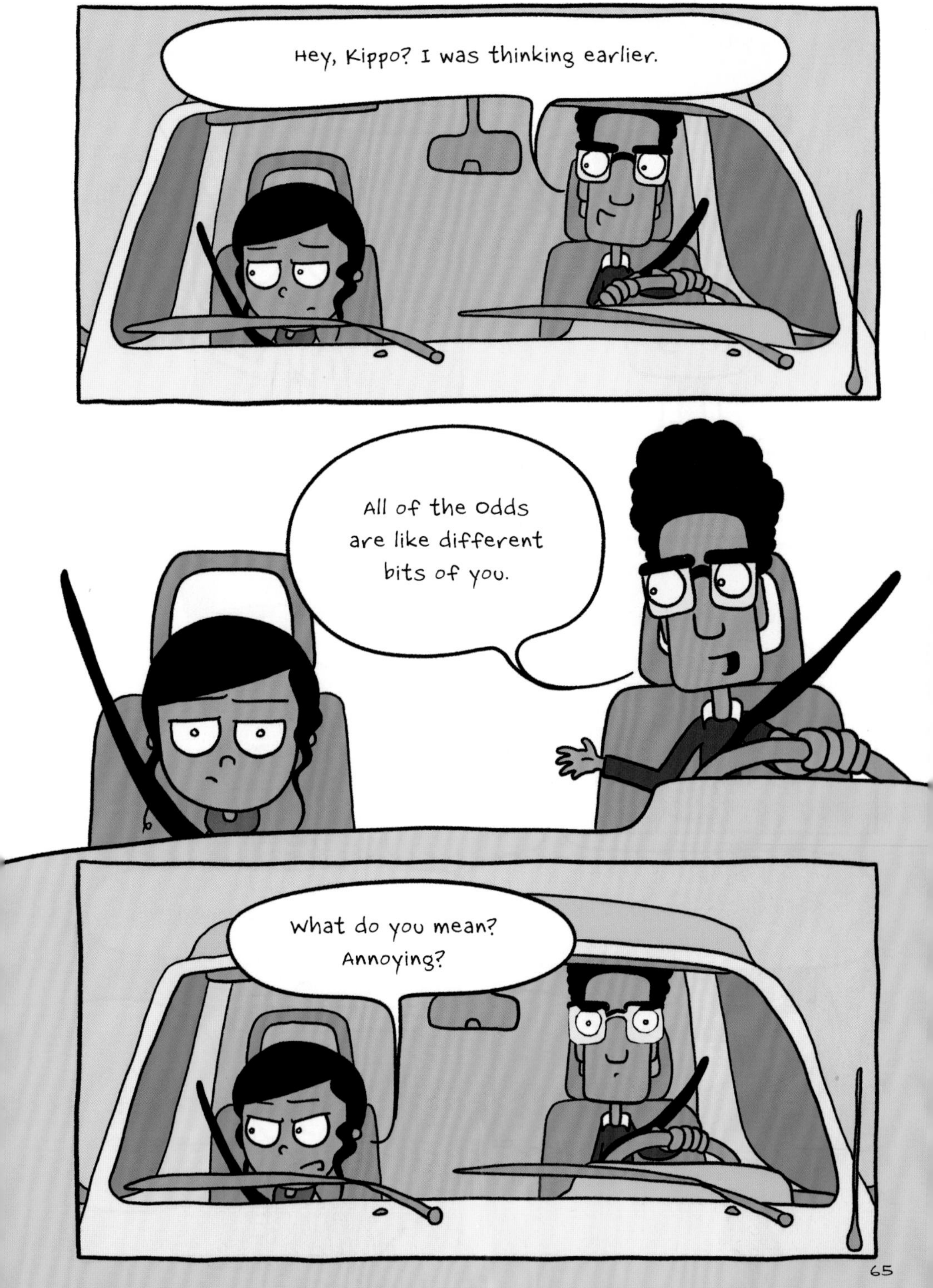
Hey, Kippo? I was thinking earlier.
All of the Odds are like different bits of you.
What do you mean? Annoying?

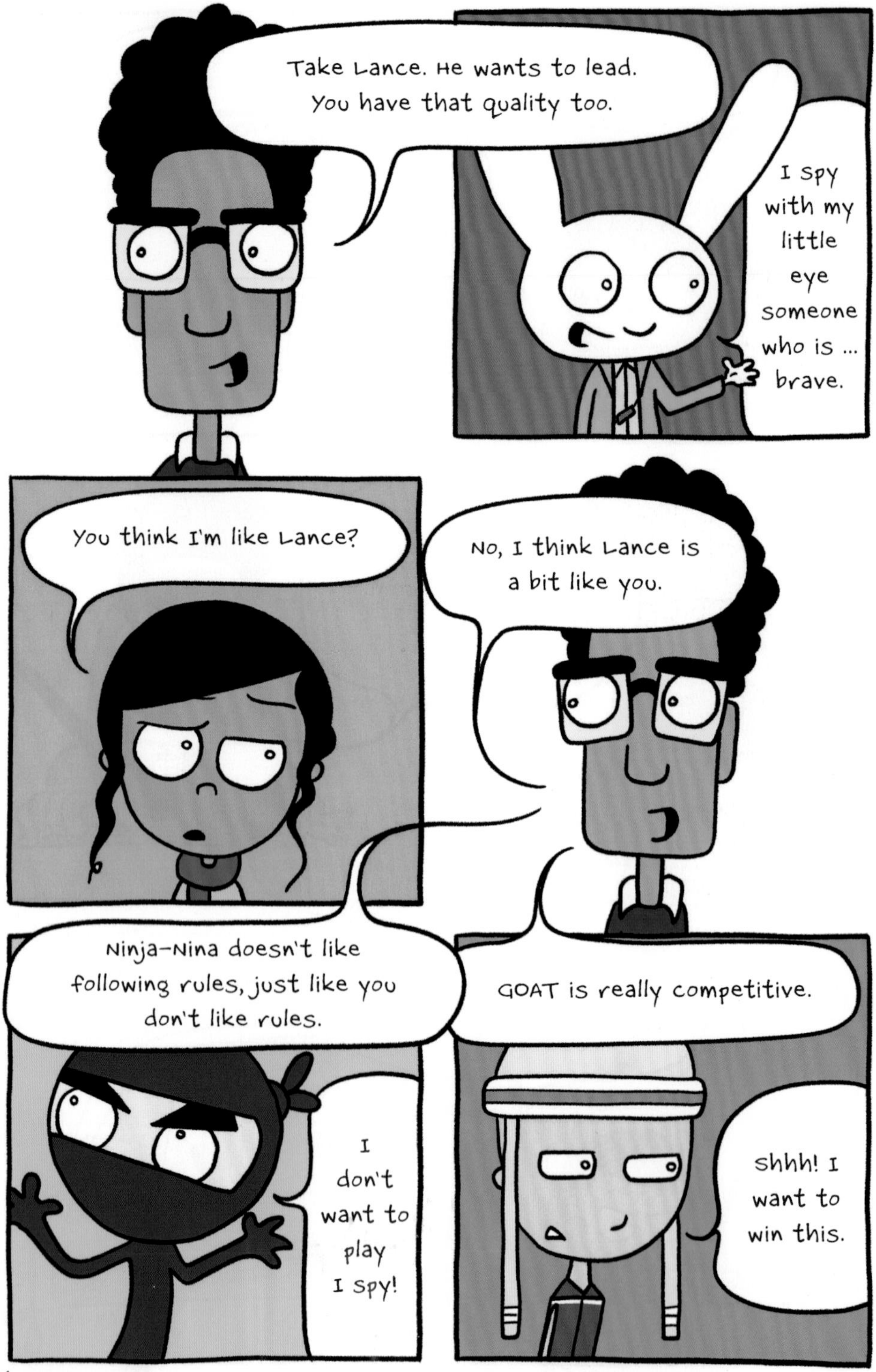
Take Lance. He wants to lead.
You have that quality too.
I spy with my little eye someone who is ... brave.
You think I'm like Lance?
No, I think Lance is a bit like you.
Ninja-Nina doesn't like following rules, just like you don't like rules.
GOAT is really competitive.
I don't want to play I spy!
Shhh! I want to win this.

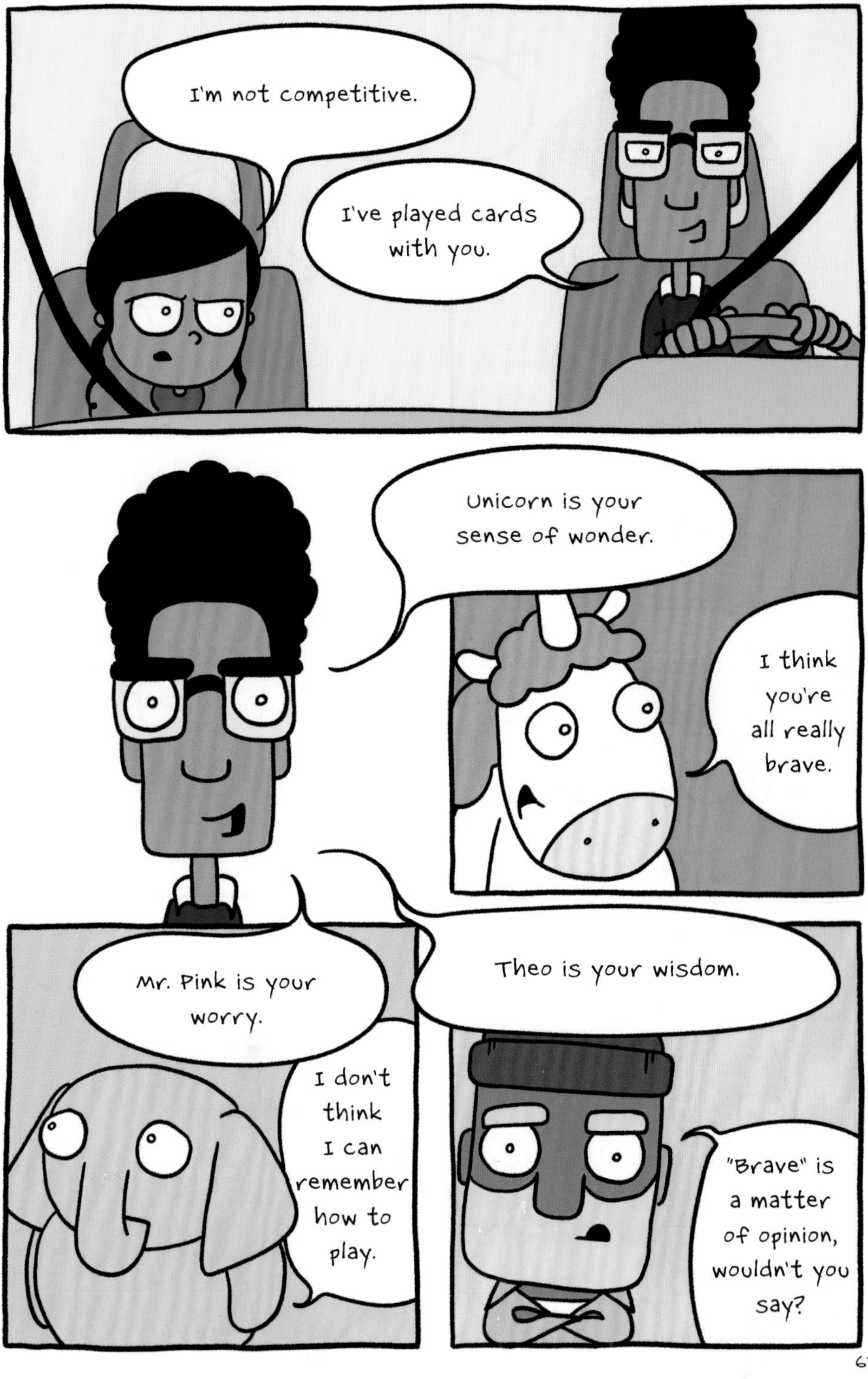
I'm not competitive.
I've played cards with you.
Unicorn is your sense of wonder.
I think you're all really brave.
Mr. Pink is your worry.
Theo is your wisdom.
I don't think I can remember how to play.
"Brave" is a matter of opinion, wouldn't you say?

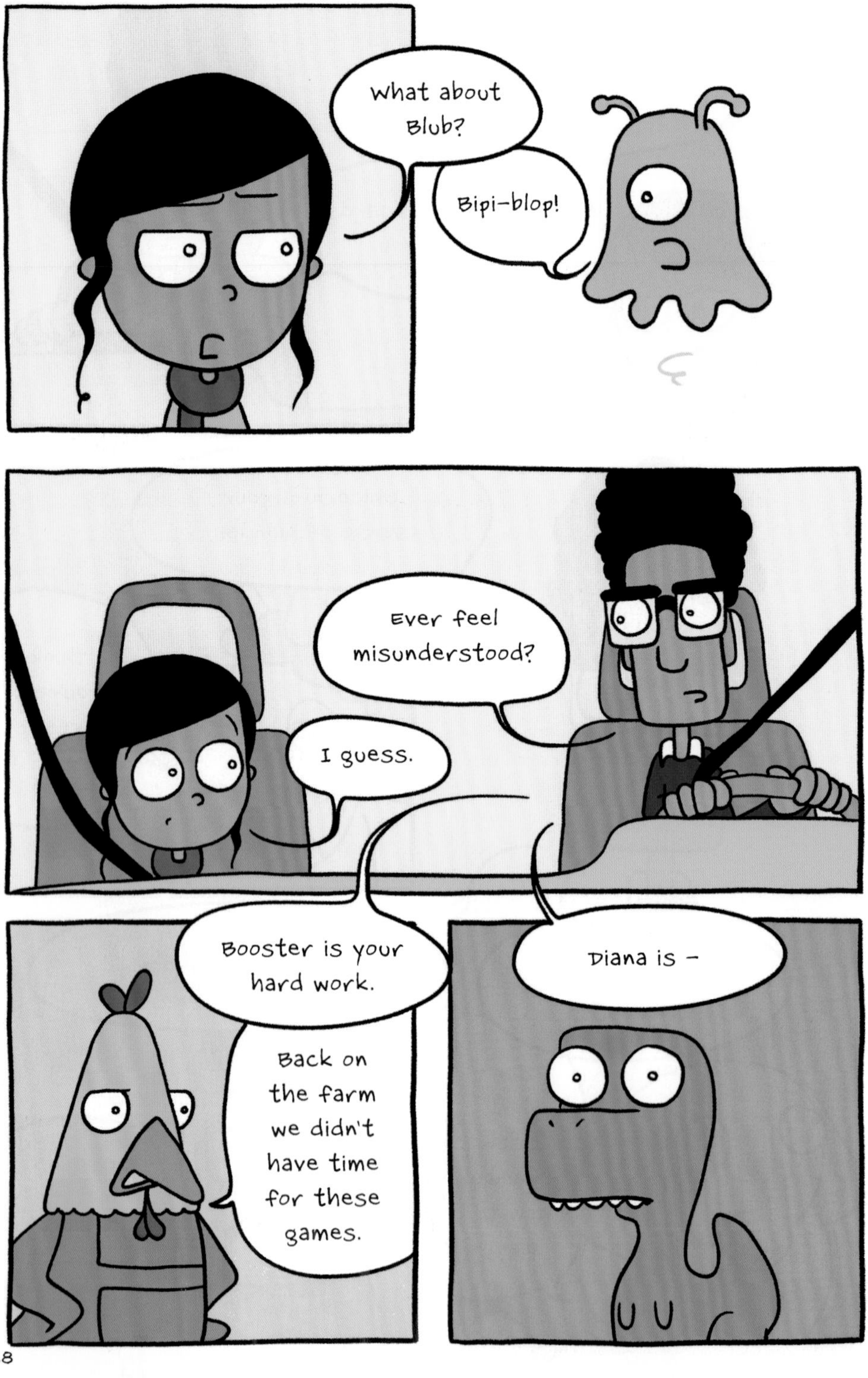
What about Blub?
Bipi-blop!
Ever feel misunderstood?
I guess.
Booster is your hard work.
Back on the farm we didn't have time for these games.
Diana is -

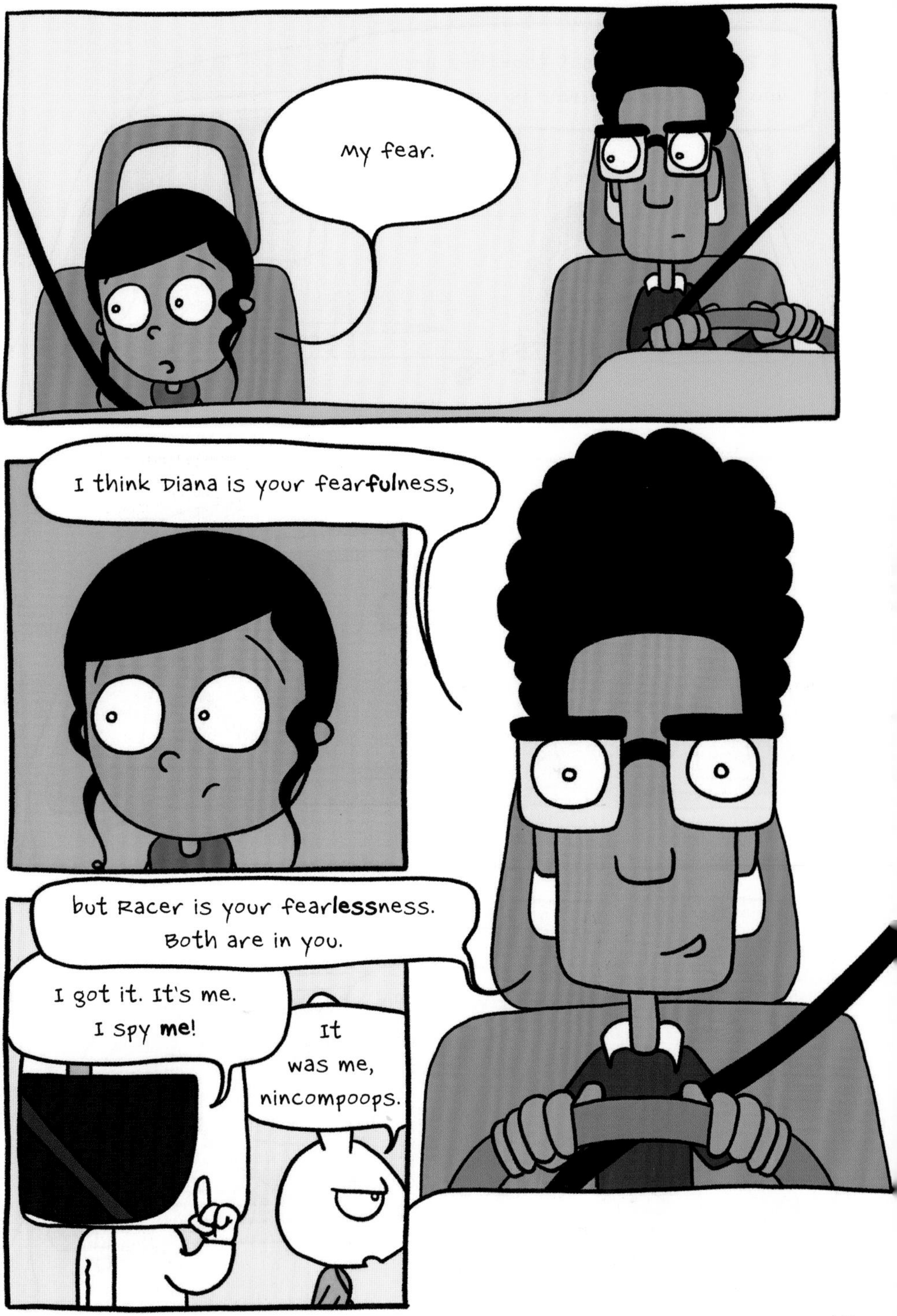
My fear.
I think Diana is your fear**ful**ness,
but Racer is your fear**less**ness.
Both are in you.
I got it. It's me.
I spy **me**!
It was me, nincompoops.

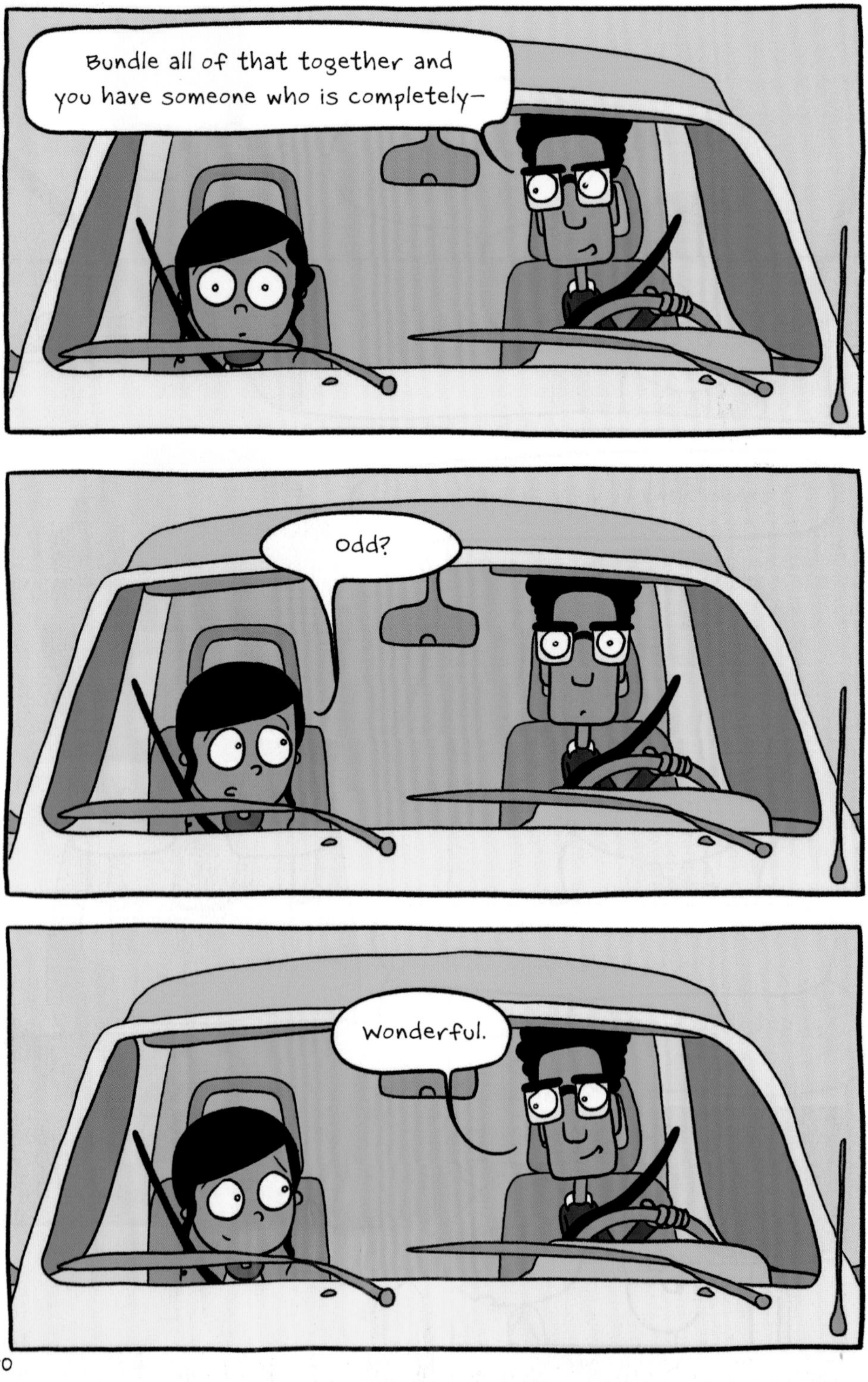
Bundle all of that together and you have someone who is completely–
odd?
Wonderful.

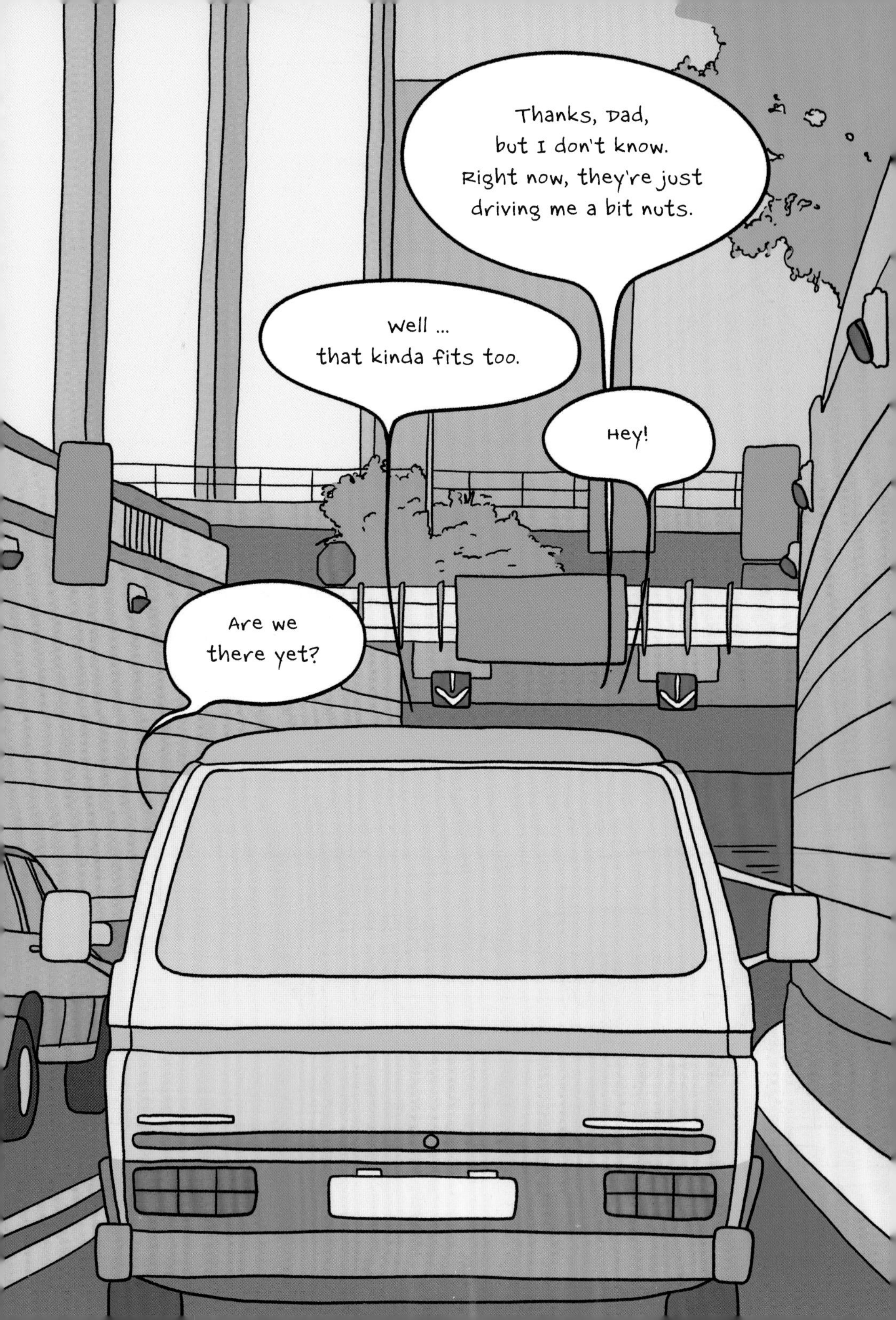
Thanks, Dad, but I don't know. Right now, they're just driving me a bit nuts.
Well ... that kinda fits too.
Hey!
Are we there yet?

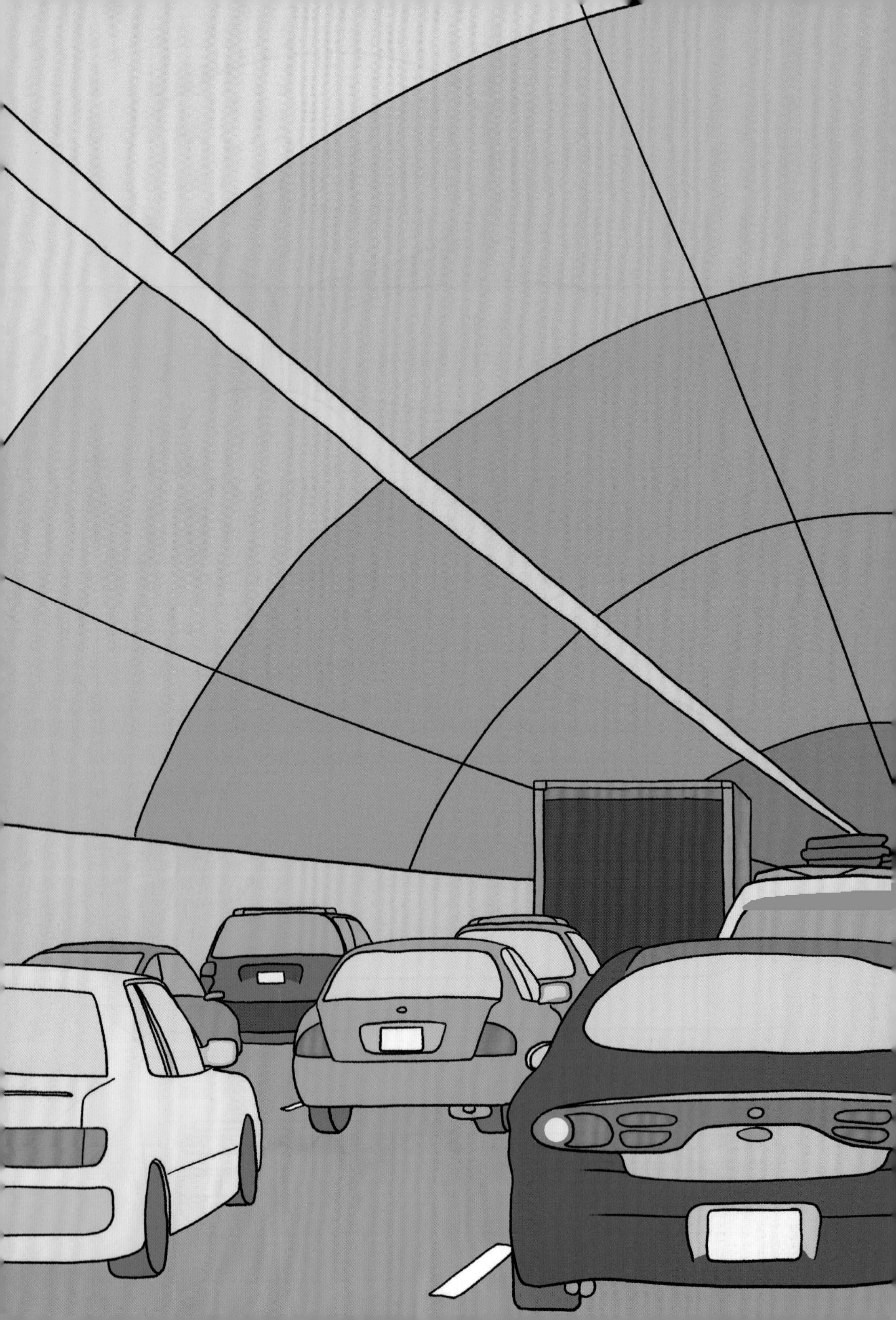

CHAPTER FOUR
An odd sort of road trip

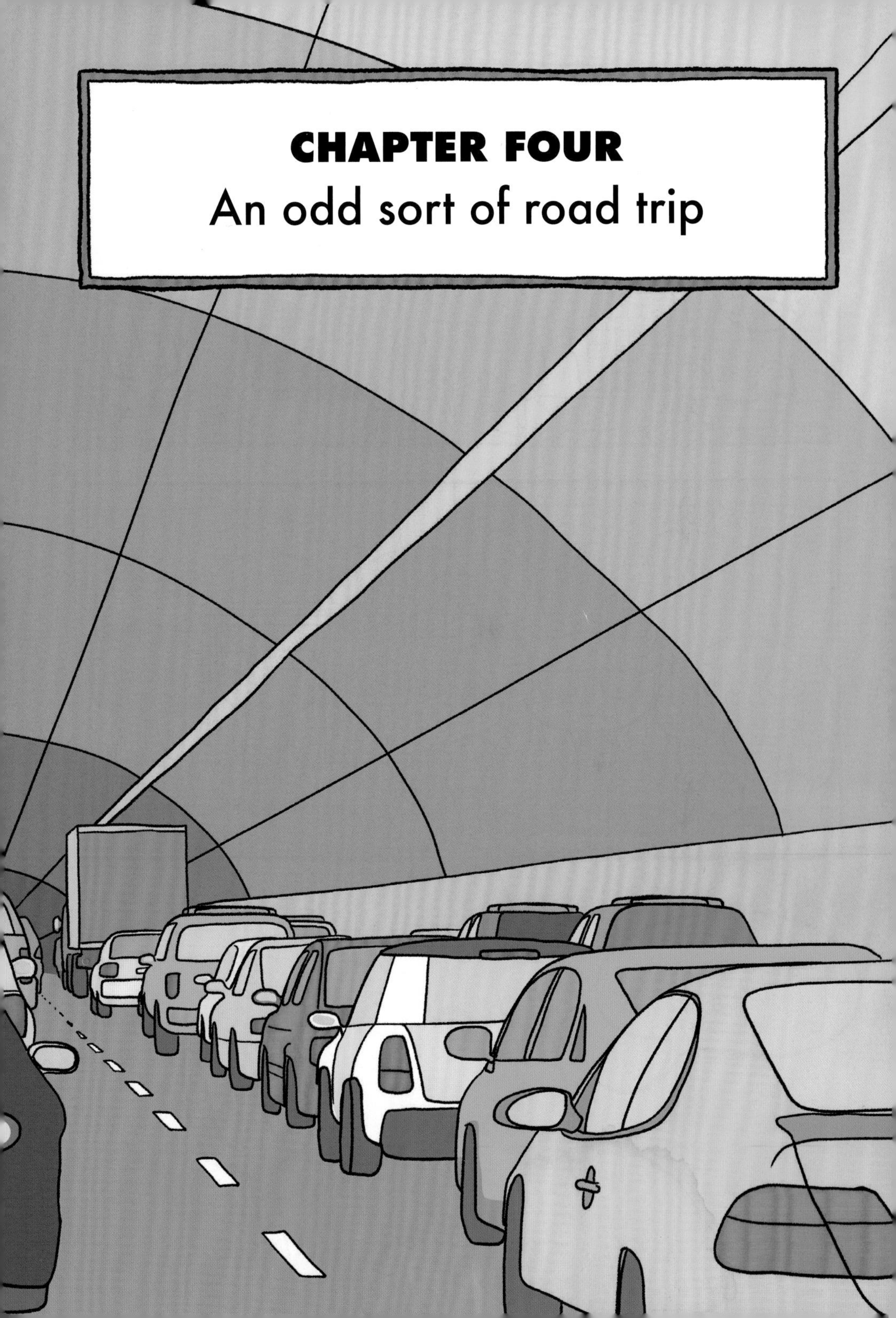

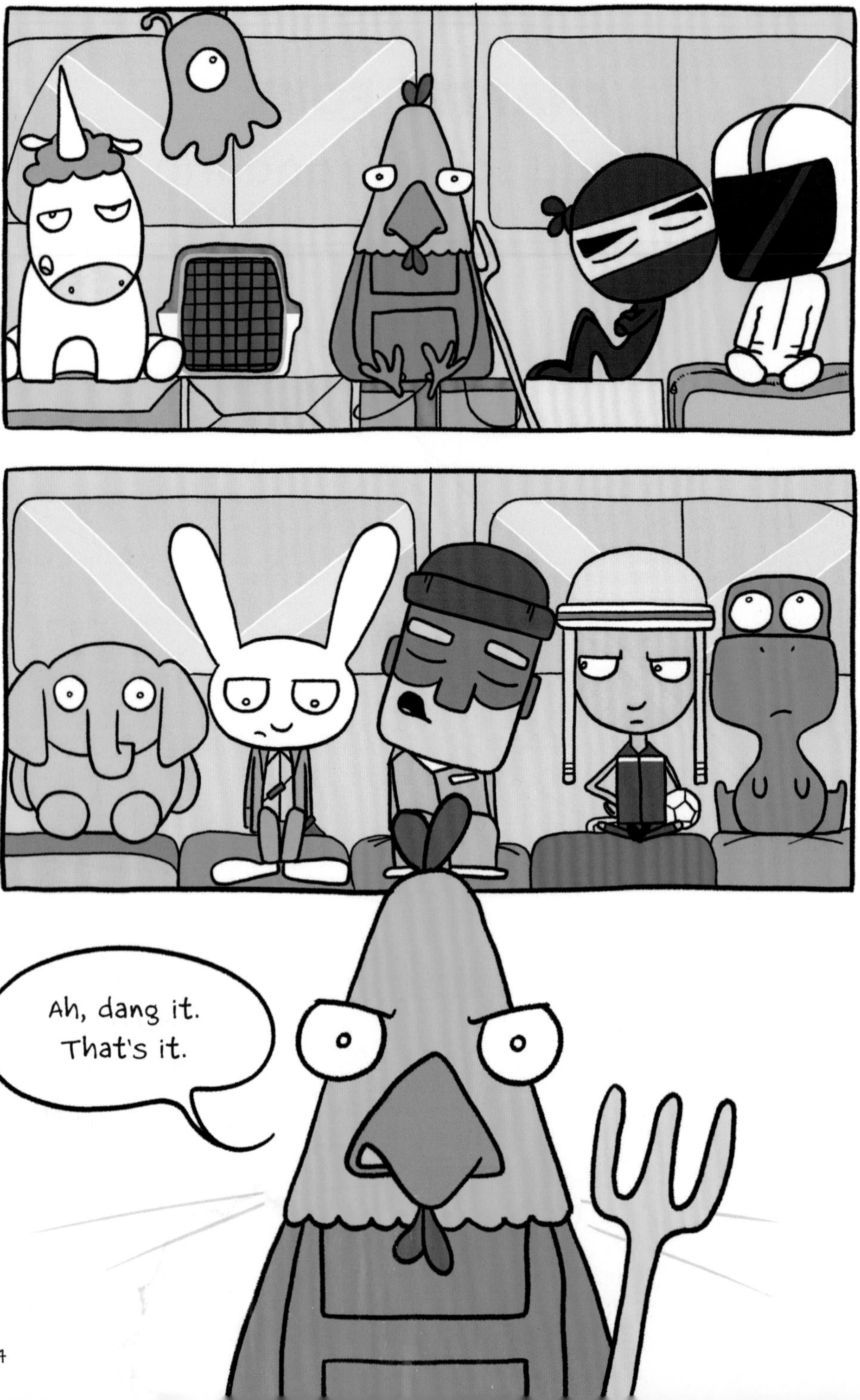
Ah, dang it.
That's it.

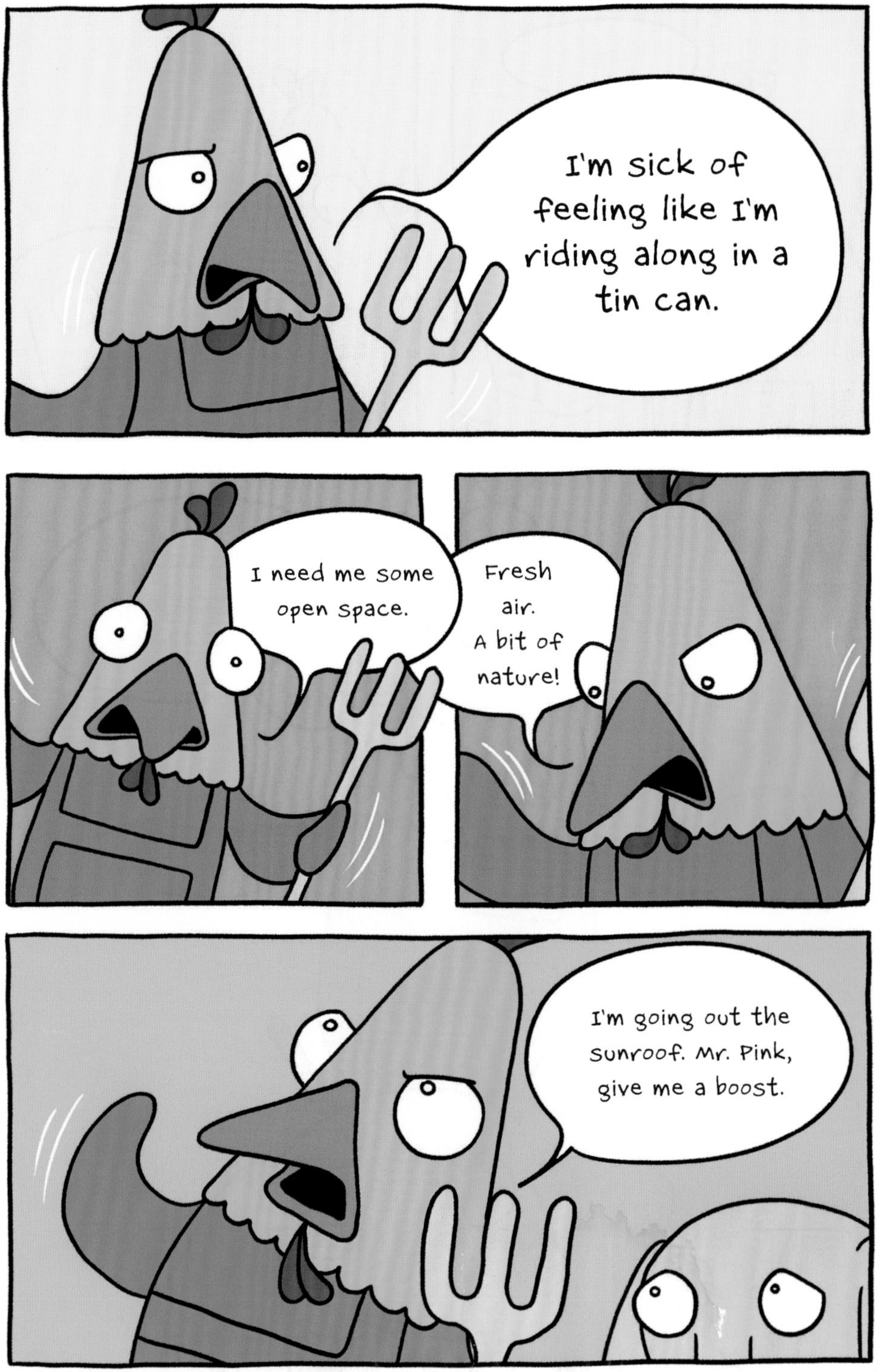
I'm sick of feeling like I'm riding along in a tin can.
I need me some open space.
Fresh air. A bit of nature!
I'm going out the sunroof. Mr. Pink, give me a boost.

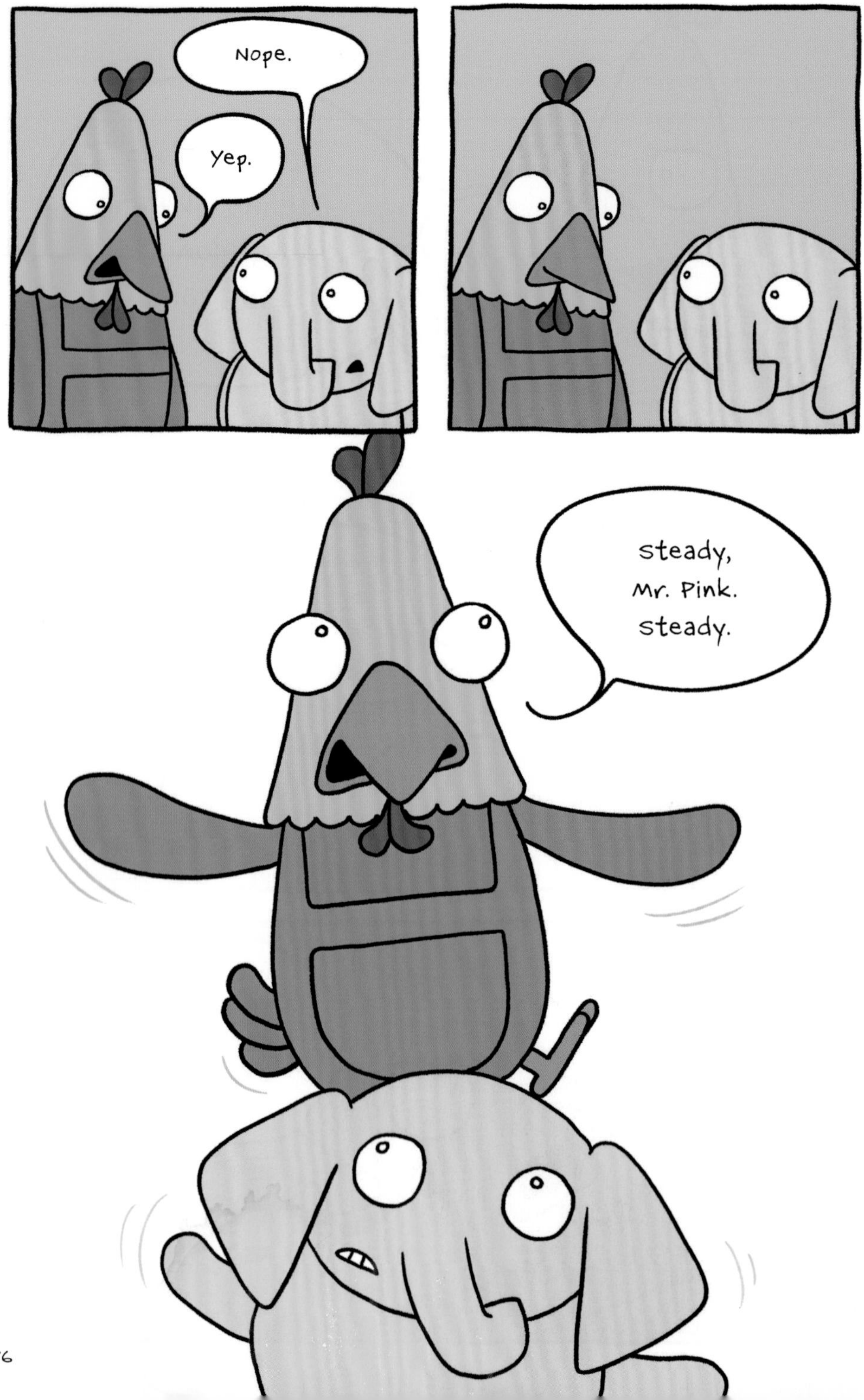
Nope.
yep.
steady,
Mr. Pink.
steady.

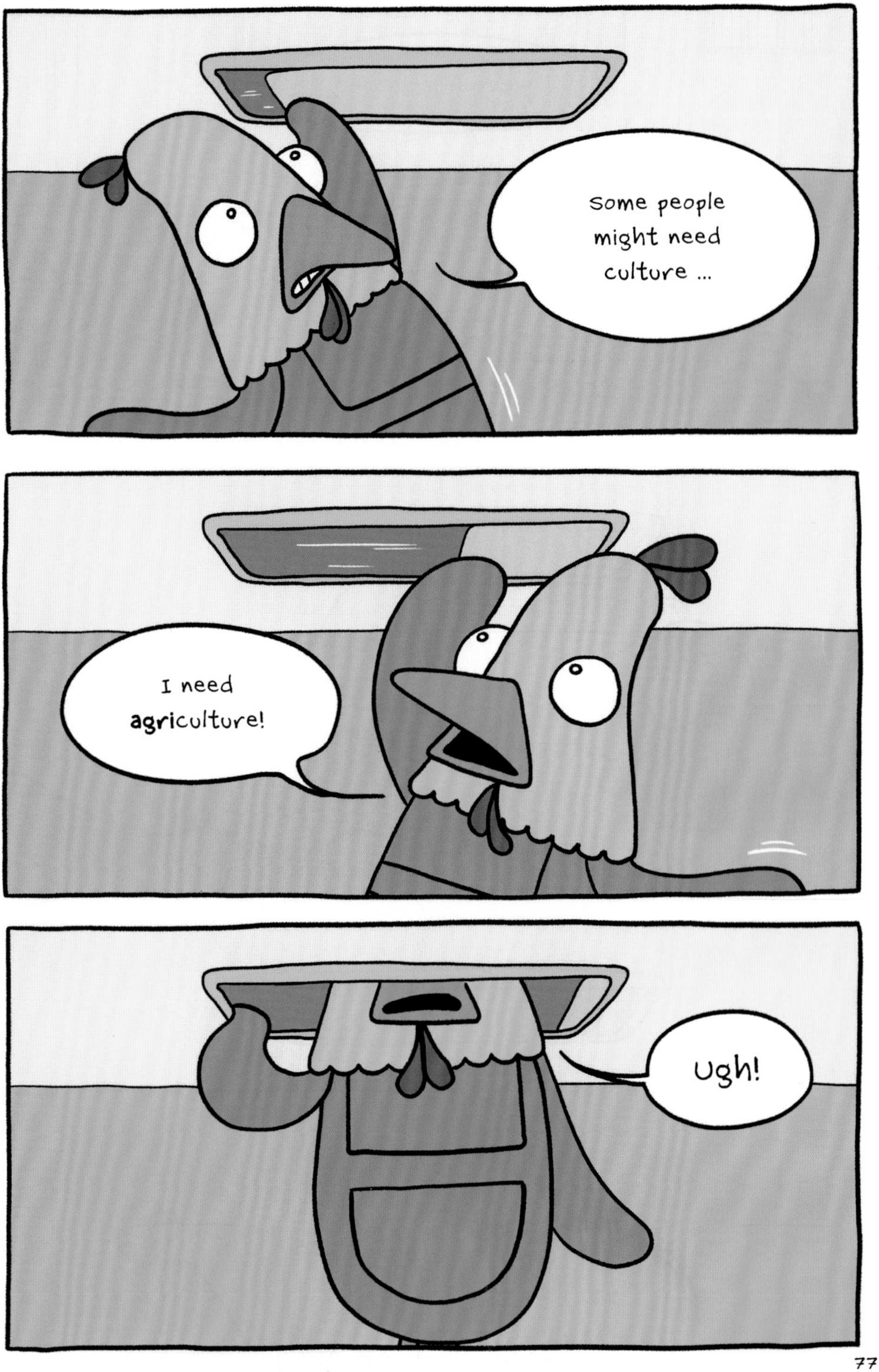
Some people might need culture ...
I need **agri**culture!
Ugh!

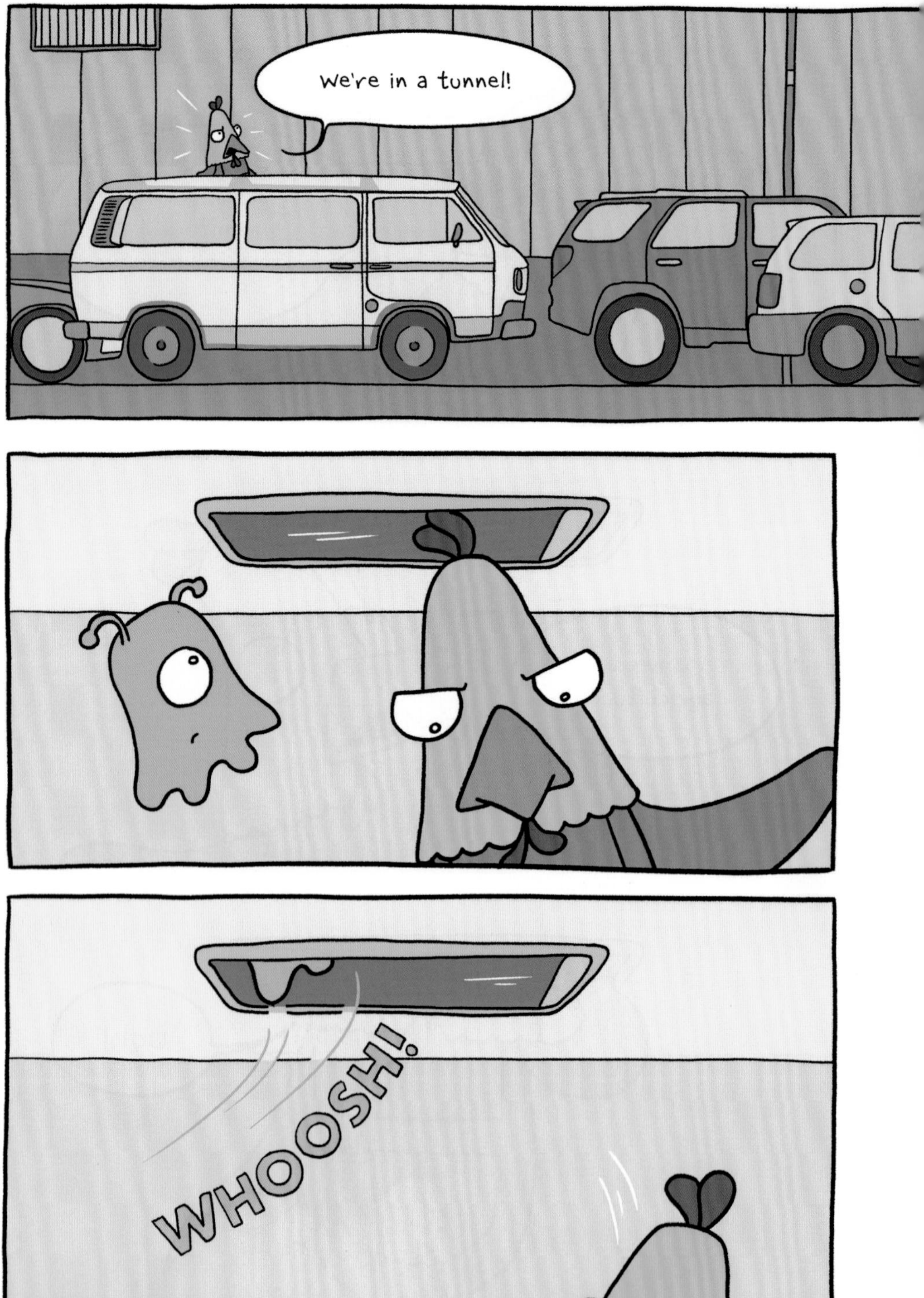
We're in a tunnel!
WHOOSH!

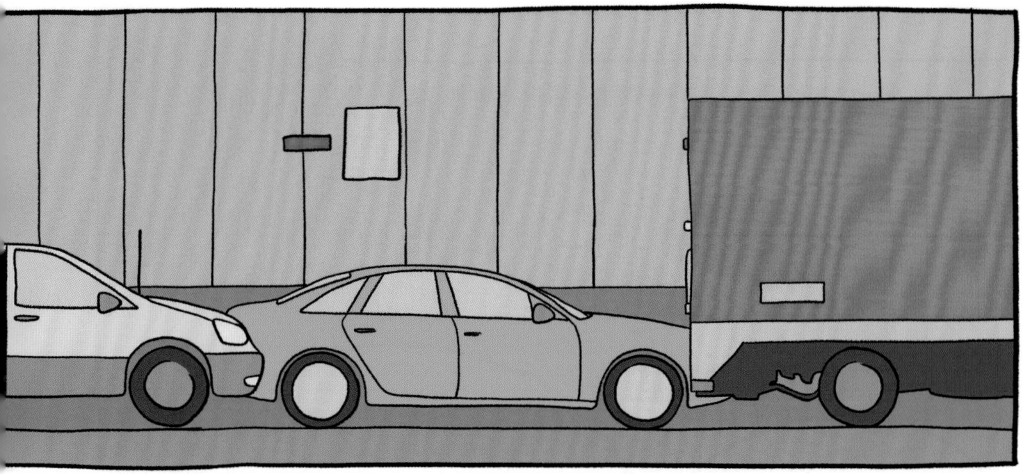

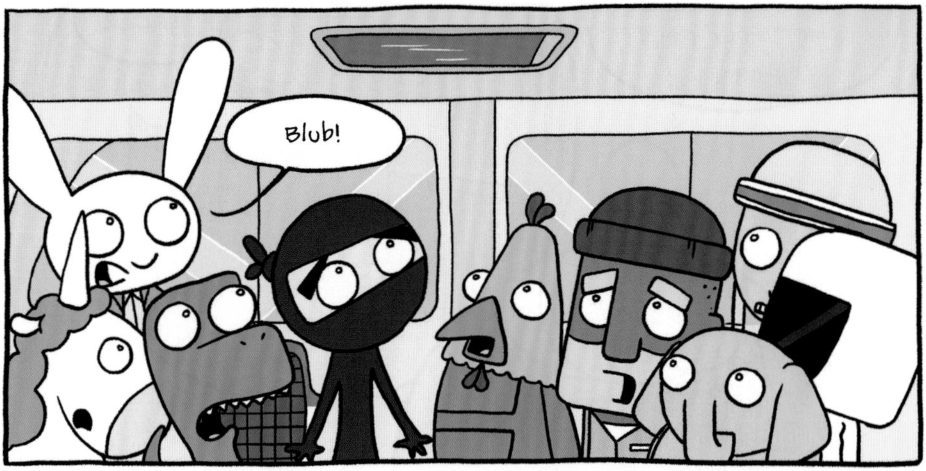
Blub!

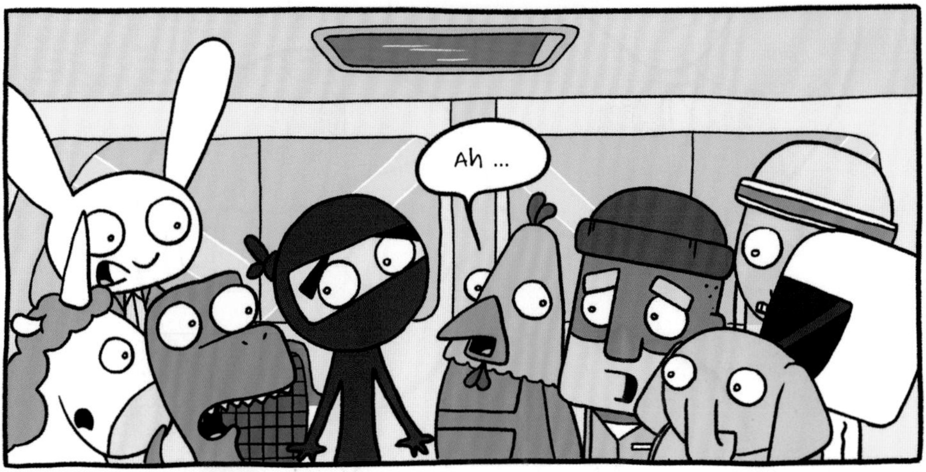
Ah ...

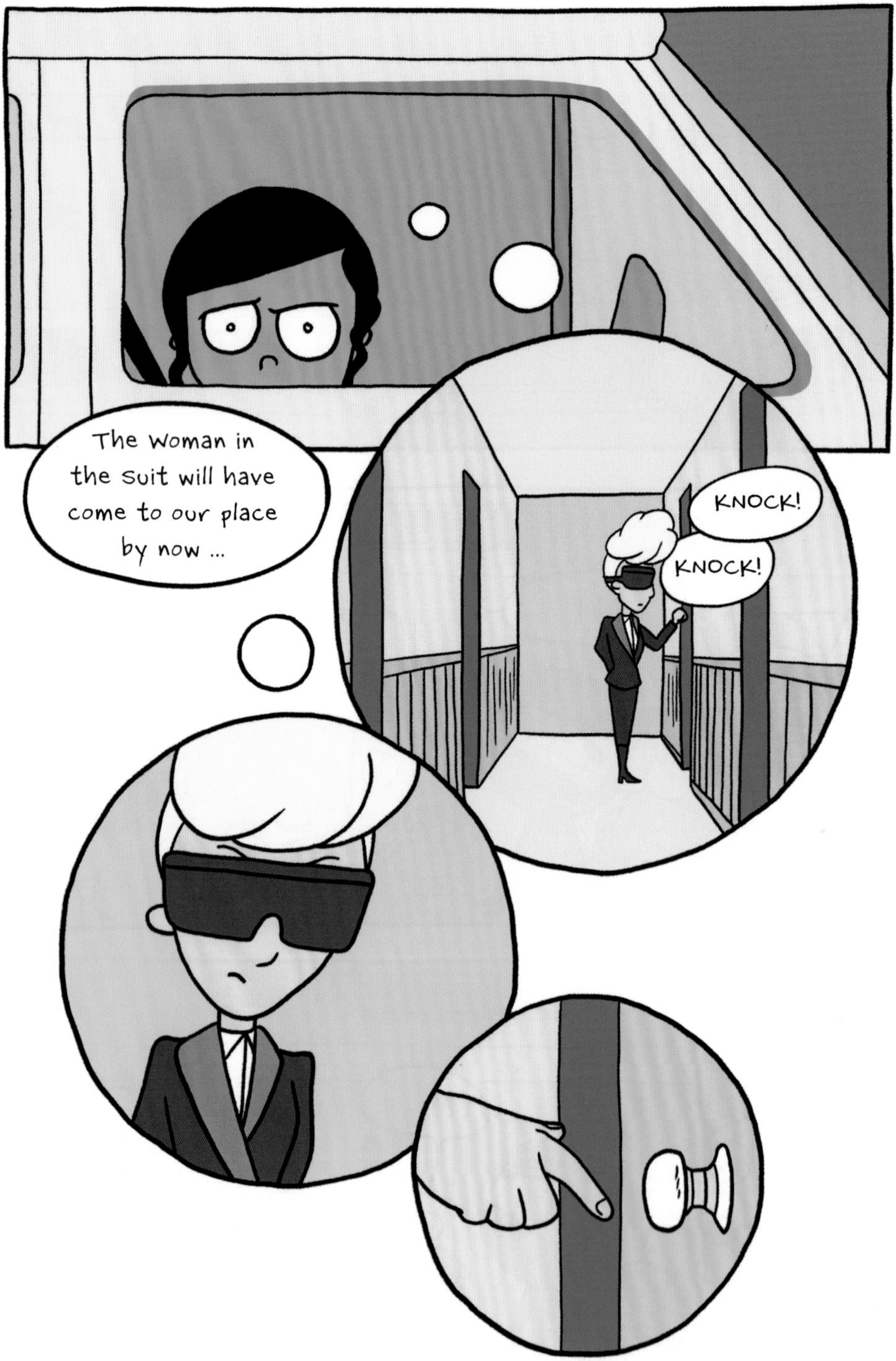

The woman in the suit will have come to our place by now ...
KNOCK!
KNOCK!

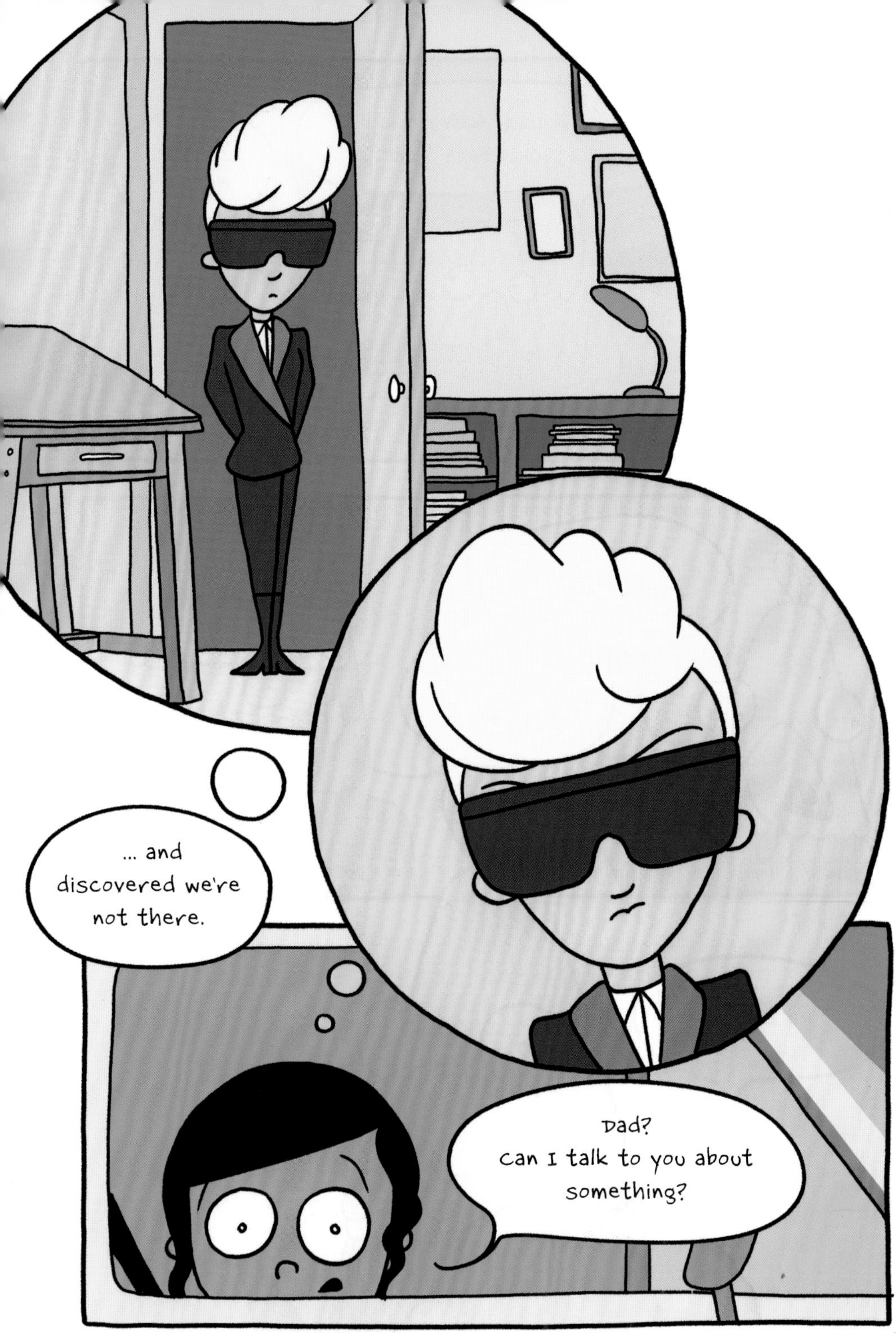
... and discovered we're not there.
Dad? Can I talk to you about something?

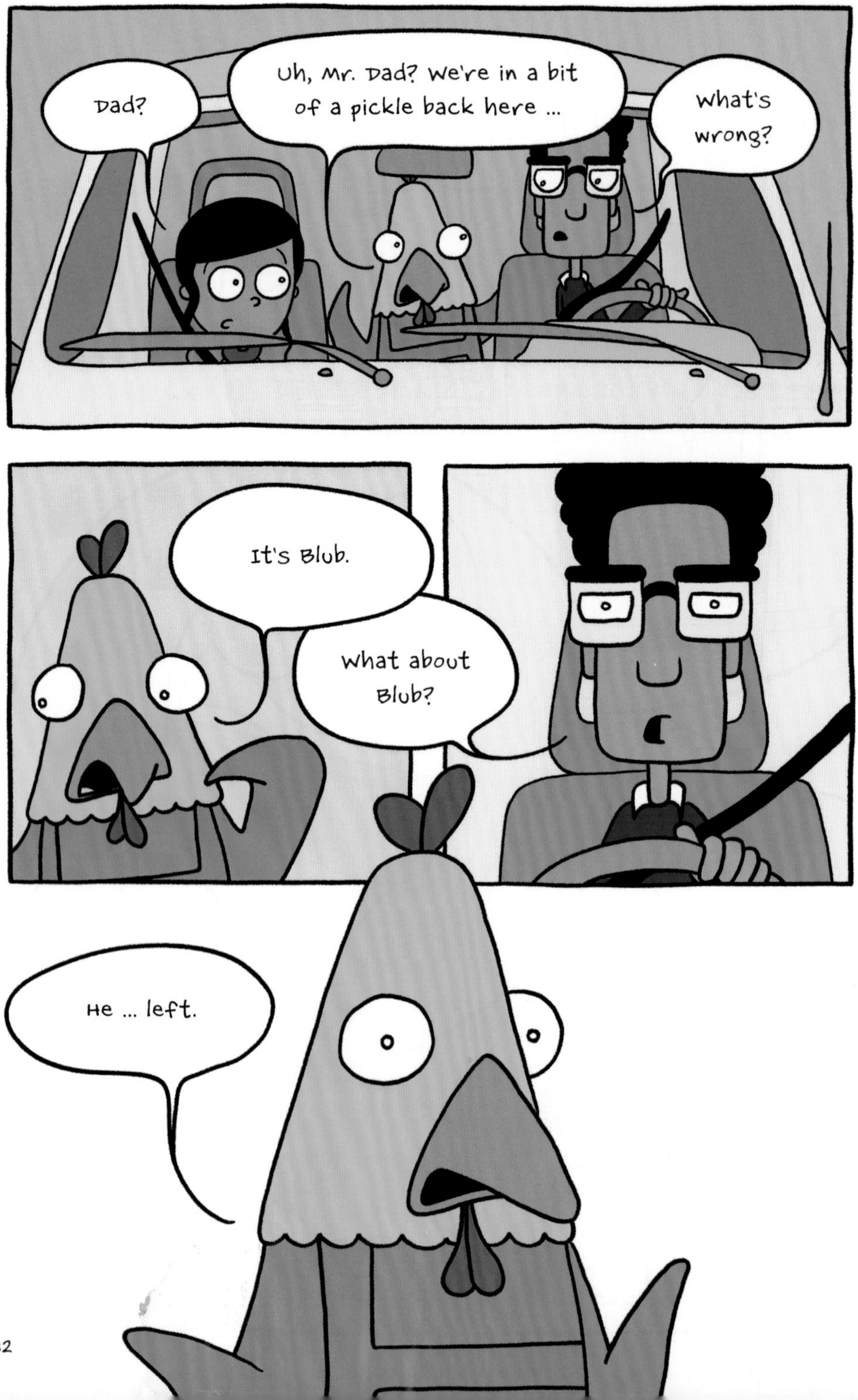
Dad?
Uh, Mr. Dad? We're in a bit of a pickle back here ...
What's wrong?
It's Blub.
What about Blub?
He ... left.

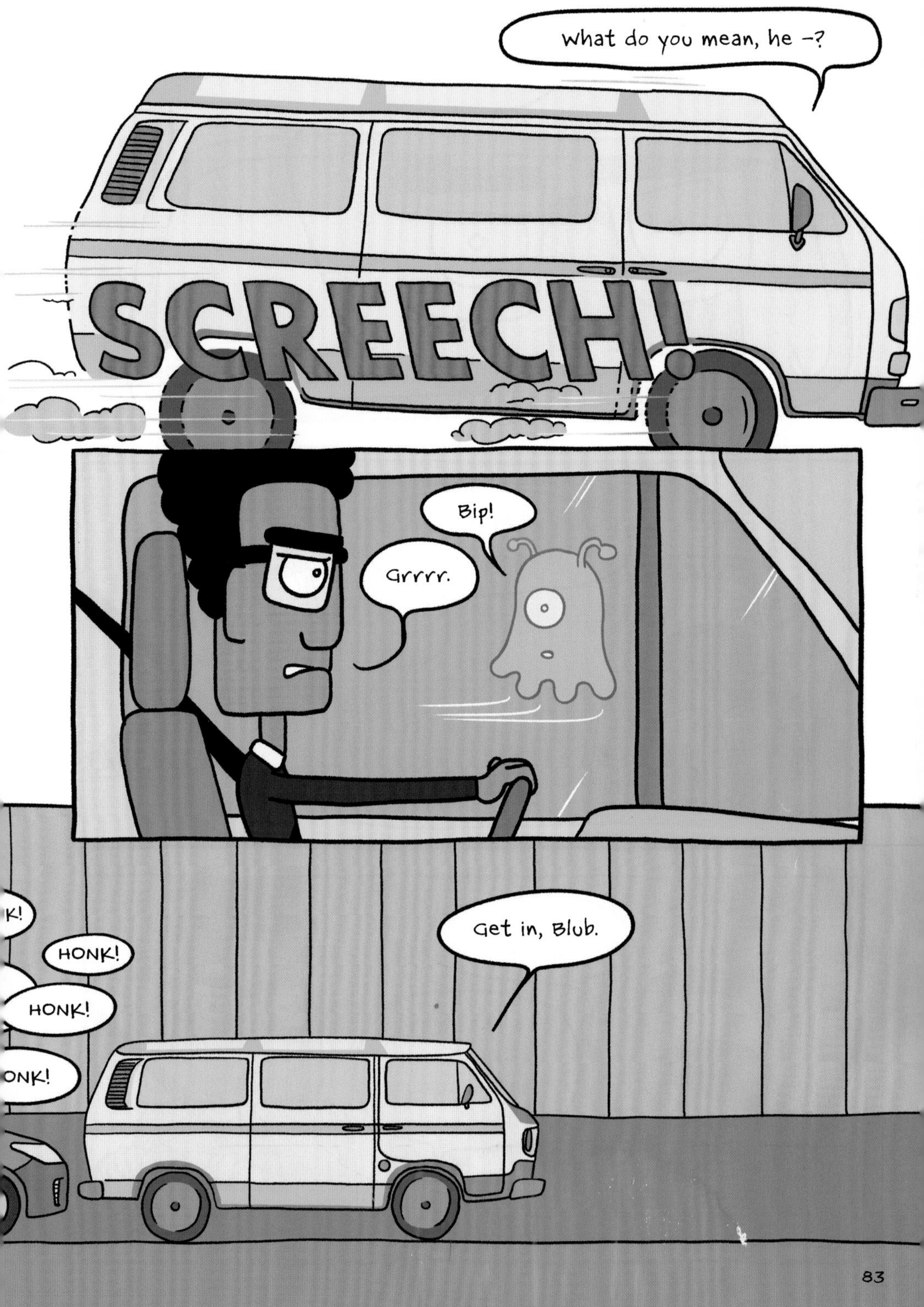

What do you mean, he –?
SCREECH!
Bip!
Grrrr.
Get in, Blub.
K!
HONK!
HONK!
ONK!

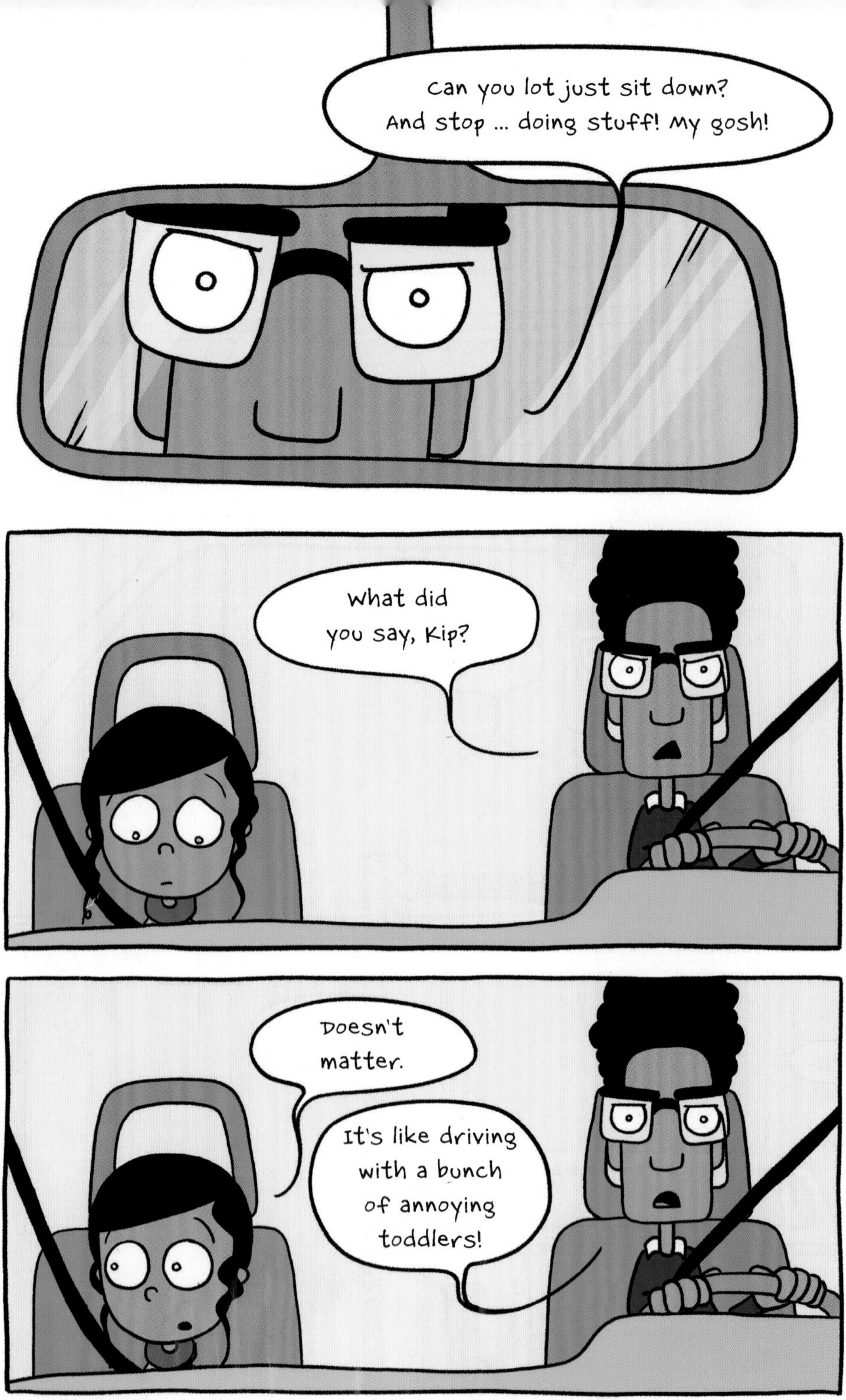
Can you lot just sit down? And stop ... doing stuff! My gosh!
What did you say, Kip?
Doesn't matter.
It's like driving with a bunch of annoying toddlers!

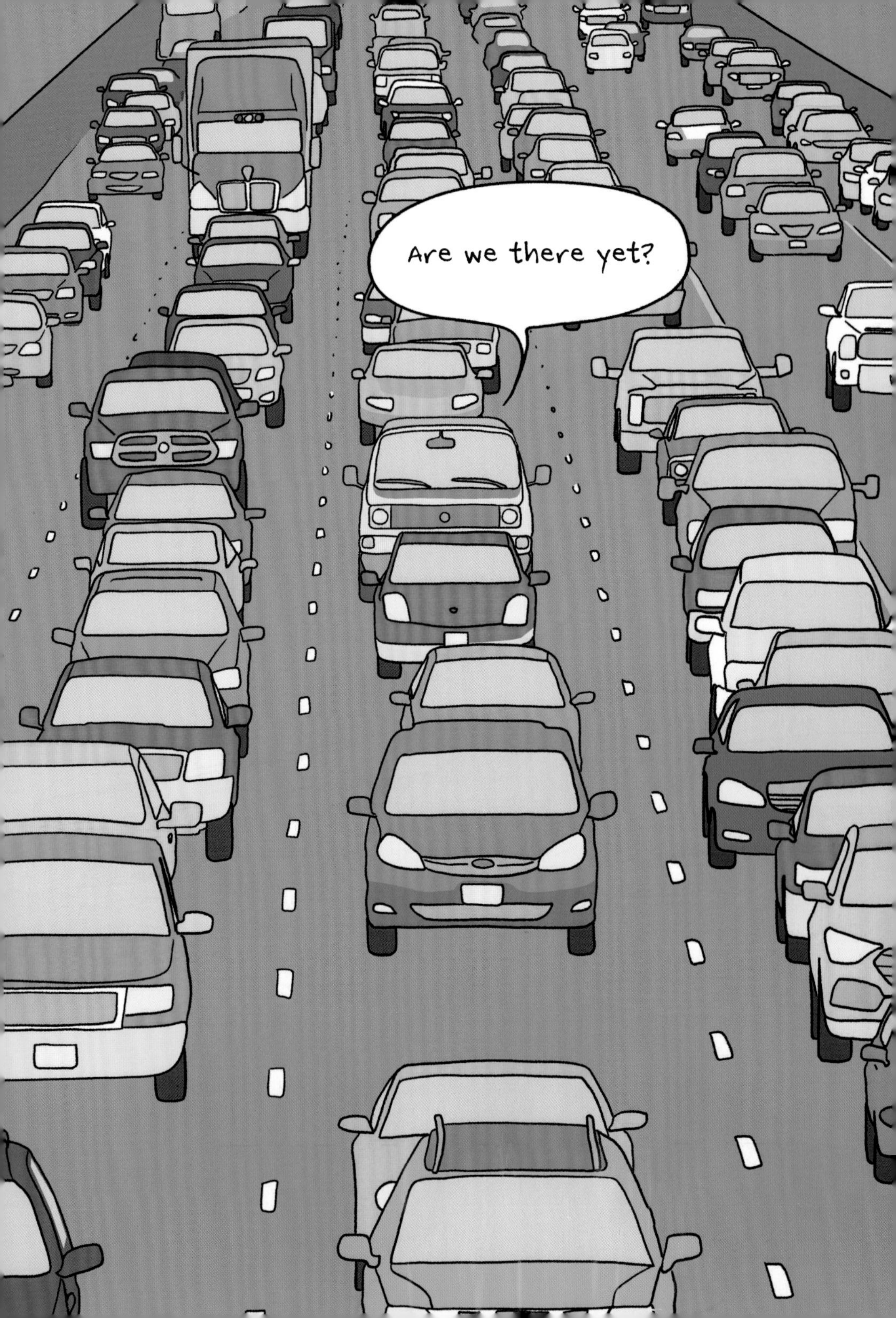
Are we there yet?

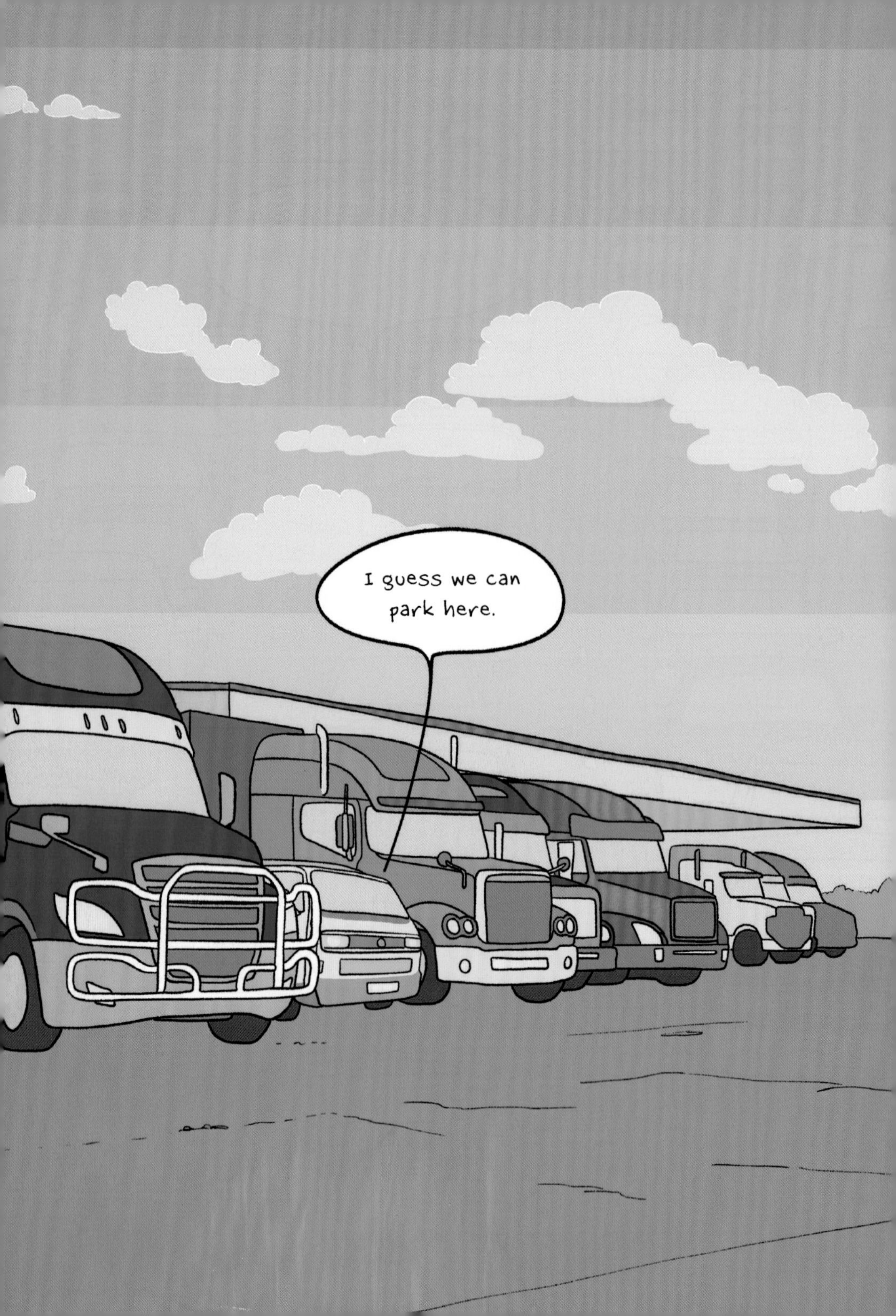
I guess we can park here.

CHAPTER FIVE
Odds in, Odds out

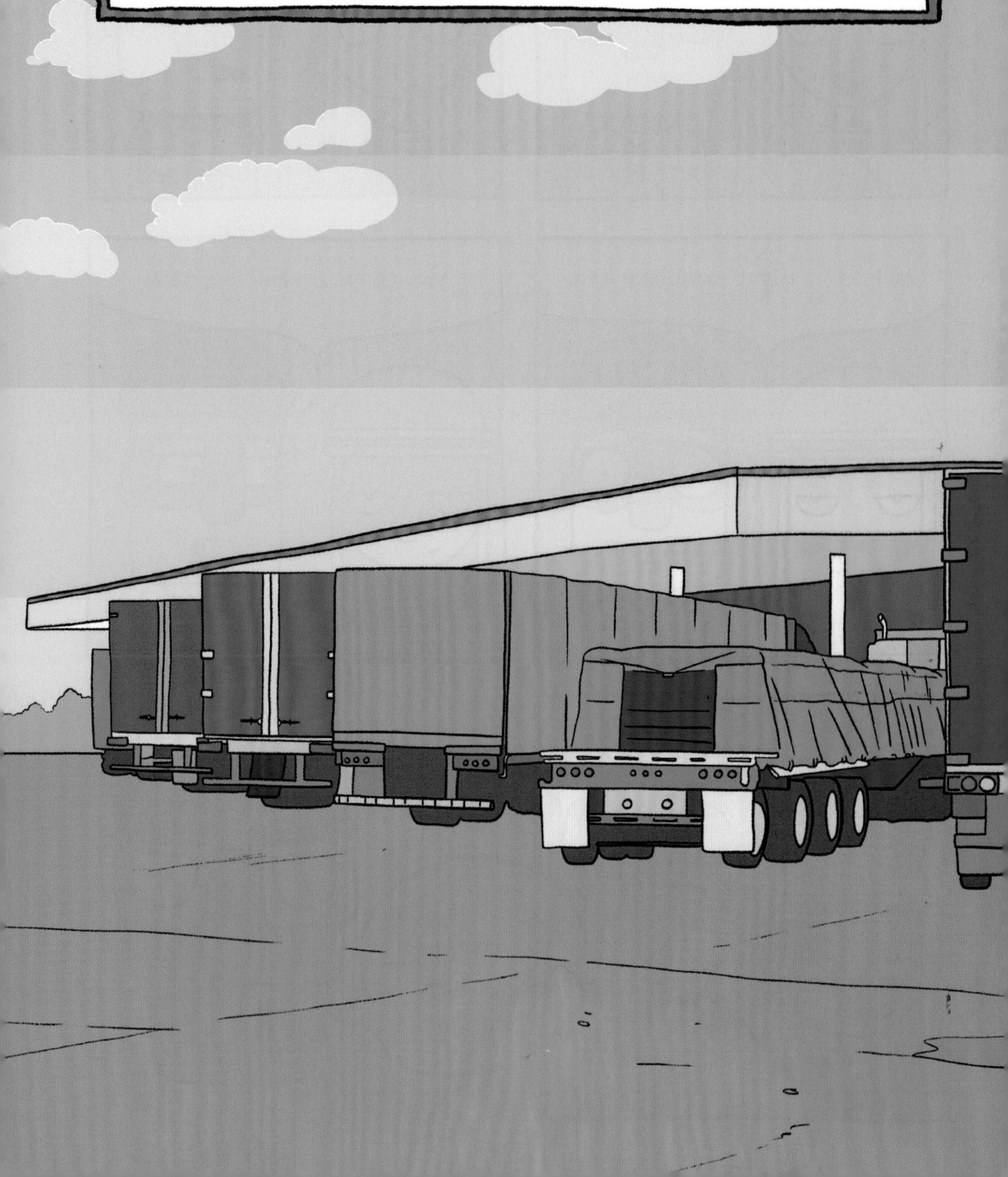

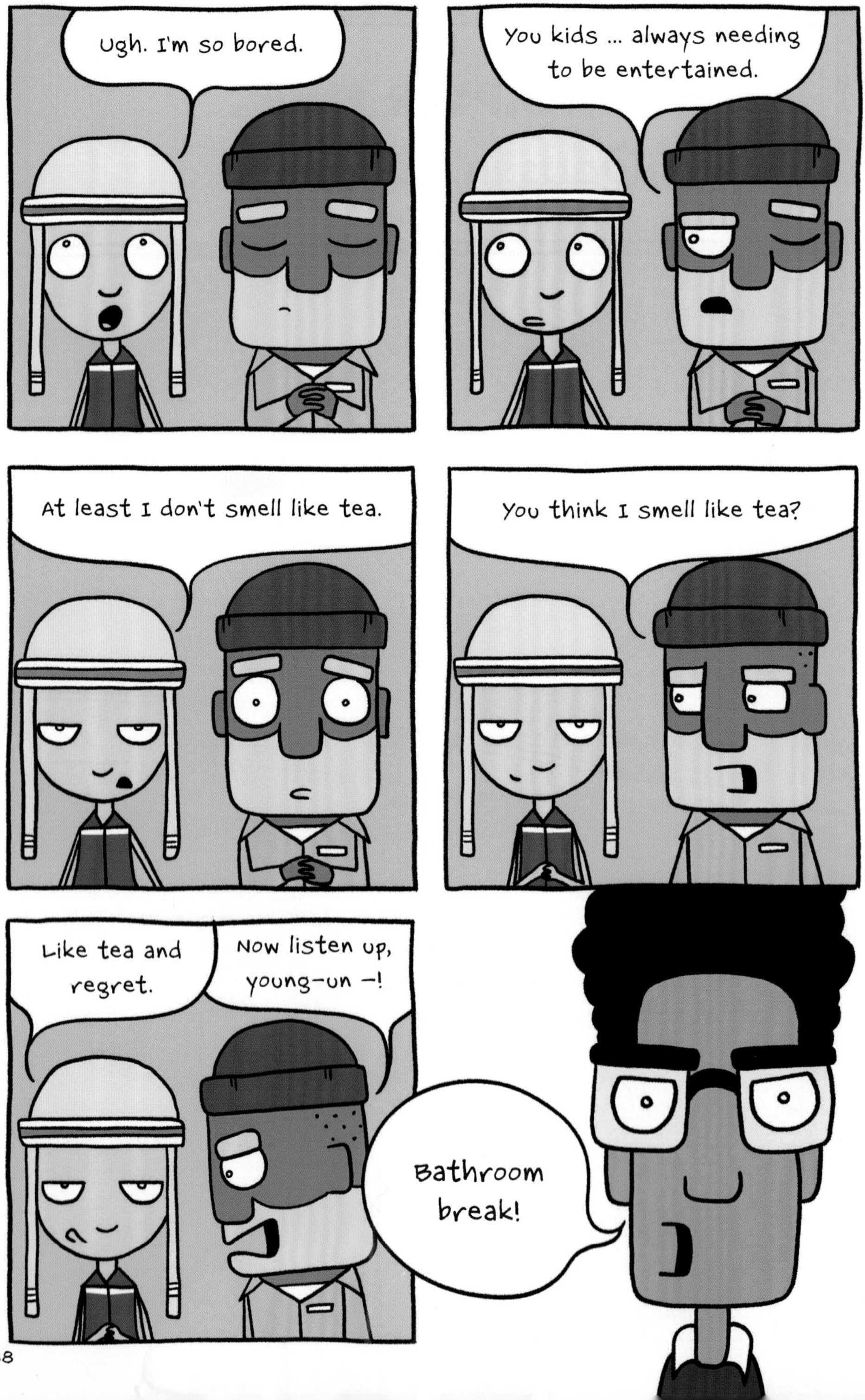
Ugh. I'm so bored.
You kids ... always needing to be entertained.
At least I don't smell like tea.
You think I smell like tea?
Like tea and regret.
Now listen up, young-un —!
Bathroom break!

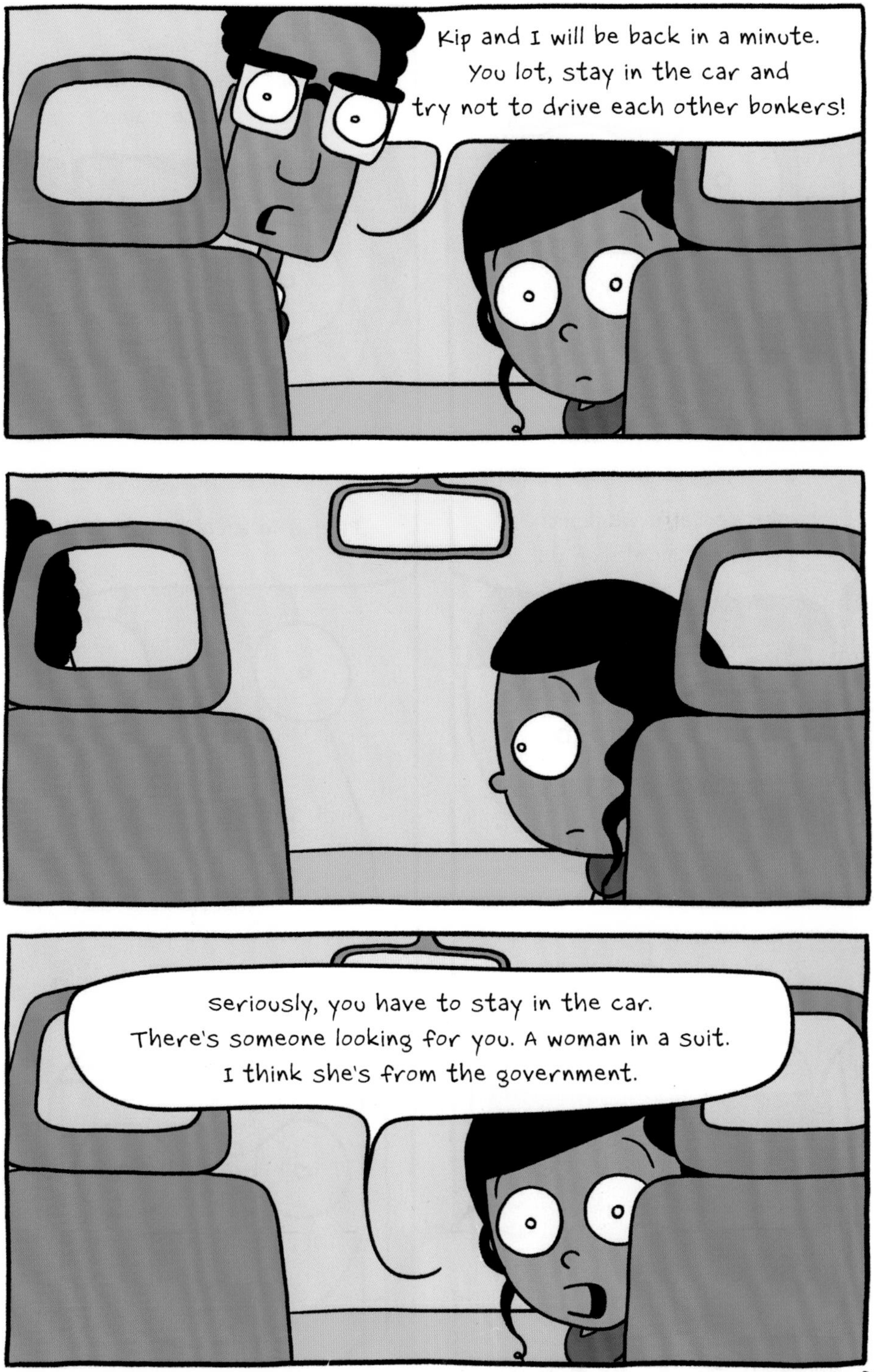
Kip and I will be back in a minute. You lot, stay in the car and try not to drive each other bonkers!
Seriously, you have to stay in the car. There's someone looking for you. A woman in a suit. I think she's from the government.

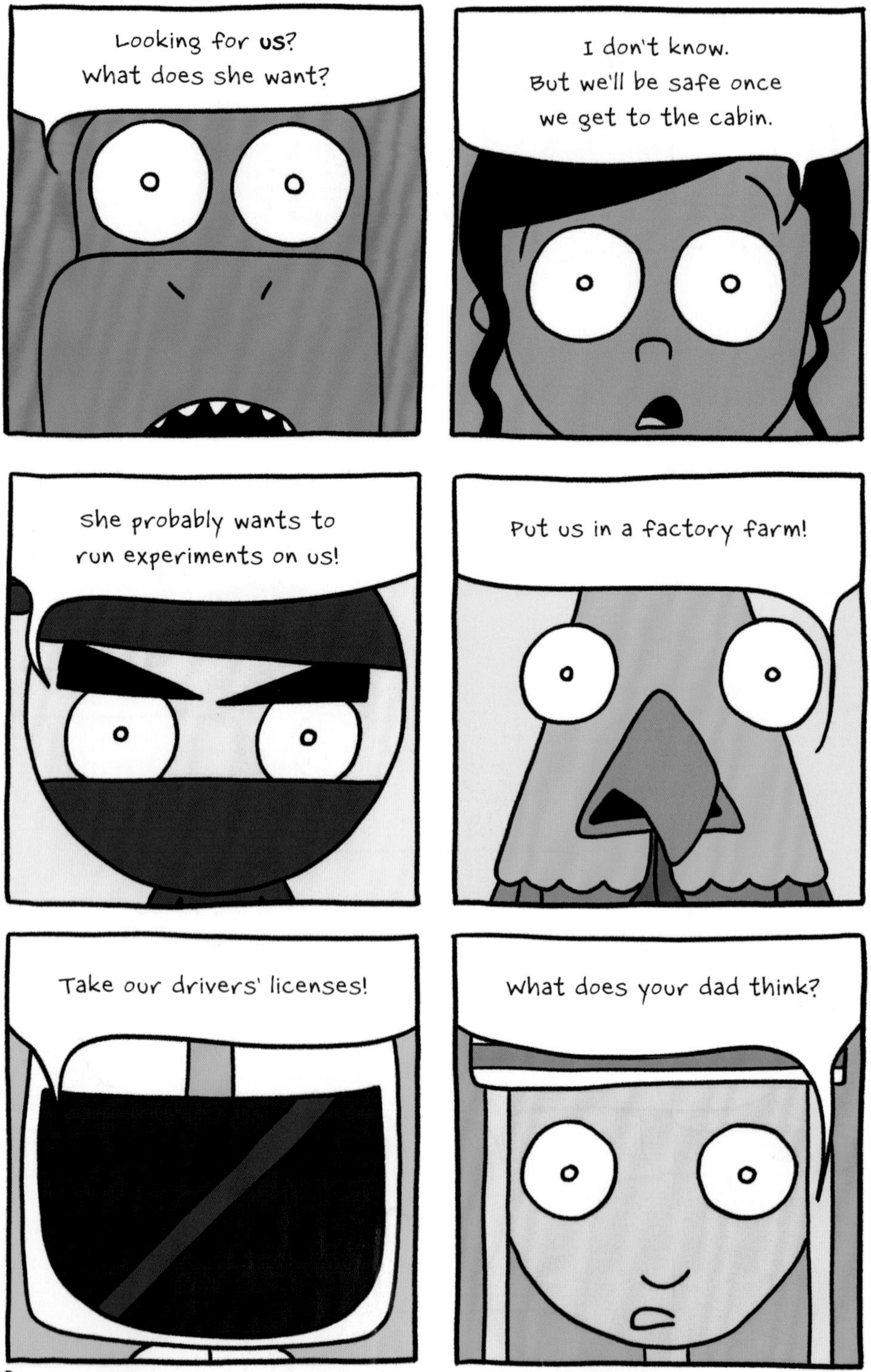

Looking for **us**? What does she want?
I don't know. But we'll be safe once we get to the cabin.
She probably wants to run experiments on us!
Put us in a factory farm!
Take our drivers' licenses!
What does your dad think?

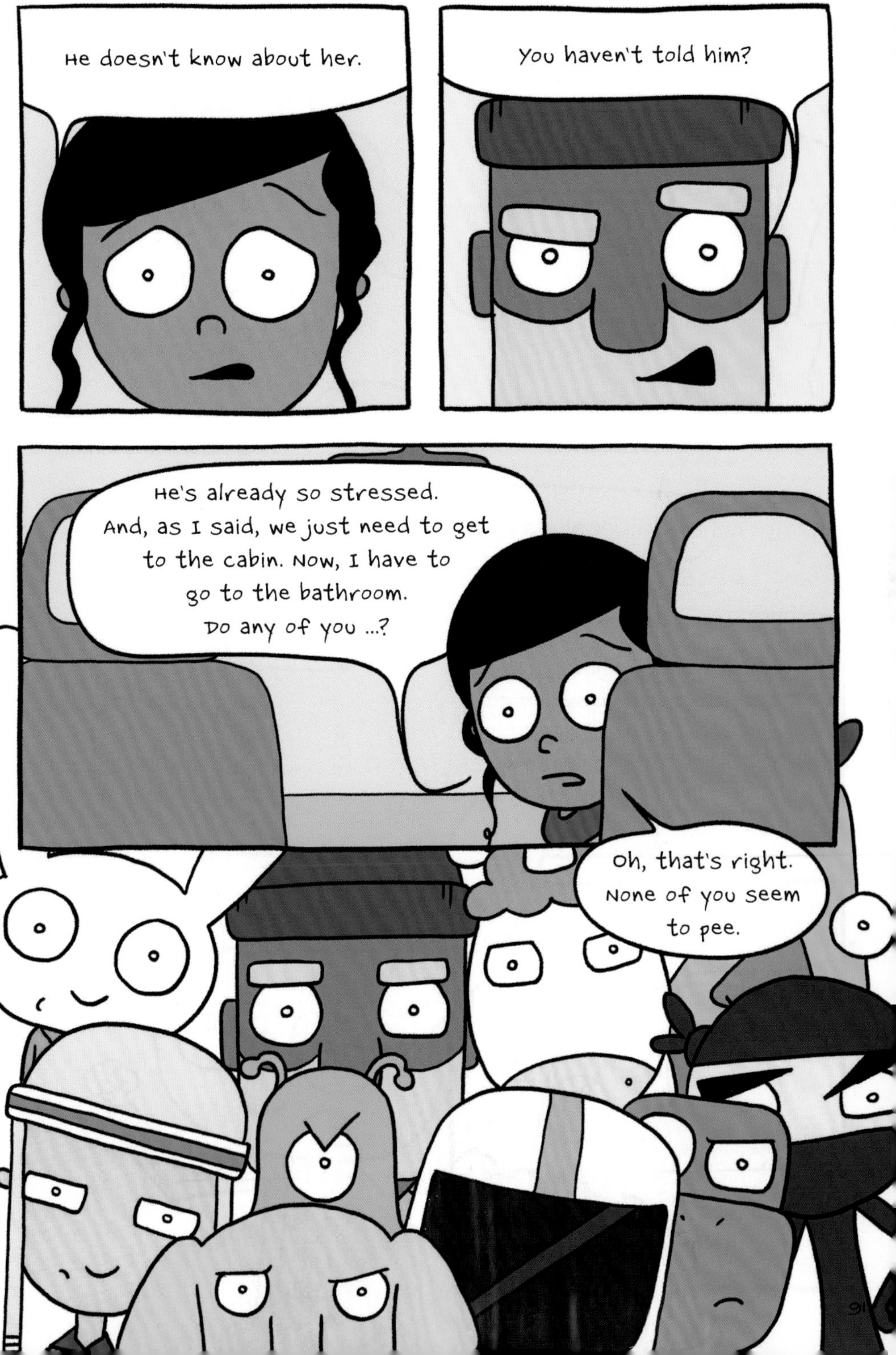
He doesn't know about her.
You haven't told him?
He's already so stressed. And, as I said, we just need to get to the cabin. Now, I have to go to the bathroom. Do any of you ...?
Oh, that's right. None of you seem to pee.

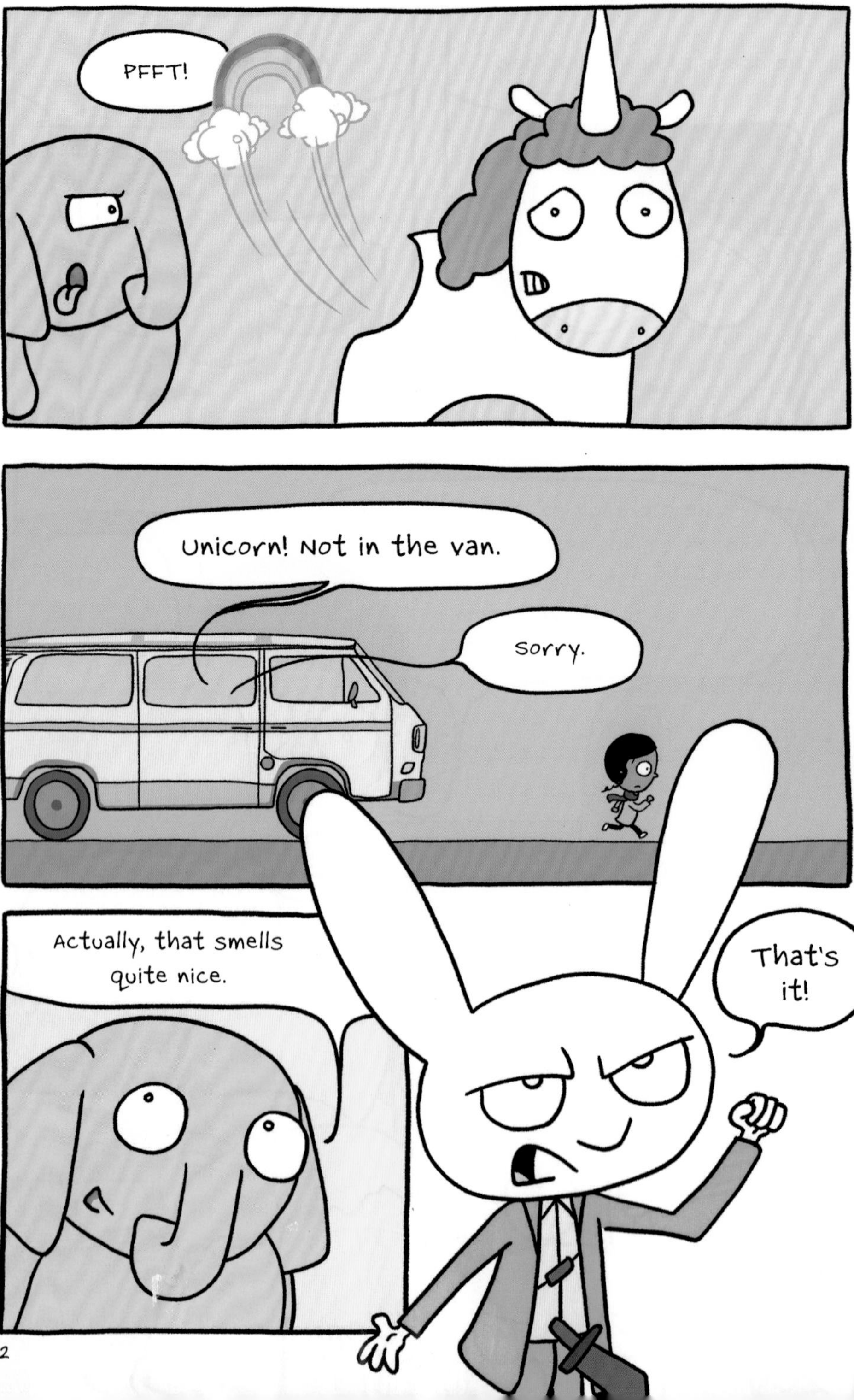
PFFT!
Unicorn! Not in the van.
sorry.
Actually, that smells quite nice.
That's it!

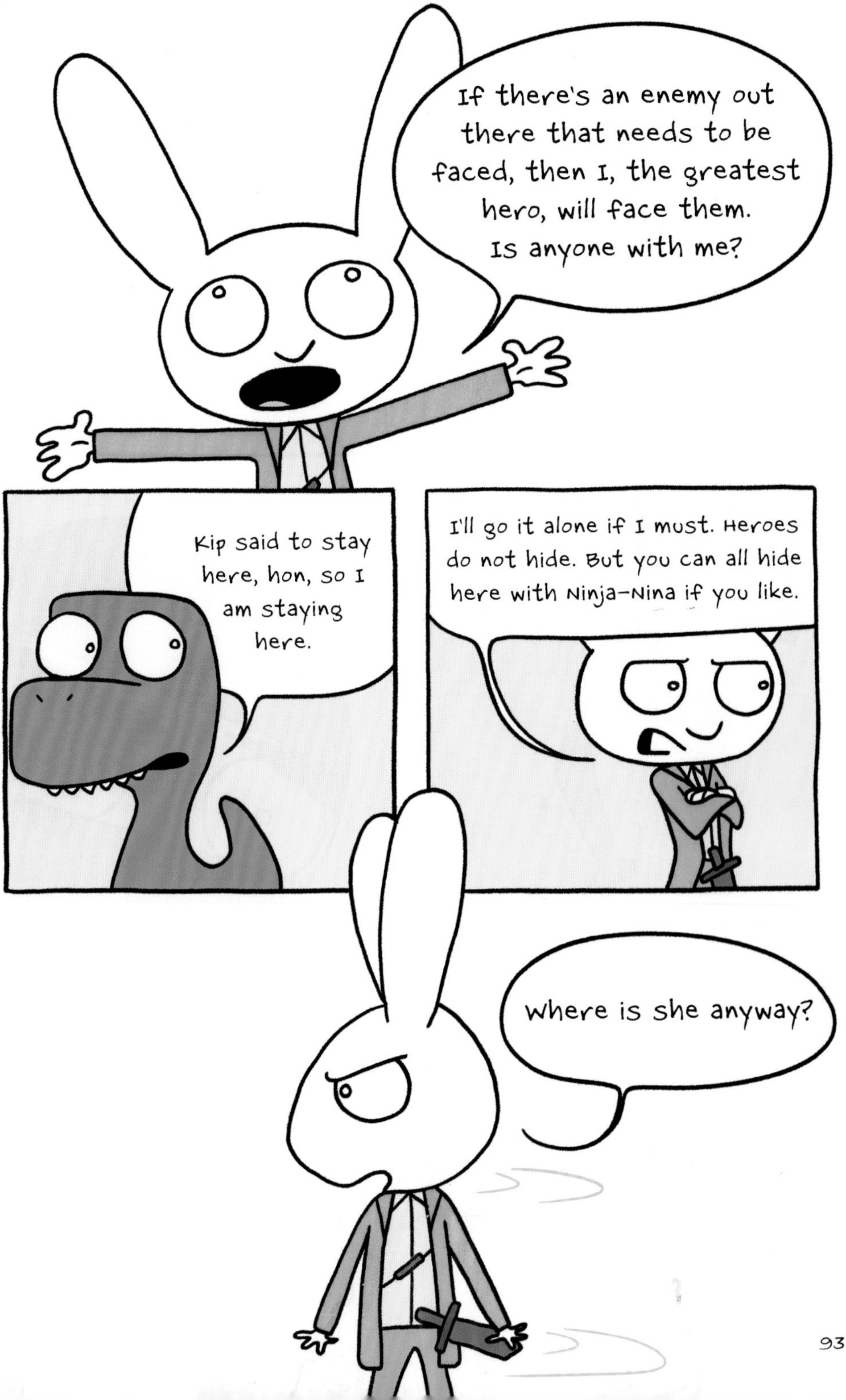
If there's an enemy out there that needs to be faced, then I, the greatest hero, will face them. Is anyone with me?
Kip said to stay here, hon, so I am staying here.
I'll go it alone if I must. Heroes do not hide. But you can all hide here with Ninja-Nina if you like.
Where is she anyway?

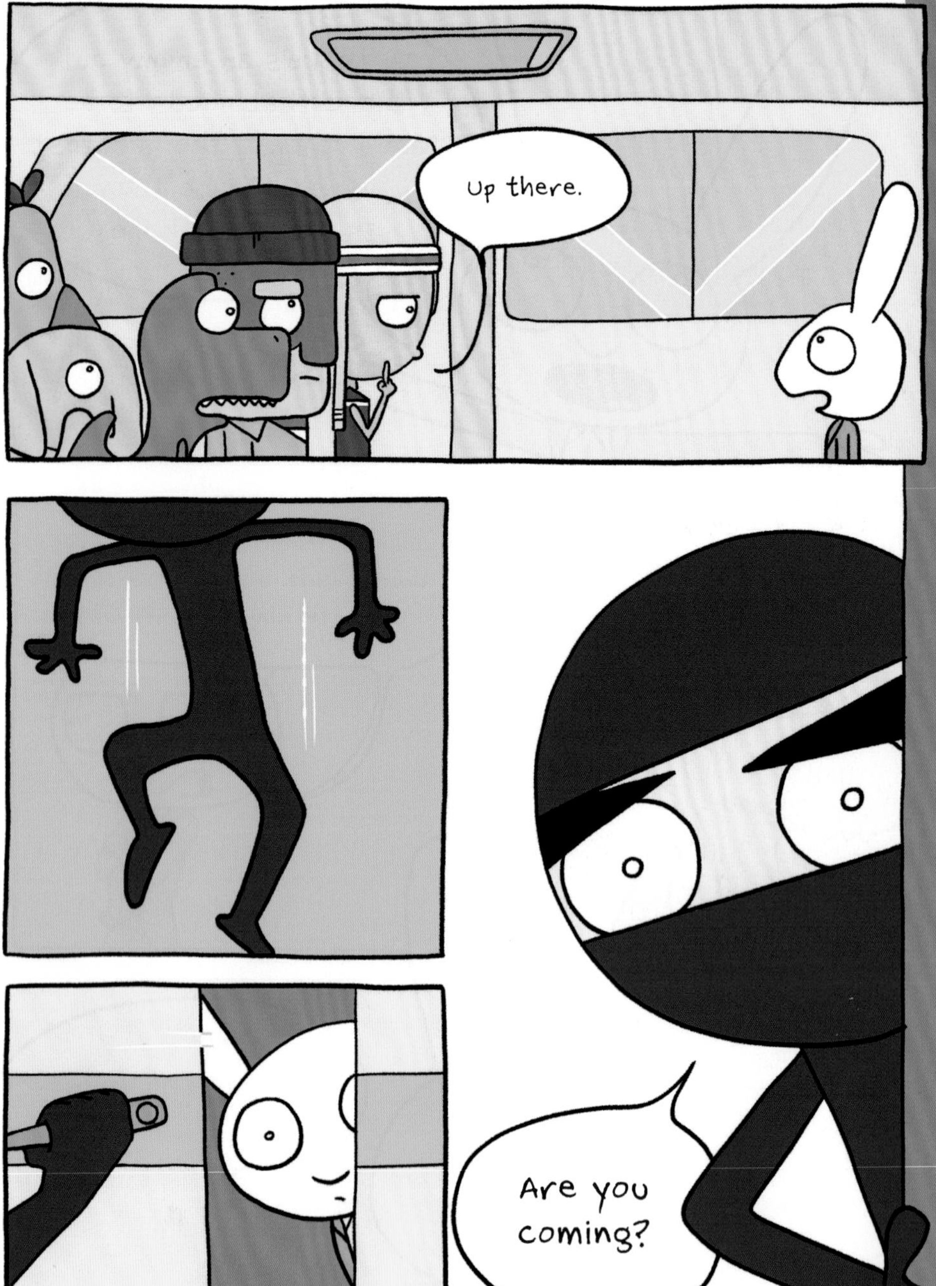
Up there.
Are you coming?

Aw, man! He took the keys with him!

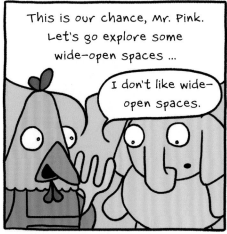

This is our chance, Mr. Pink. Let's go explore some wide-open spaces ...

I don't like wide-open spaces.

Stick our feet in the dirt ...

My feet are fluffy.

It's time to find a farm, break a sweat, and do some hard work!

No, thank you.

Mr. Pink, has anyone ever told you you're a bit ... **soft**?

And squishy.

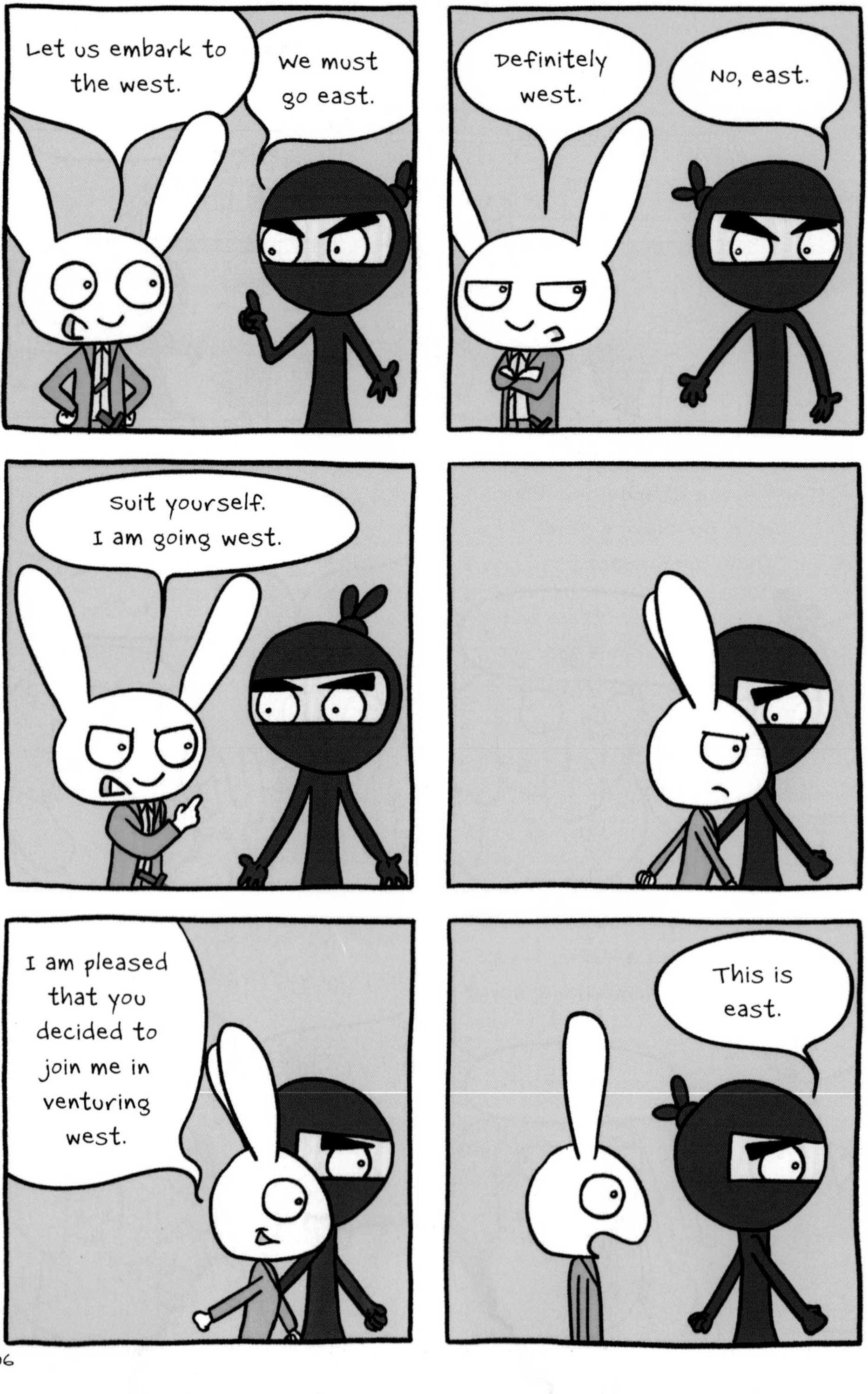
Let us embark to the west.
We must go east.
Definitely west.
No, east.
Suit yourself. I am going west.
I am pleased that you decided to join me in venturing west.
This is east.

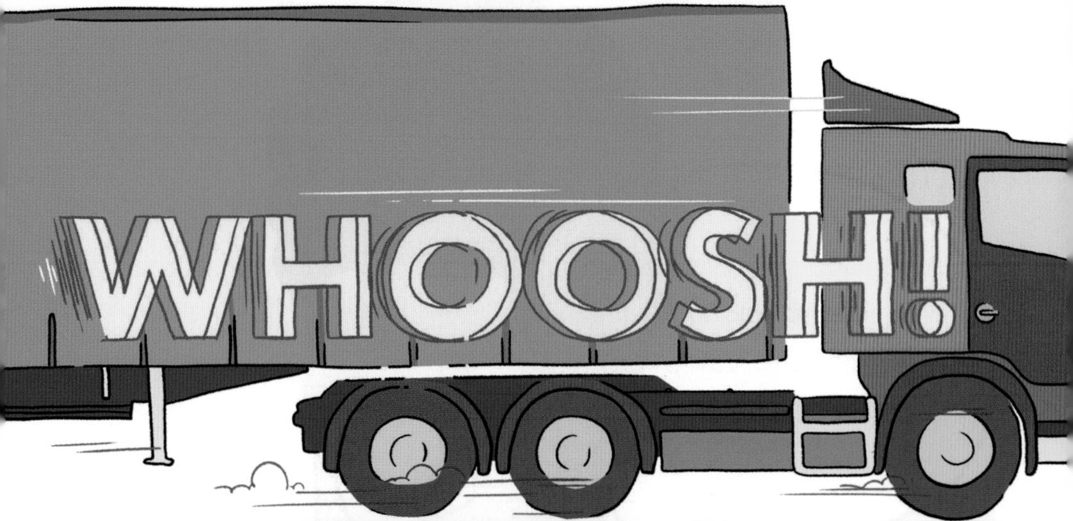
WHOOSH!

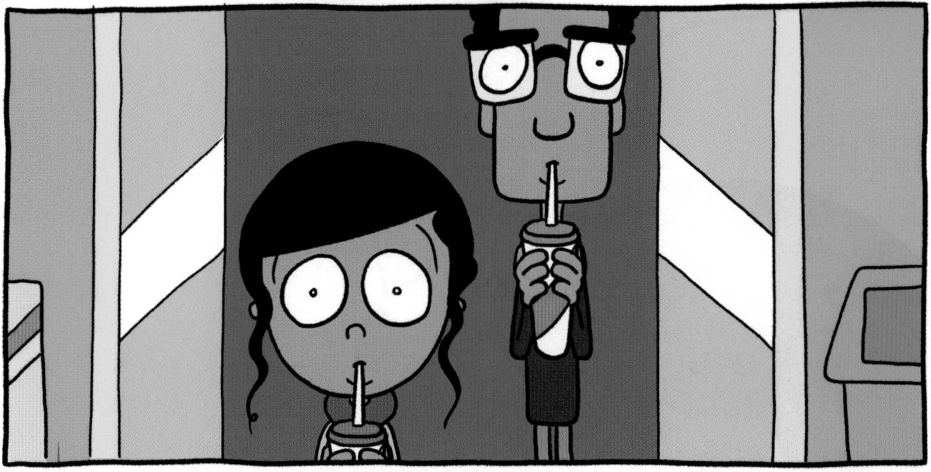

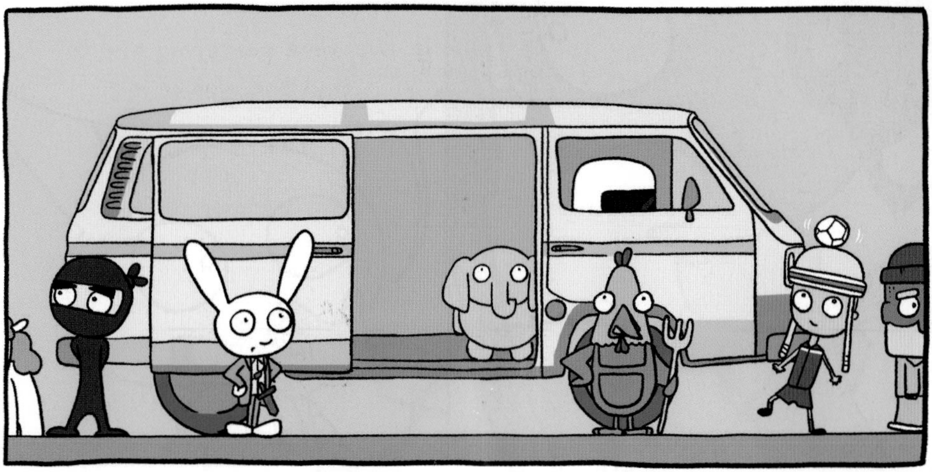

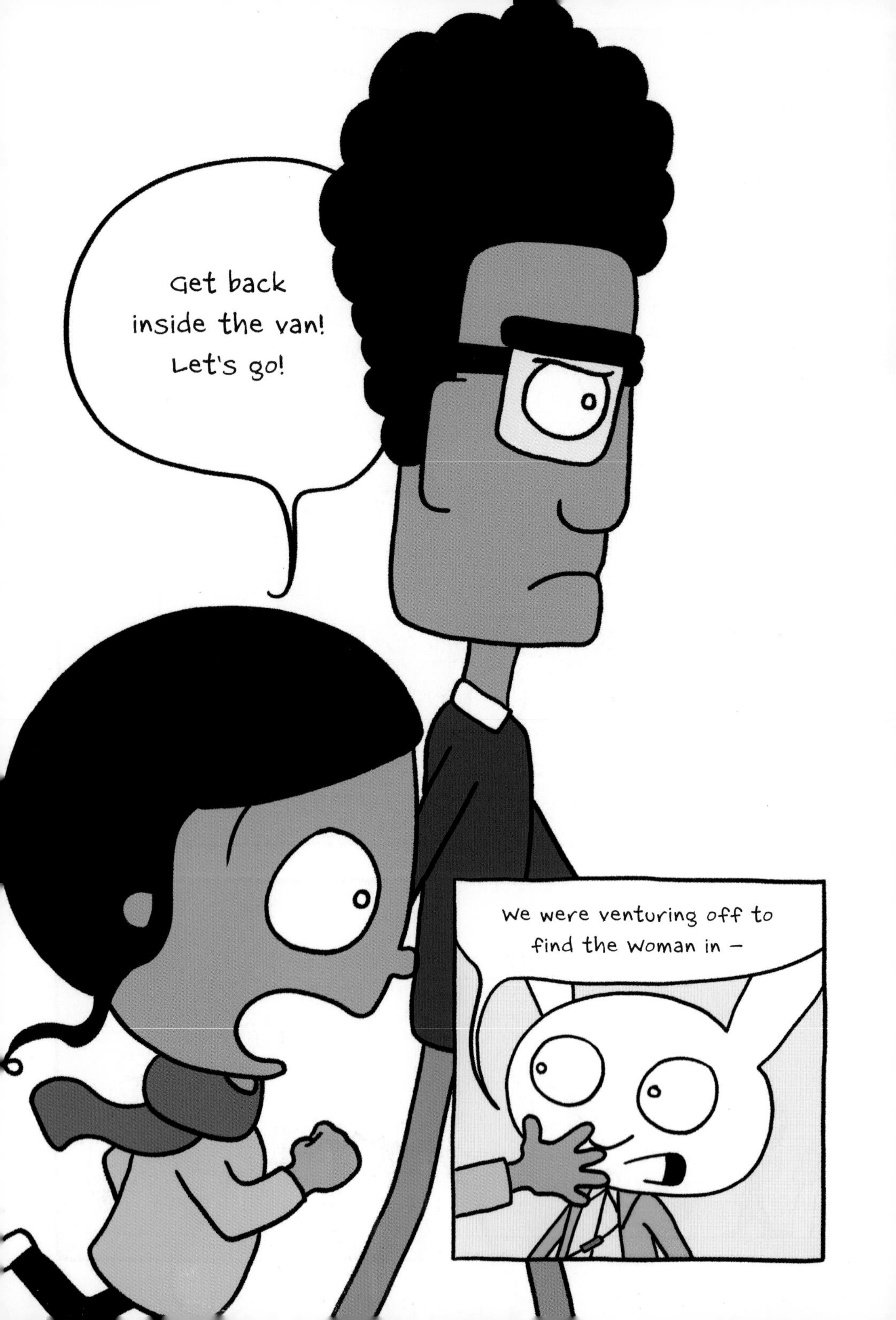
Get back inside the van! Let's go!
We were venturing off to find the woman in –

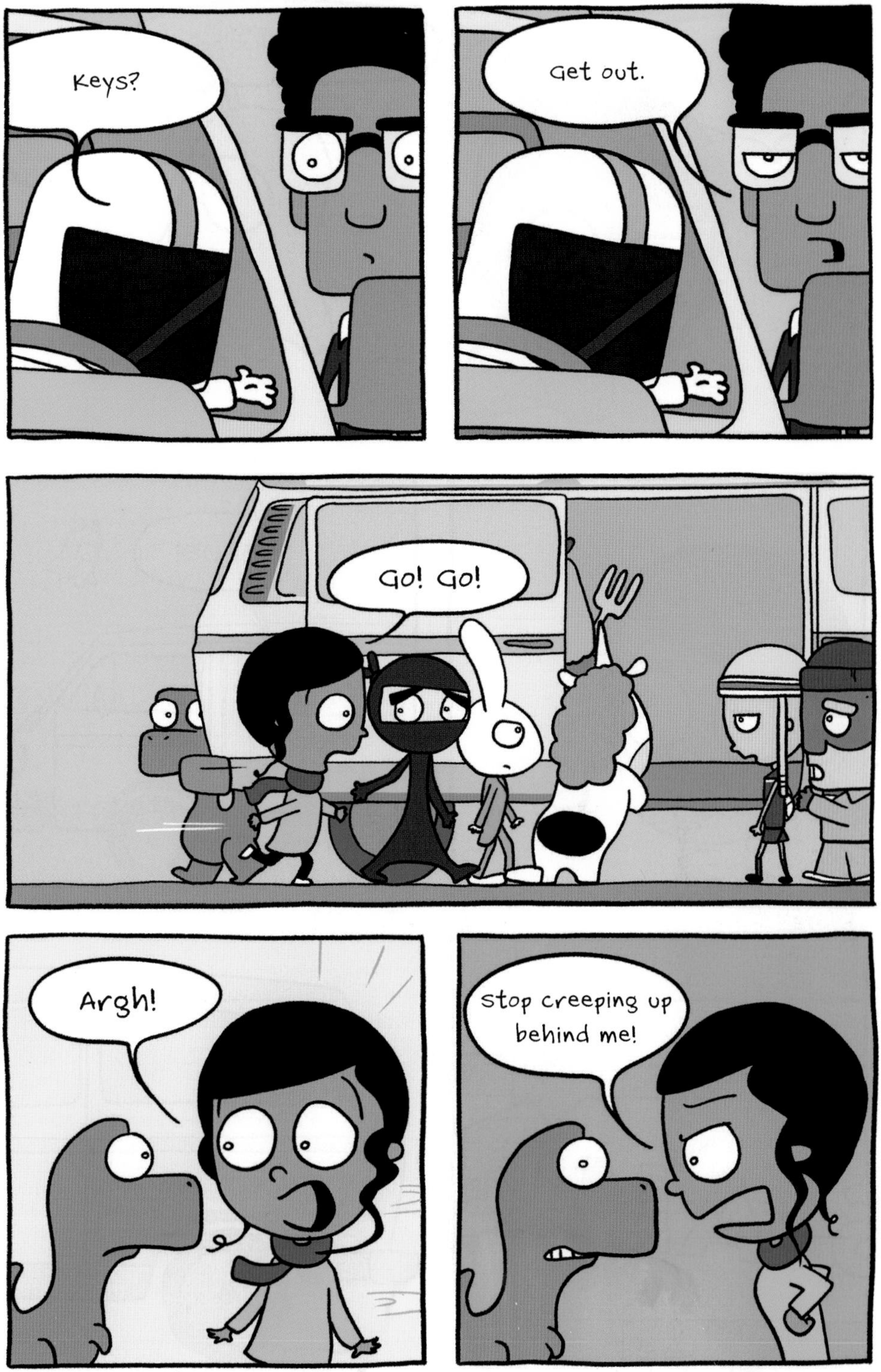
Keys?
Get out.
Go! Go!
Argh!
Stop creeping up behind me!

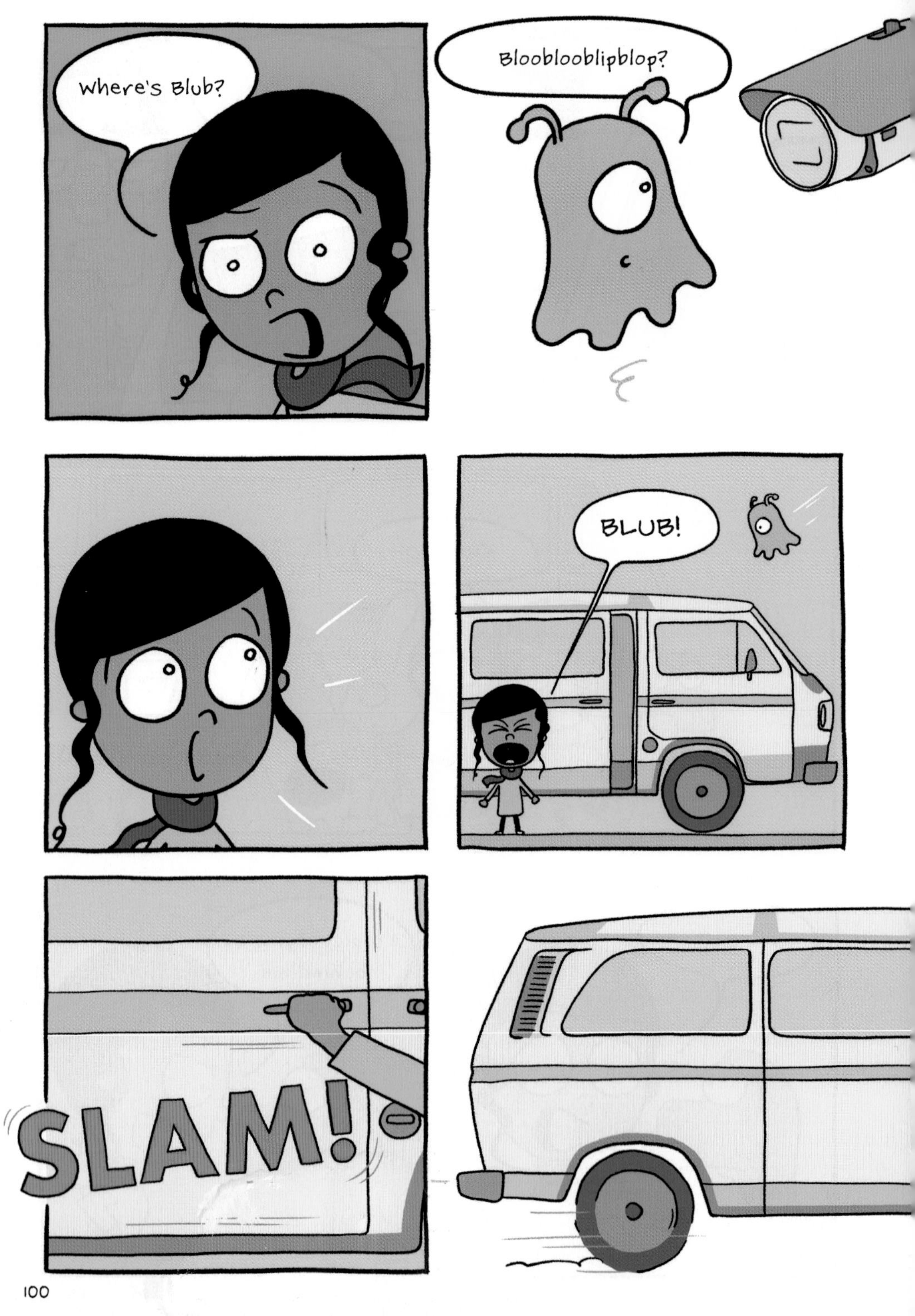
Where's Blub?
Bloobloobliplop?
BLUB!
SLAM!

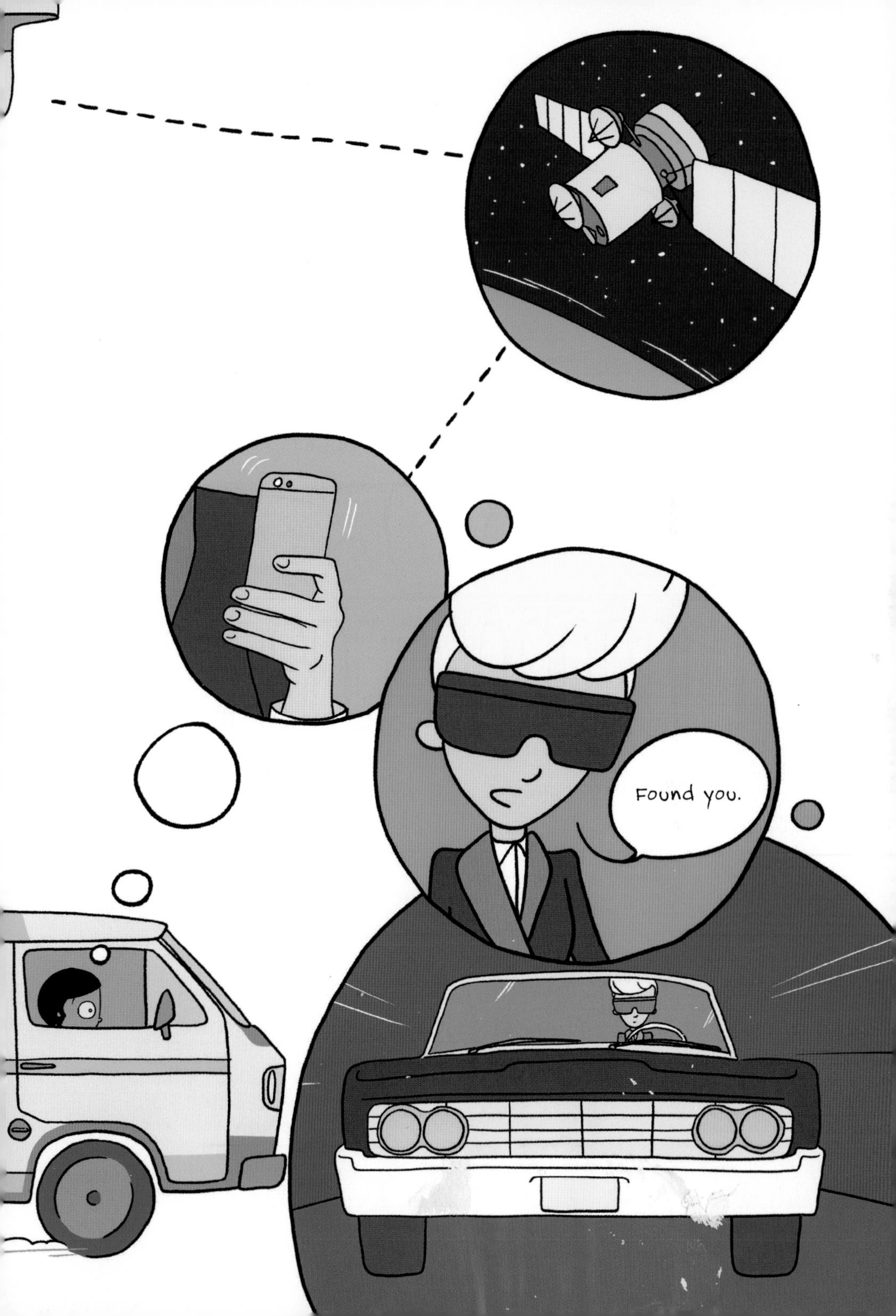
Found you.

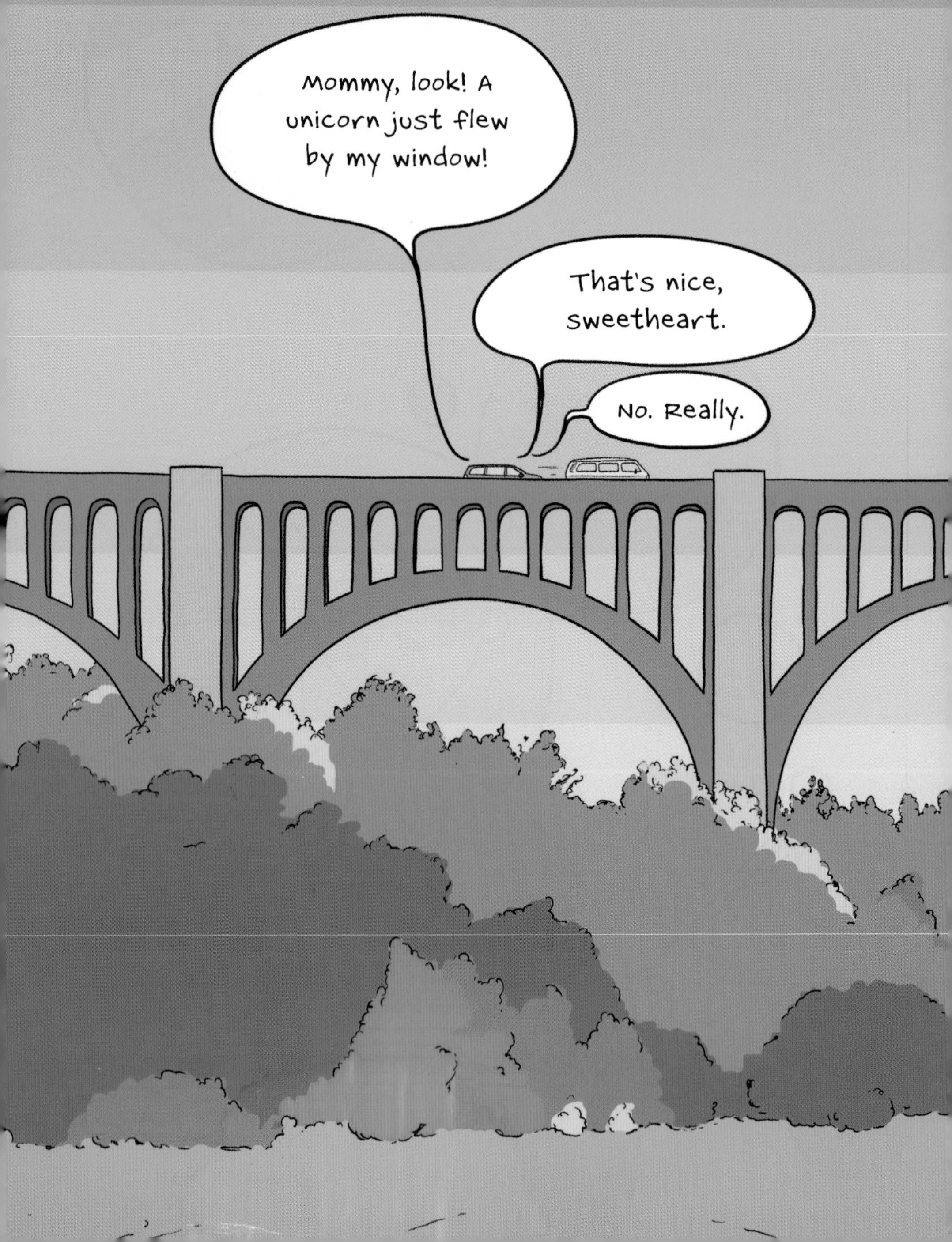
Mommy, look! A unicorn just flew by my window!
That's nice, sweetheart.
No. Really.

CHAPTER SIX
An odd detour

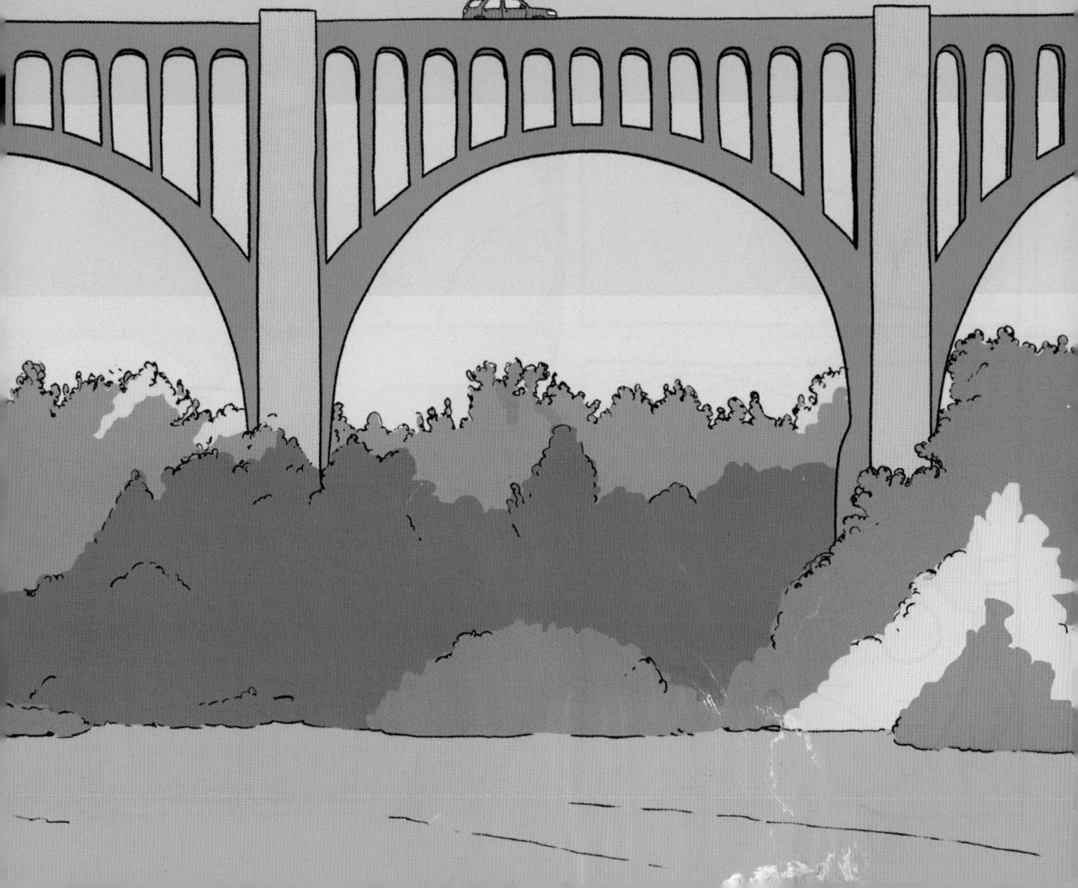

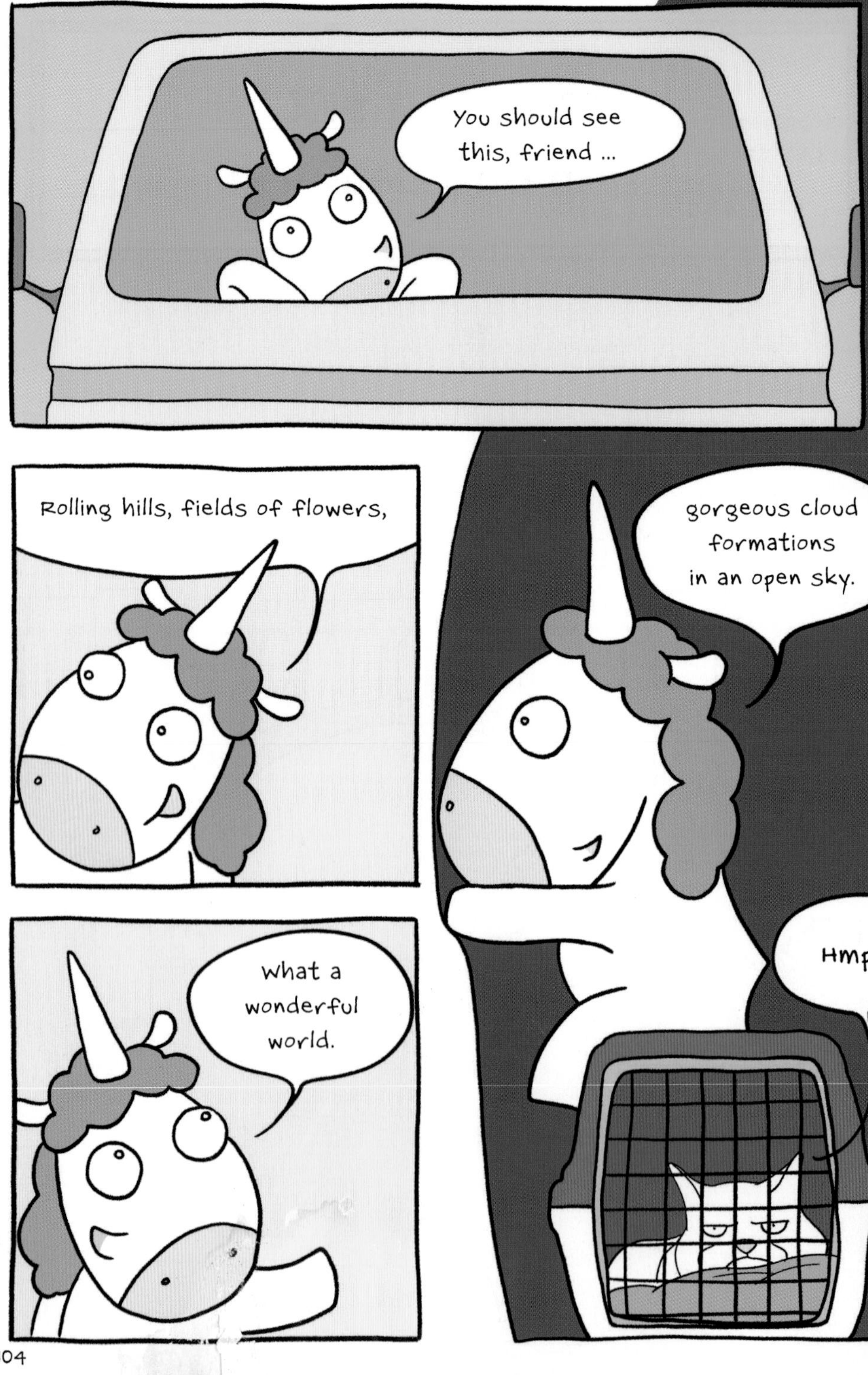
You should see this, friend ...
Rolling hills, fields of flowers,
gorgeous cloud formations in an open sky.
What a wonderful world.
Hmpf.

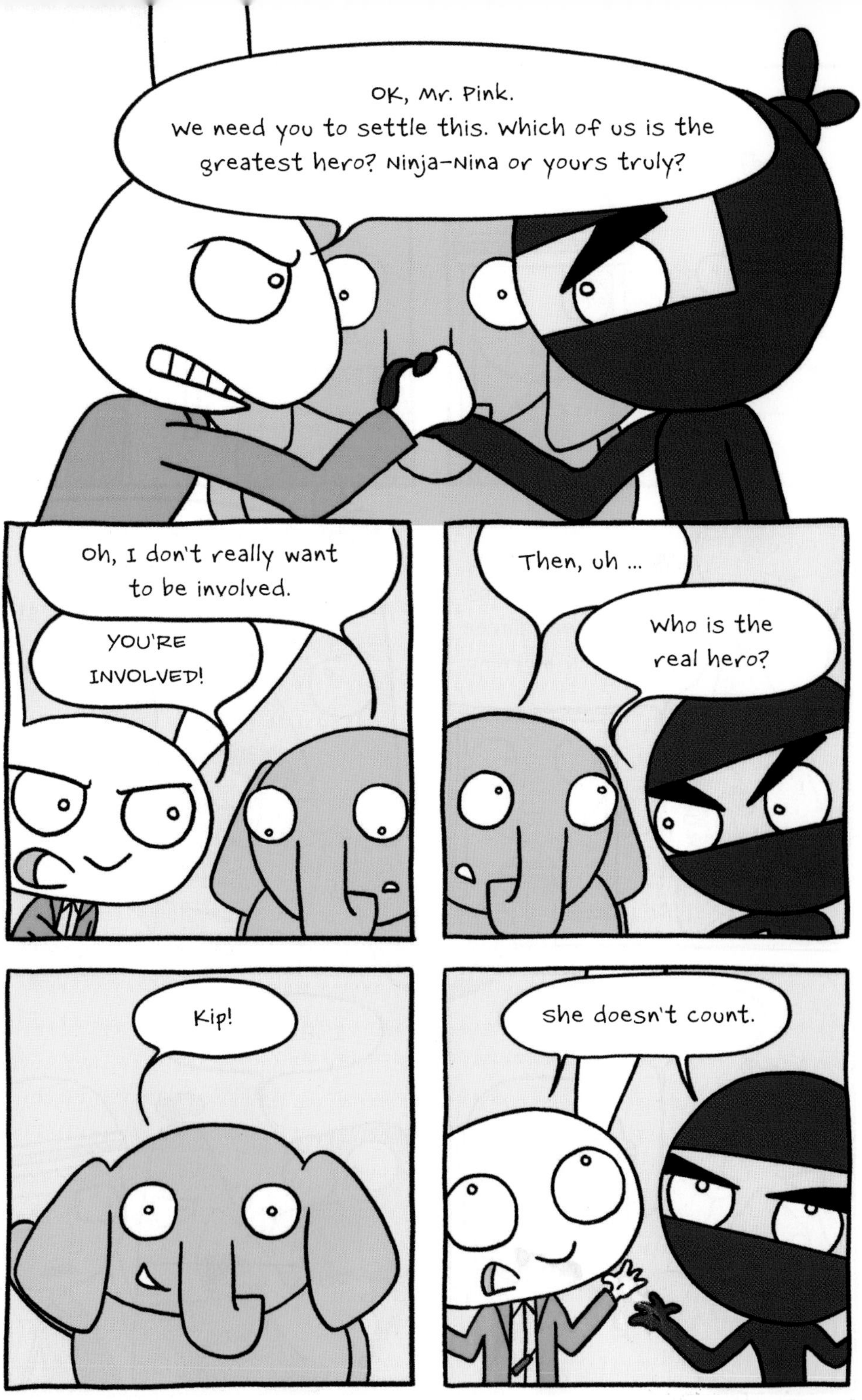
OK, Mr. Pink.
We need you to settle this. Which of us is the greatest hero? Ninja-Nina or yours truly?
Oh, I don't really want to be involved.
YOU'RE INVOLVED!
Then, uh ...
Who is the real hero?
Kip!
She doesn't count.

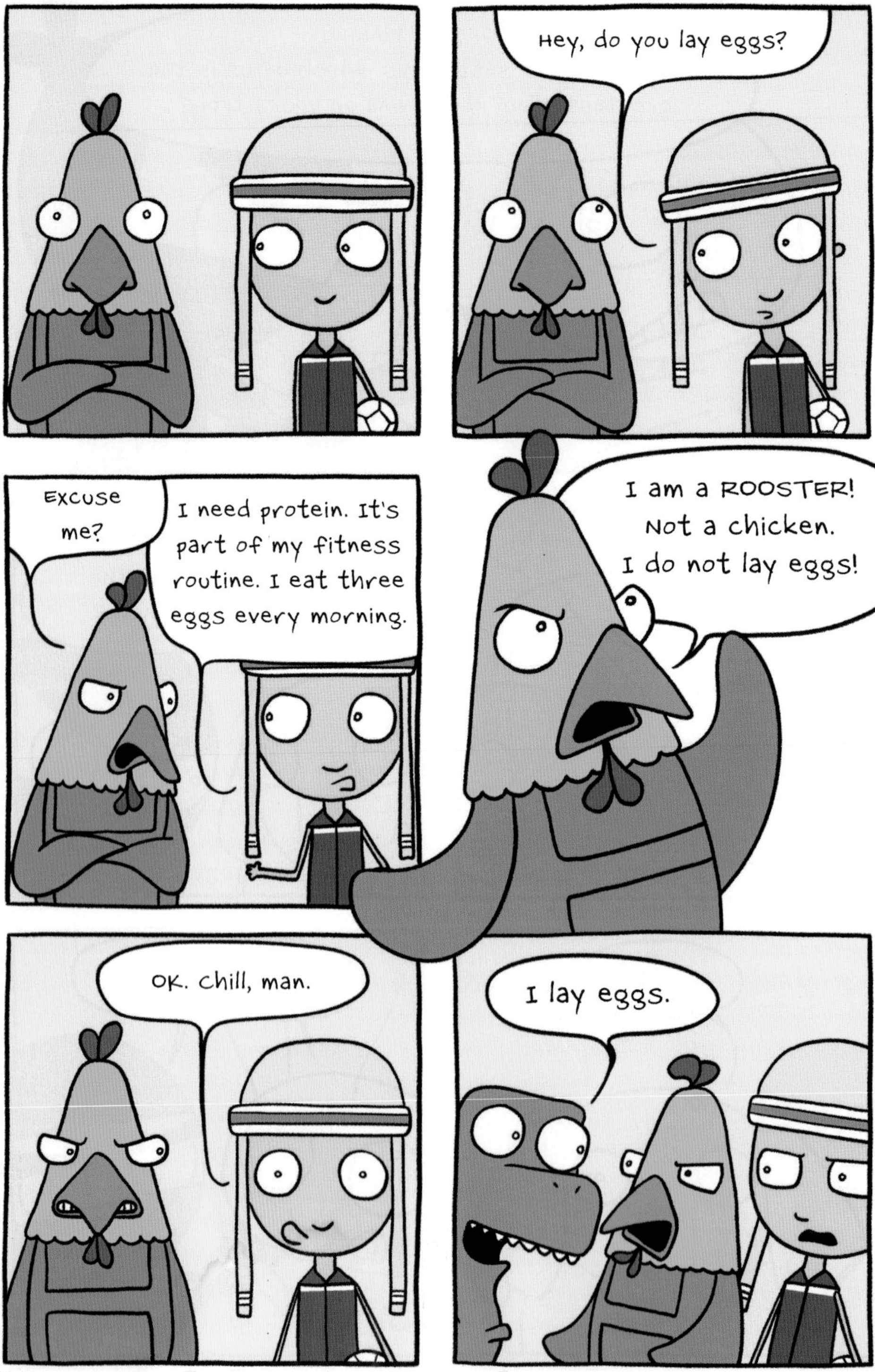
Hey, do you lay eggs?
Excuse me?
I need protein. It's part of my fitness routine. I eat three eggs every morning.
I am a ROOSTER! Not a chicken. I do not lay eggs!
OK. Chill, man.
I lay eggs.

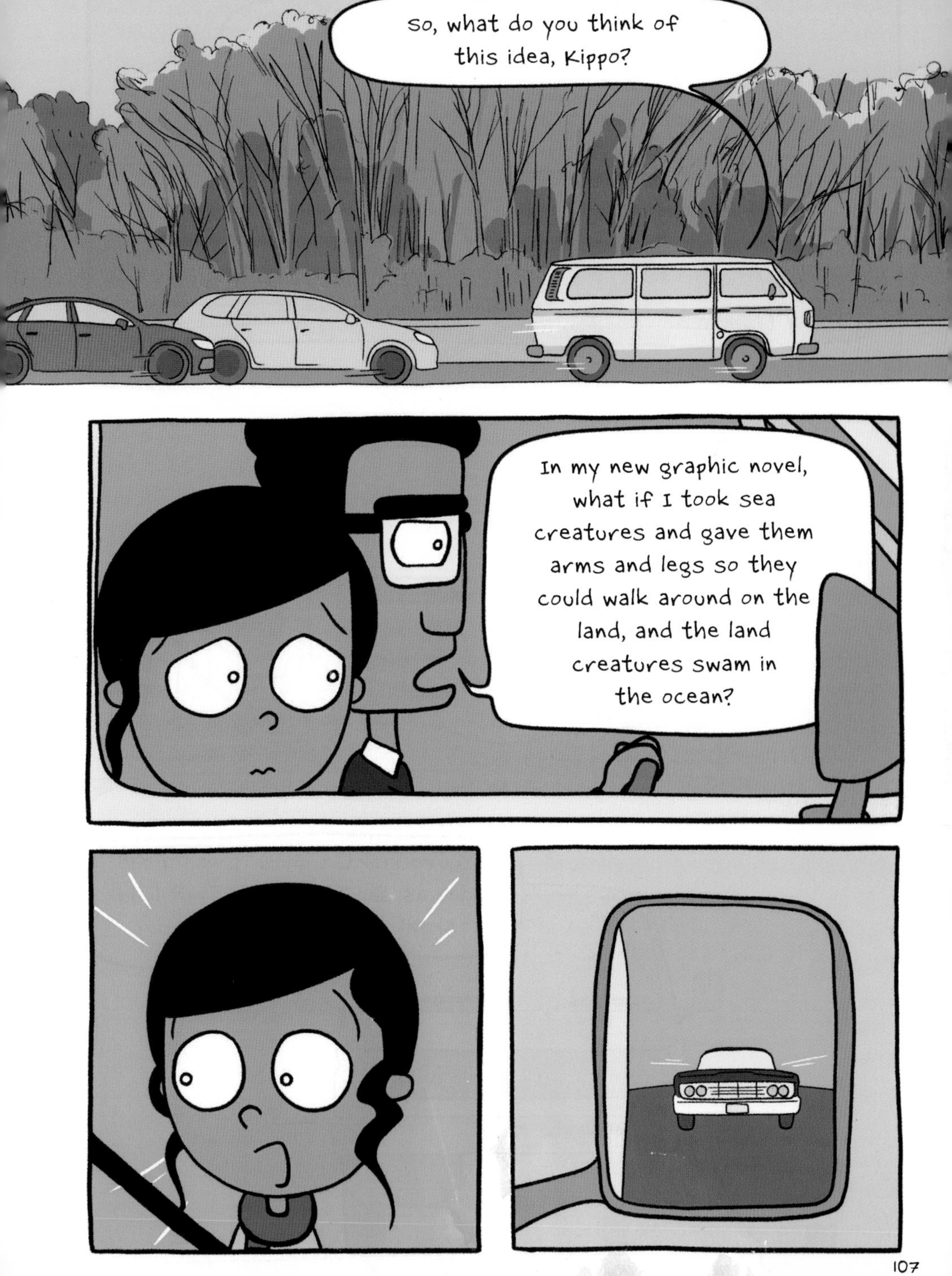
So, what do you think of this idea, Kippo?
In my new graphic novel, what if I took sea creatures and gave them arms and legs so they could walk around on the land, and the land creatures swam in the ocean?

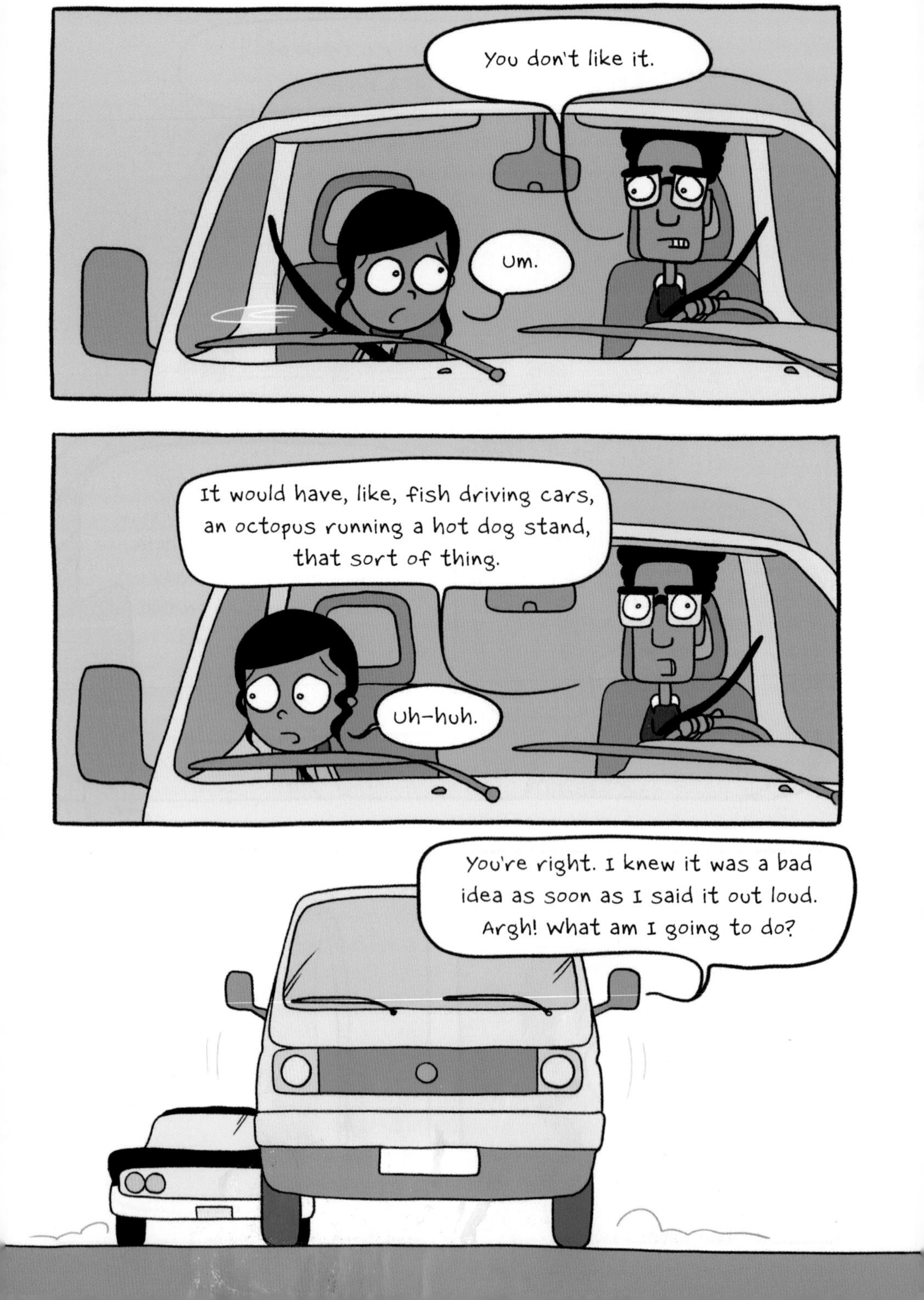
You don't like it.
Um.
It would have, like, fish driving cars, an octopus running a hot dog stand, that sort of thing.
Uh-huh.
You're right. I knew it was a bad idea as soon as I said it out loud. Argh! What am I going to do?

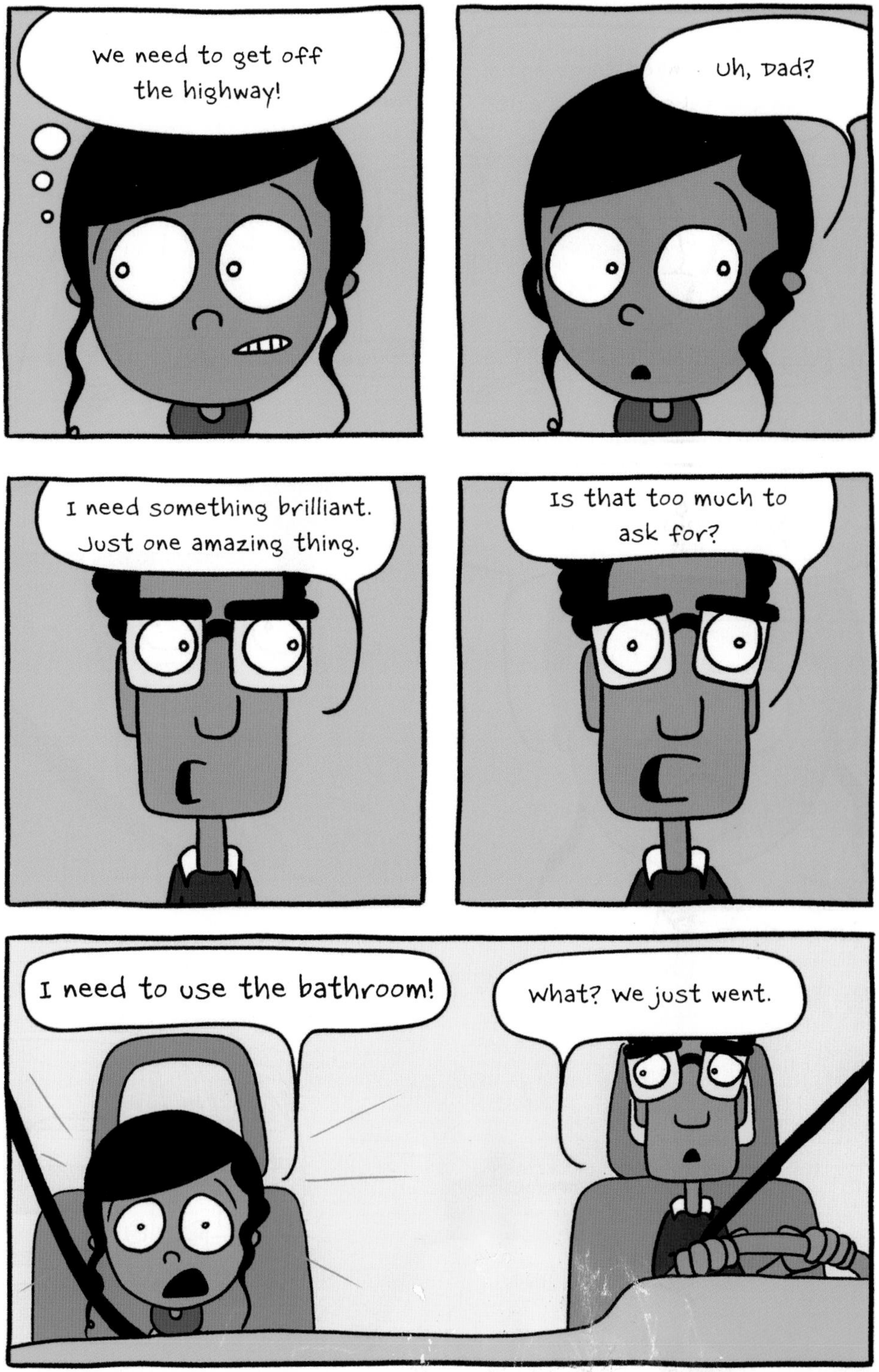
We need to get off the highway!
Uh, Dad?
I need something brilliant. Just one amazing thing.
Is that too much to ask for?
I need to use the bathroom!
What? We just went.

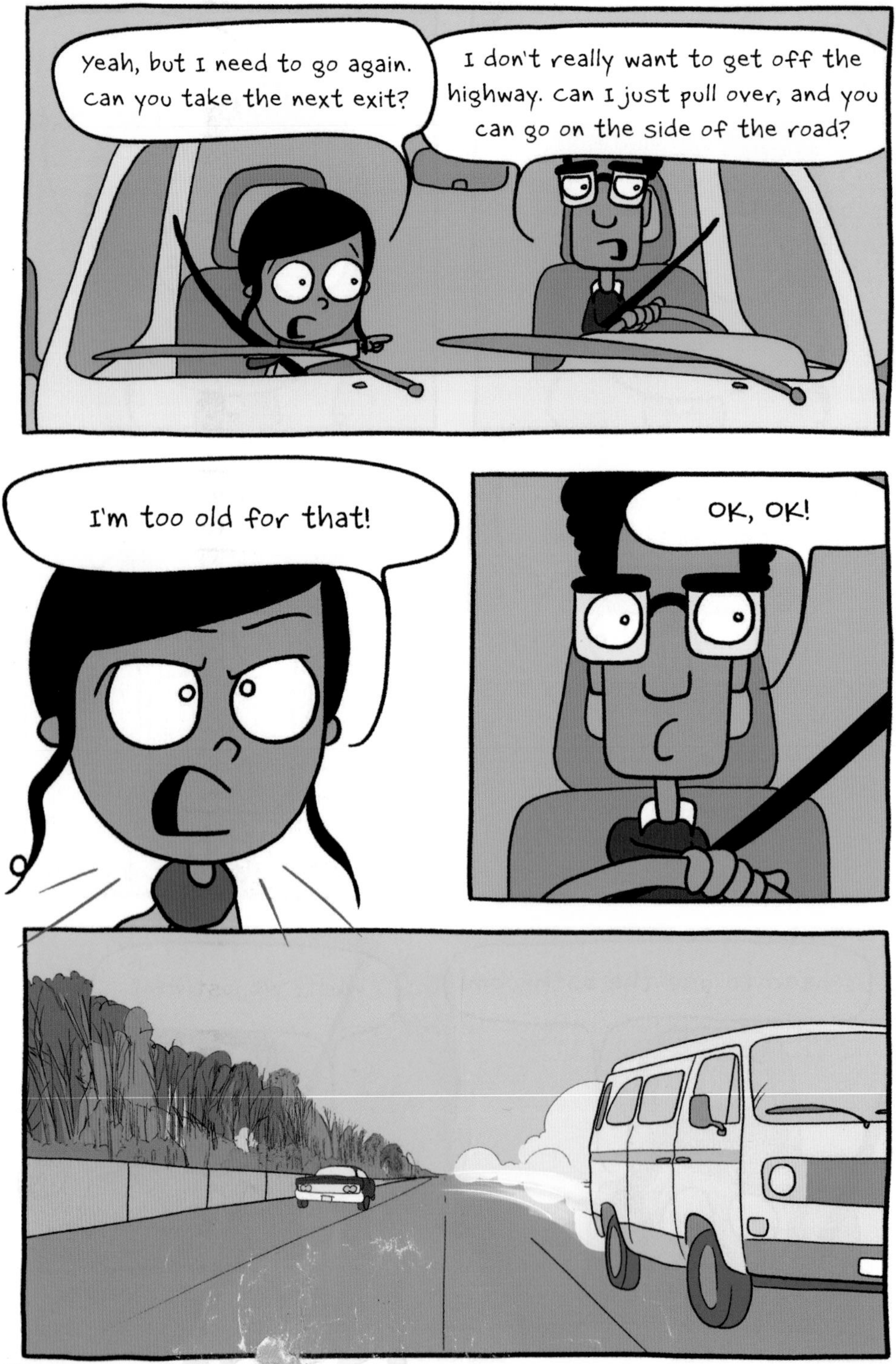

Yeah, but I need to go again. Can you take the next exit?
I don't really want to get off the highway. Can I just pull over, and you can go on the side of the road?
I'm too old for that!
OK, OK!

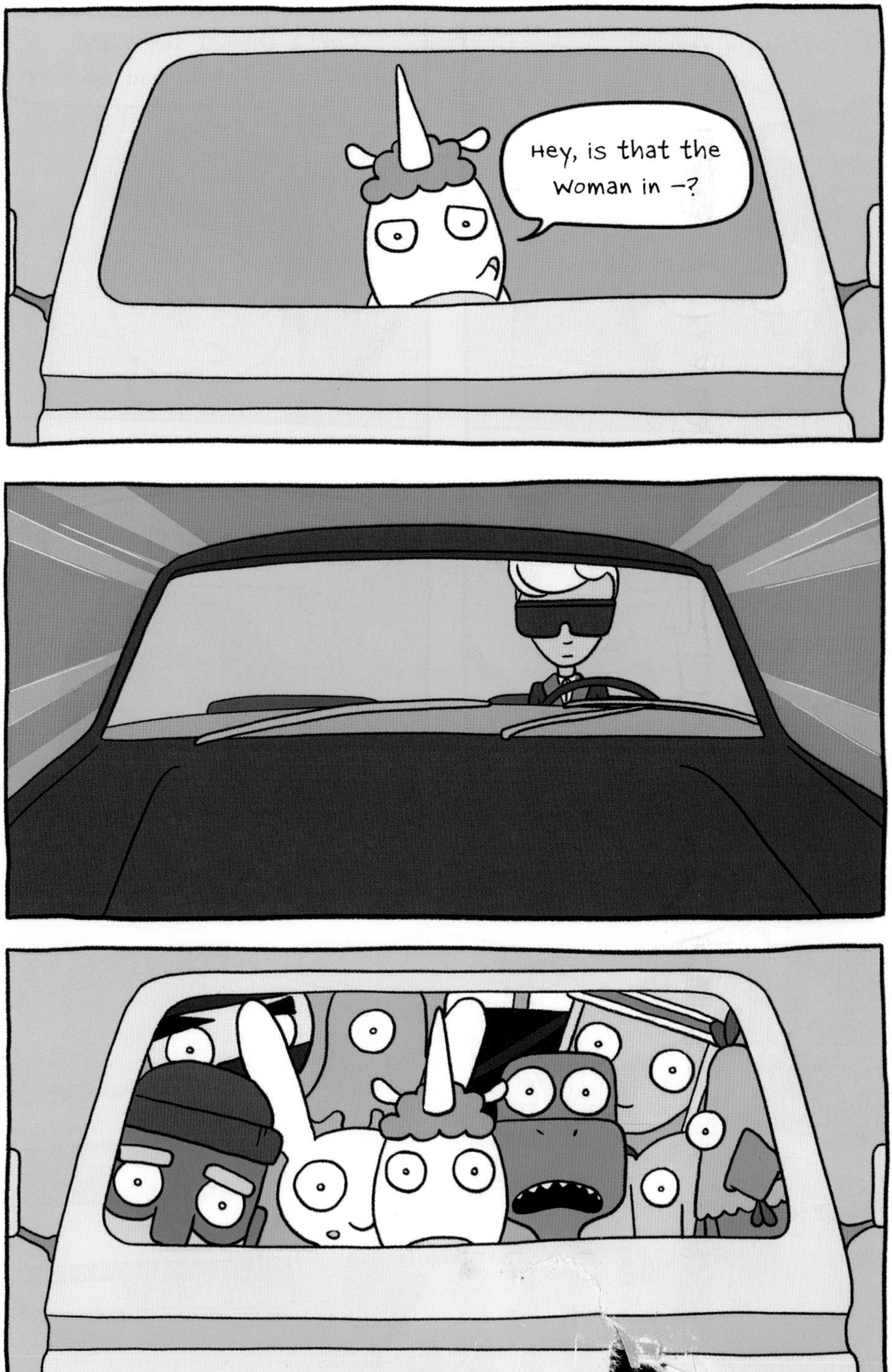
Hey, is that the woman in —?

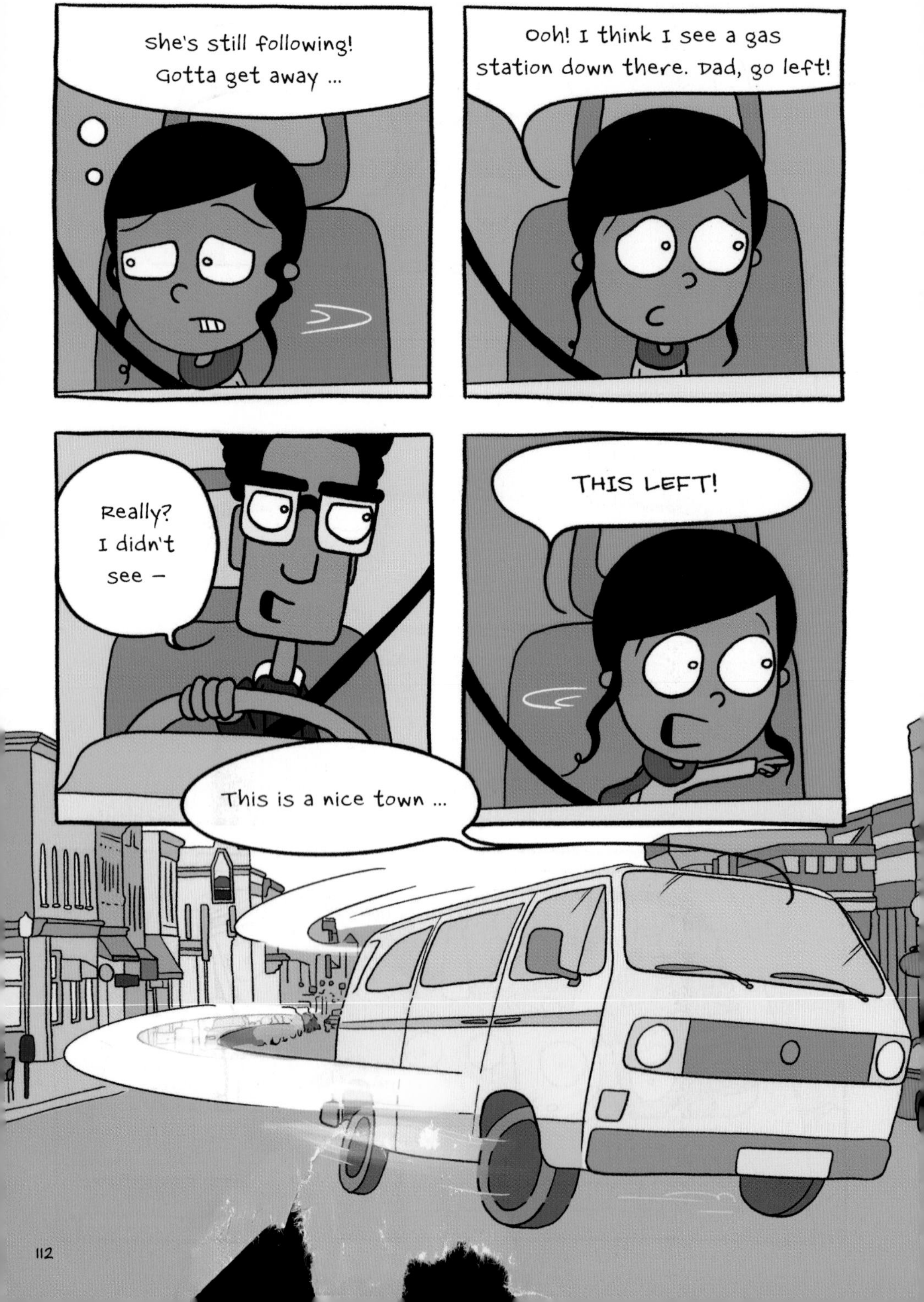
she's still following!
Gotta get away ...
Ooh! I think I see a gas station down there. Dad, go left!
Really? I didn't see –
THIS LEFT!
This is a nice town ...

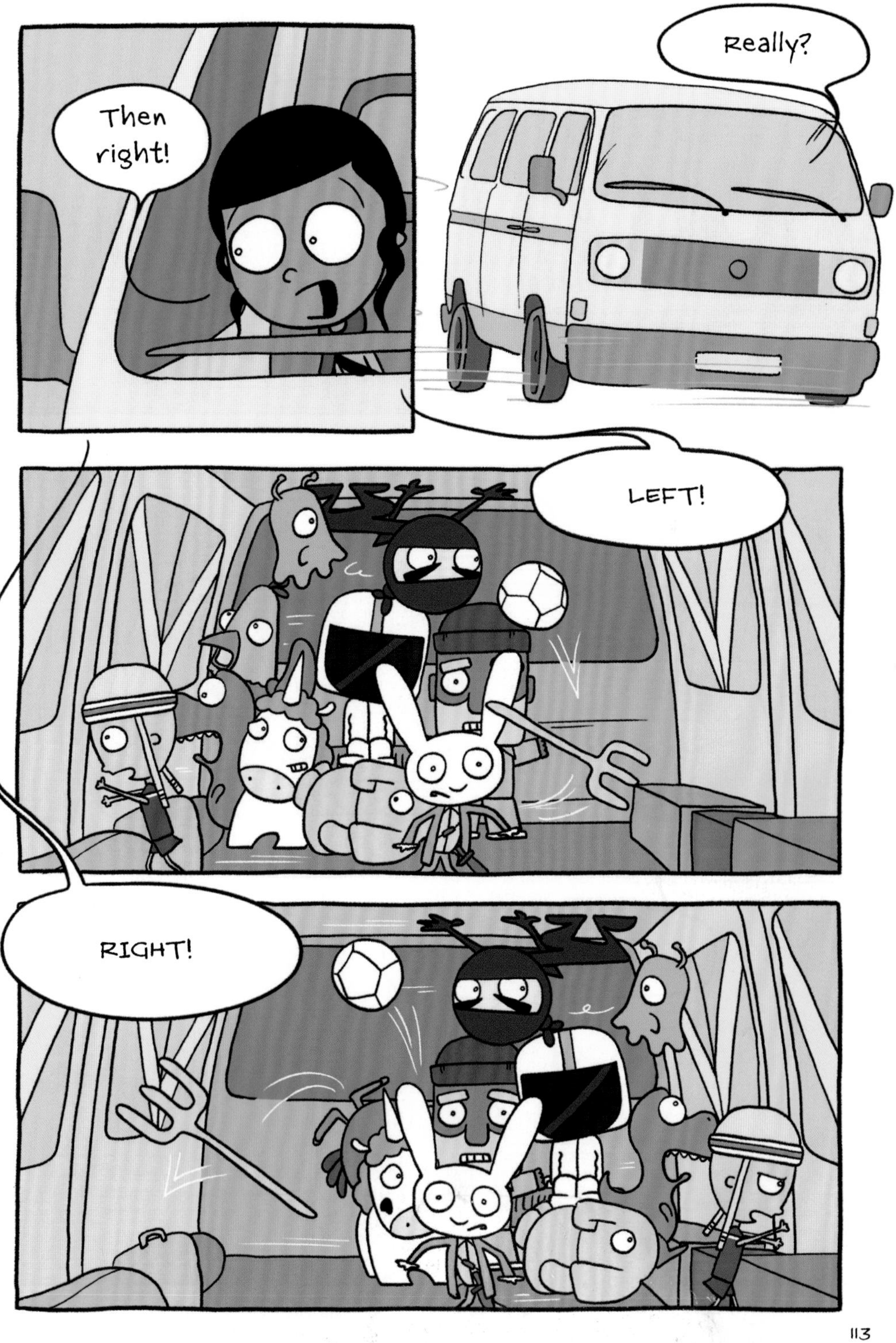
Then right!
Really?
LEFT!
RIGHT!

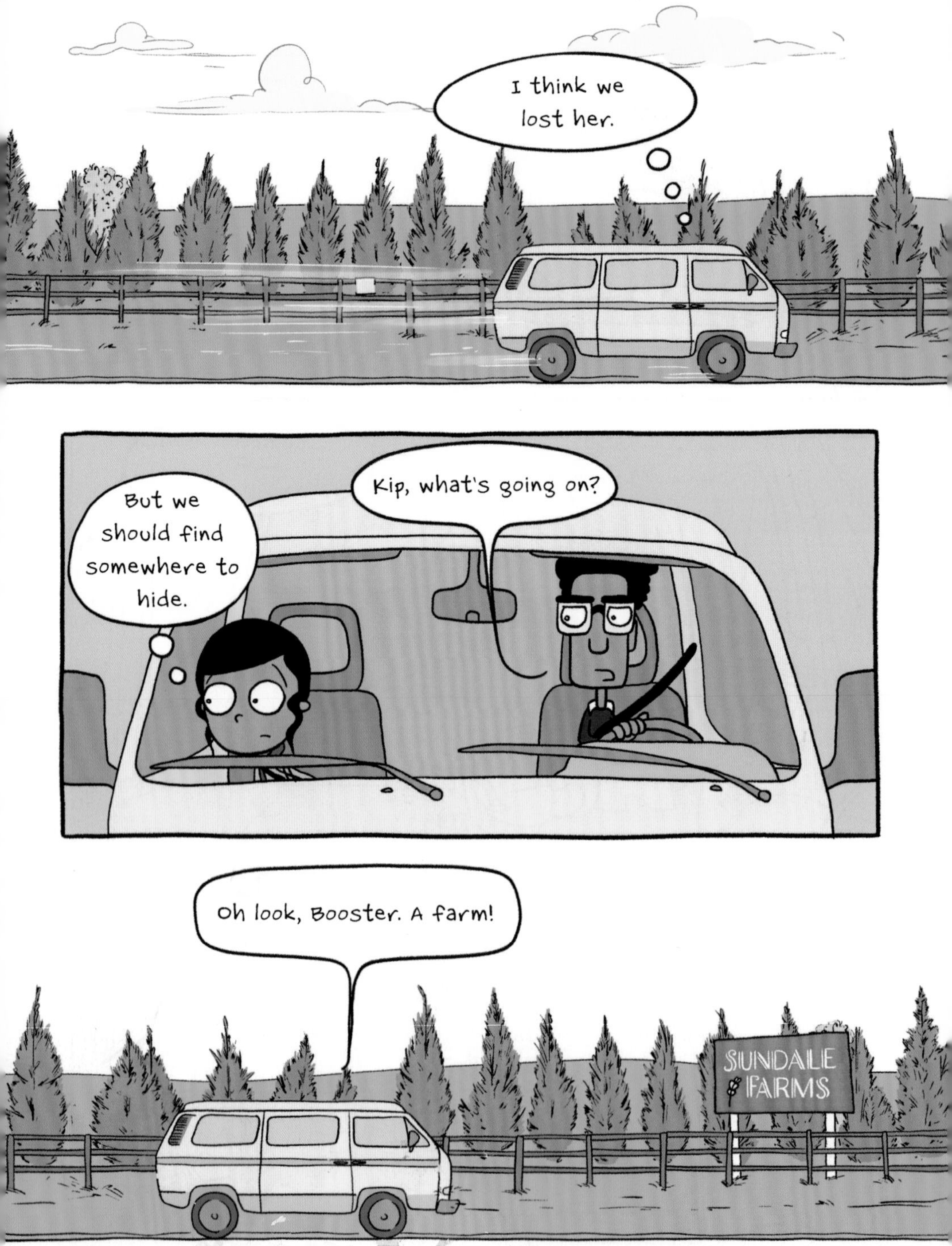
I think we lost her.
But we should find somewhere to hide.
Kip, what's going on?
Oh look, Booster. A farm!
SUNDALE FARMS

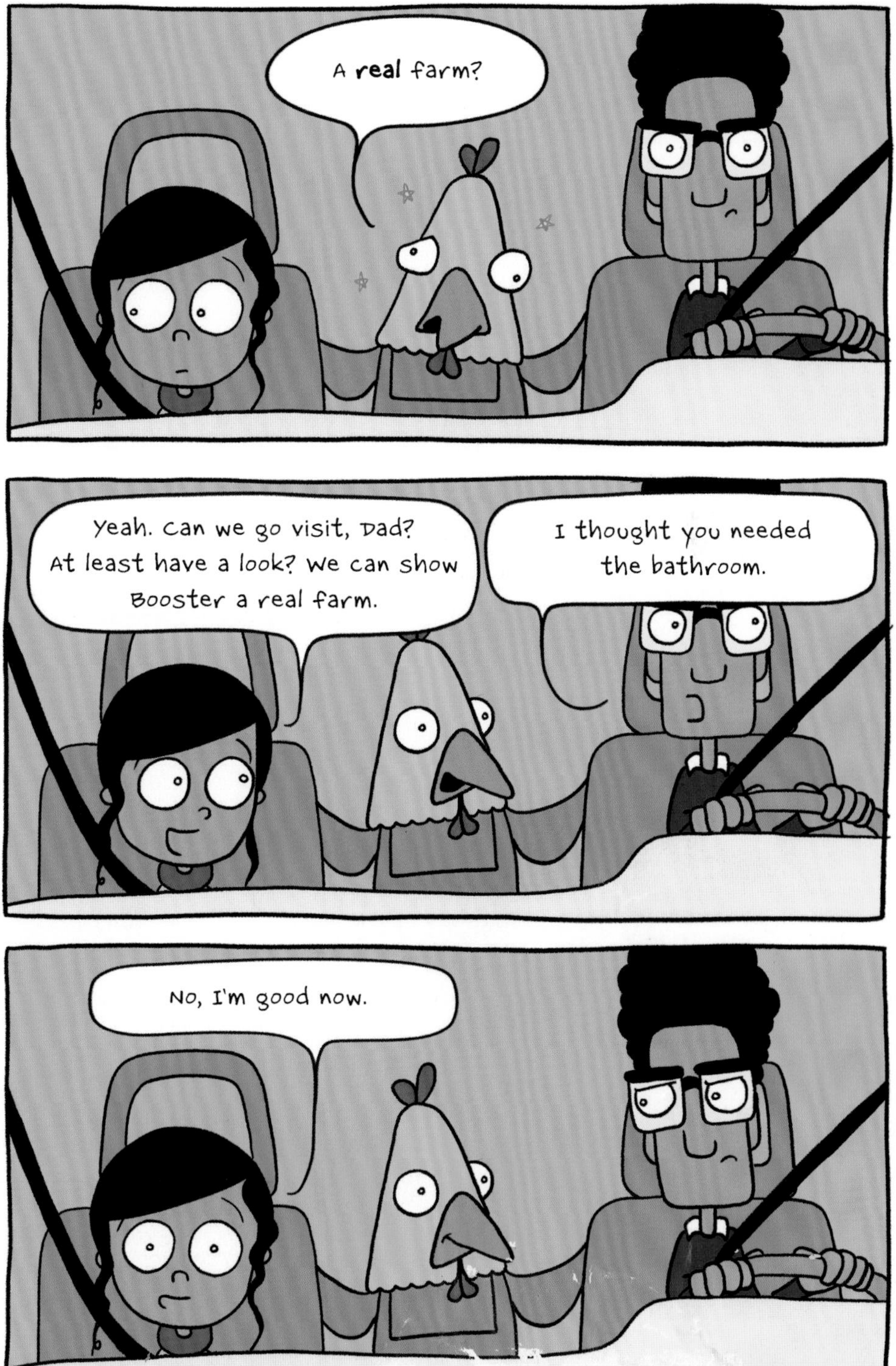
A **real** farm?
Yeah. Can we go visit, Dad? At least have a look? We can show Booster a real farm.
I thought you needed the bathroom.
No, I'm good now.

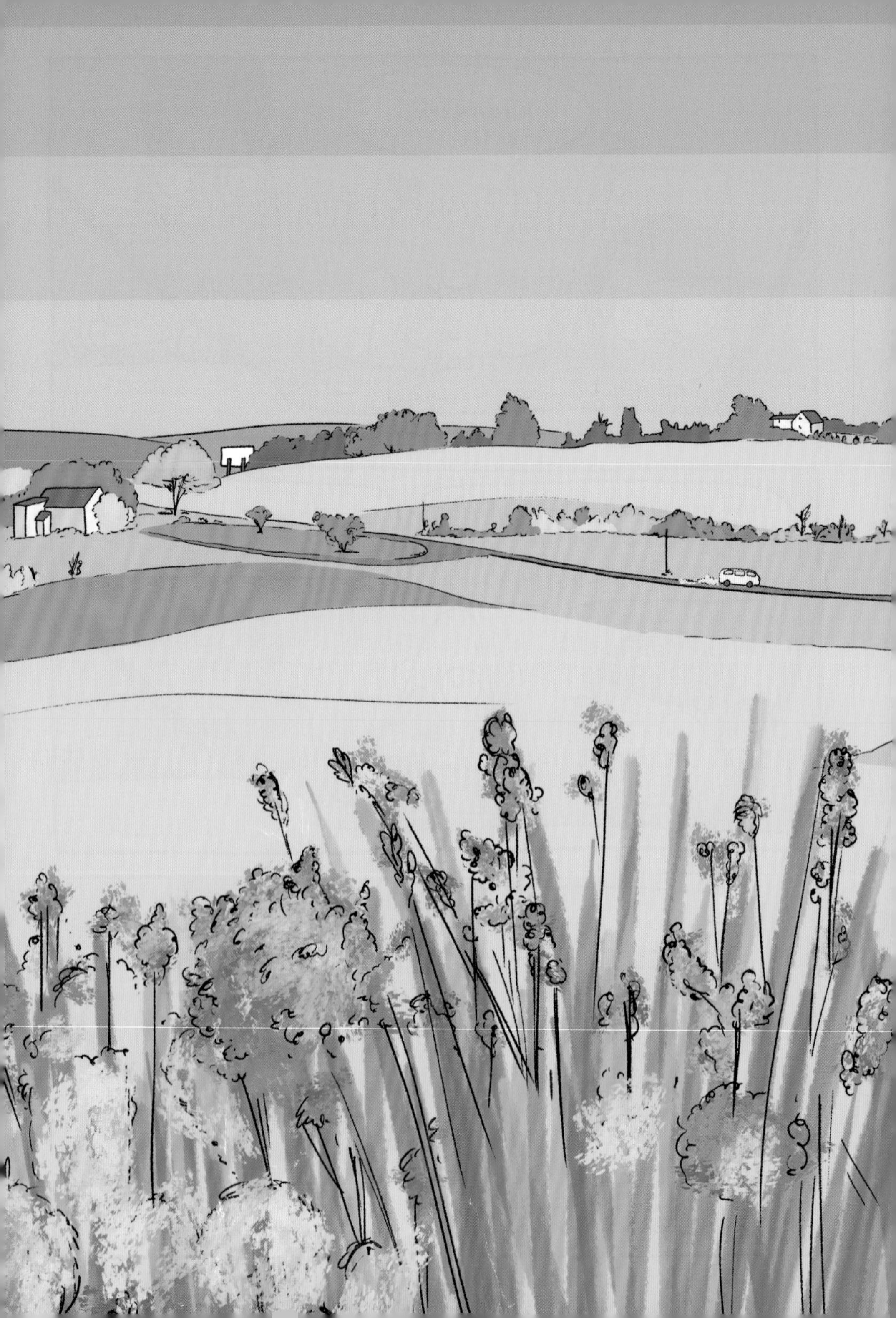

CHAPTER SEVEN
The Odds take a farm tour

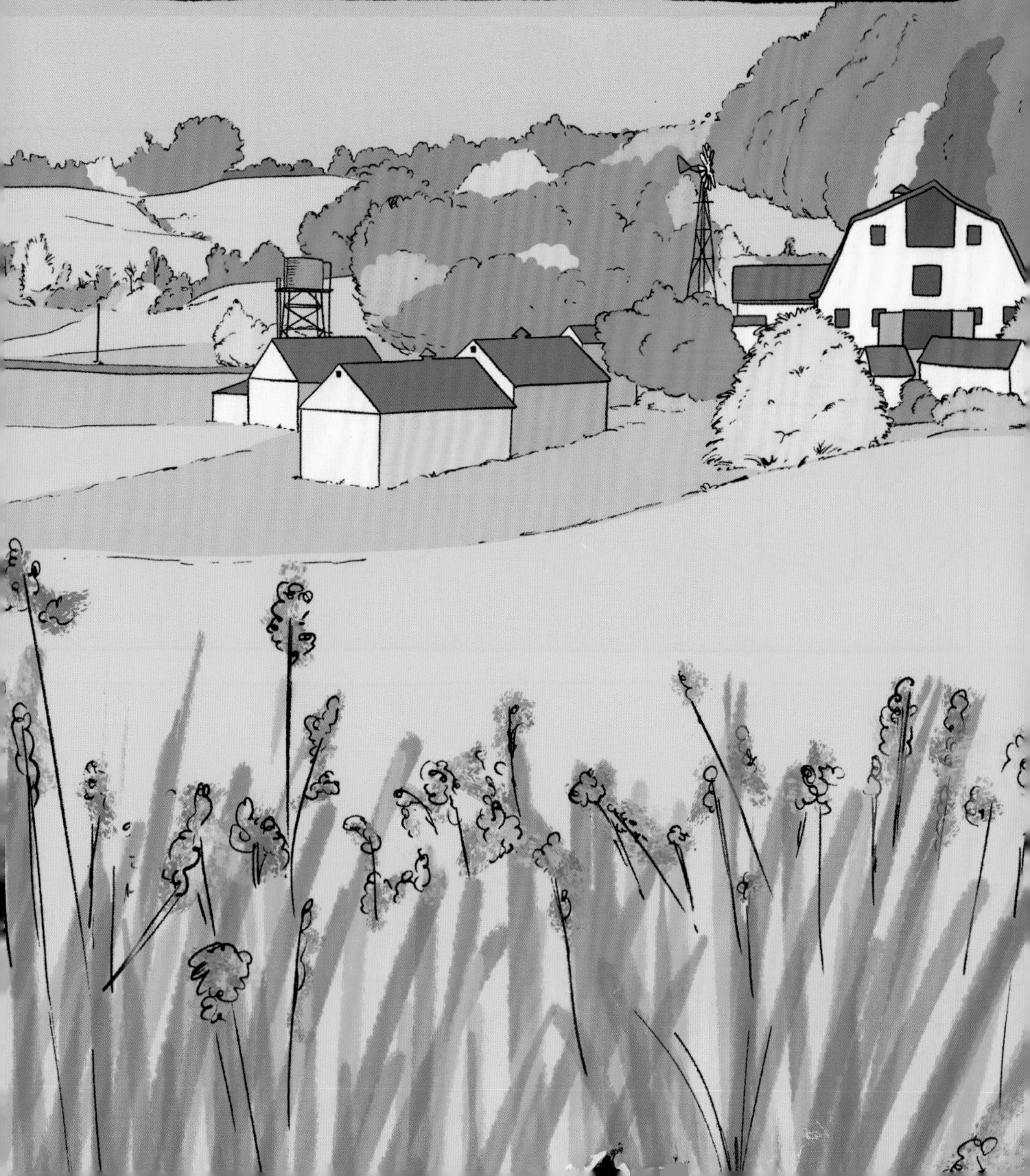

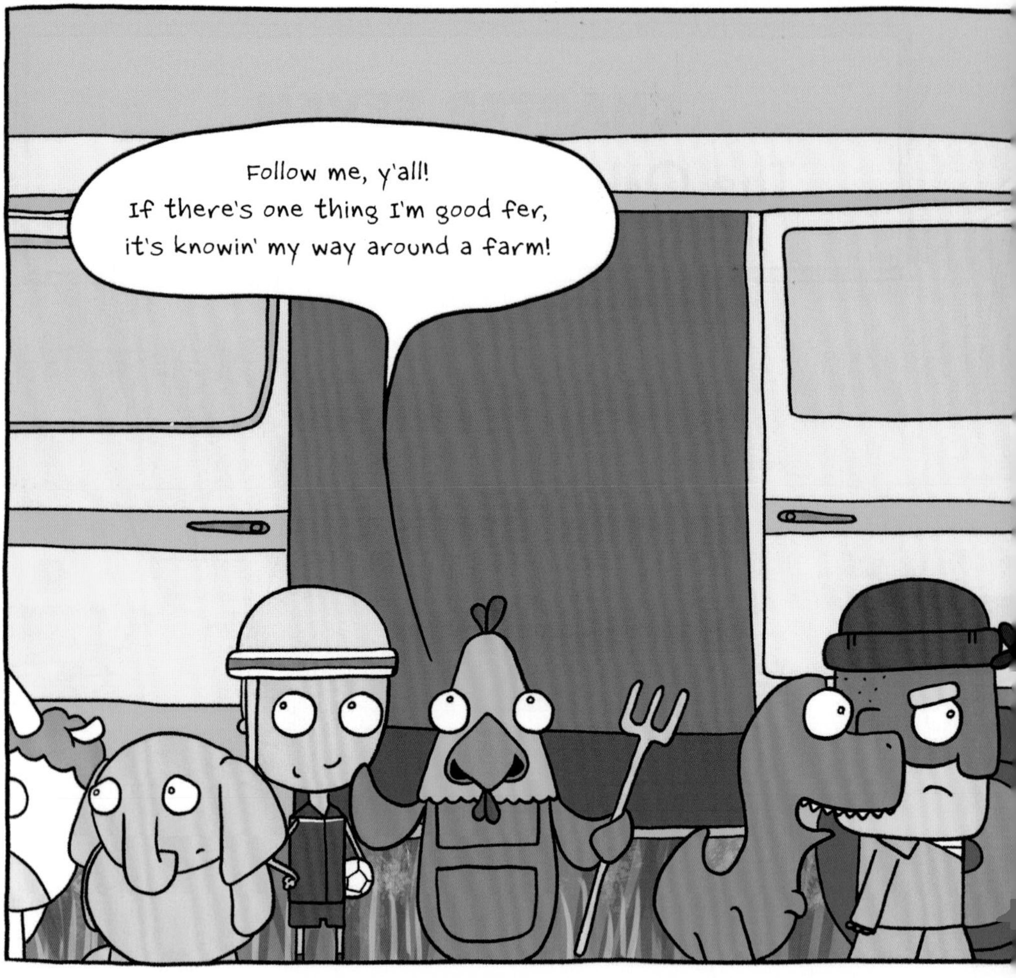
Follow me, y'all!
If there's one thing I'm good fer,
it's knowin' my way around a farm!

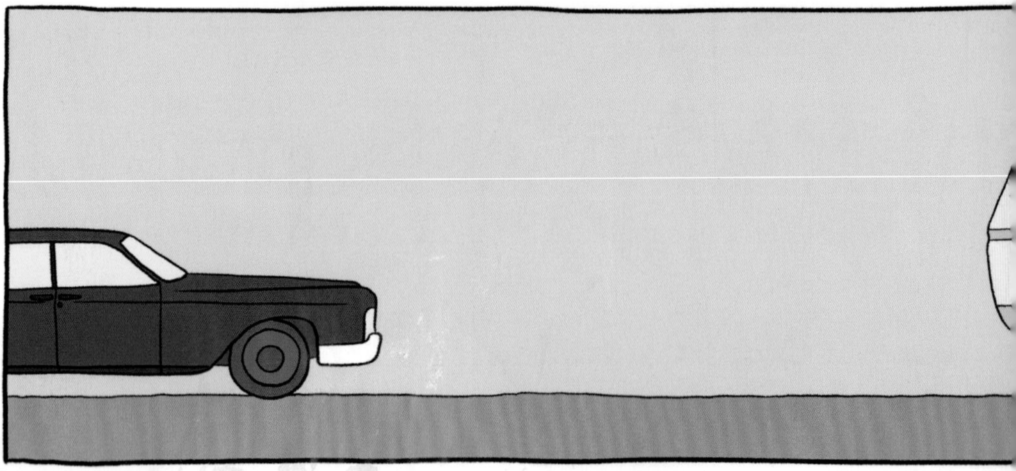

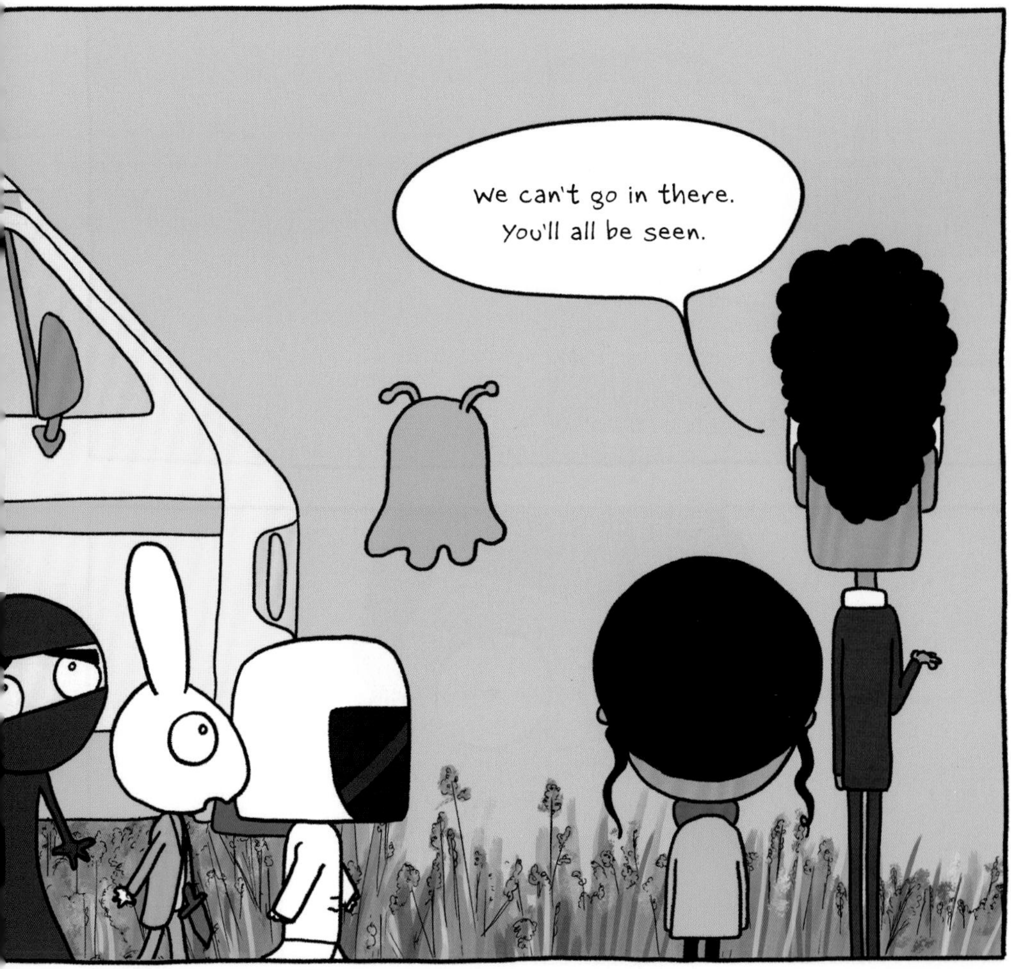
We can't go in there.
You'll all be seen.

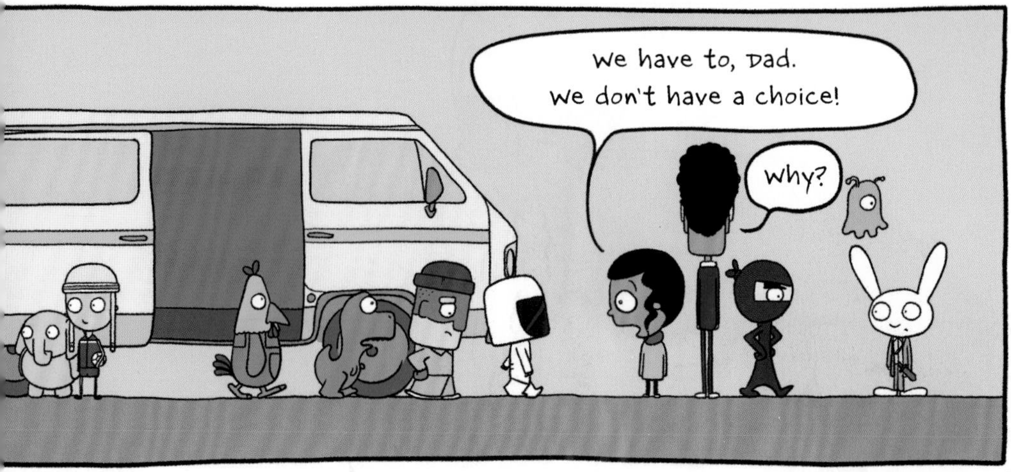
We have to, Dad.
We don't have a choice!
Why?

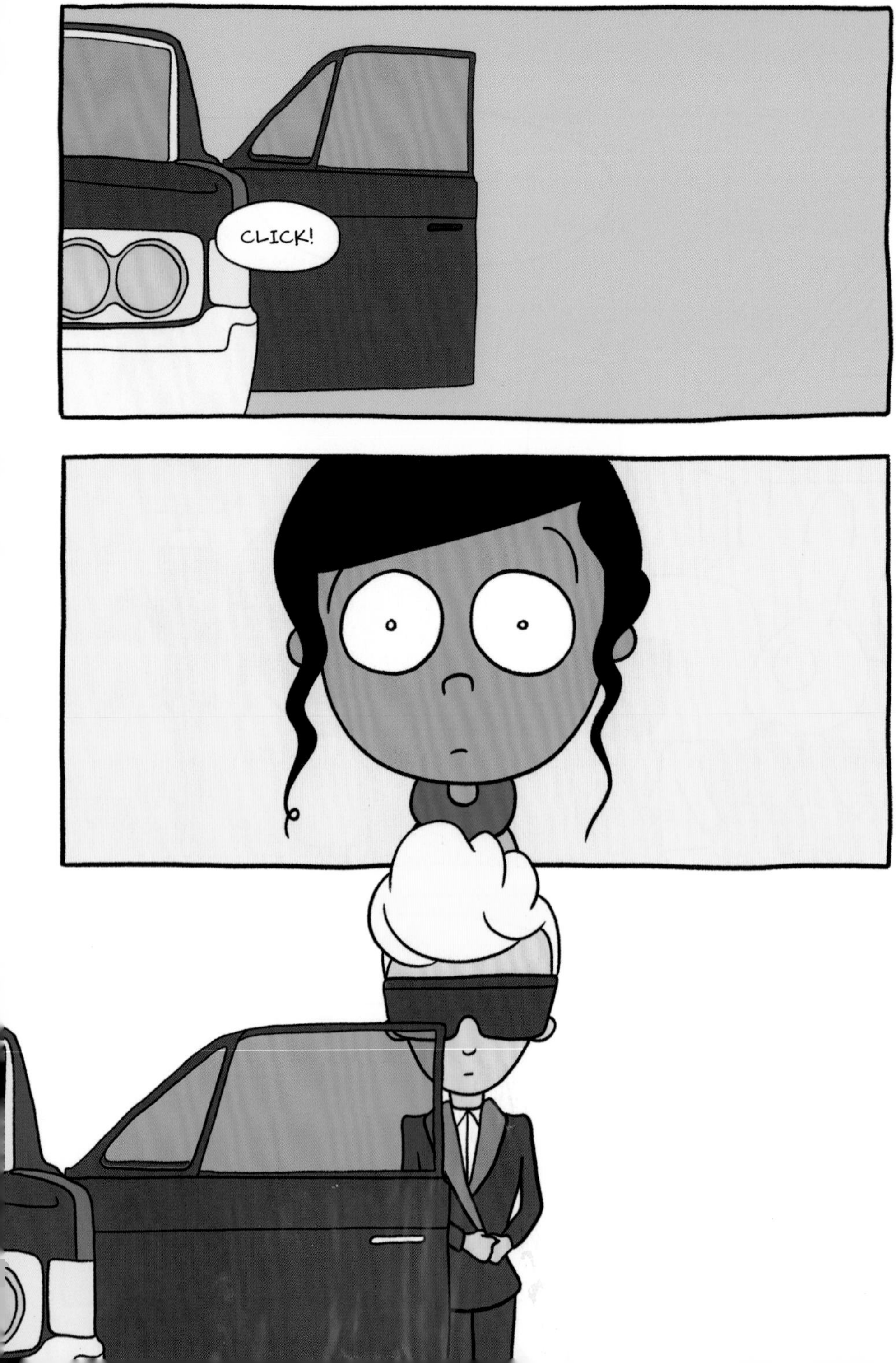
CLICK!

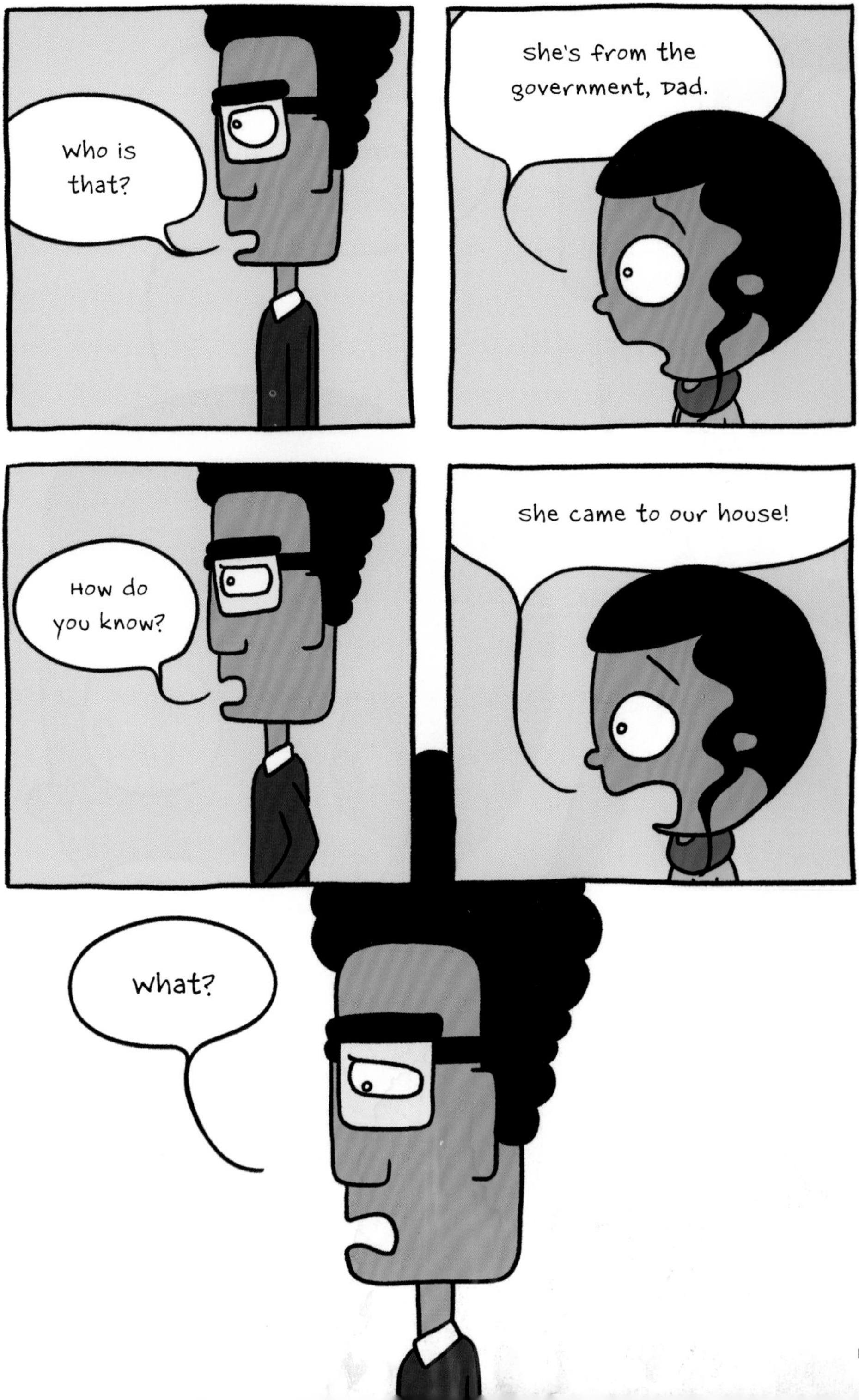
Who is that?
She's from the government, Dad.
How do you know?
She came to our house!
What?

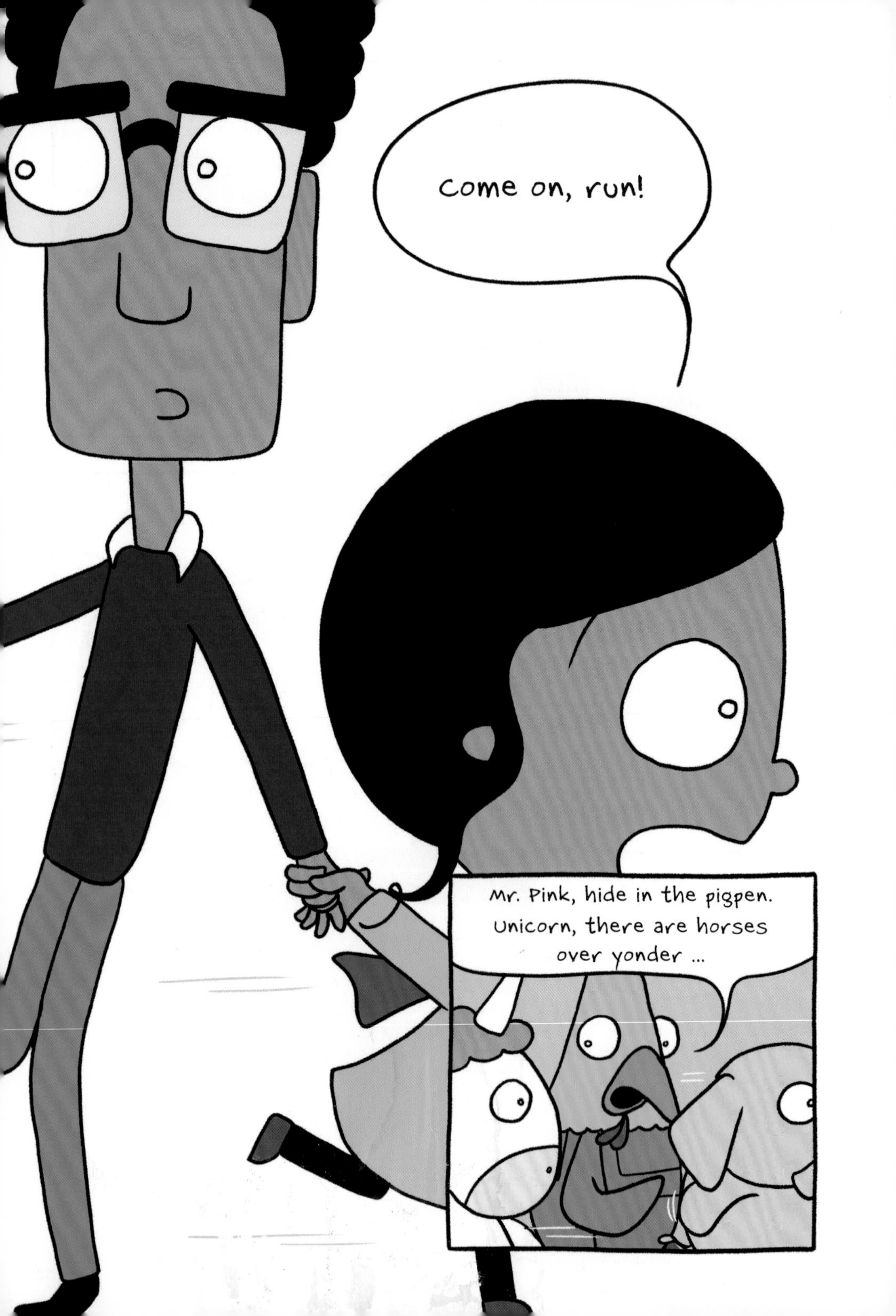
Come on, run!
Mr. Pink, hide in the pigpen. Unicorn, there are horses over yonder ...

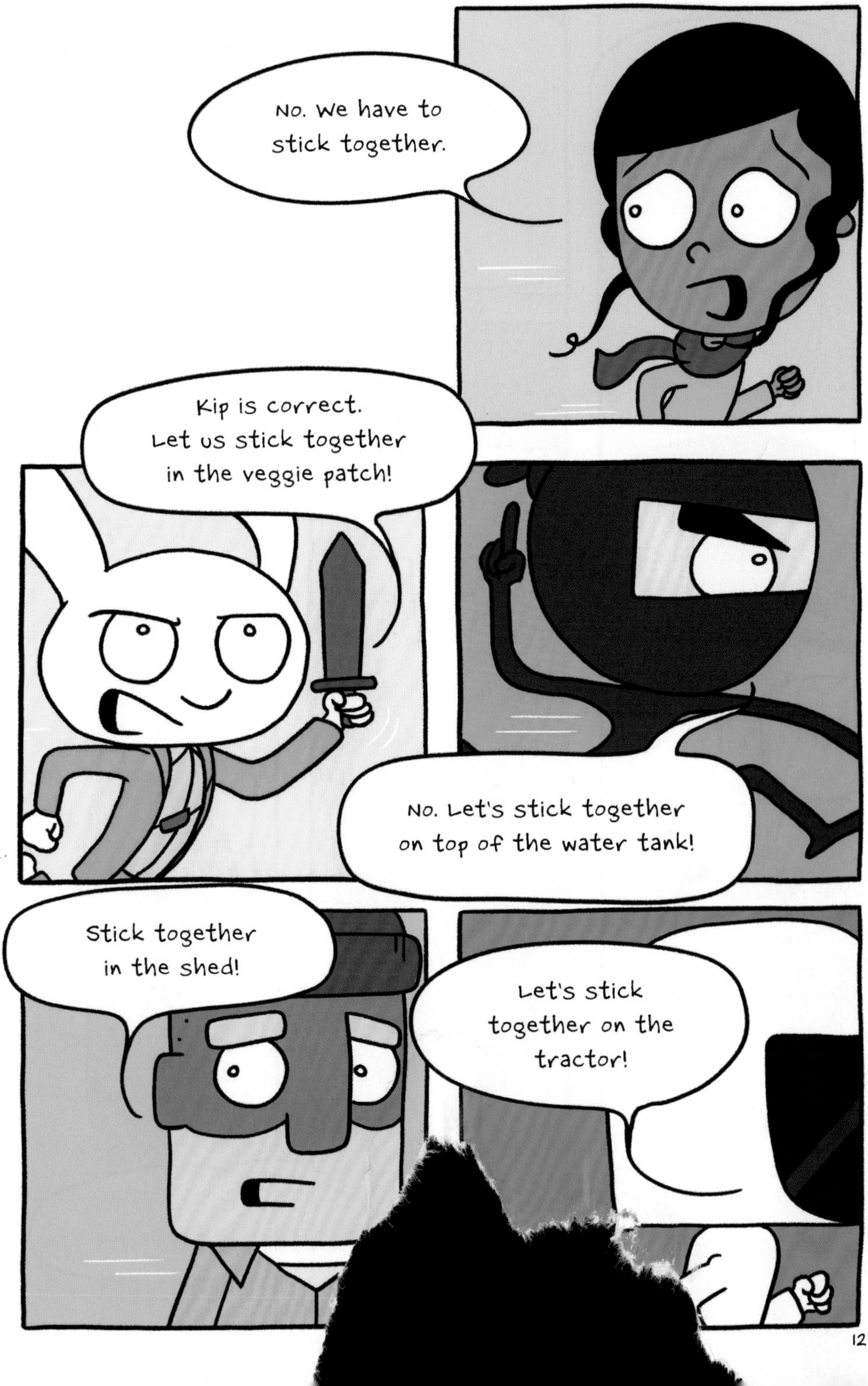
No. We have to stick together.
Kip is correct. Let us stick together in the veggie patch!
No. Let's stick together on top of the water tank!
Stick together in the shed!
Let's stick together on the tractor!

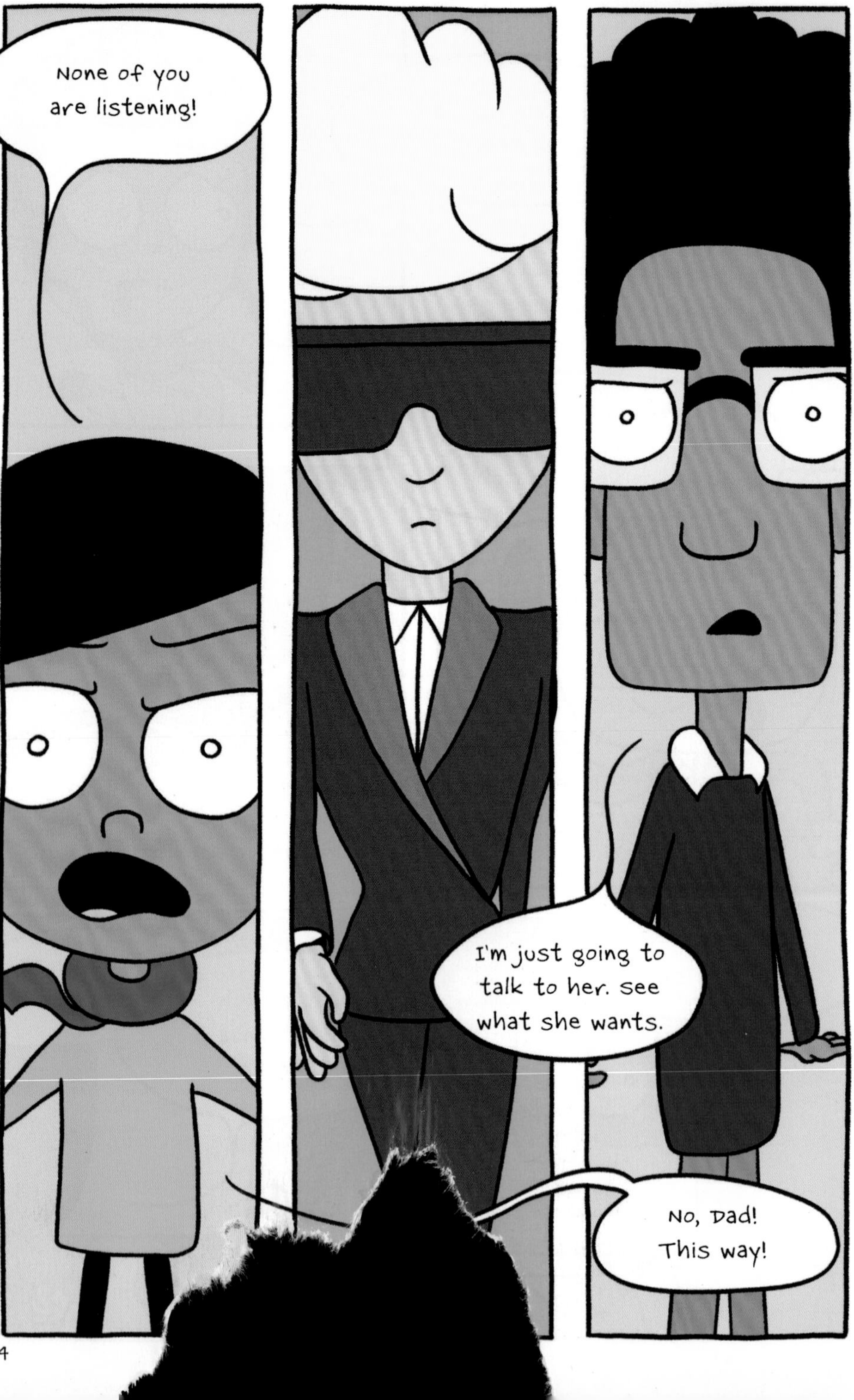
None of you are listening!
I'm just going to talk to her. see what she wants.
No, Dad! This way!

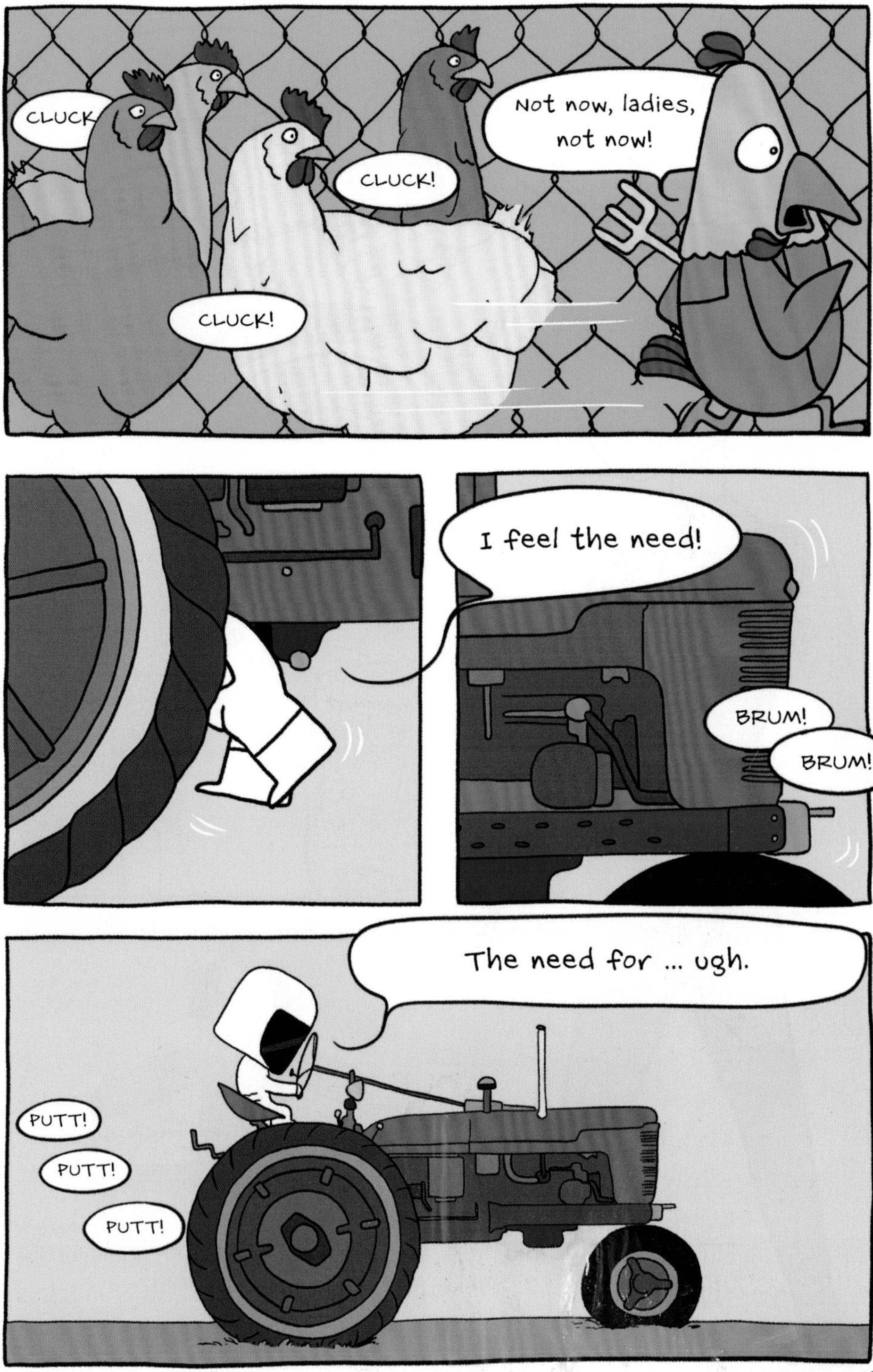
CLUCK
CLUCK!
CLUCK!
Not now, ladies, not now!
I feel the need!
BRUM!
BRUM!
The need for ... ugh.
PUTT!
PUTT!
PUTT!

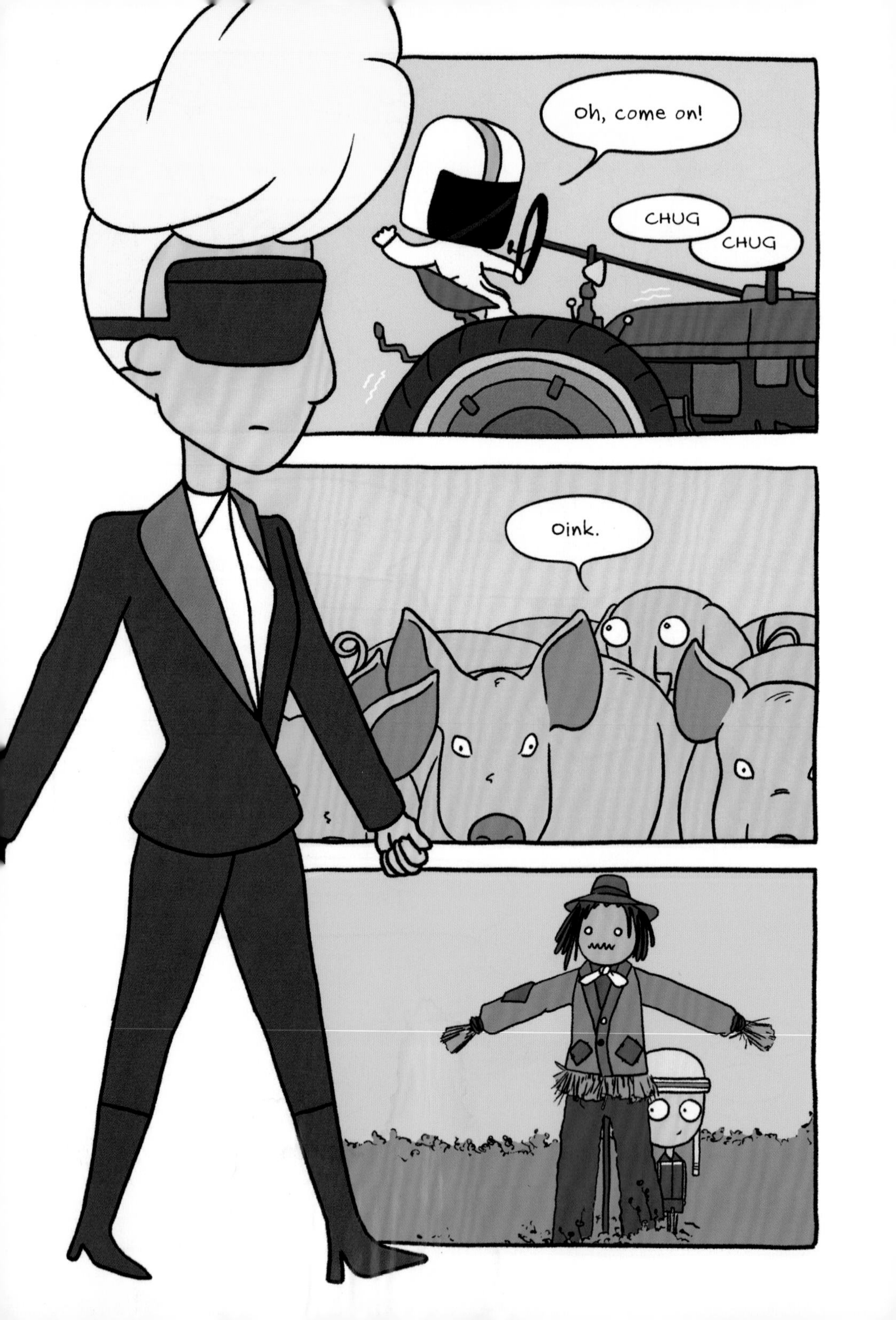
Oh, come on!
CHUG
CHUG
Oink.

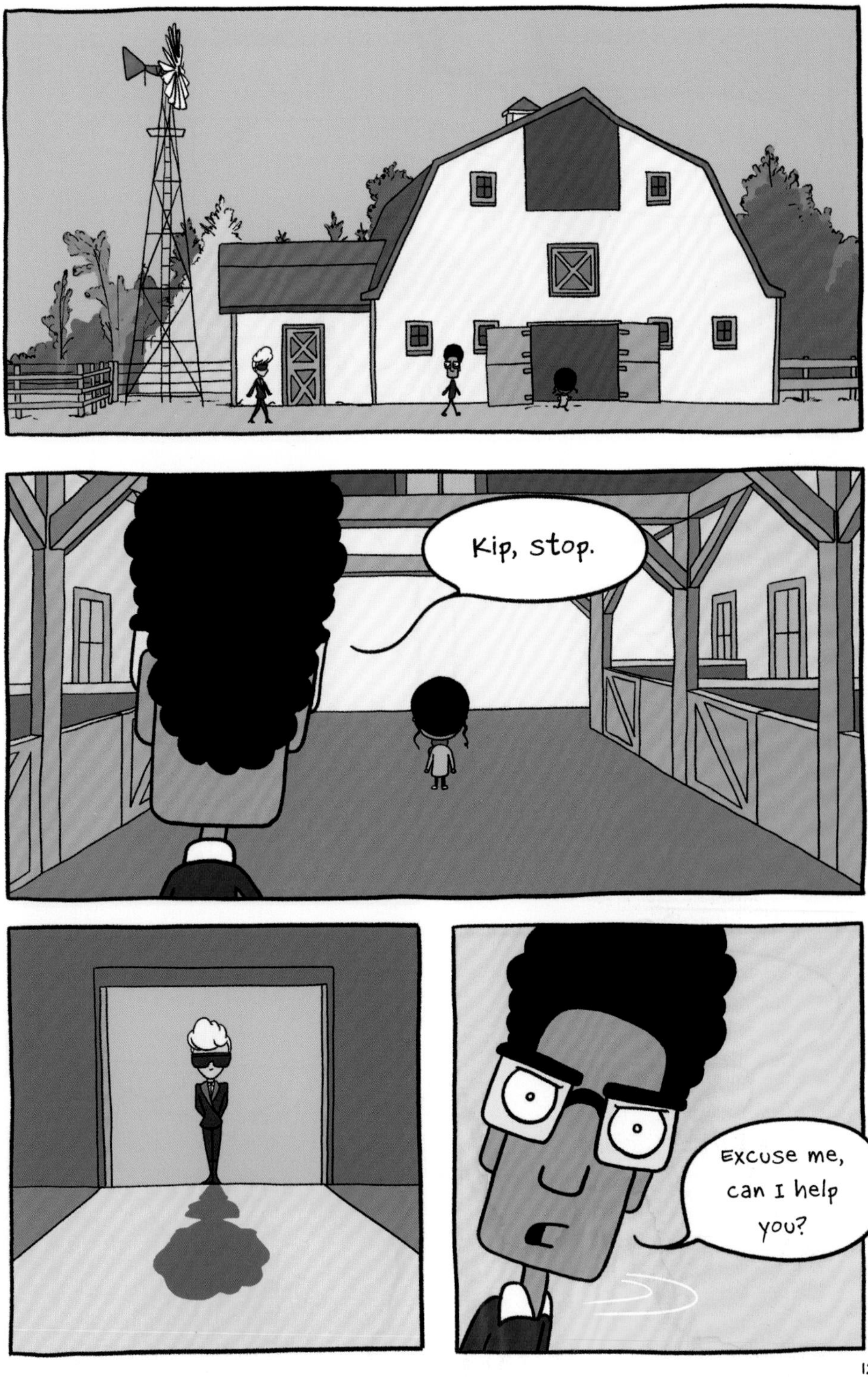
Kip, stop.
Excuse me, can I help you?

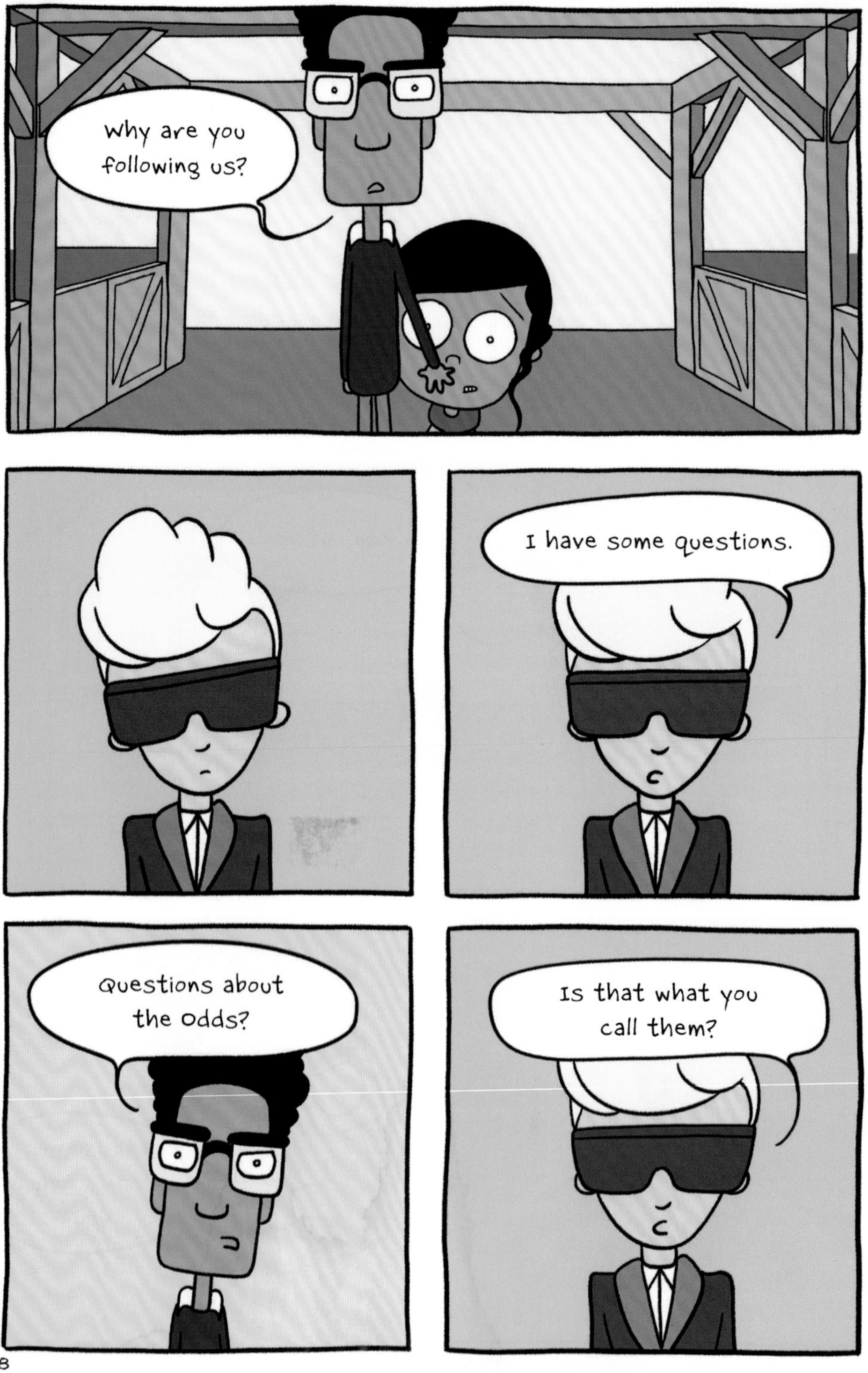
Why are you following us?
I have some questions.
Questions about the odds?
Is that what you call them?

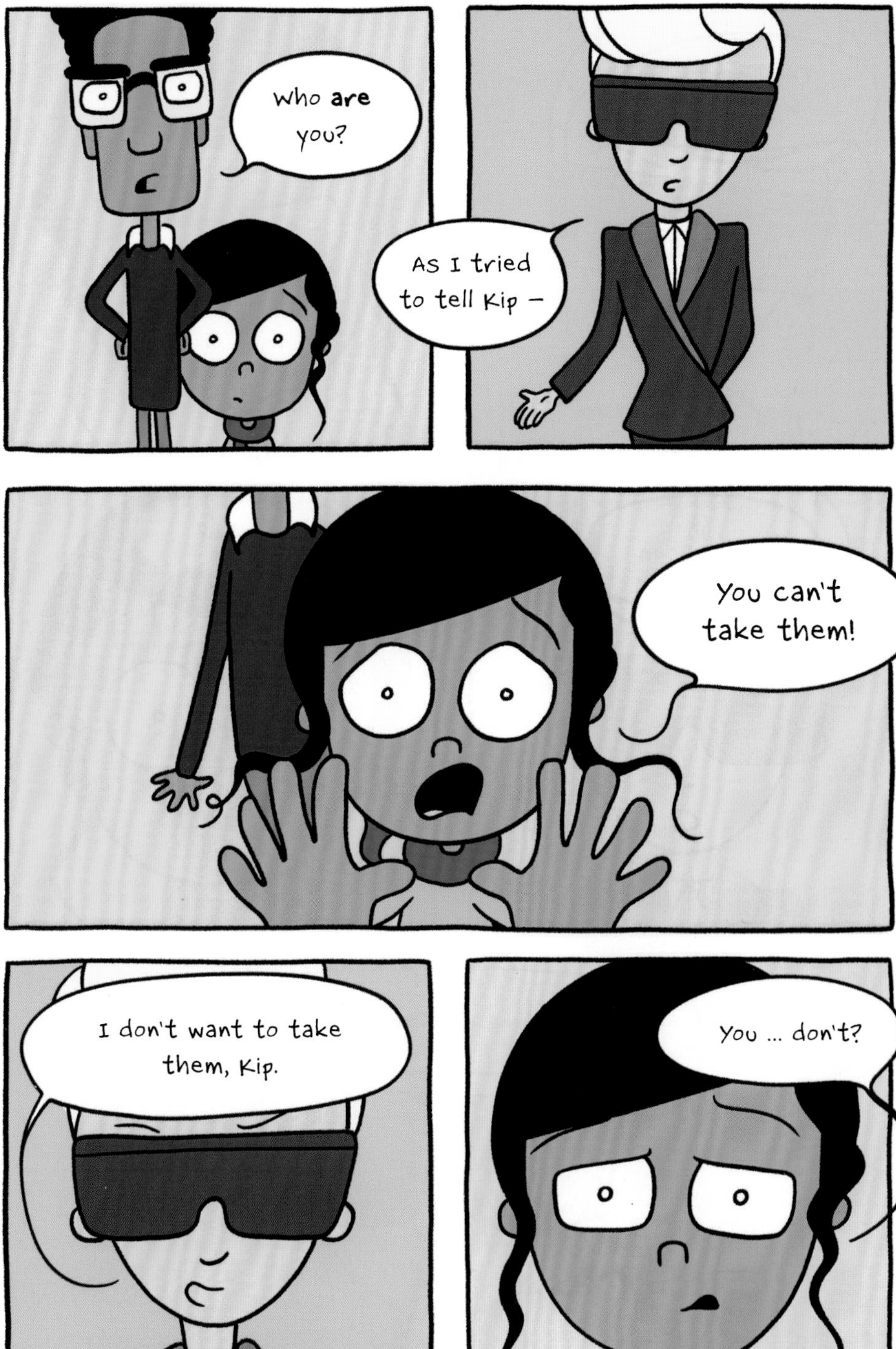
Who **are** you?
As I tried to tell Kip —
You can't take them!
I don't want to take them, Kip.
You ... don't?

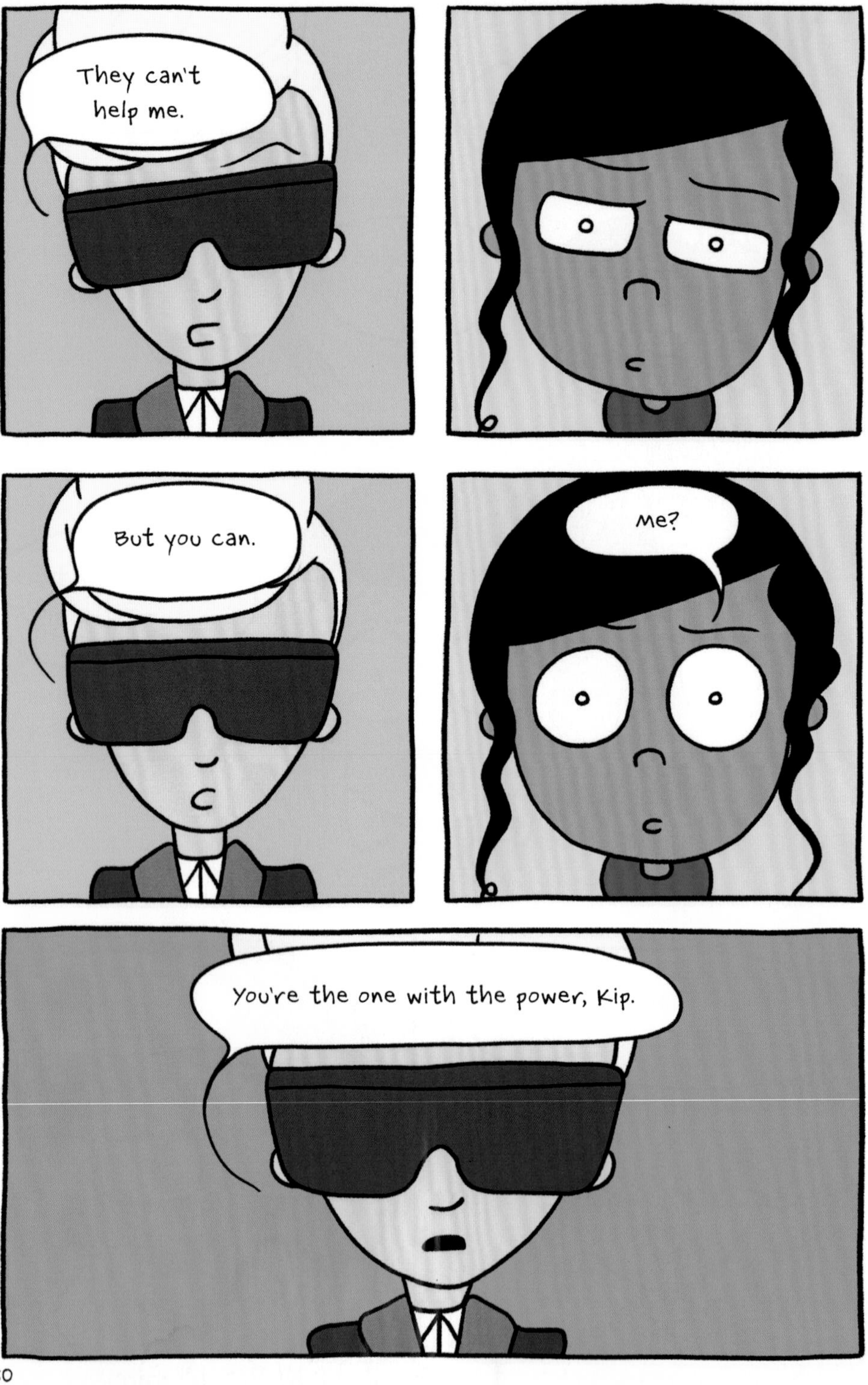
They can't help me.
But you can.
Me?
You're the one with the power, Kip.

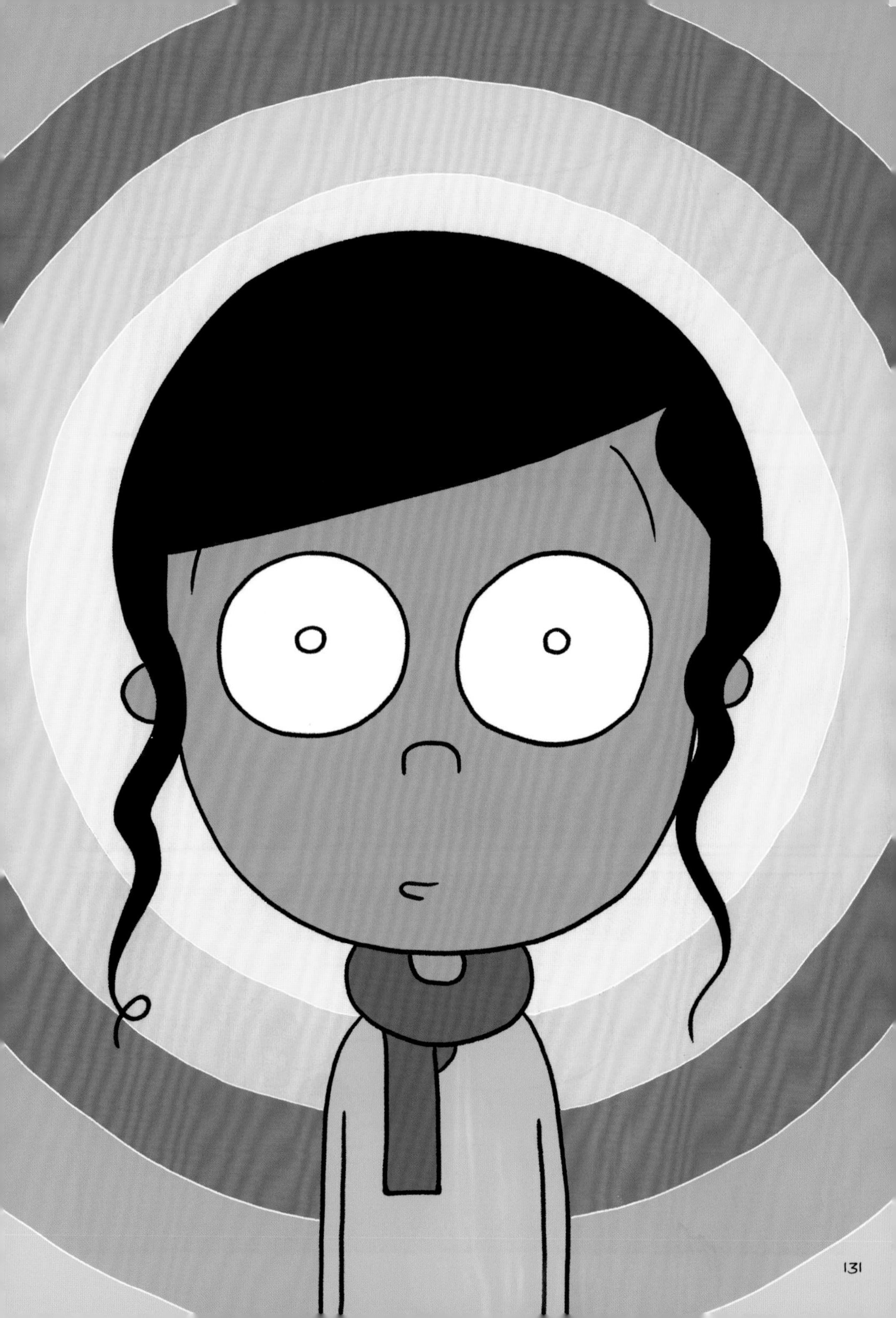

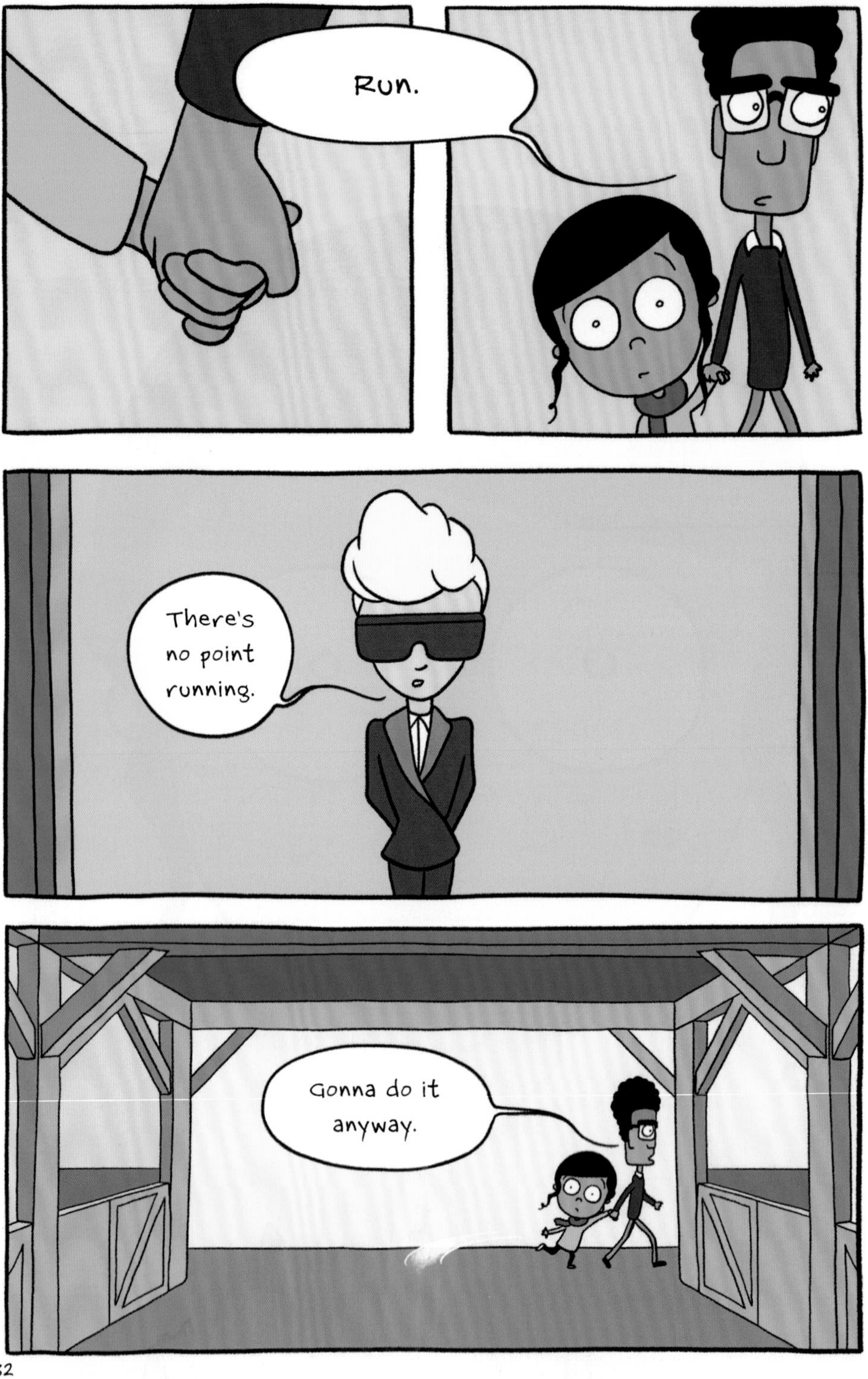
Run.
There's no point running.
Gonna do it anyway.

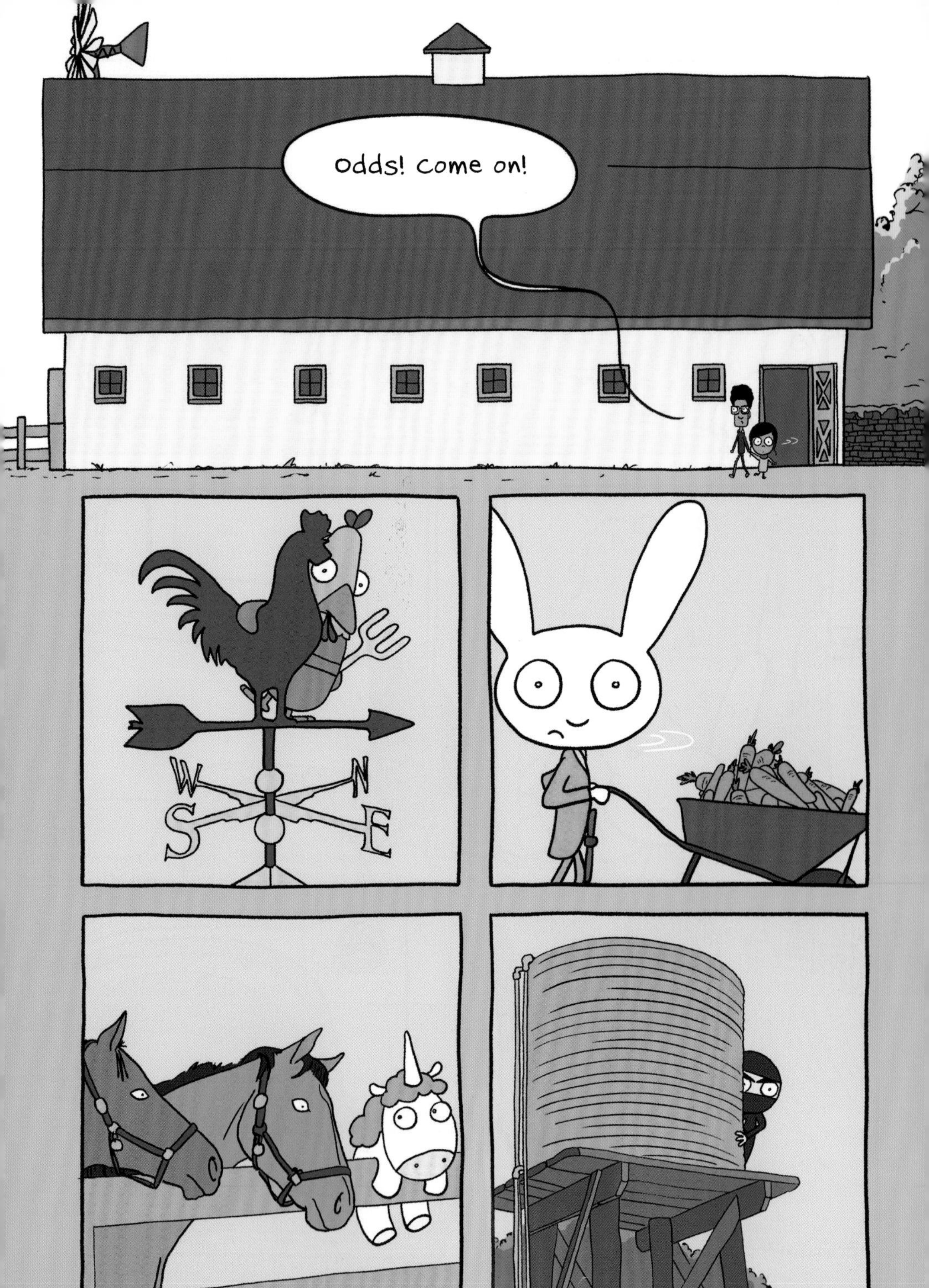
Odds! Come on!
W
N
S
E

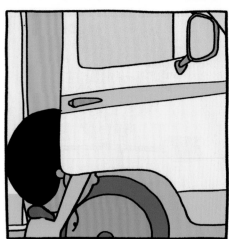

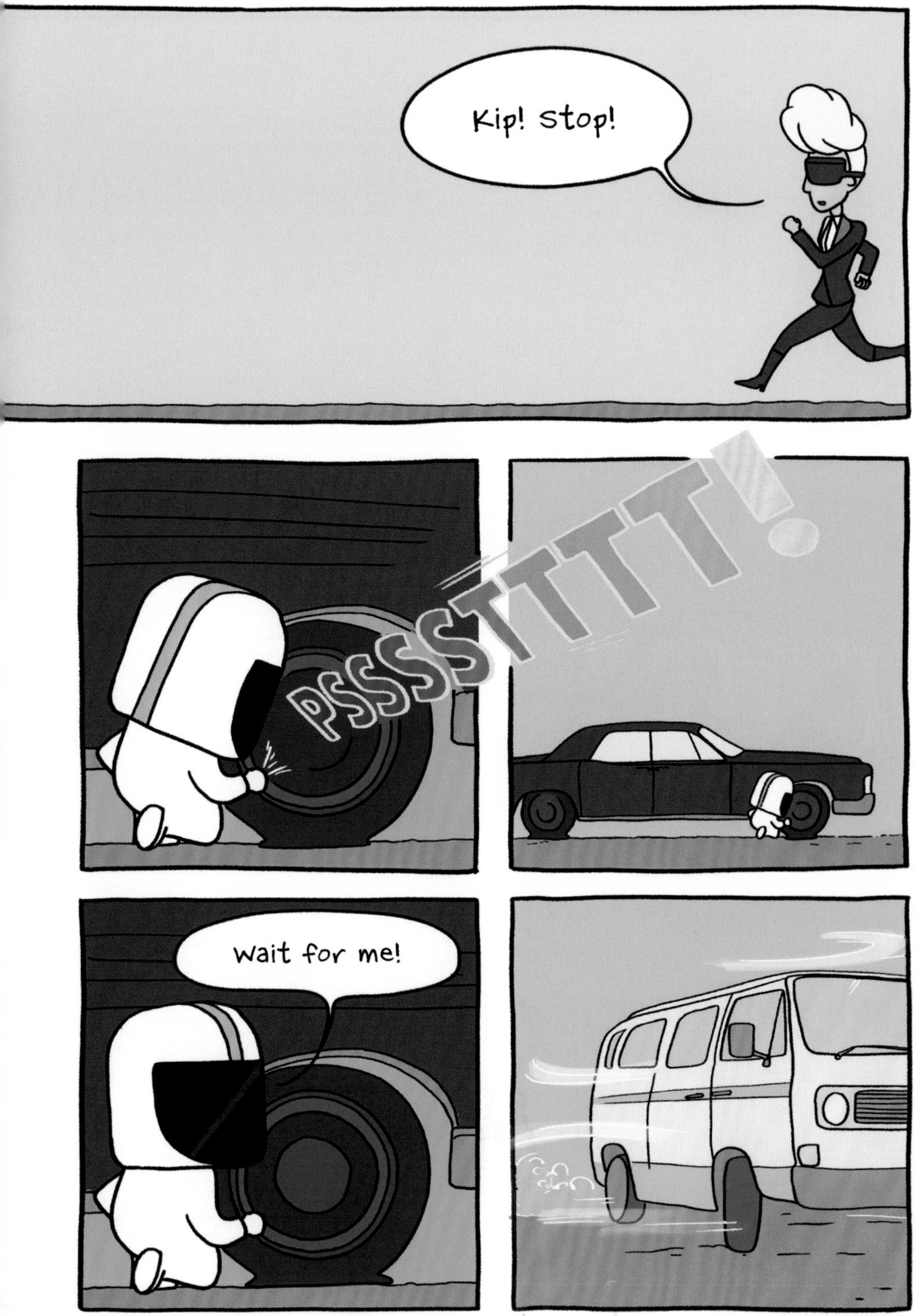
Kip! Stop!
PSSSSTTTT!
Wait for me!

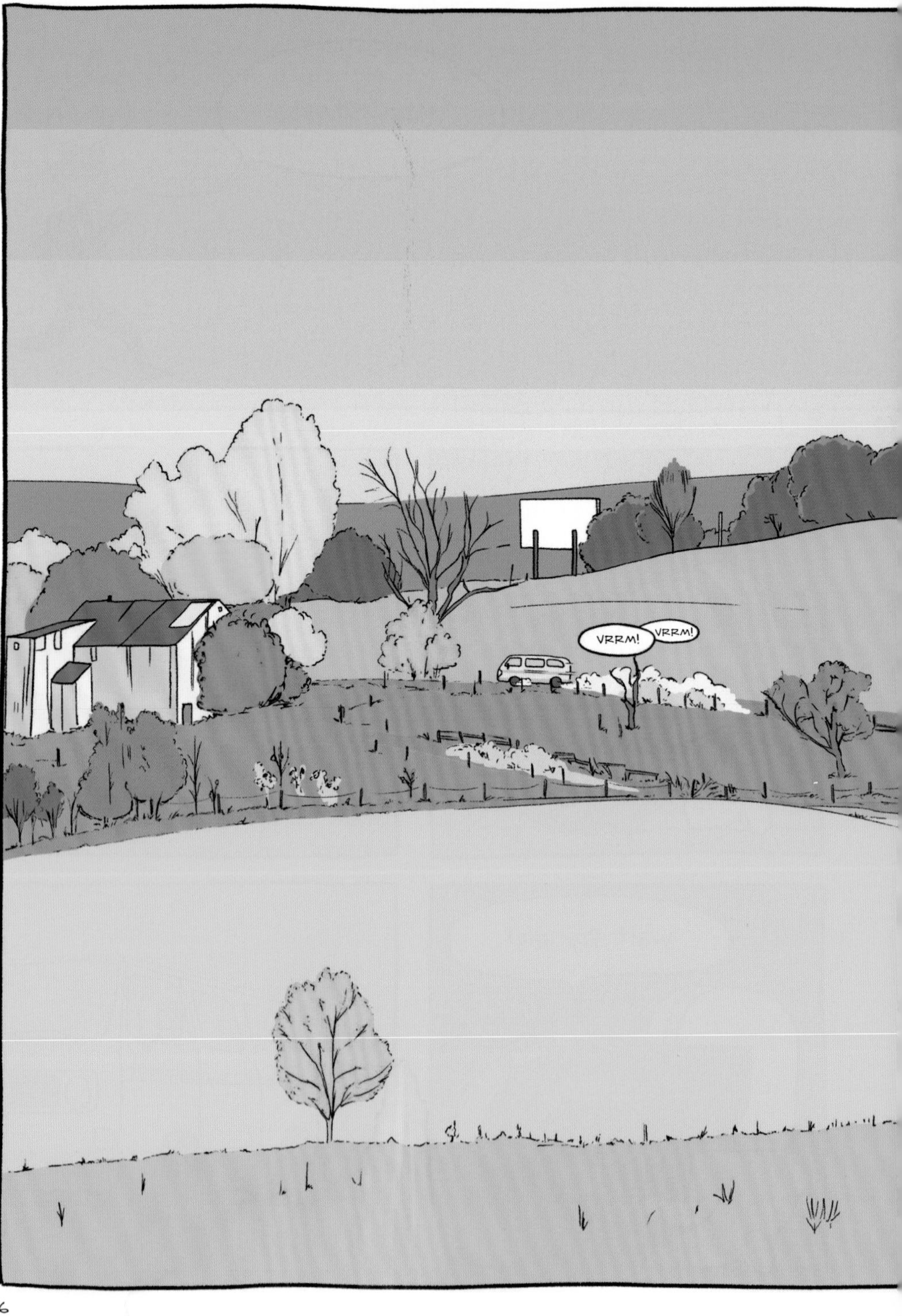
VRRM!
VRRM!

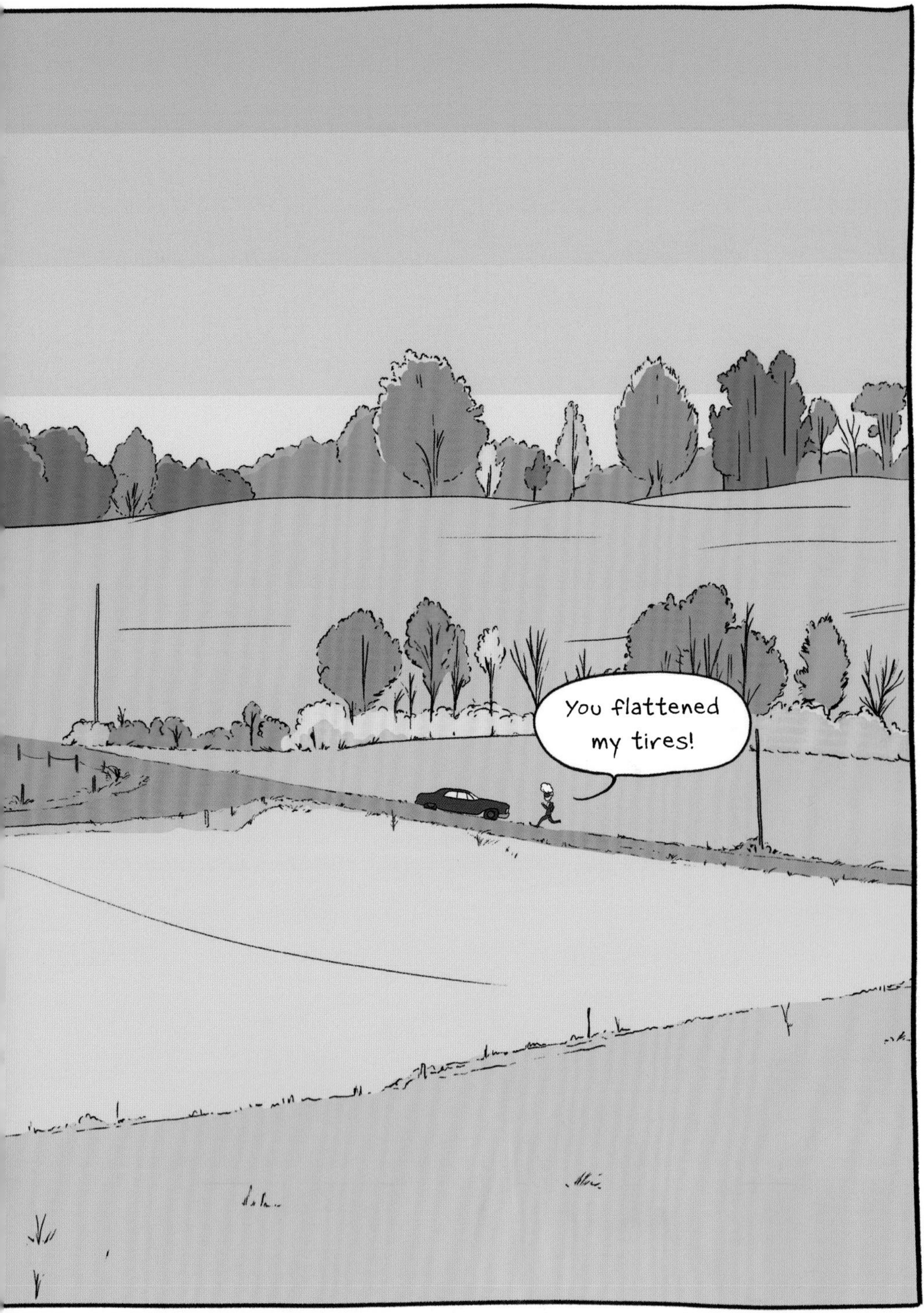
You flattened my tires!

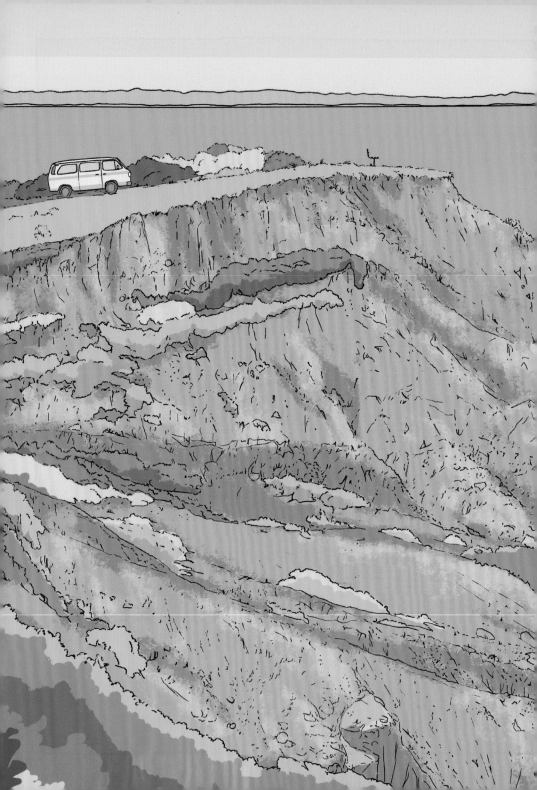

CHAPTER EIGHT
An odd moment of peace

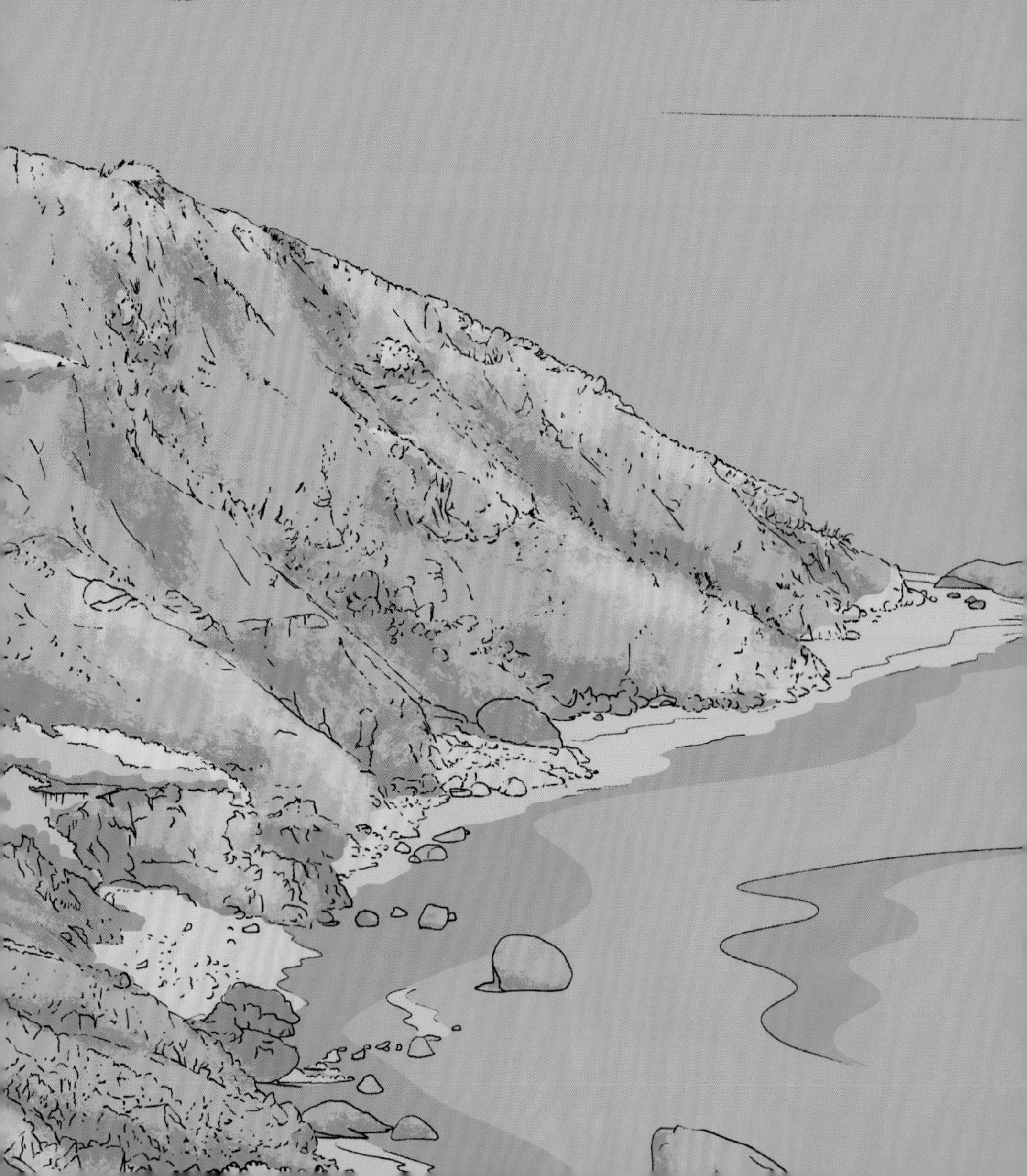

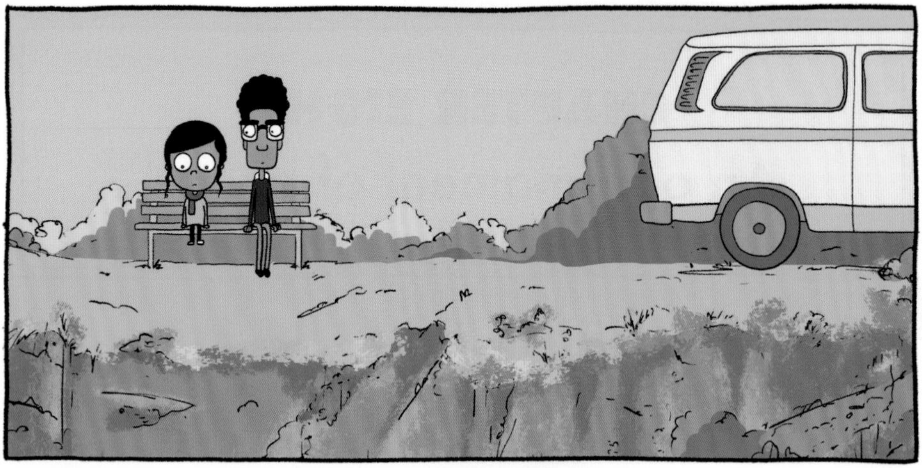

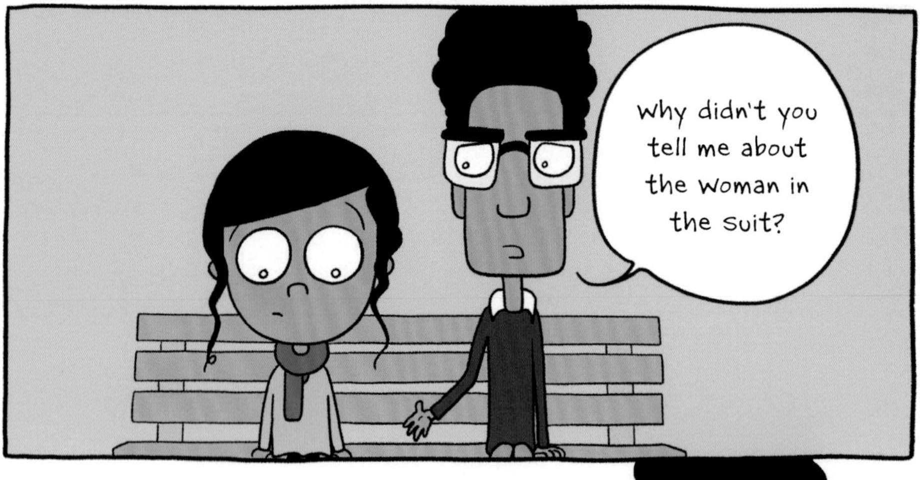
Why didn't you tell me about the woman in the suit?

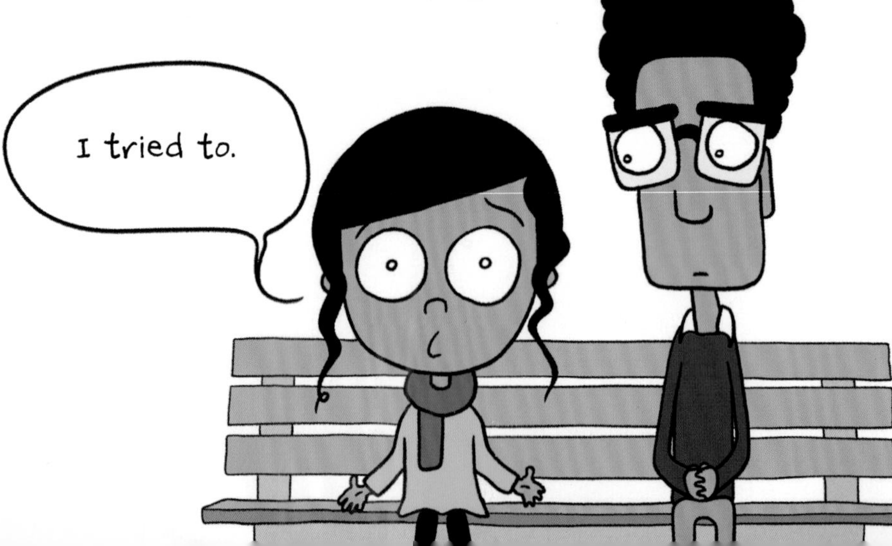
I tried to.

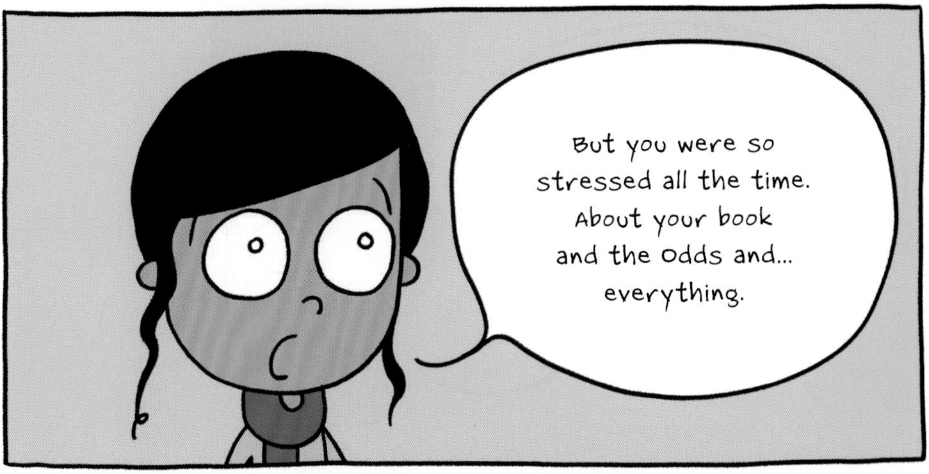
But you were so stressed all the time. About your book and the odds and... everything.

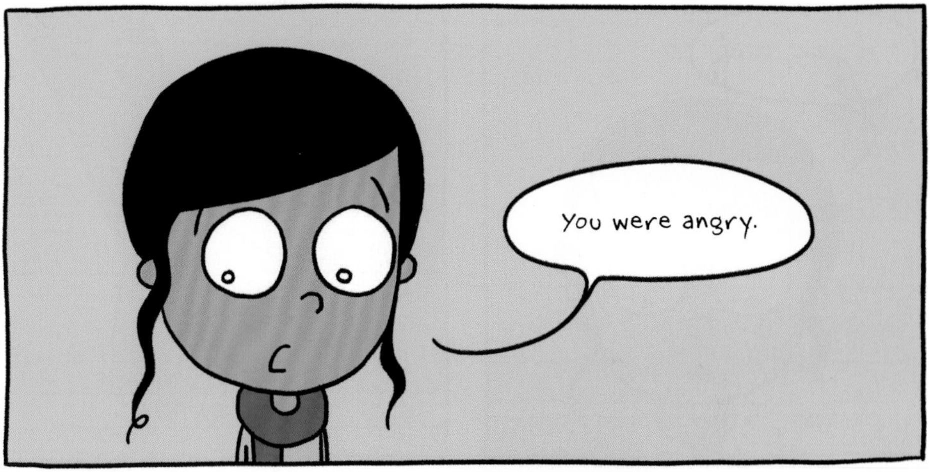
You were angry.

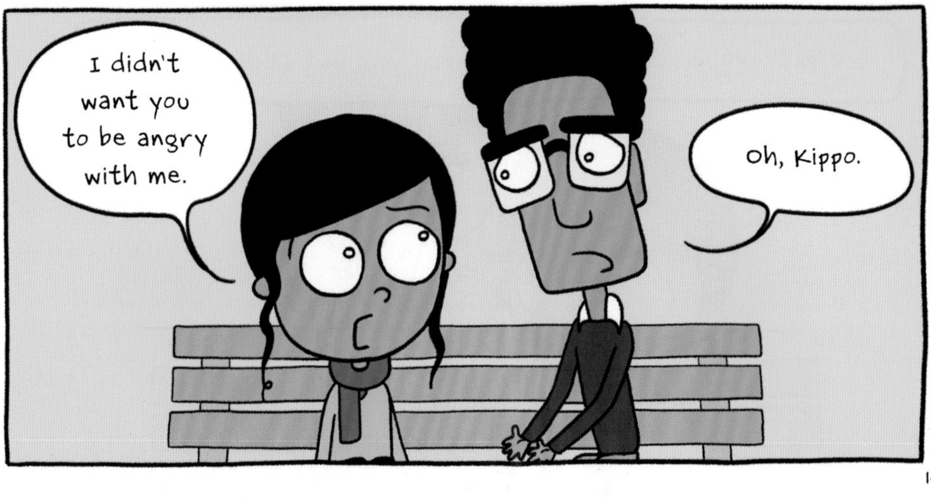
I didn't want you to be angry with me.
Oh, Kippo.

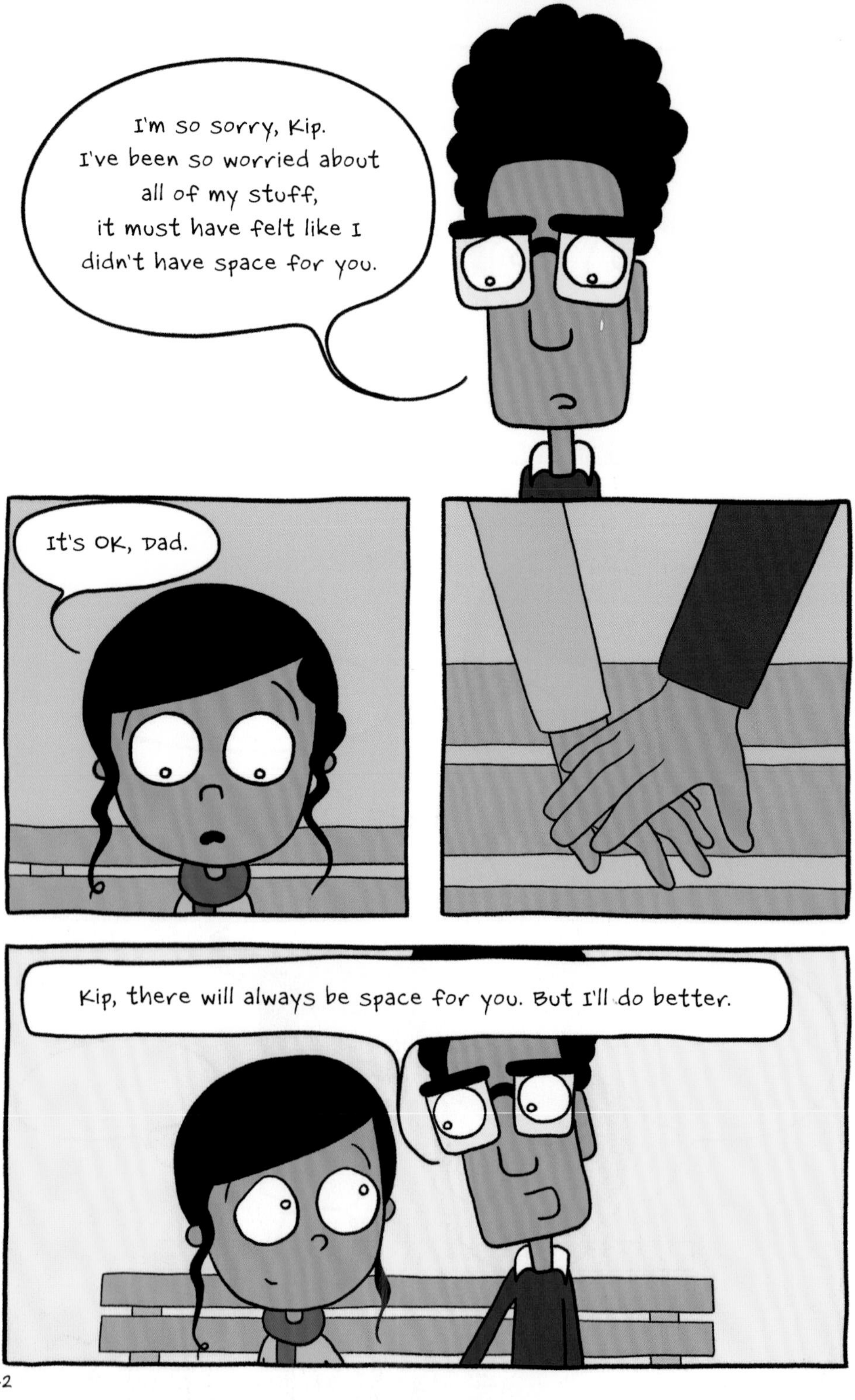
I'm so sorry, Kip. I've been so worried about all of my stuff, it must have felt like I didn't have space for you.
It's OK, Dad.
Kip, there will always be space for you. But I'll do better.

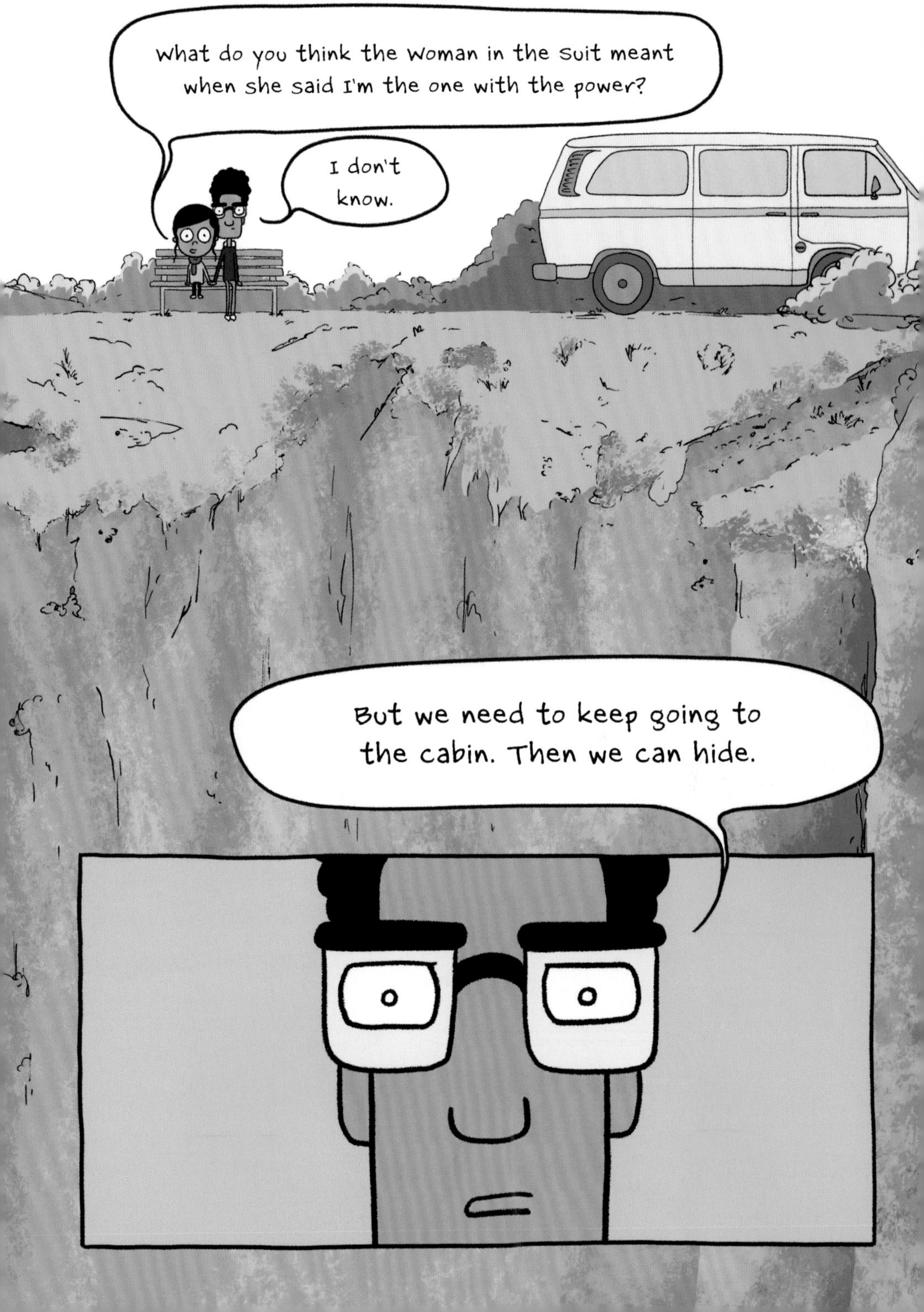
What do you think the woman in the suit meant when she said I'm the one with the power?
I don't know.
But we need to keep going to the cabin. Then we can hide.

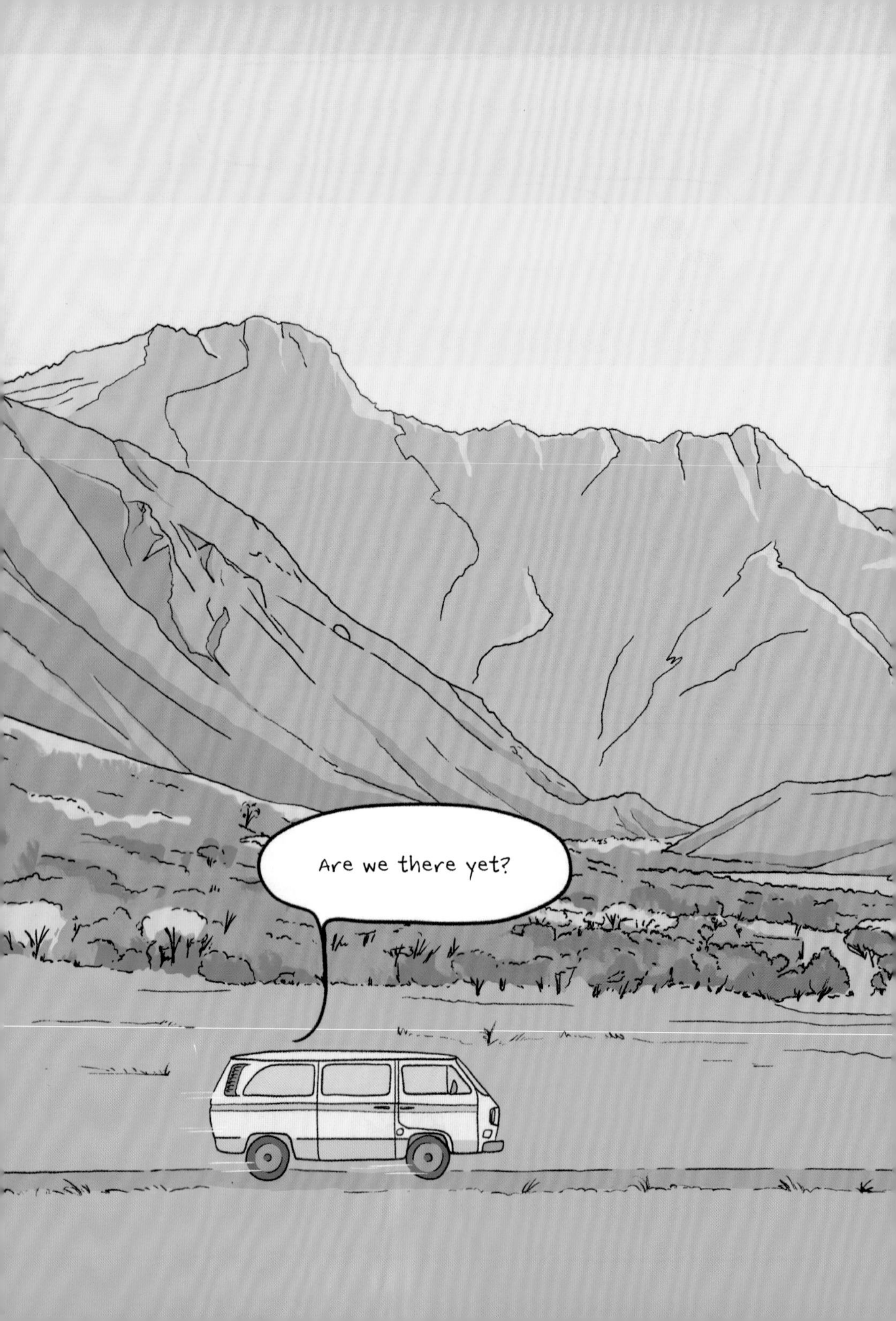
Are we there yet?

CHAPTER NINE
The Odds can't stop fighting

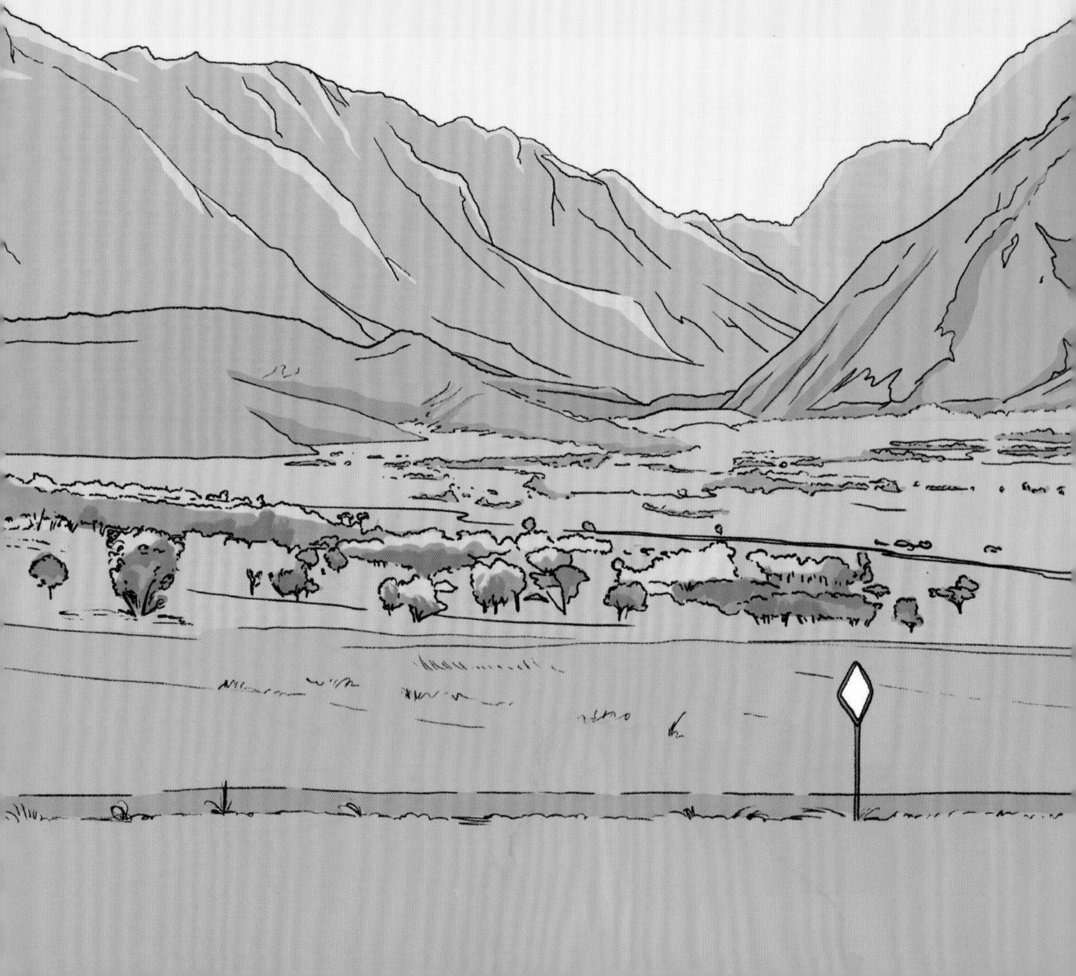

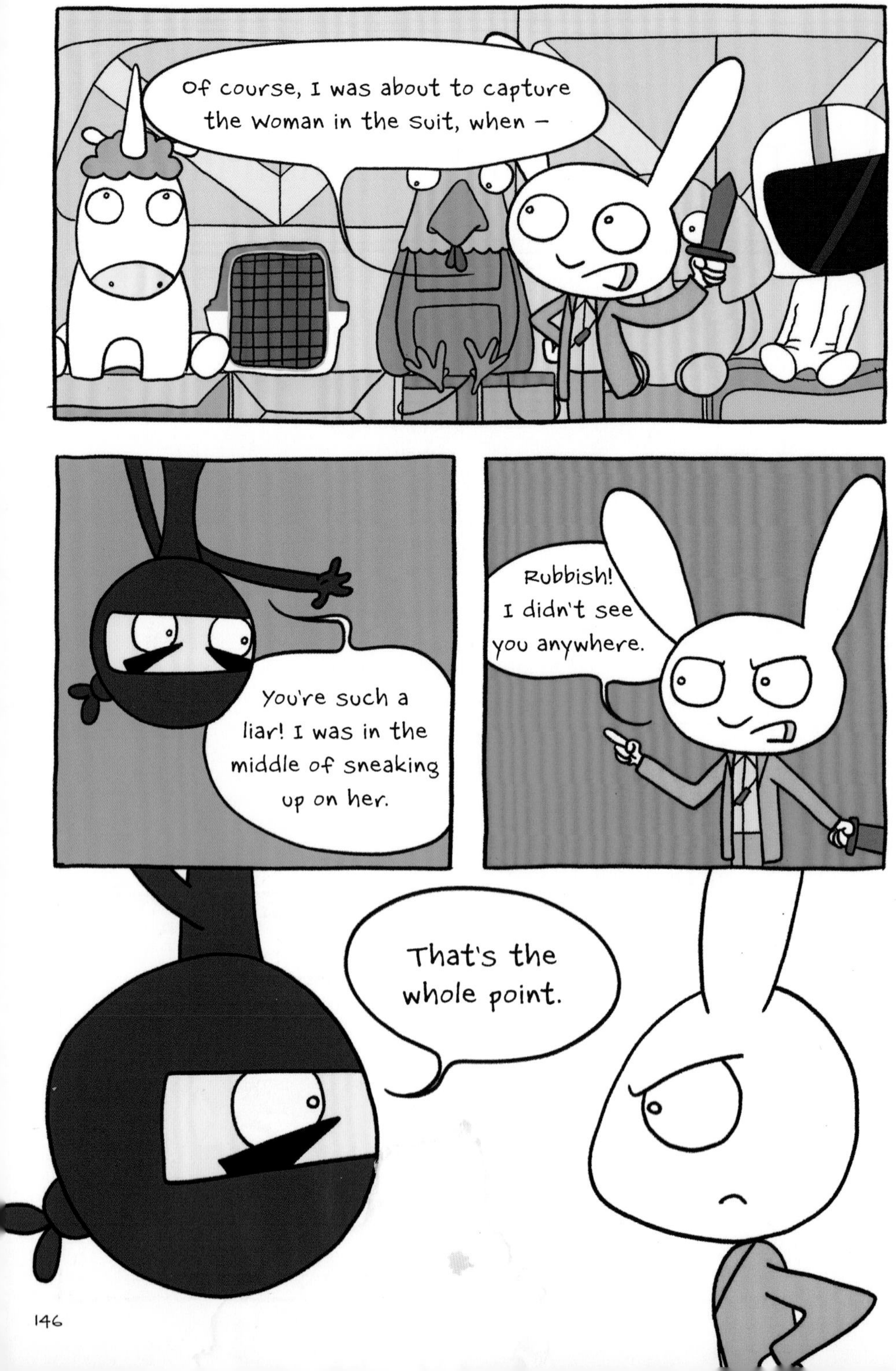

Of course, I was about to capture the woman in the suit, when –
You're such a liar! I was in the middle of sneaking up on her.
Rubbish! I didn't see you anywhere.
That's the whole point.

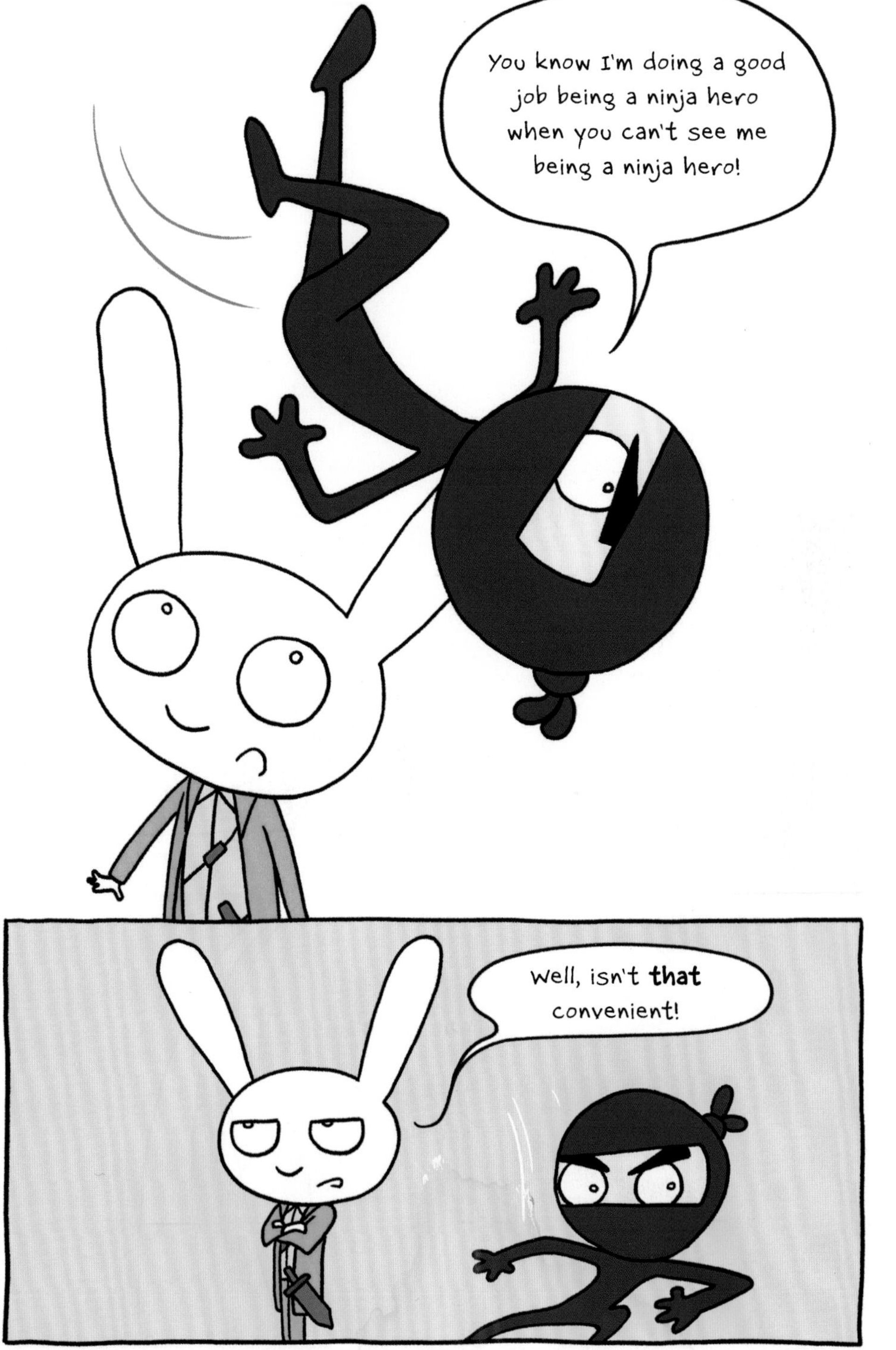
You know I'm doing a good job being a ninja hero when you can't see me being a ninja hero!
Well, isn't **that** convenient!

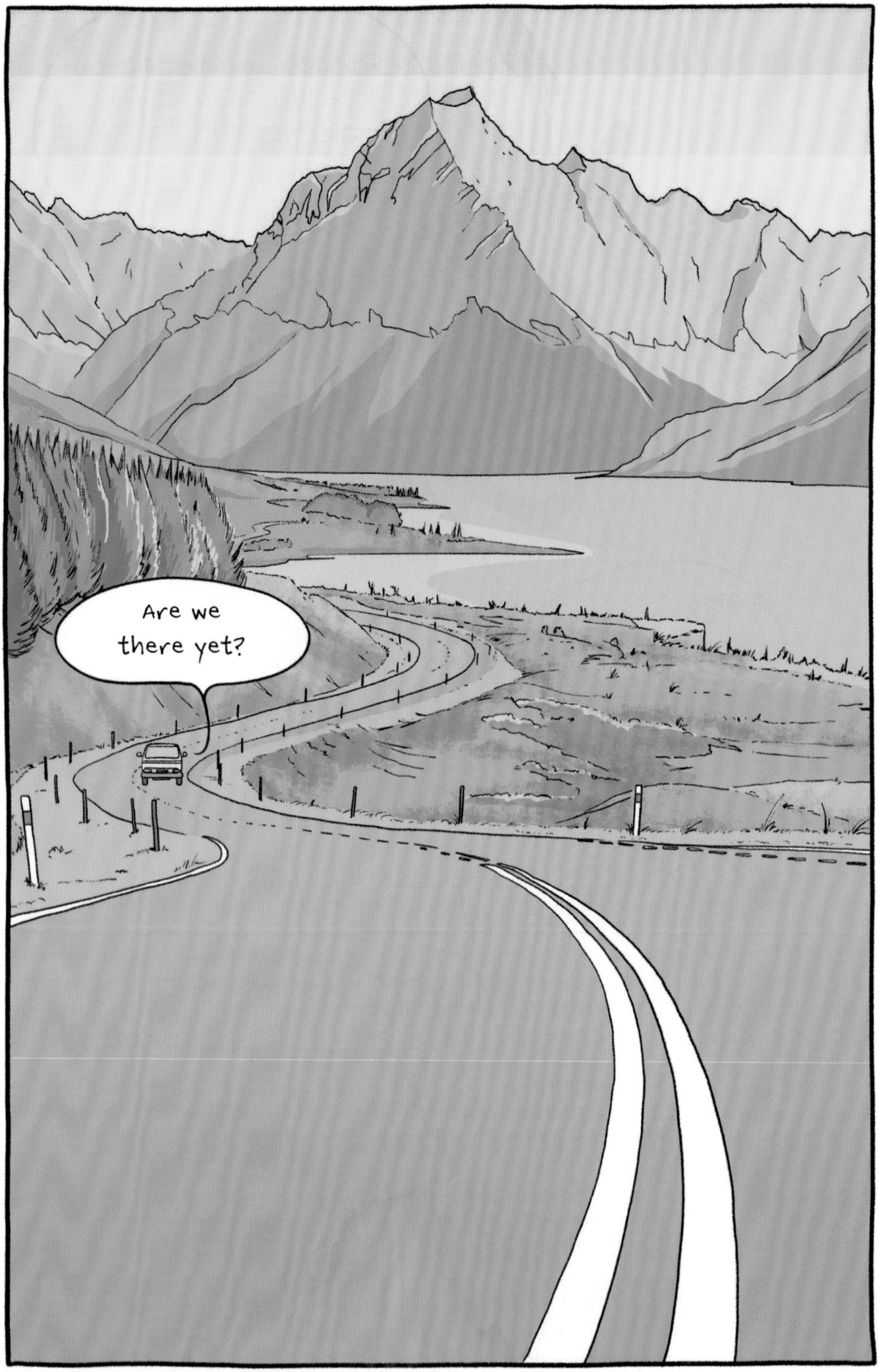
Are we there yet?

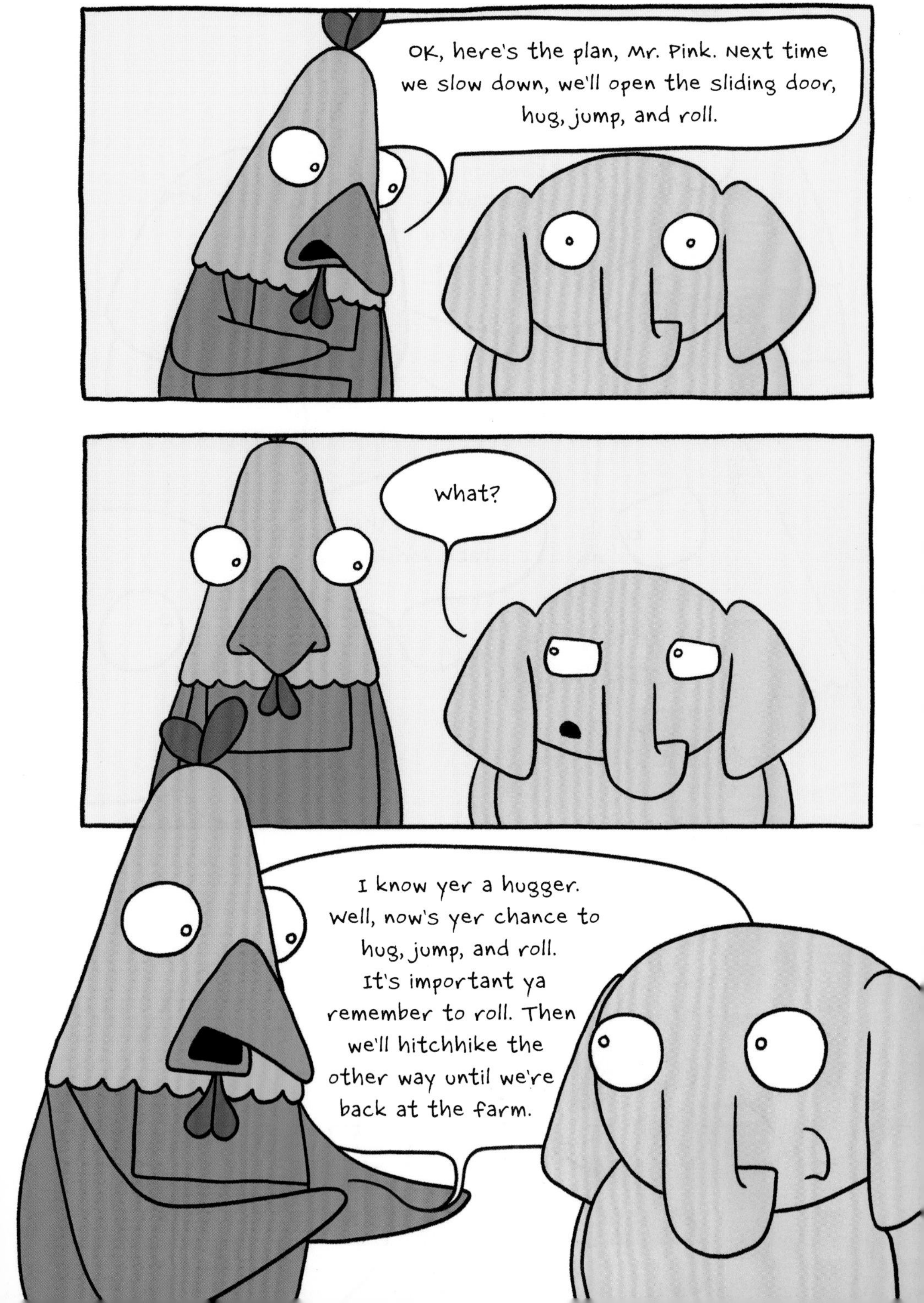
OK, here's the plan, Mr. Pink. Next time we slow down, we'll open the sliding door, hug, jump, and roll.
What?
I know yer a hugger. Well, now's yer chance to hug, jump, and roll. It's important ya remember to roll. Then we'll hitchhike the other way until we're back at the farm.

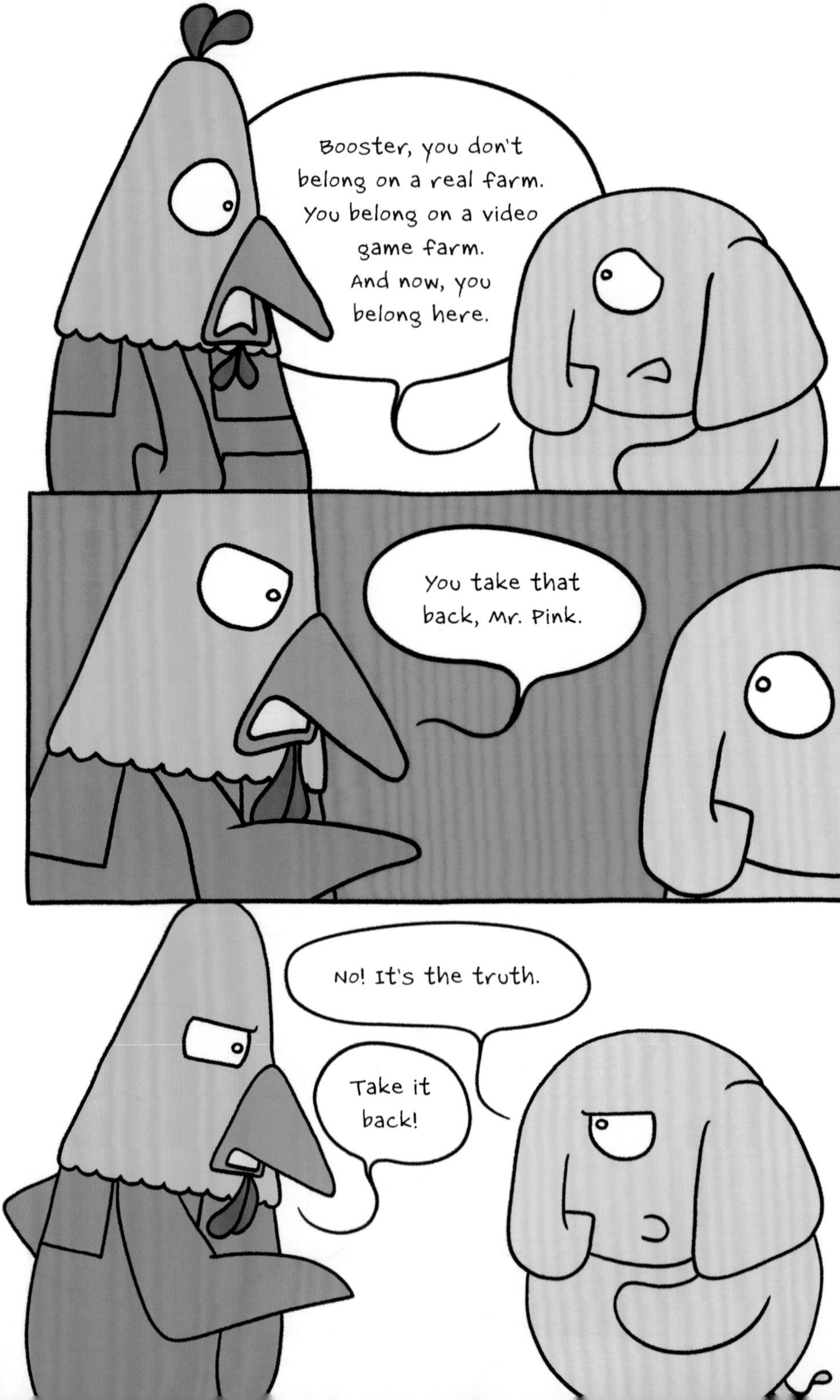
Booster, you don't belong on a real farm. You belong on a video game farm. And now, you belong here.
You take that back, Mr. Pink.
No! It's the truth.
Take it back!

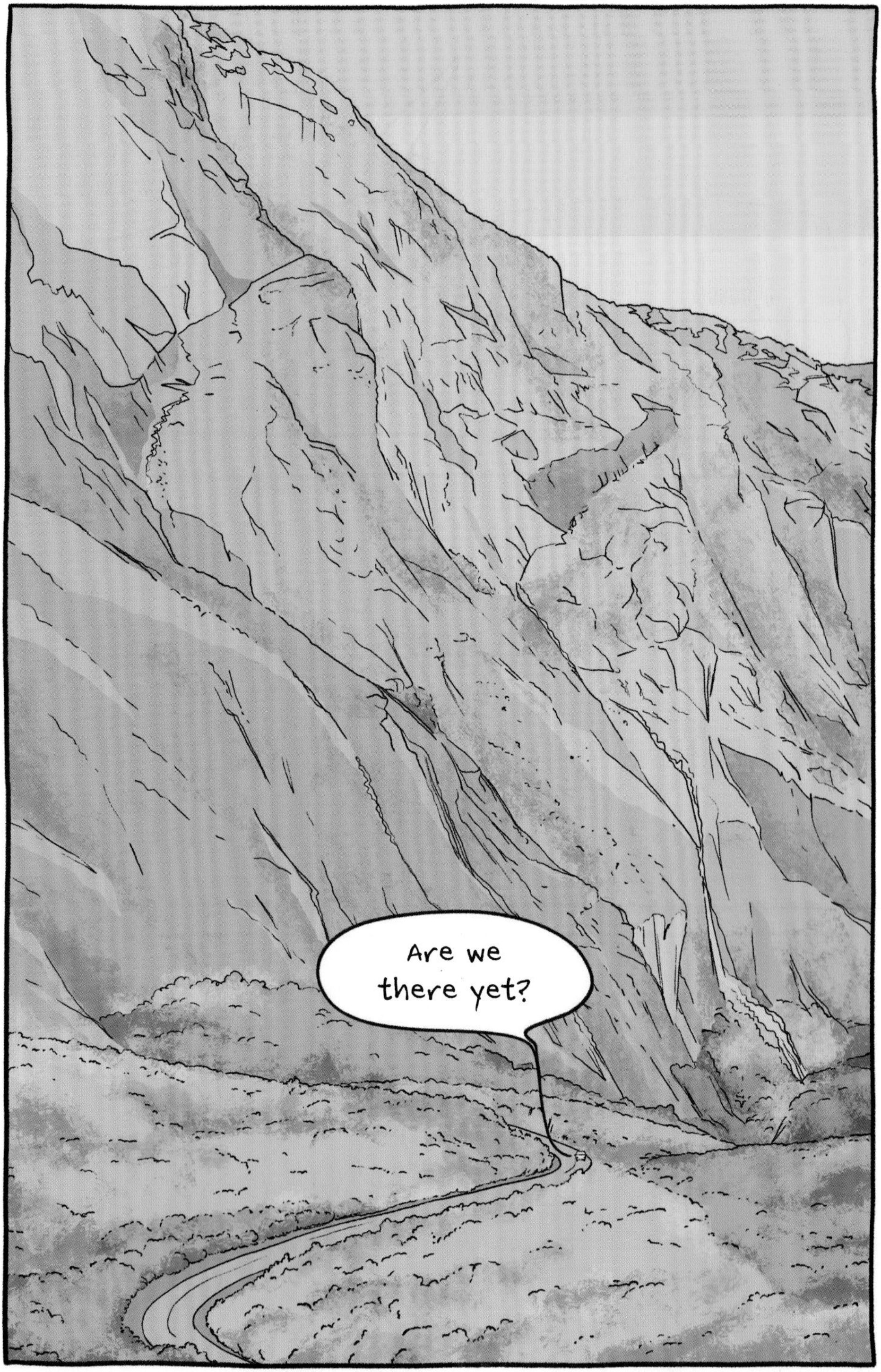
Are we there yet?

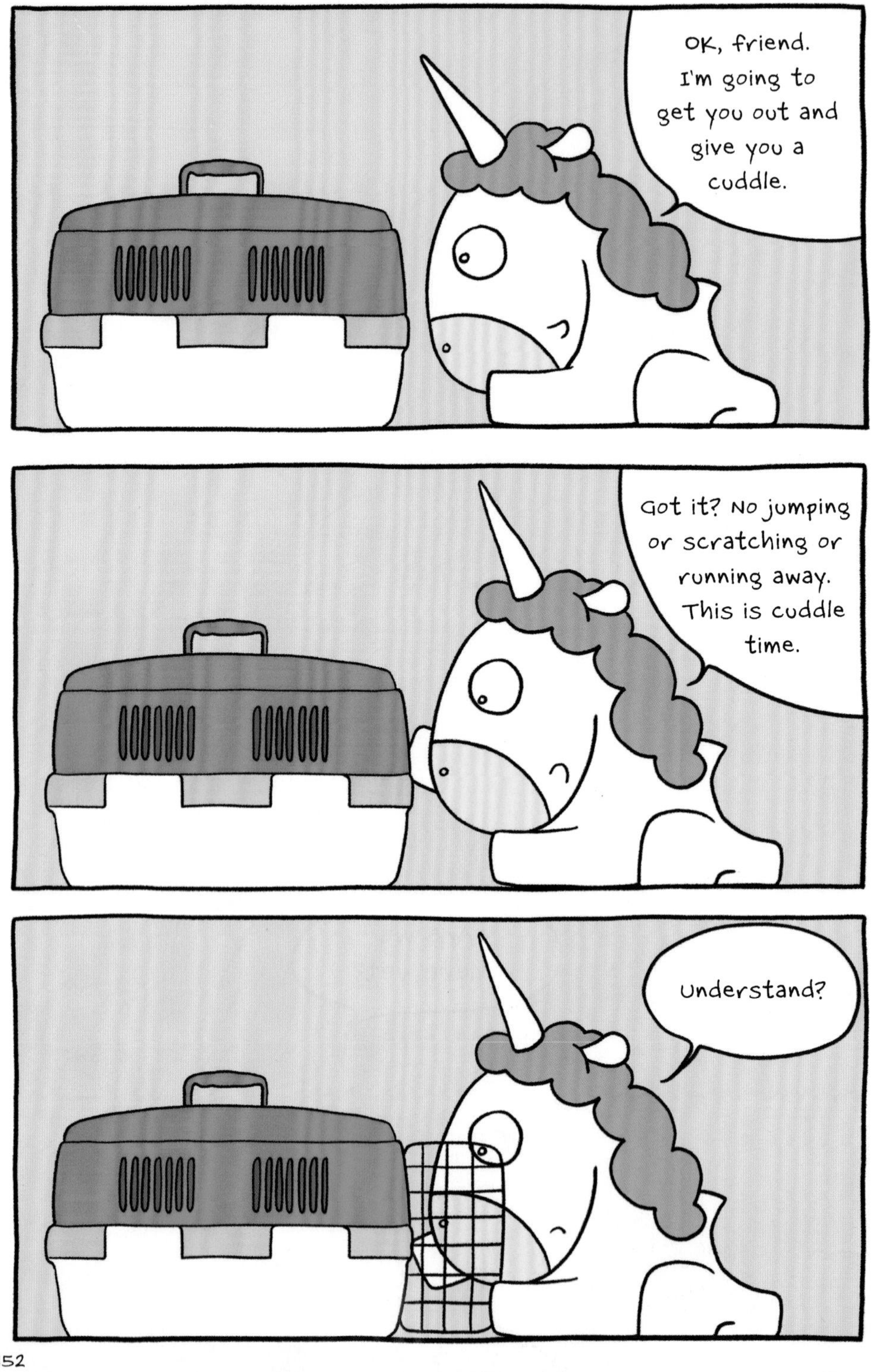
OK, friend. I'm going to get you out and give you a cuddle.
Got it? No jumping or scratching or running away. This is cuddle time.
Understand?

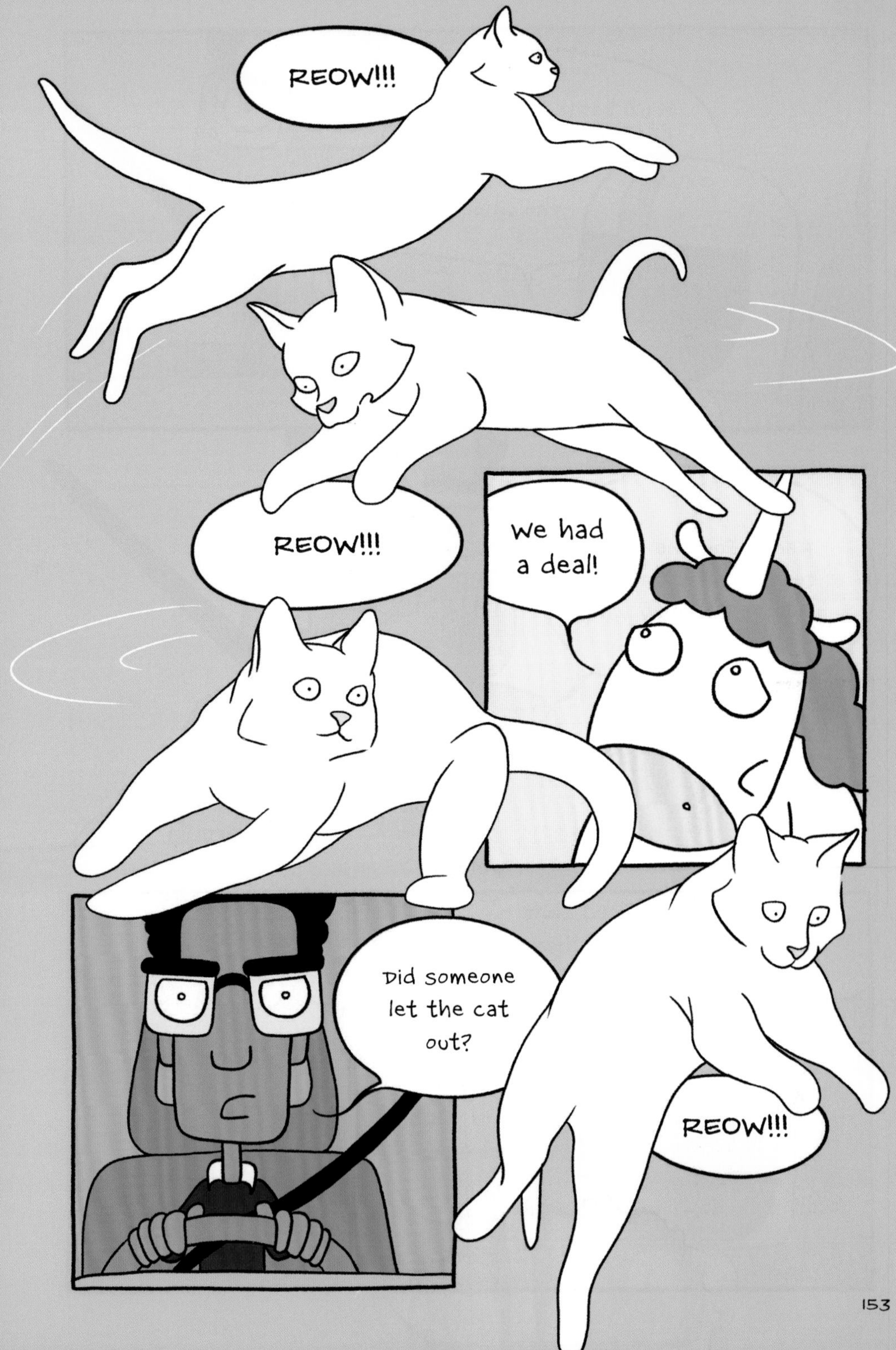
REOW!!!
REOW!!!
We had a deal!
Did someone let the cat out?
REOW!!!

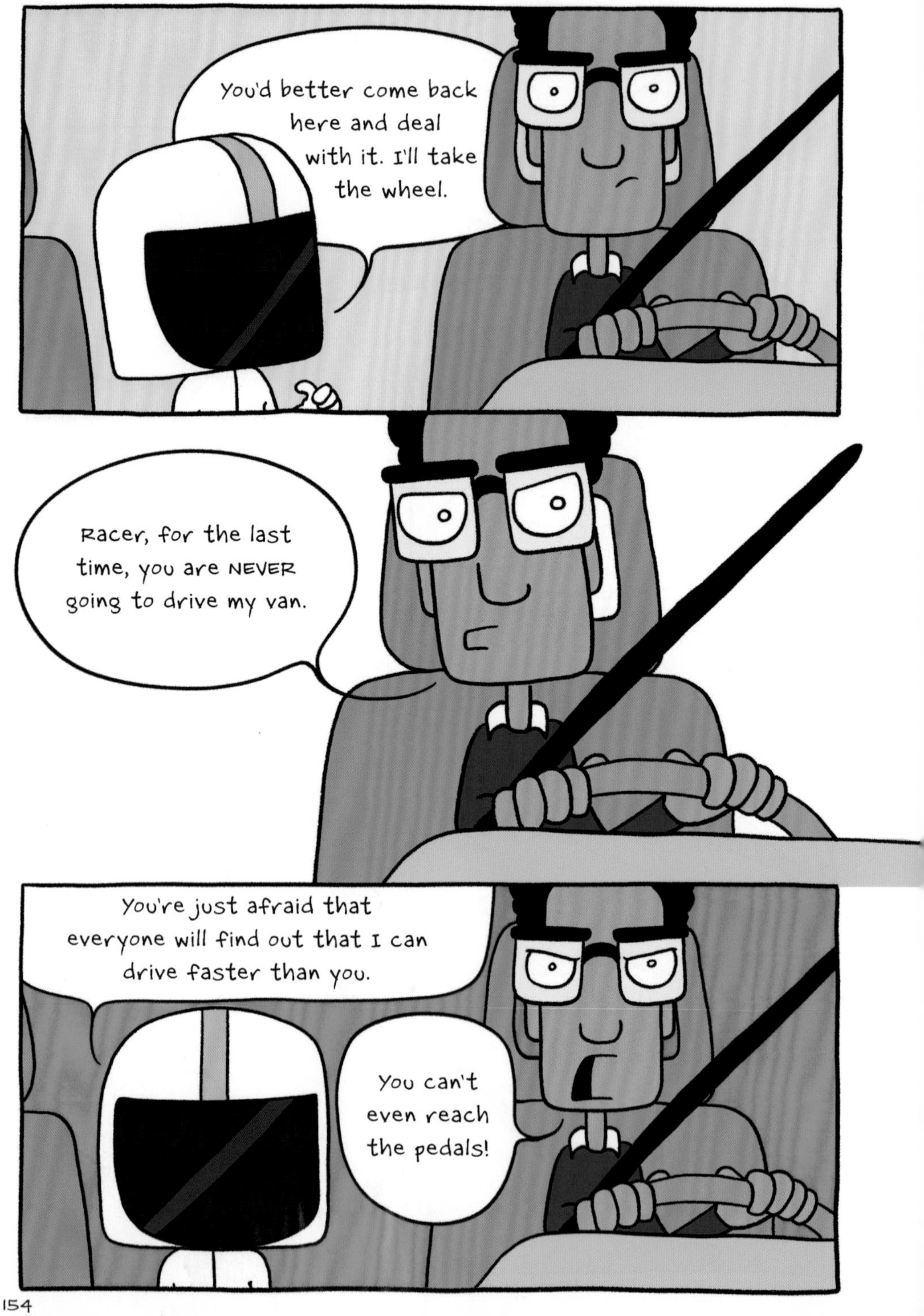
You'd better come back here and deal with it. I'll take the wheel.
Racer, for the last time, you are NEVER going to drive my van.
You're just afraid that everyone will find out that I can drive faster than you.
You can't even reach the pedals!

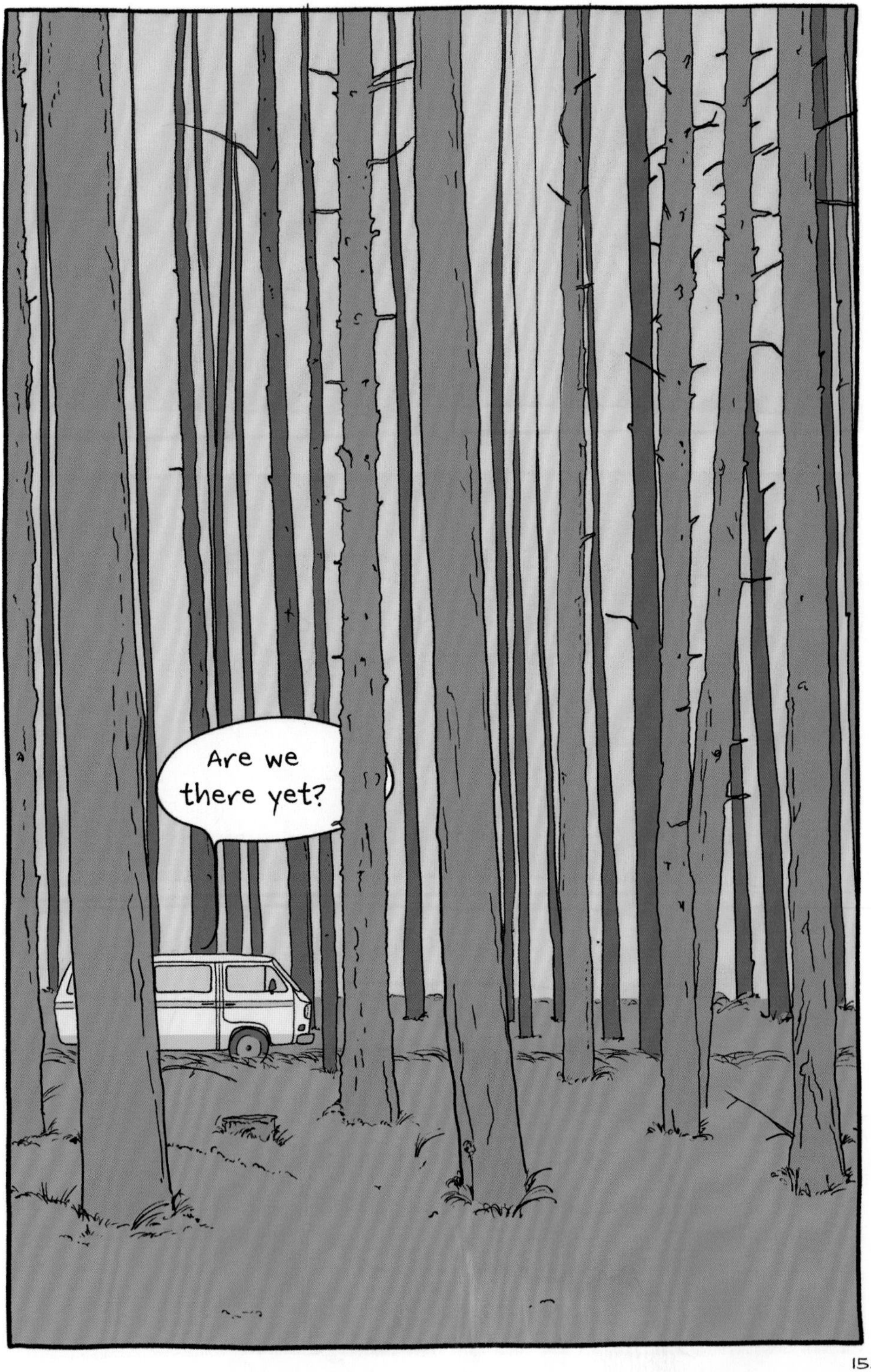
Are we there yet?

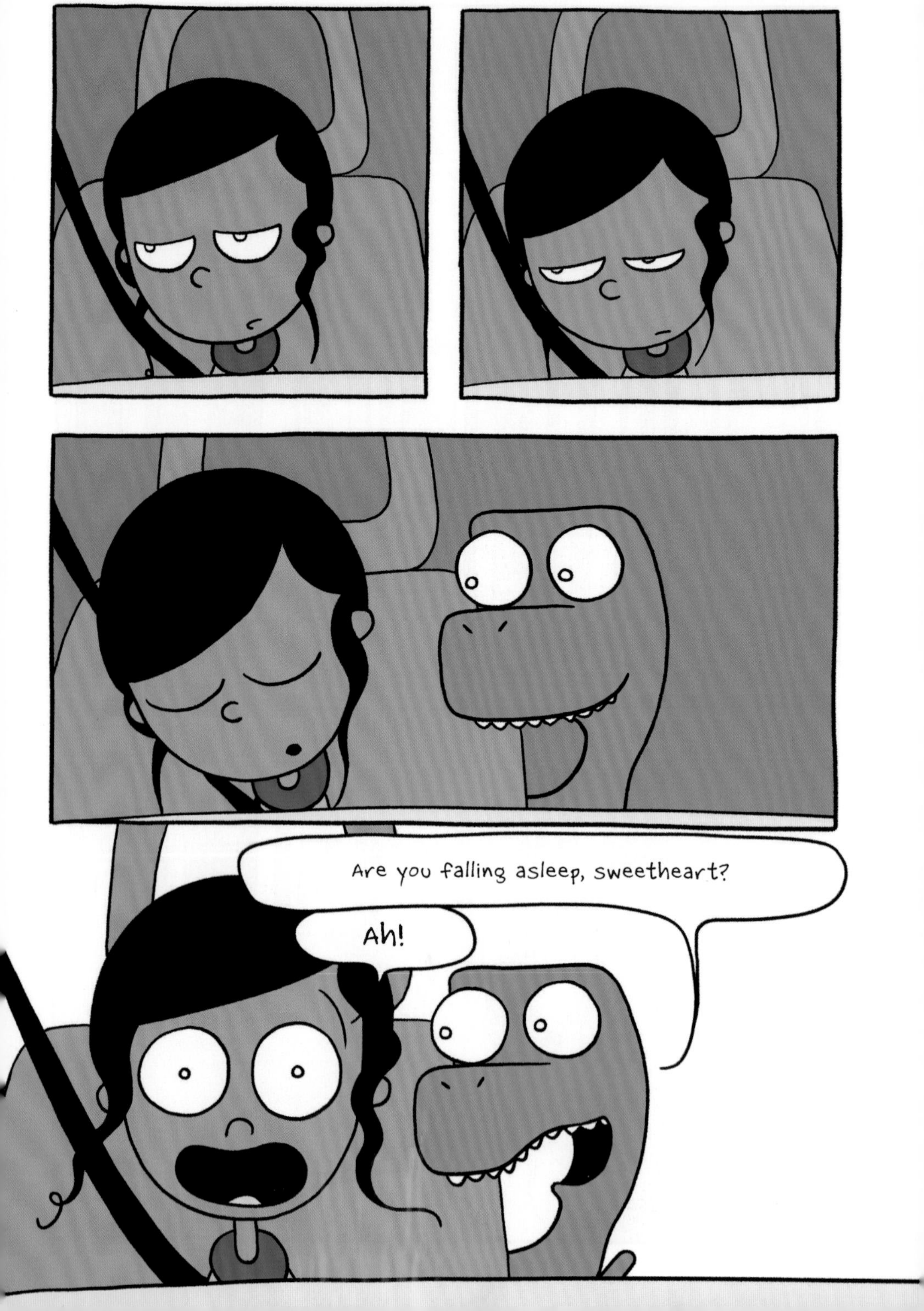
Are you falling asleep, sweetheart?
Ah!

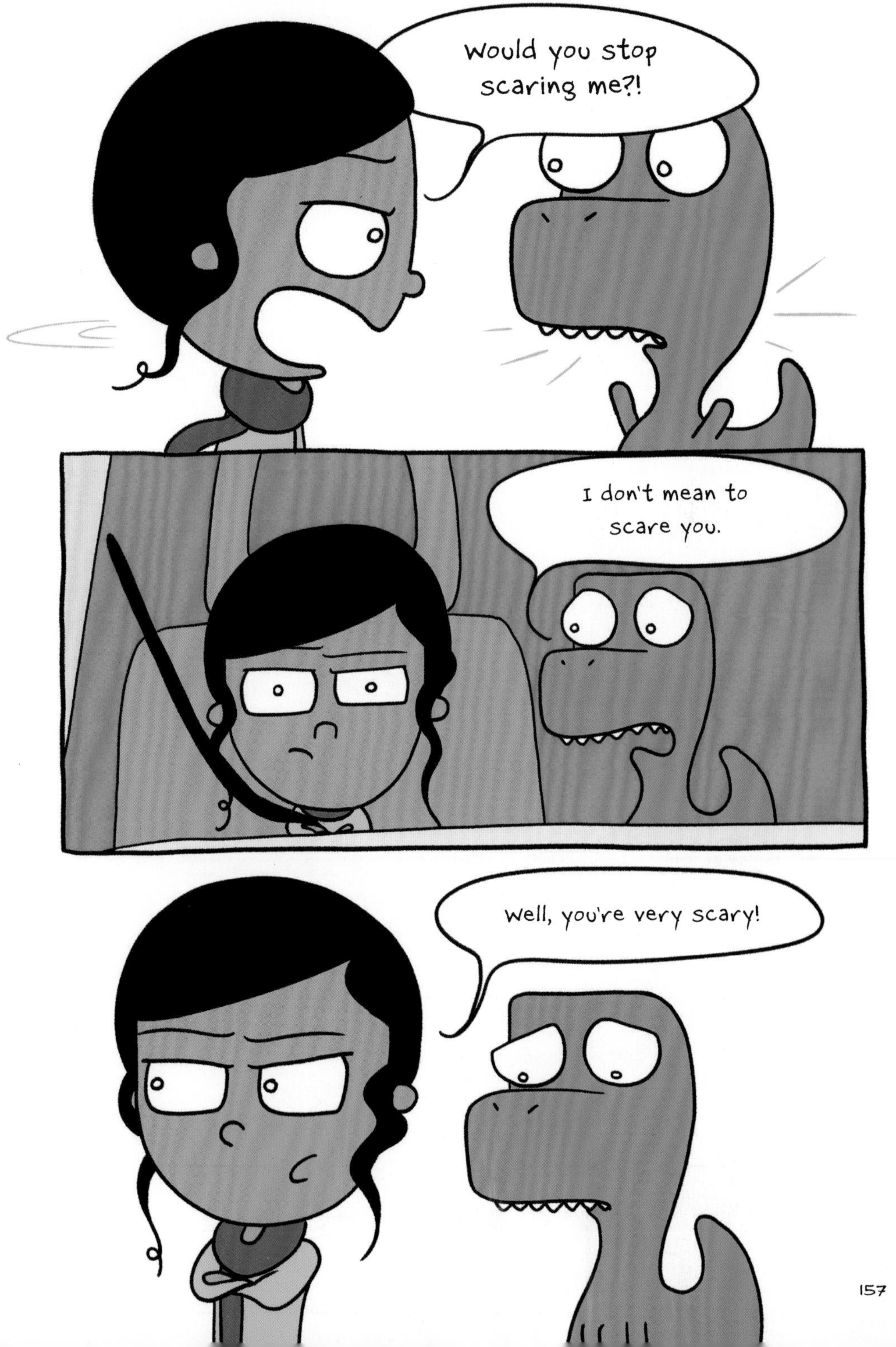
Would you stop scaring me?!
I don't mean to scare you.
Well, you're very scary!

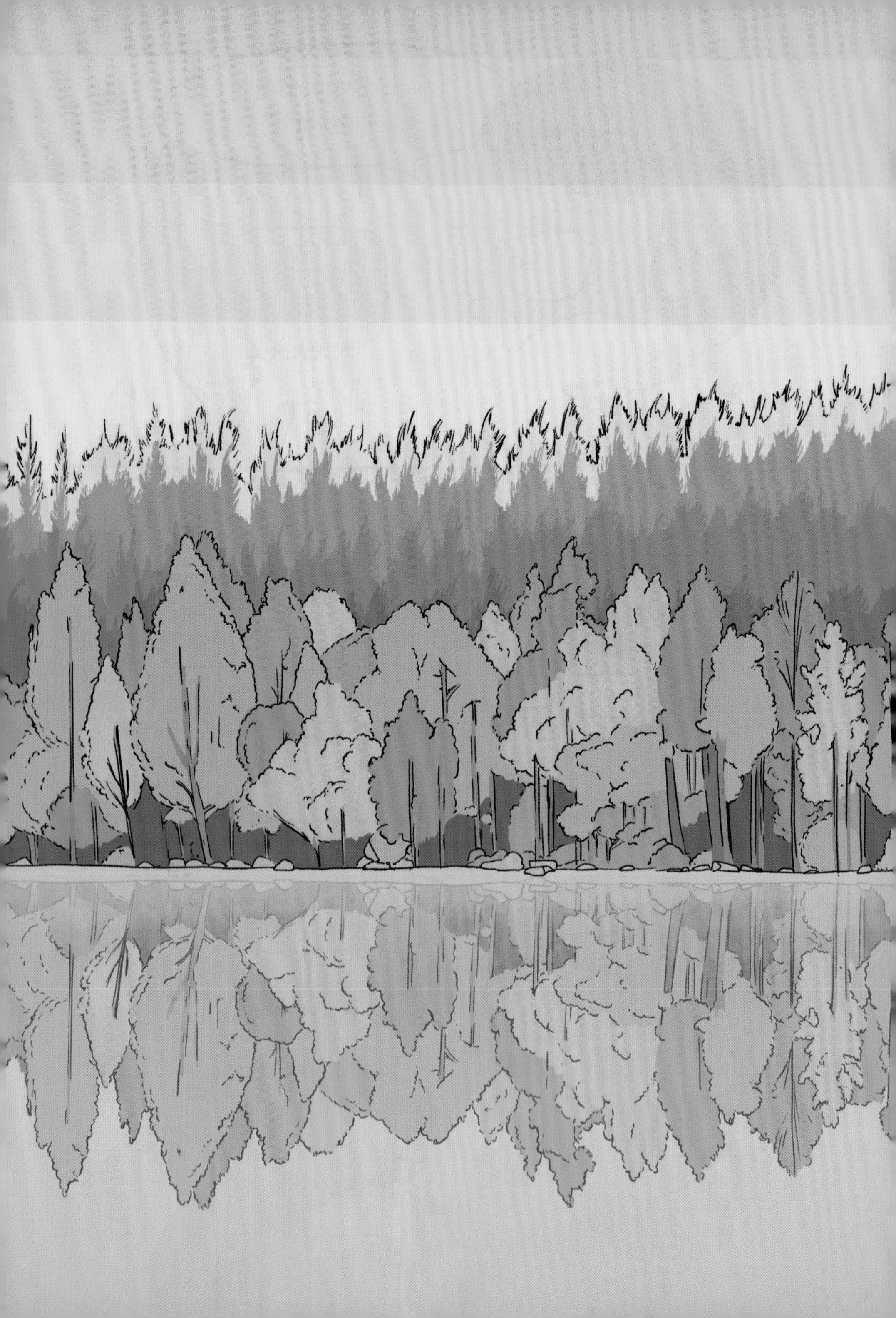

CHAPTER TEN
The Odds arrive

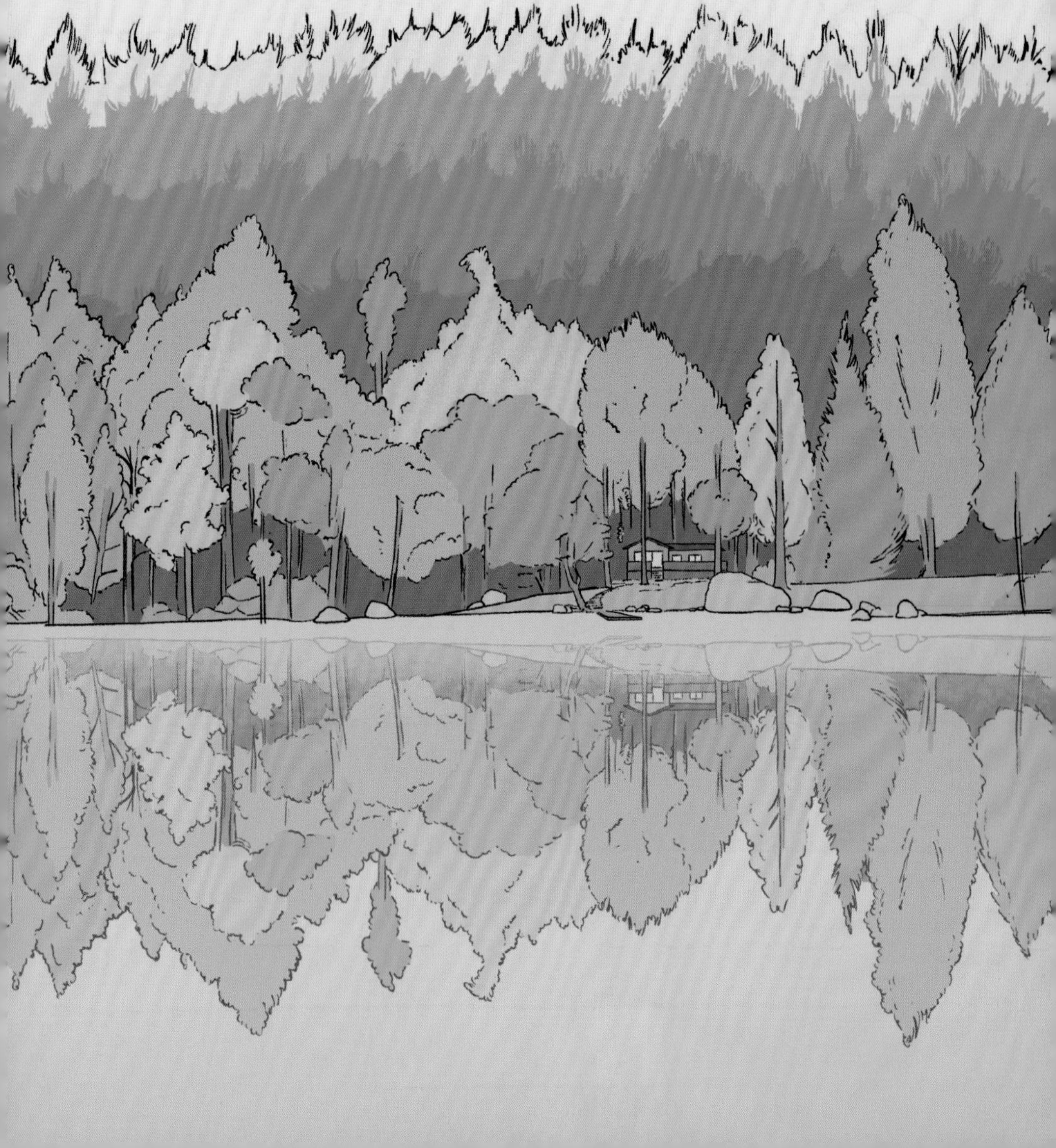

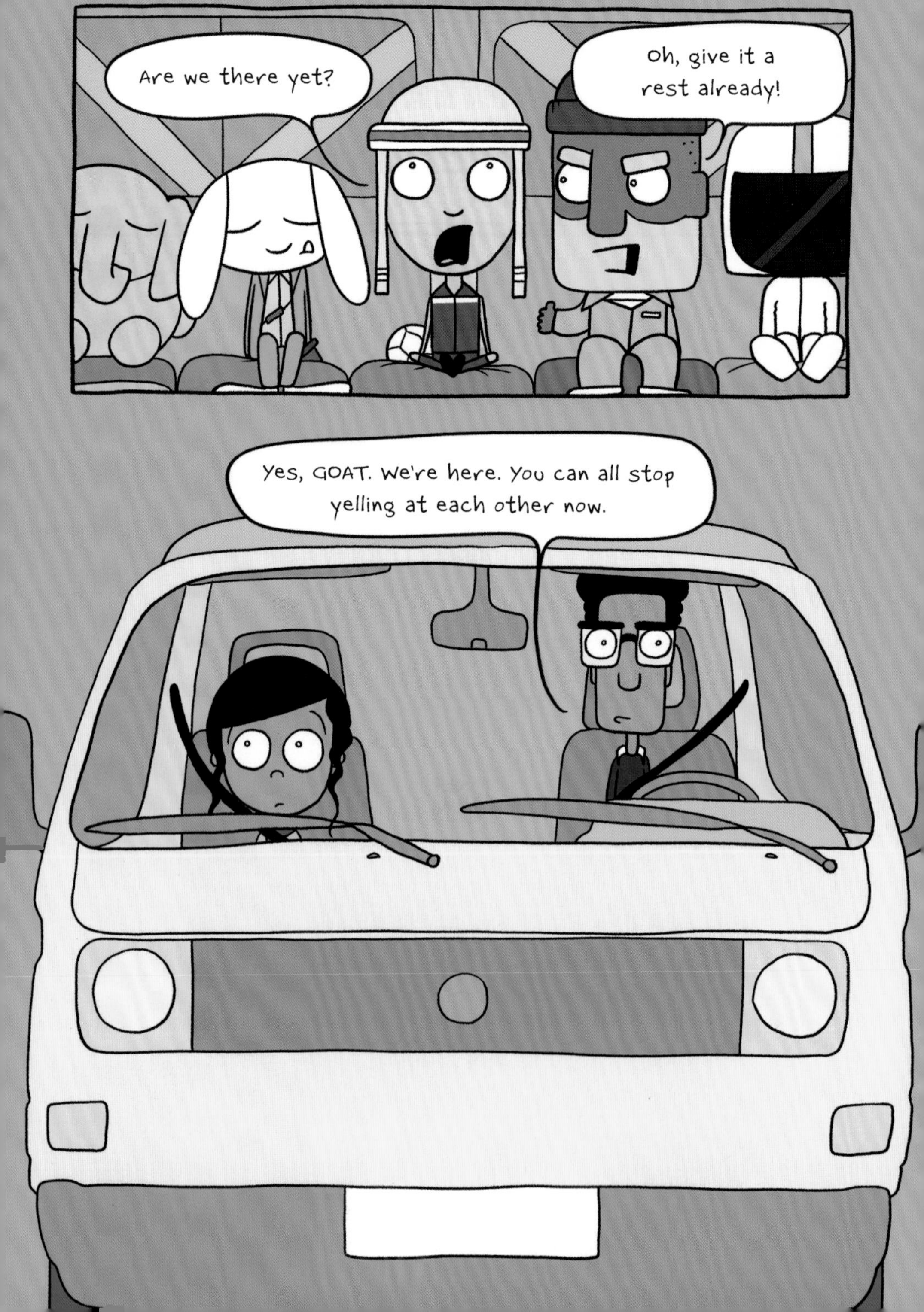
Are we there yet?
Oh, give it a rest already!
Yes, GOAT. We're here. You can all stop yelling at each other now.

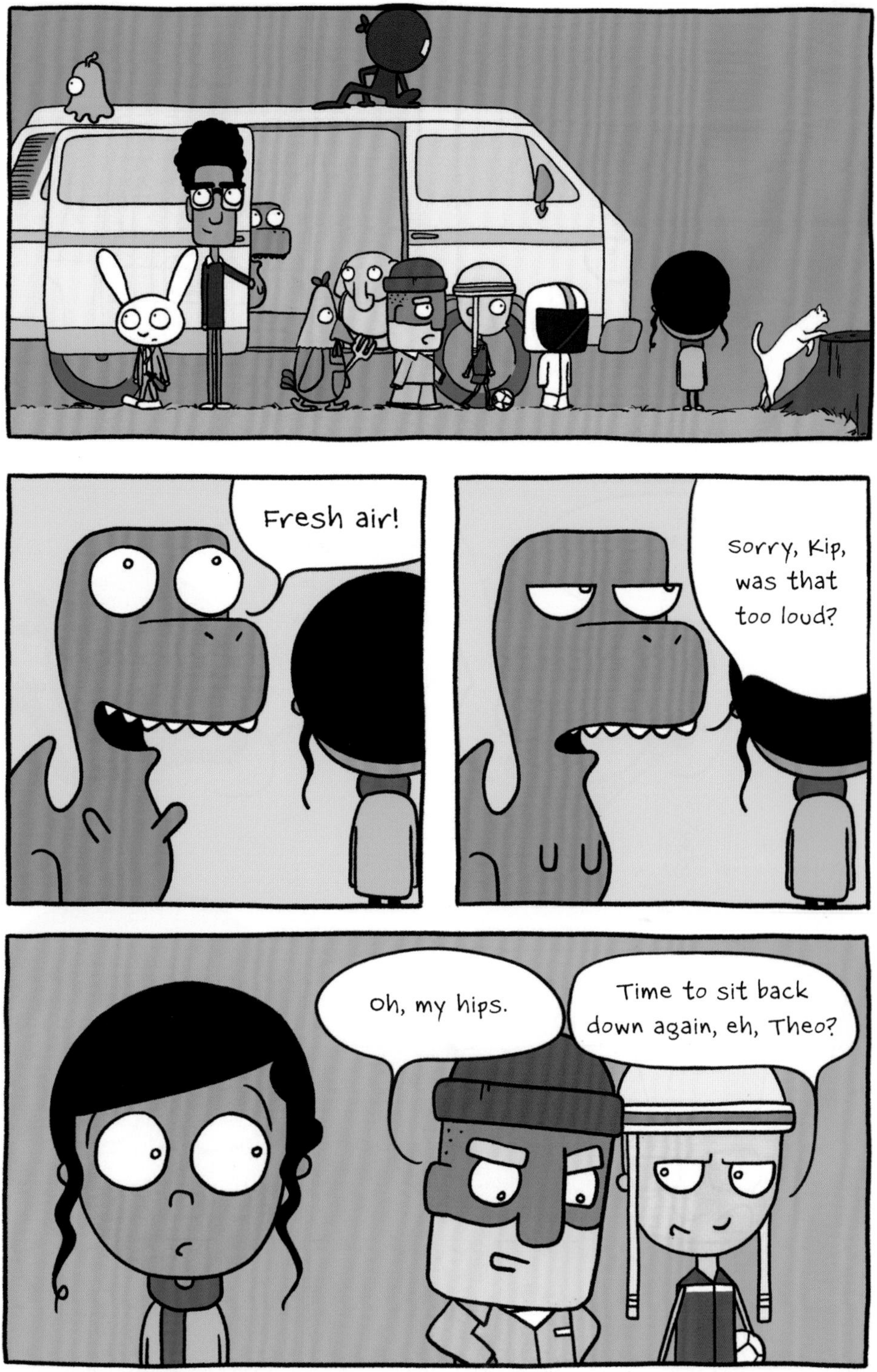
Fresh air!
Sorry, Kip, was that too loud?
Oh, my hips.
Time to sit back down again, eh, Theo?

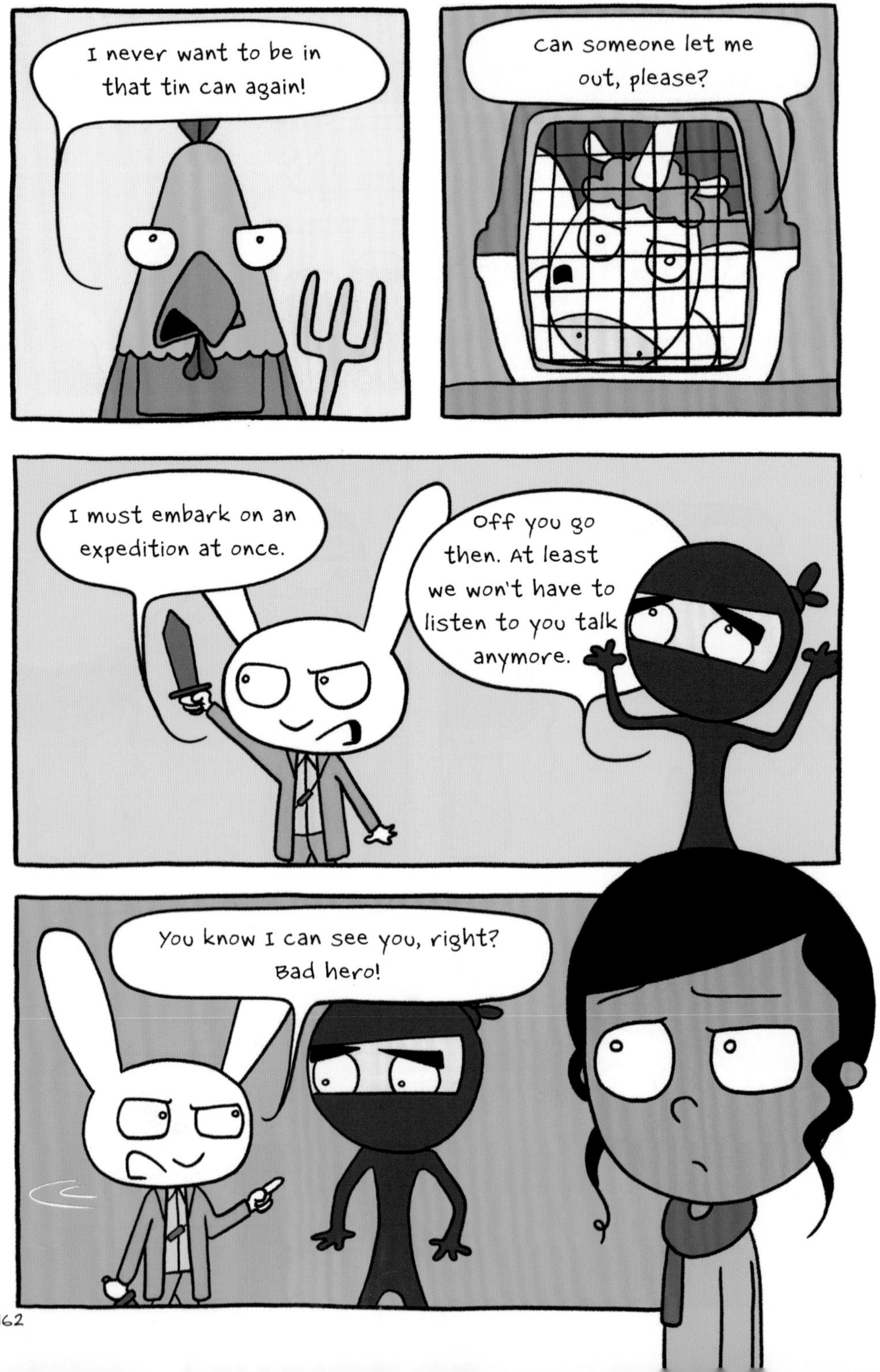
I never want to be in that tin can again!
Can someone let me out, please?
I must embark on an expedition at once.
Off you go then. At least we won't have to listen to you talk anymore.
You know I can see you, right? Bad hero!

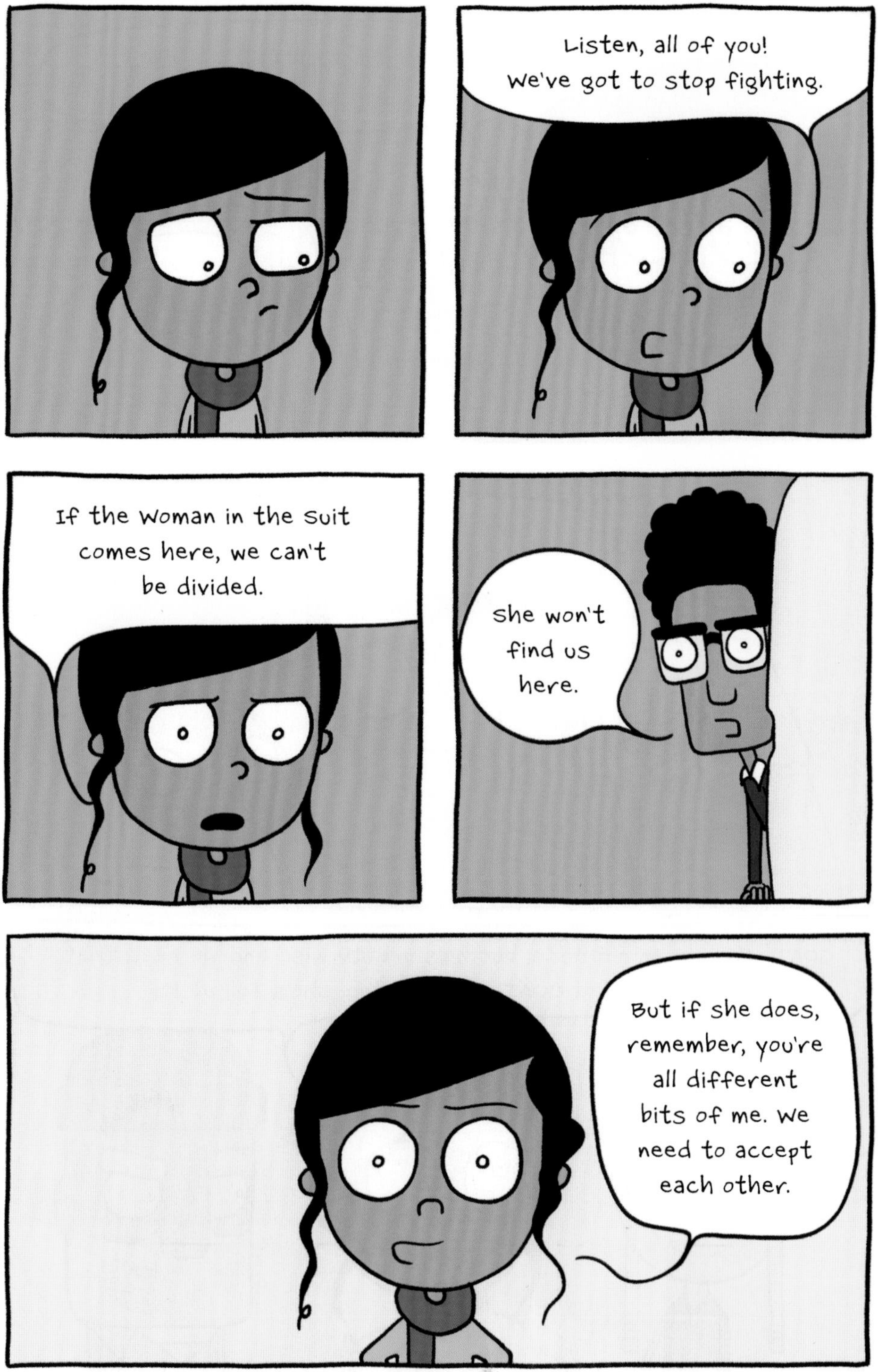
Listen, all of you! We've got to stop fighting.
If the woman in the suit comes here, we can't be divided.
She won't find us here.
But if she does, remember, you're all different bits of me. We need to accept each other.

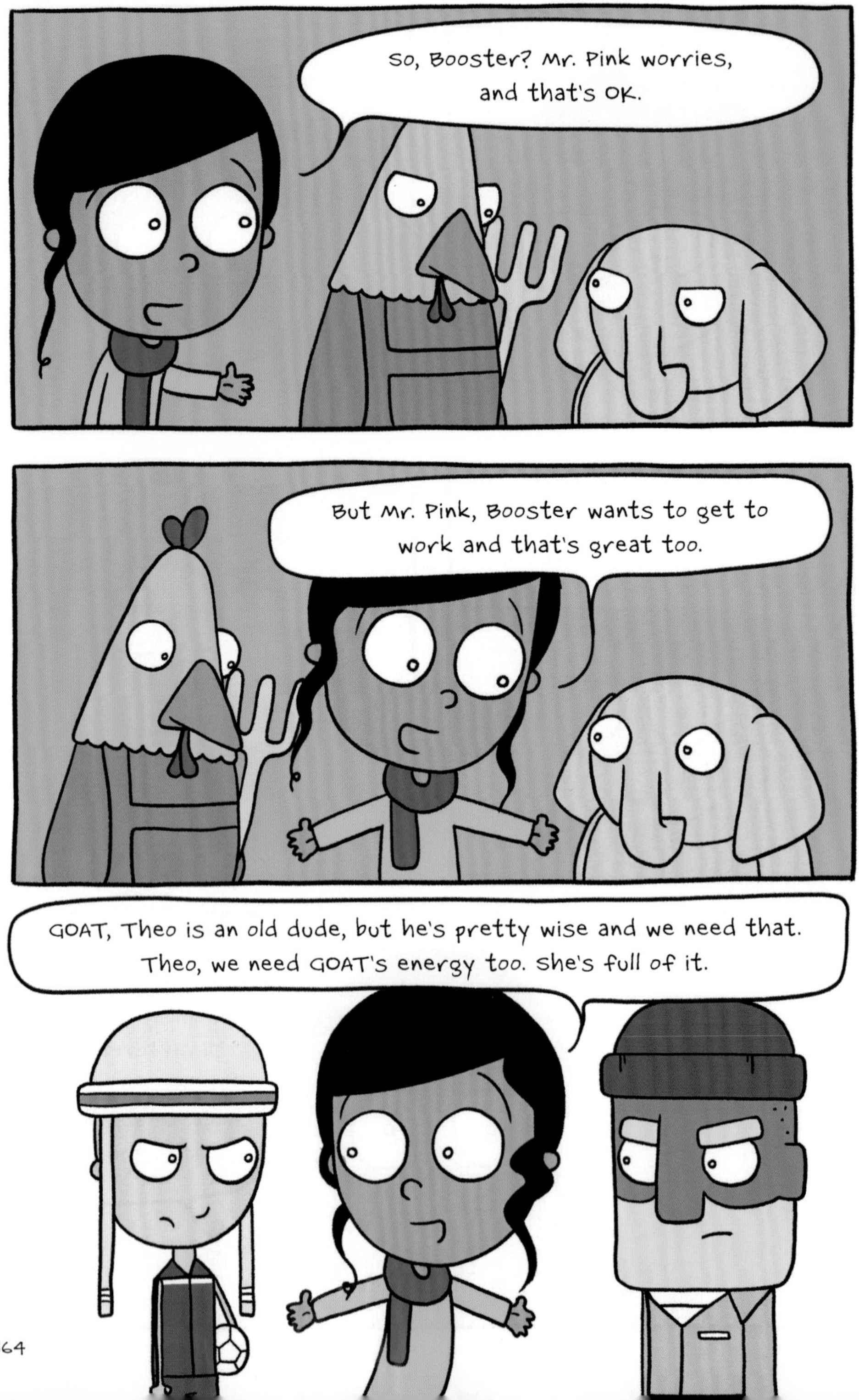
So, Booster? Mr. Pink worries, and that's OK.
But Mr. Pink, Booster wants to get to work and that's great too.
GOAT, Theo is an old dude, but he's pretty wise and we need that. Theo, we need GOAT's energy too. She's full of it.

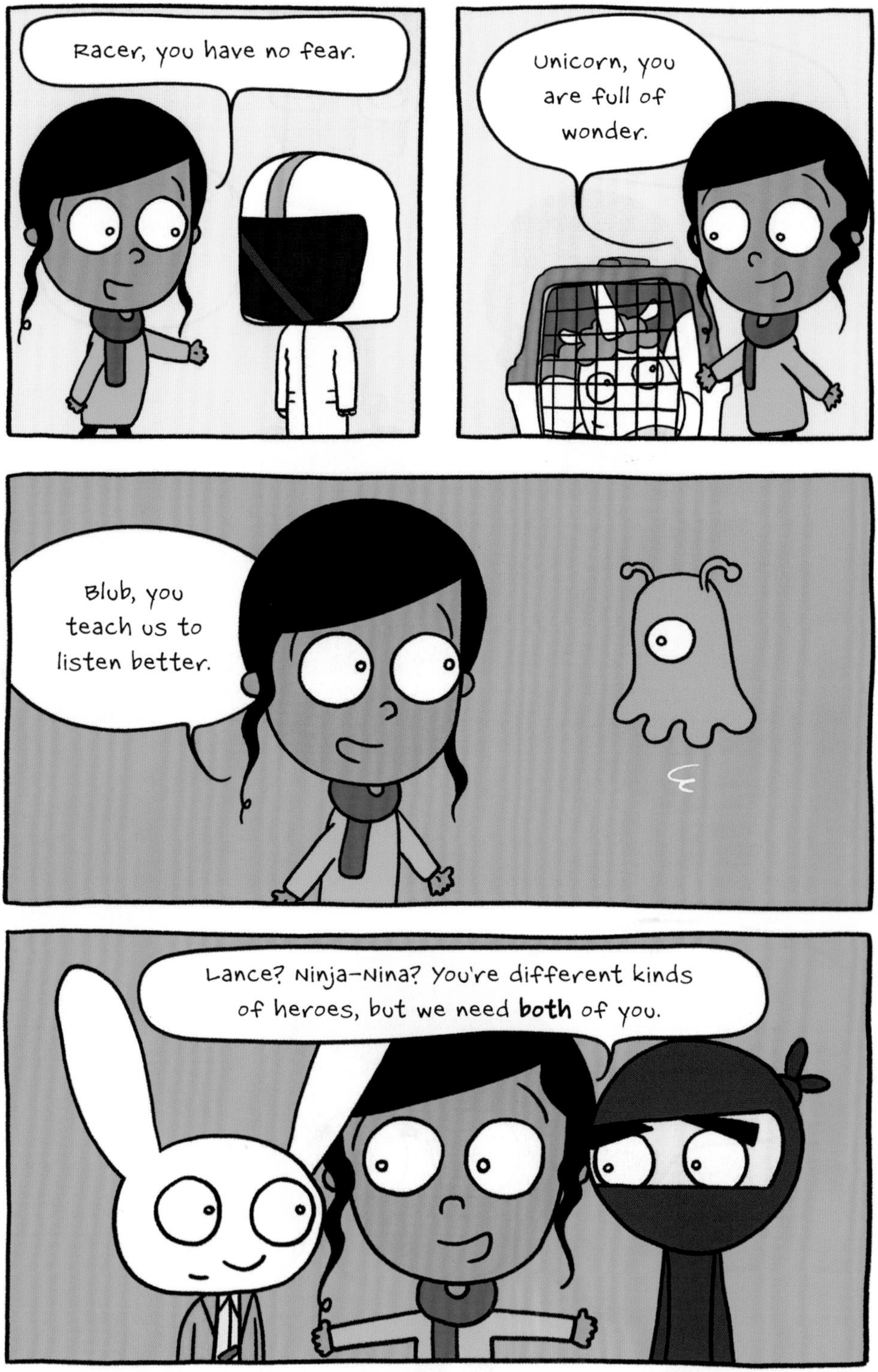
Racer, you have no fear.
Unicorn, you are full of wonder.
Blub, you teach us to listen better.
Lance? Ninja-Nina? You're different kinds of heroes, but we need **both** of you.

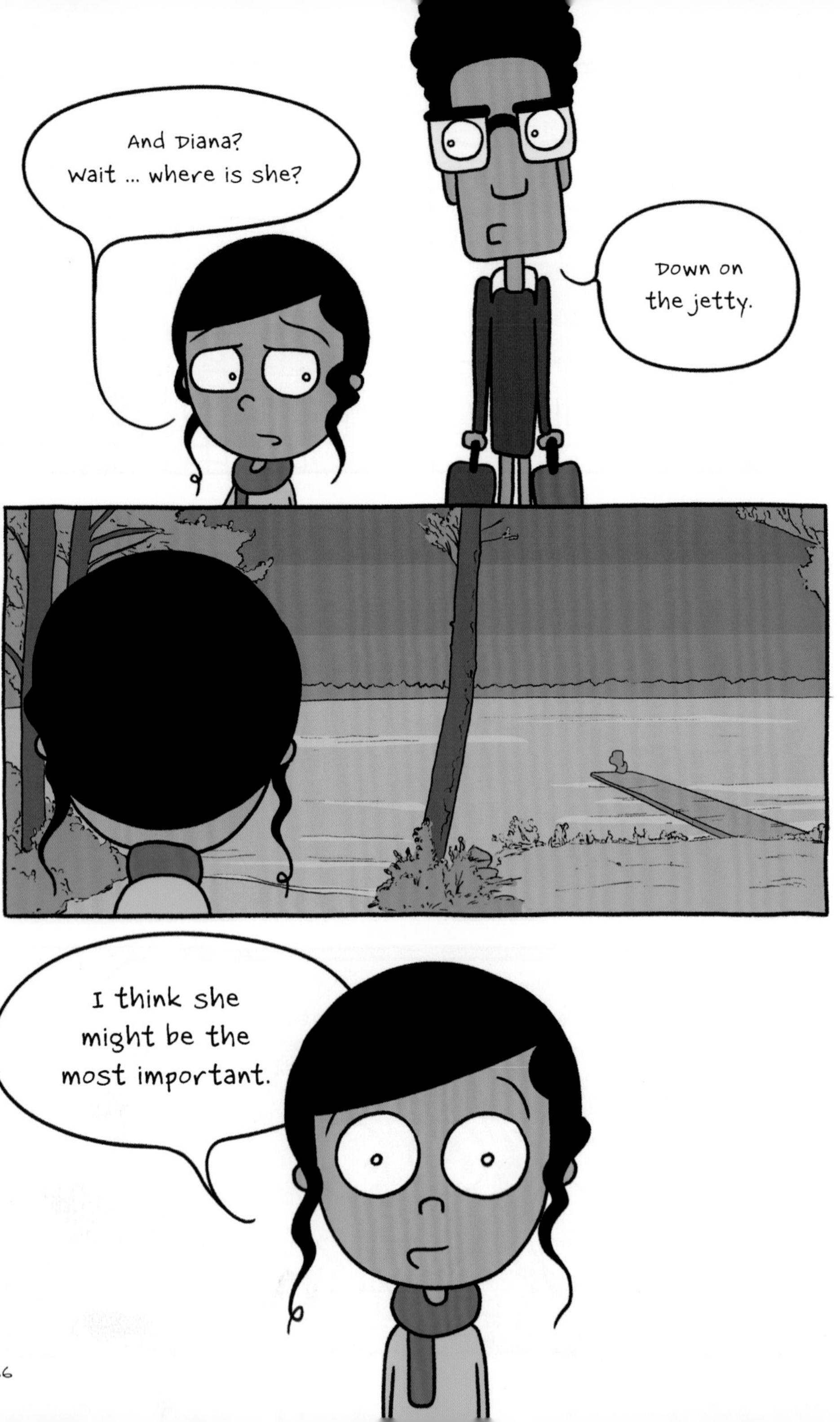
And Diana?
Wait ... where is she?
Down on the jetty.
I think she might be the most important.

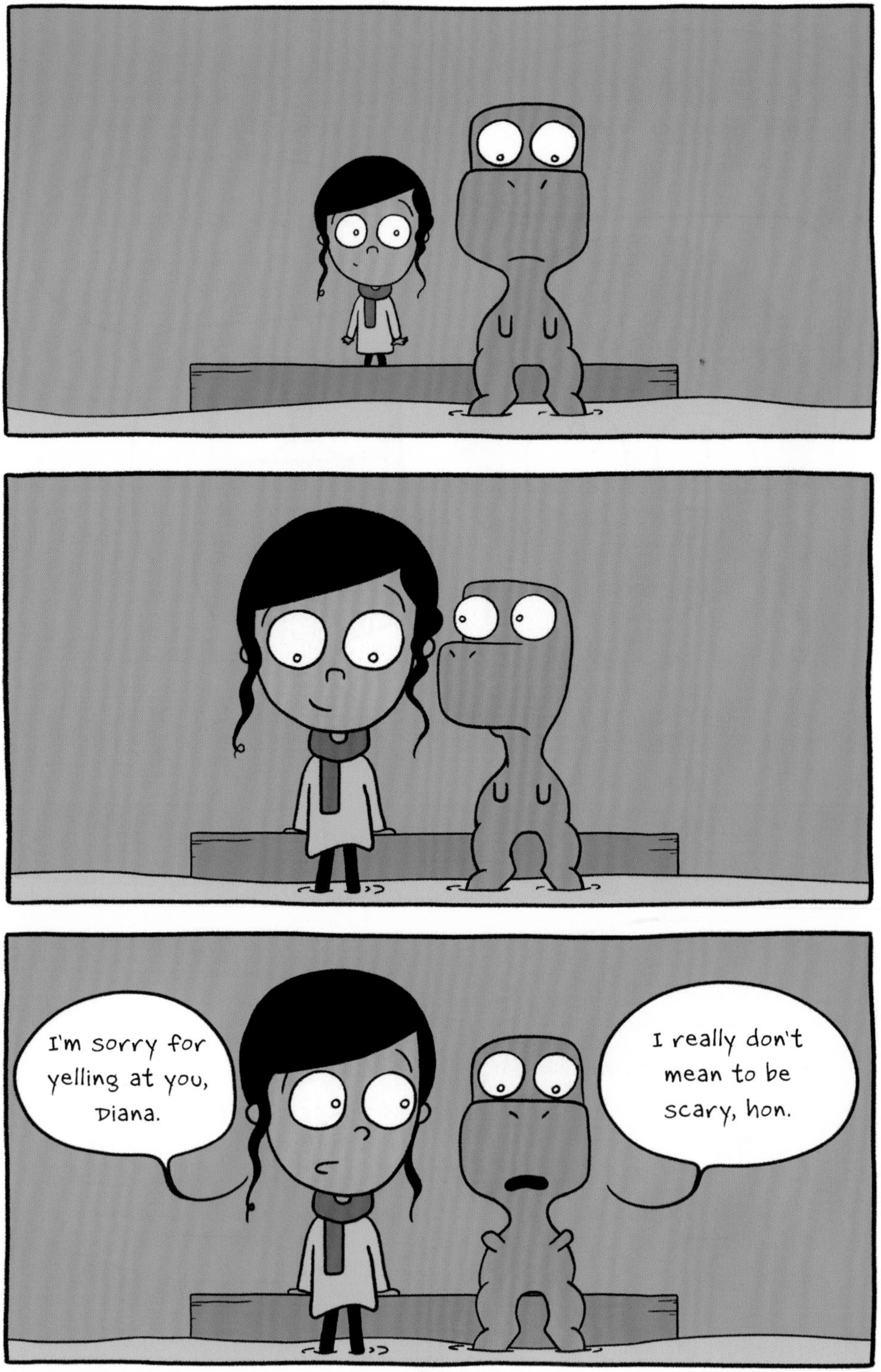
I'm sorry for yelling at you, Diana.
I really don't mean to be scary, hon.

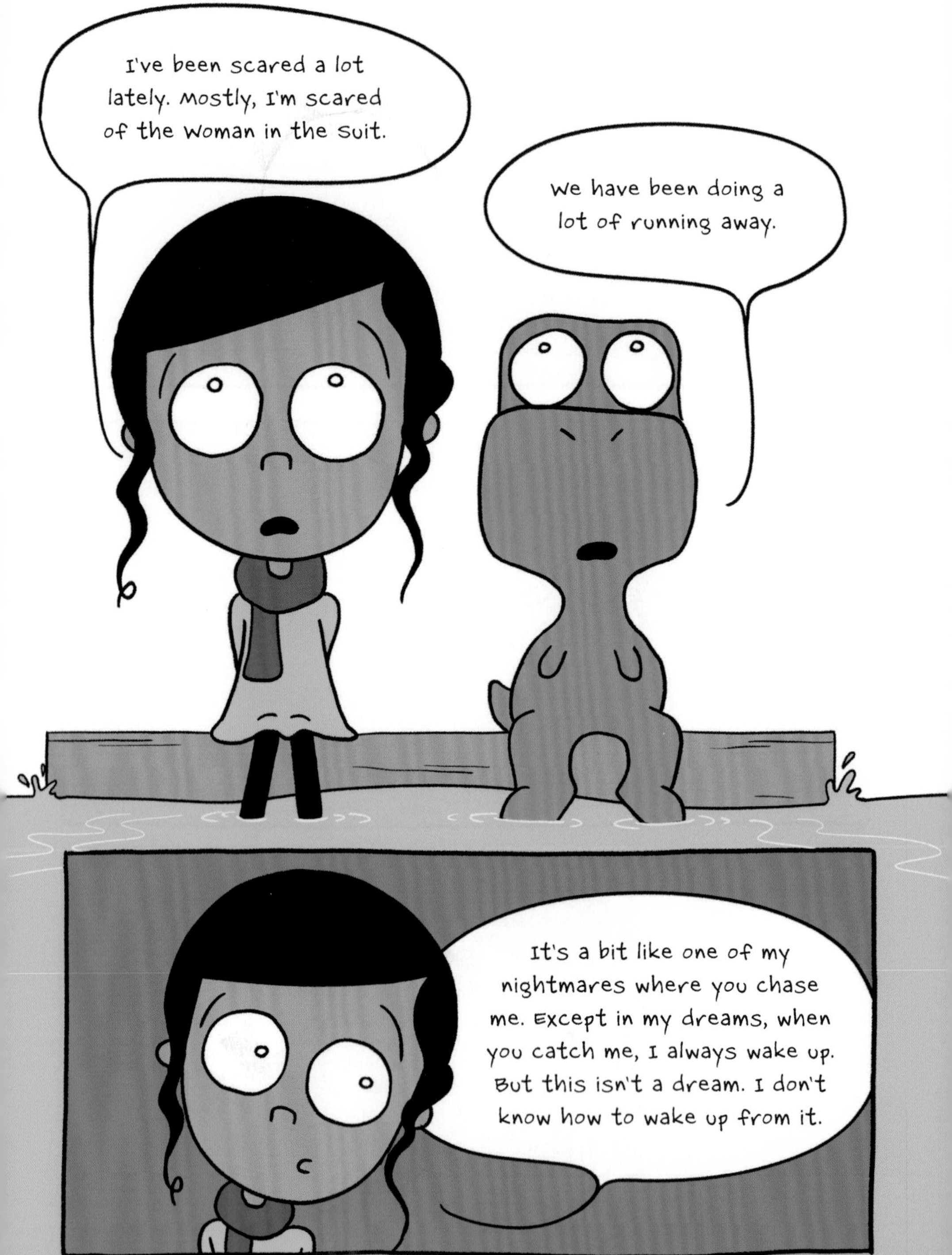
I've been scared a lot lately. Mostly, I'm scared of the woman in the suit.
We have been doing a lot of running away.
It's a bit like one of my nightmares where you chase me. Except in my dreams, when you catch me, I always wake up. But this isn't a dream. I don't know how to wake up from it.

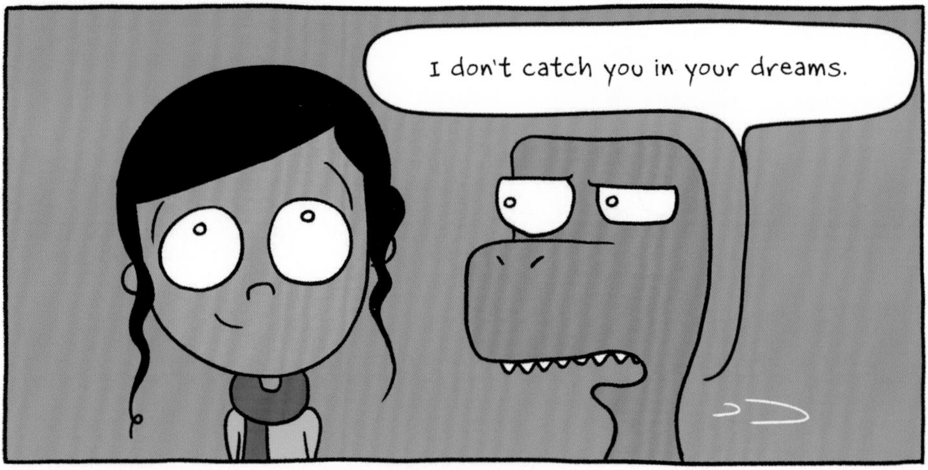
I don't catch you in your dreams.

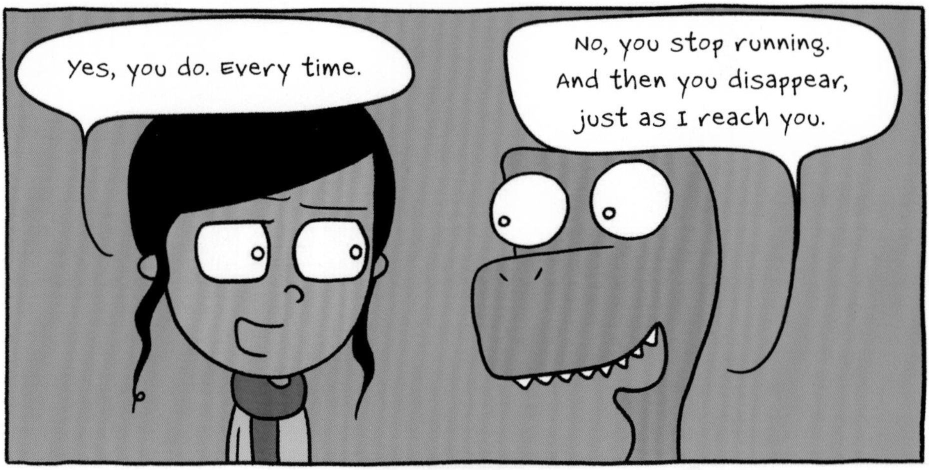
Yes, you do. Every time.
No, you stop running. And then you disappear, just as I reach you.

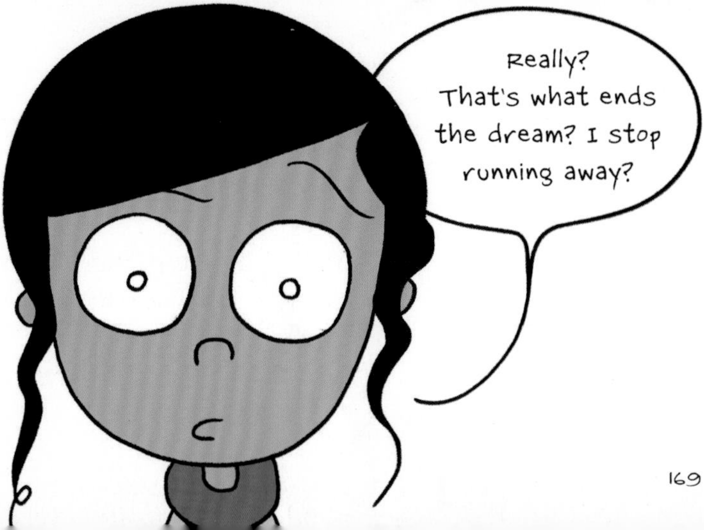
Really? That's what ends the dream? I stop running away?

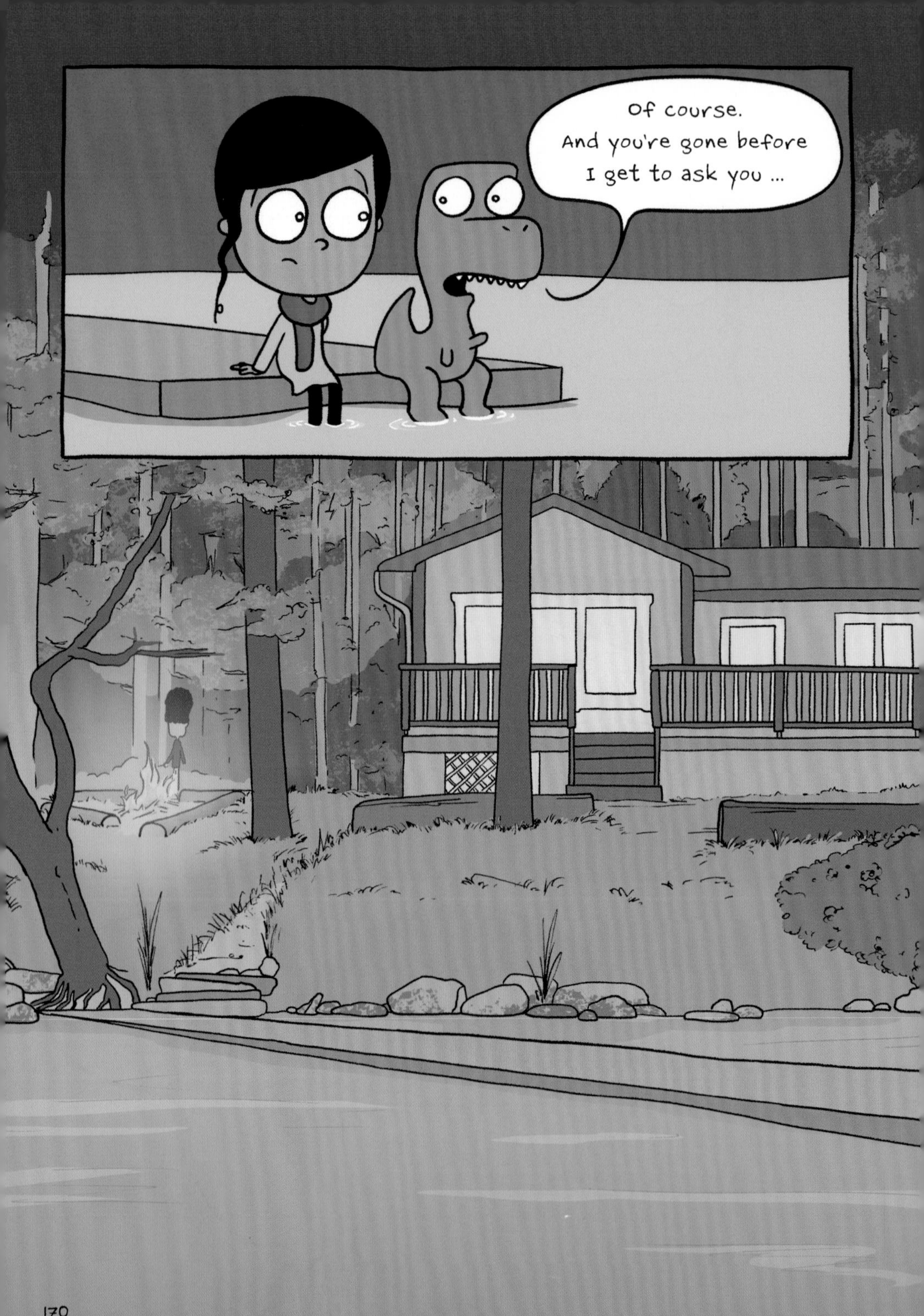
Of course.
And you're gone before
I get to ask you ...

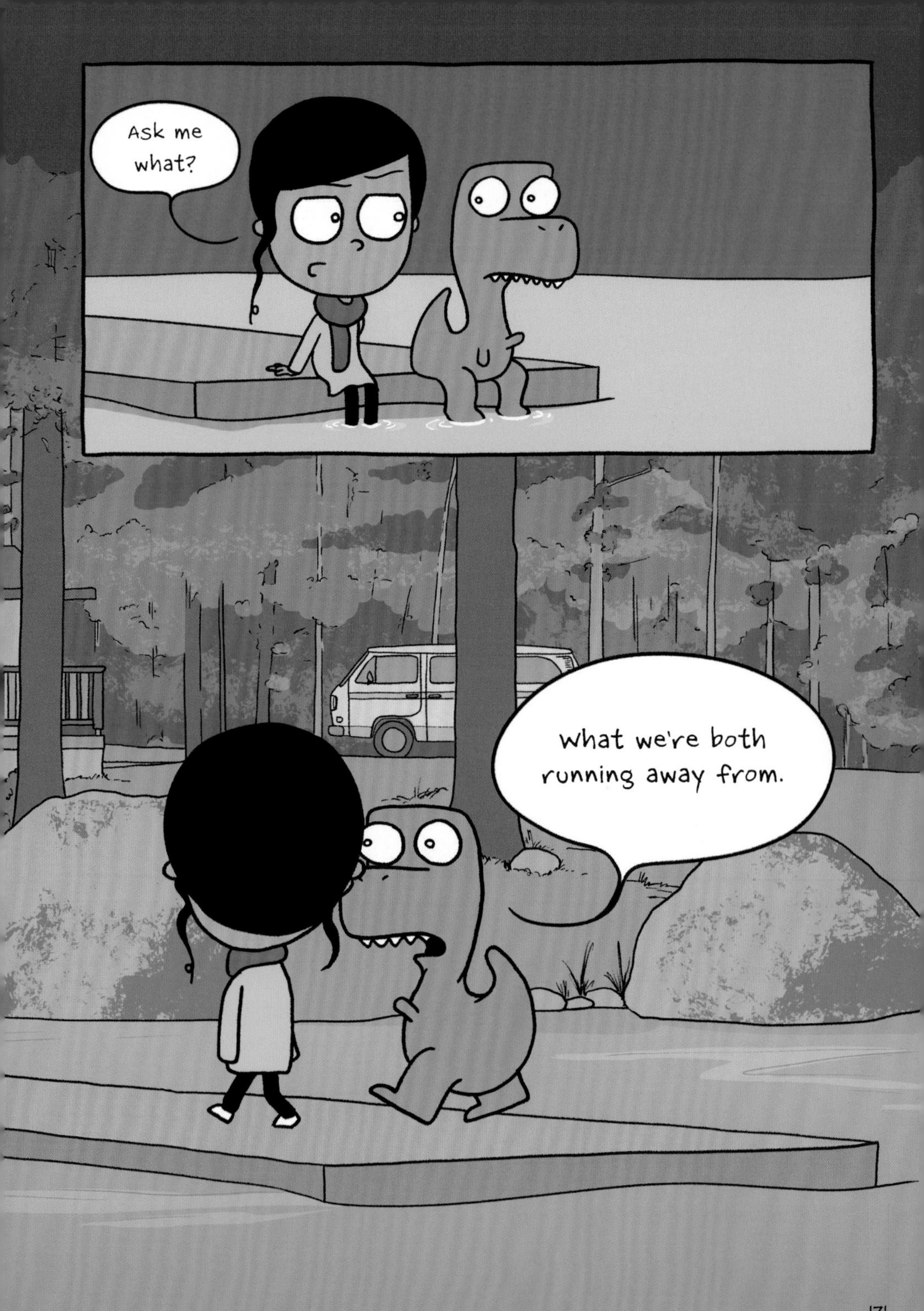
Ask me what?
what we're both running away from.

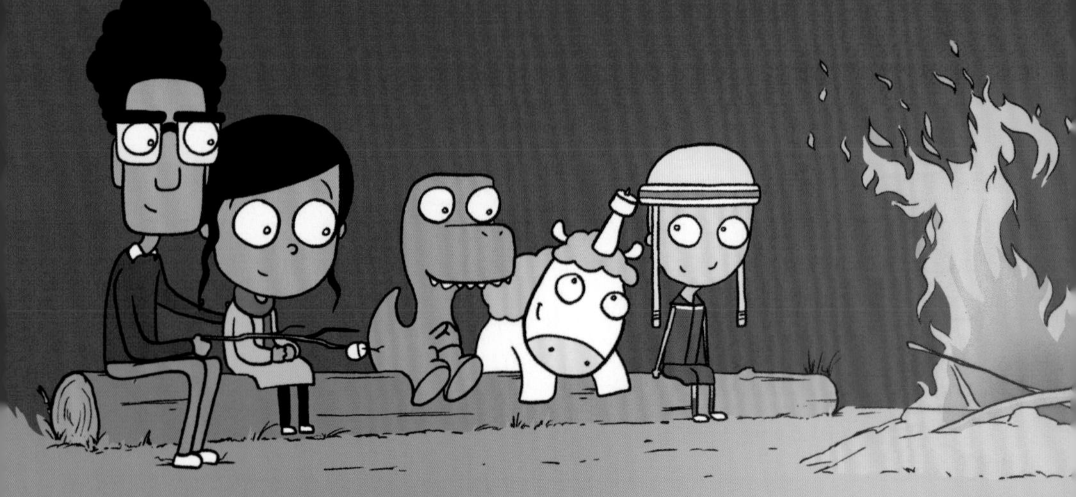

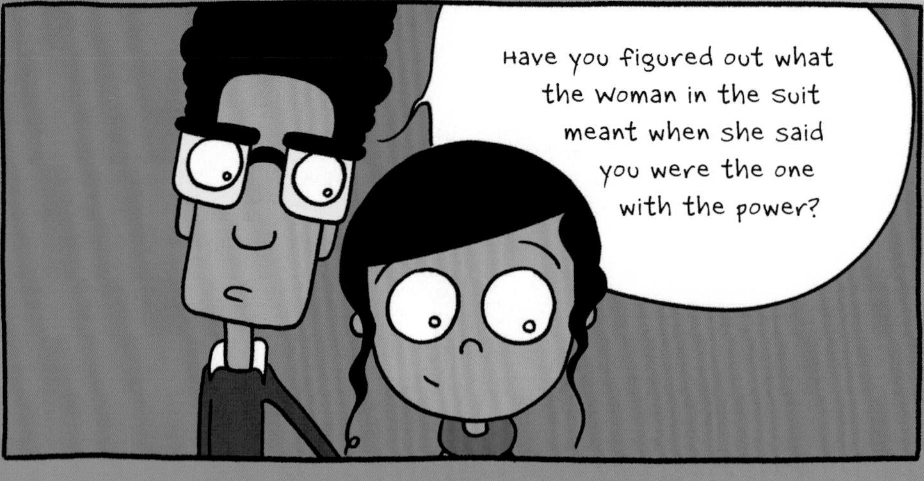
Have you figured out what the Woman in the suit meant when she said you were the one with the power?

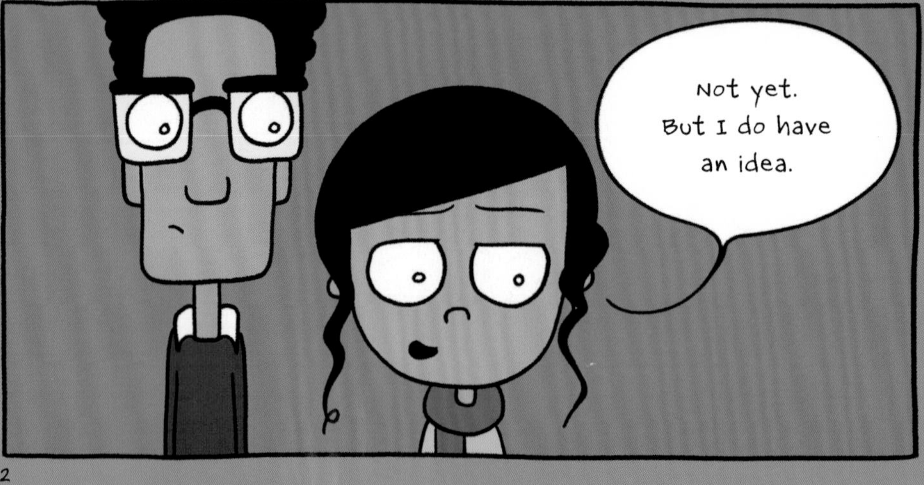
Not yet. But I do have an idea.

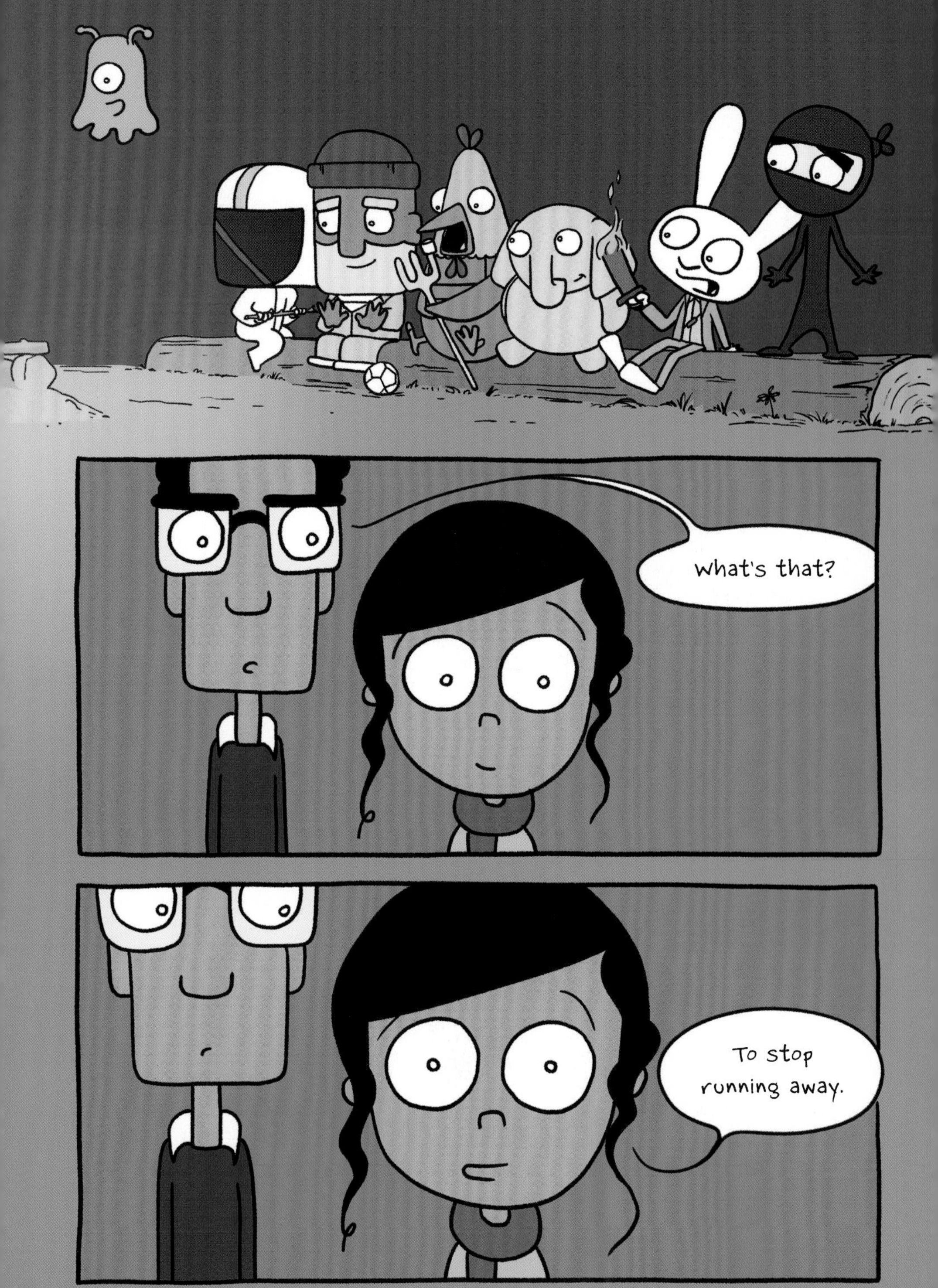
what's that?
To stop running away.

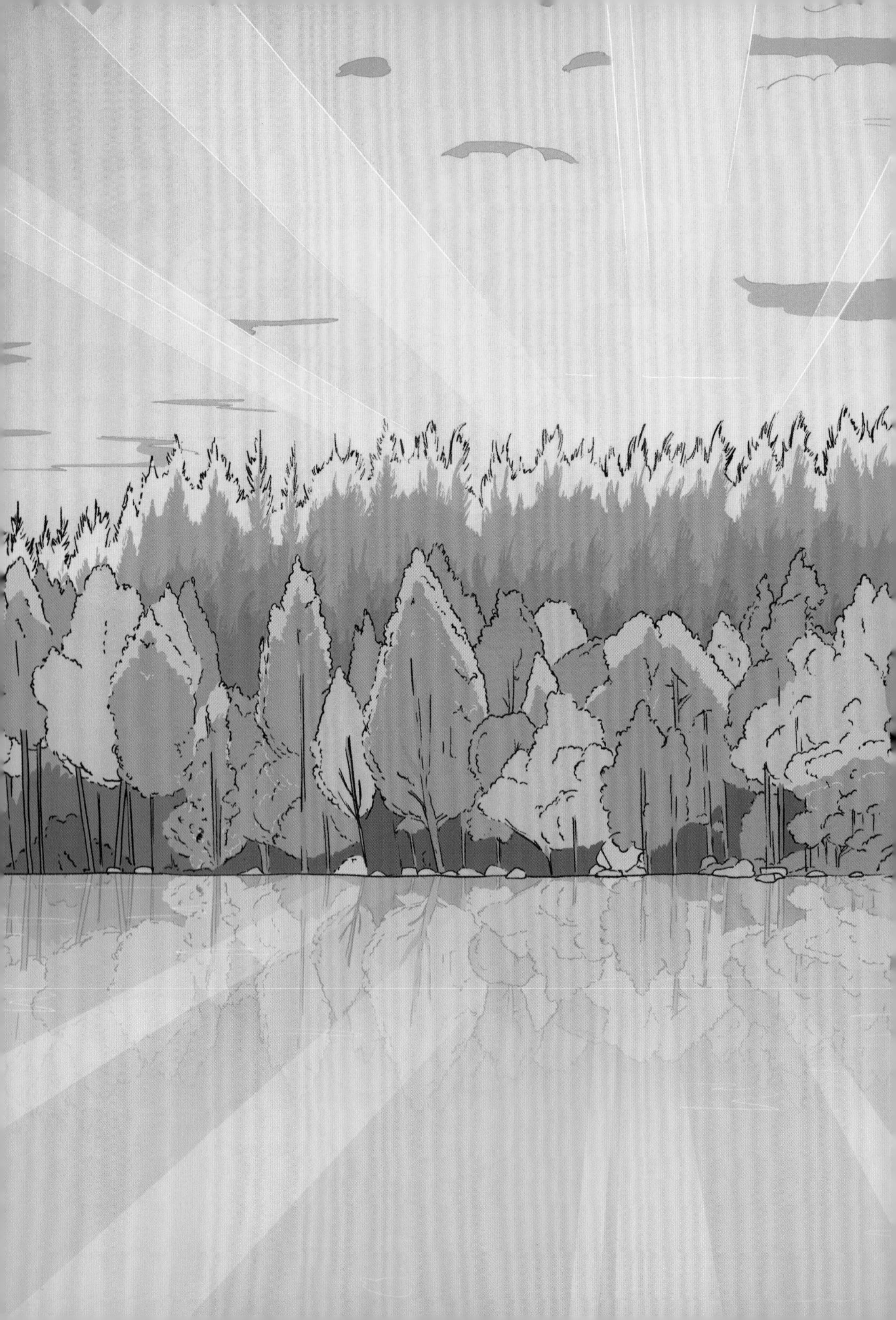

CHAPTER ELEVEN
An oddity of Odds

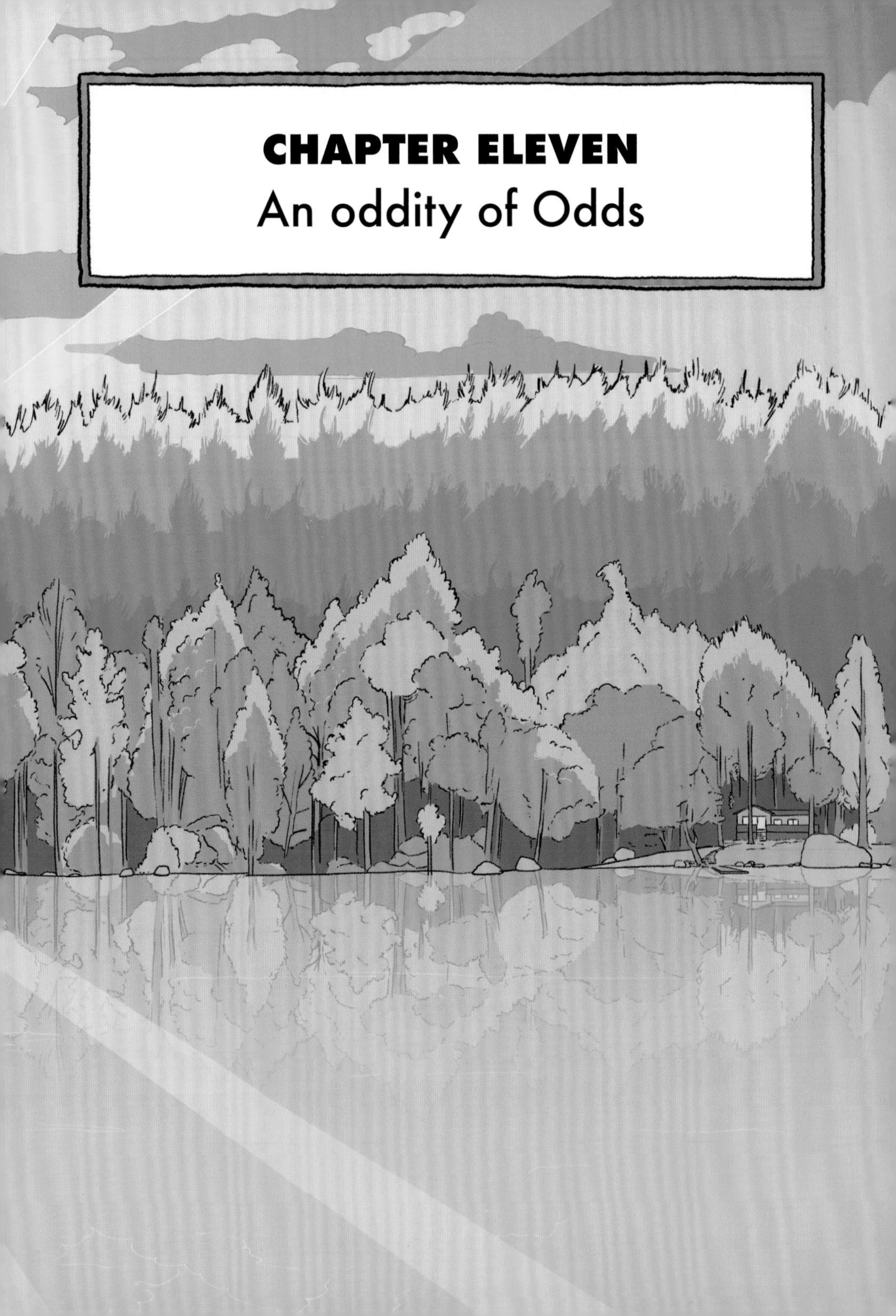

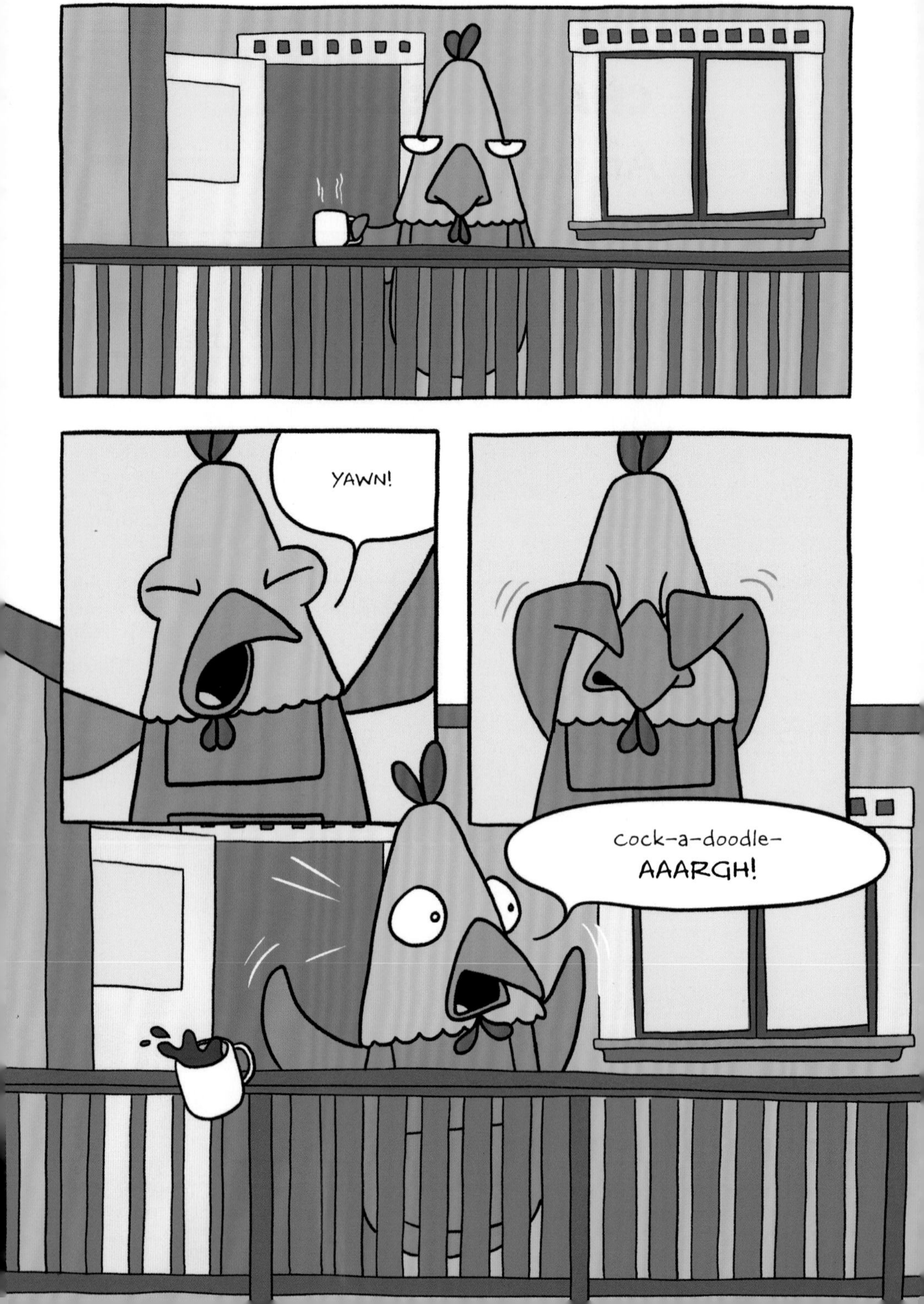
YAWN!
cock-a-doodle-
AAAARGH!

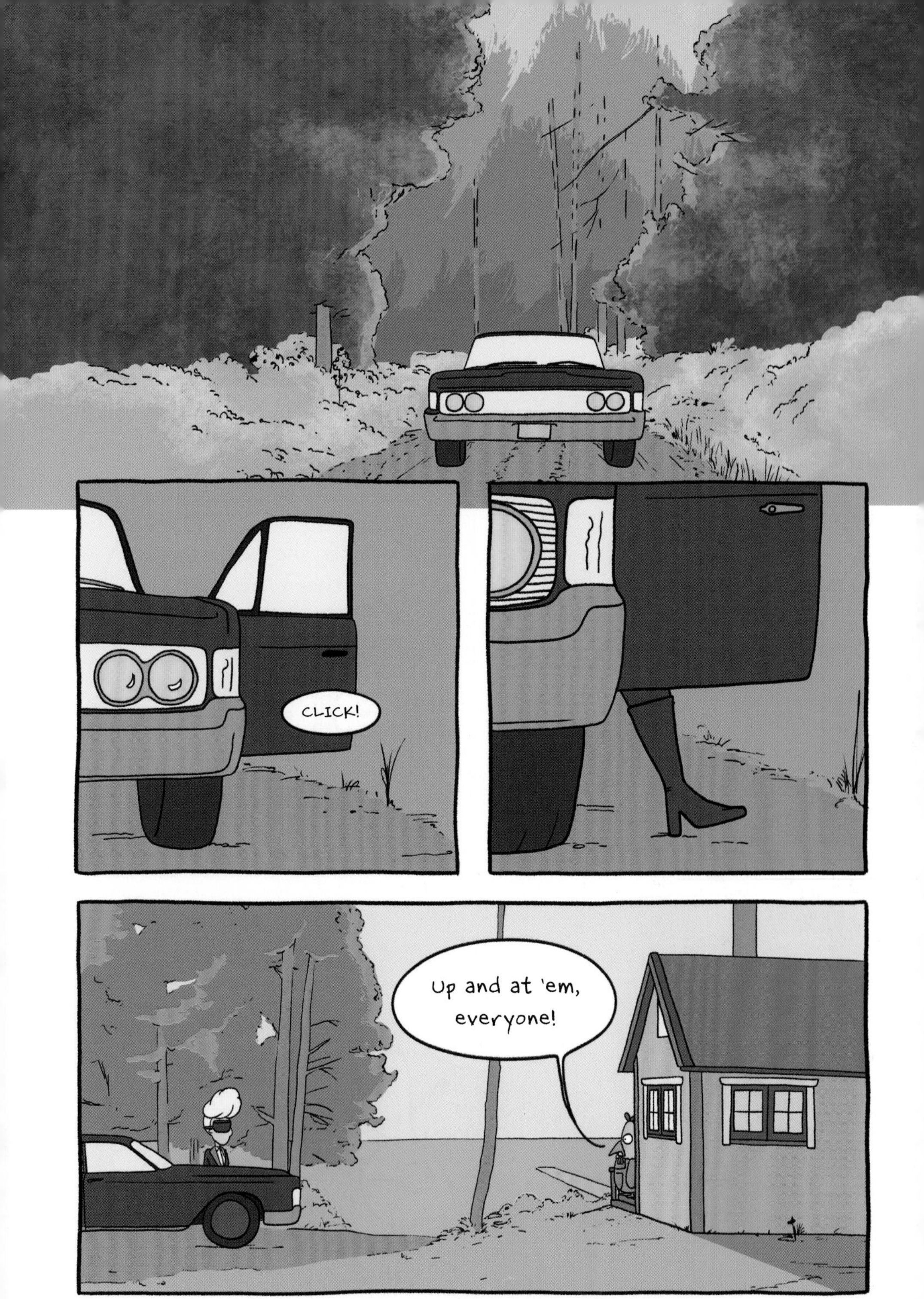
CLICK!
Up and at 'em, everyone!

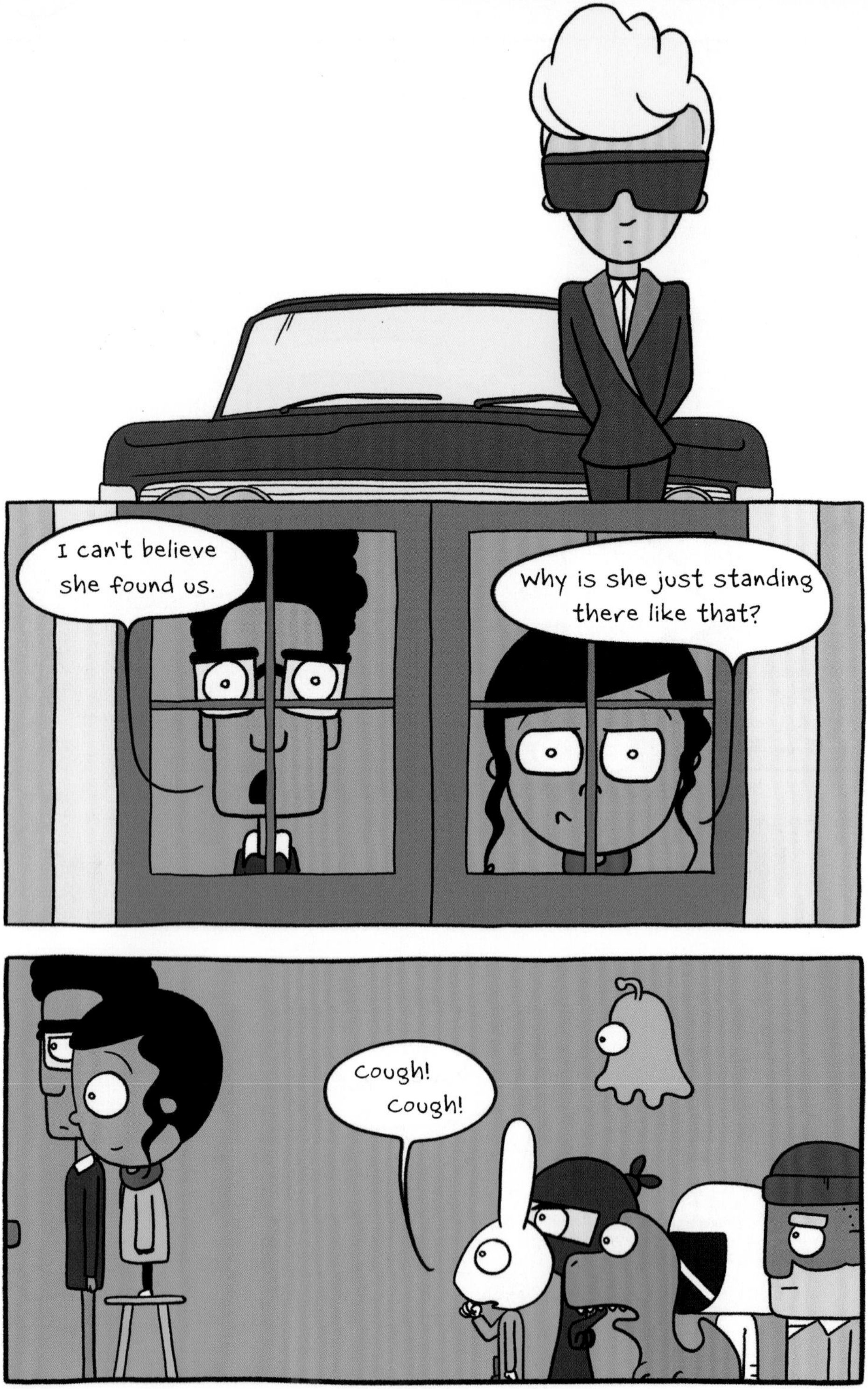
I can't believe she found us.
Why is she just standing there like that?
cough! cough!

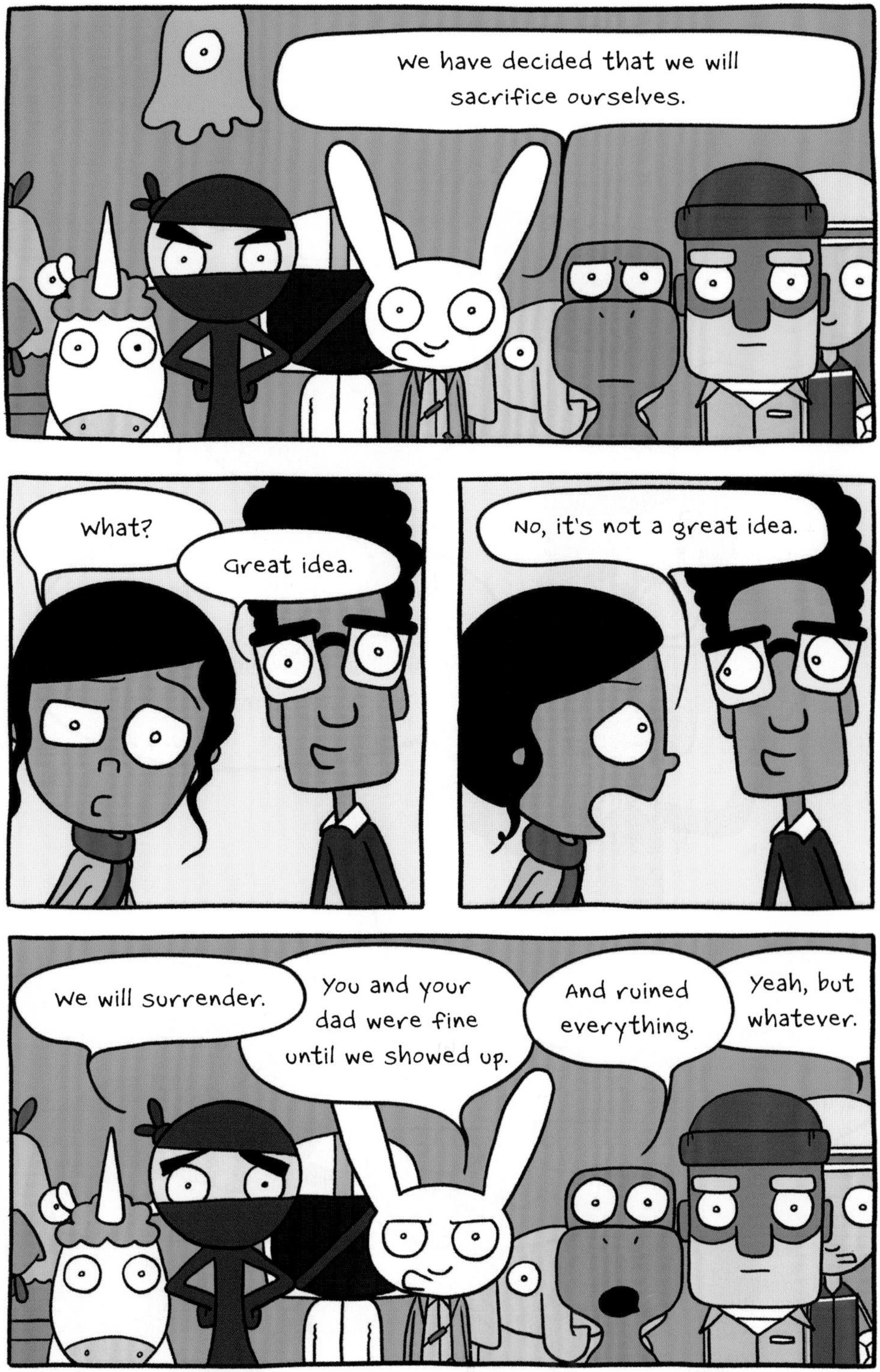
We have decided that we will sacrifice ourselves.
What?
Great idea.
No, it's not a great idea.
We will surrender.
You and your dad were fine until we showed up.
And ruined everything.
Yeah, but whatever.

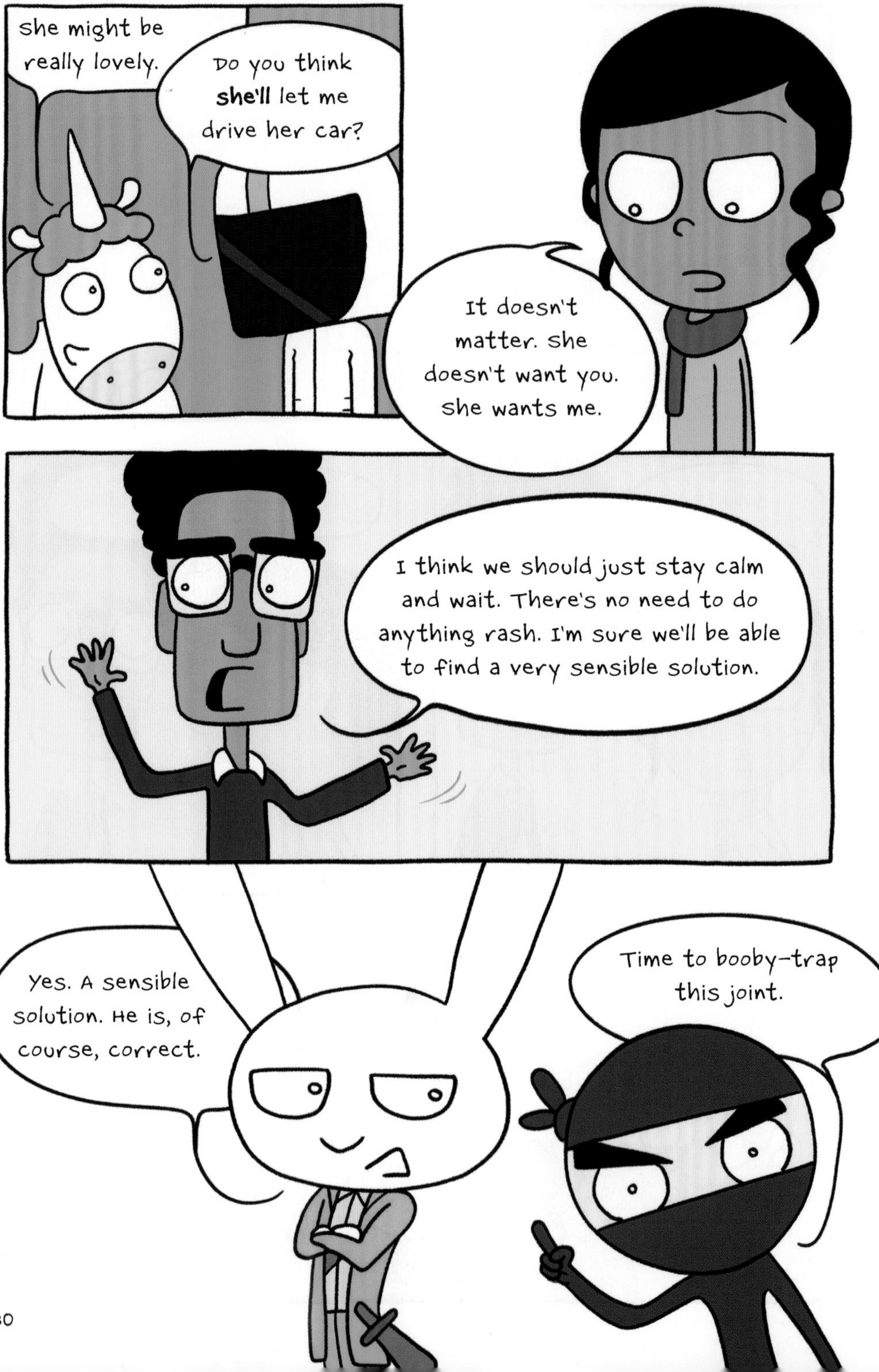

she might be really lovely.
Do you think **she'll** let me drive her car?
It doesn't matter. She doesn't want you. She wants me.
I think we should just stay calm and wait. There's no need to do anything rash. I'm sure we'll be able to find a very sensible solution.
Yes. A sensible solution. He is, of course, correct.
Time to booby-trap this joint.

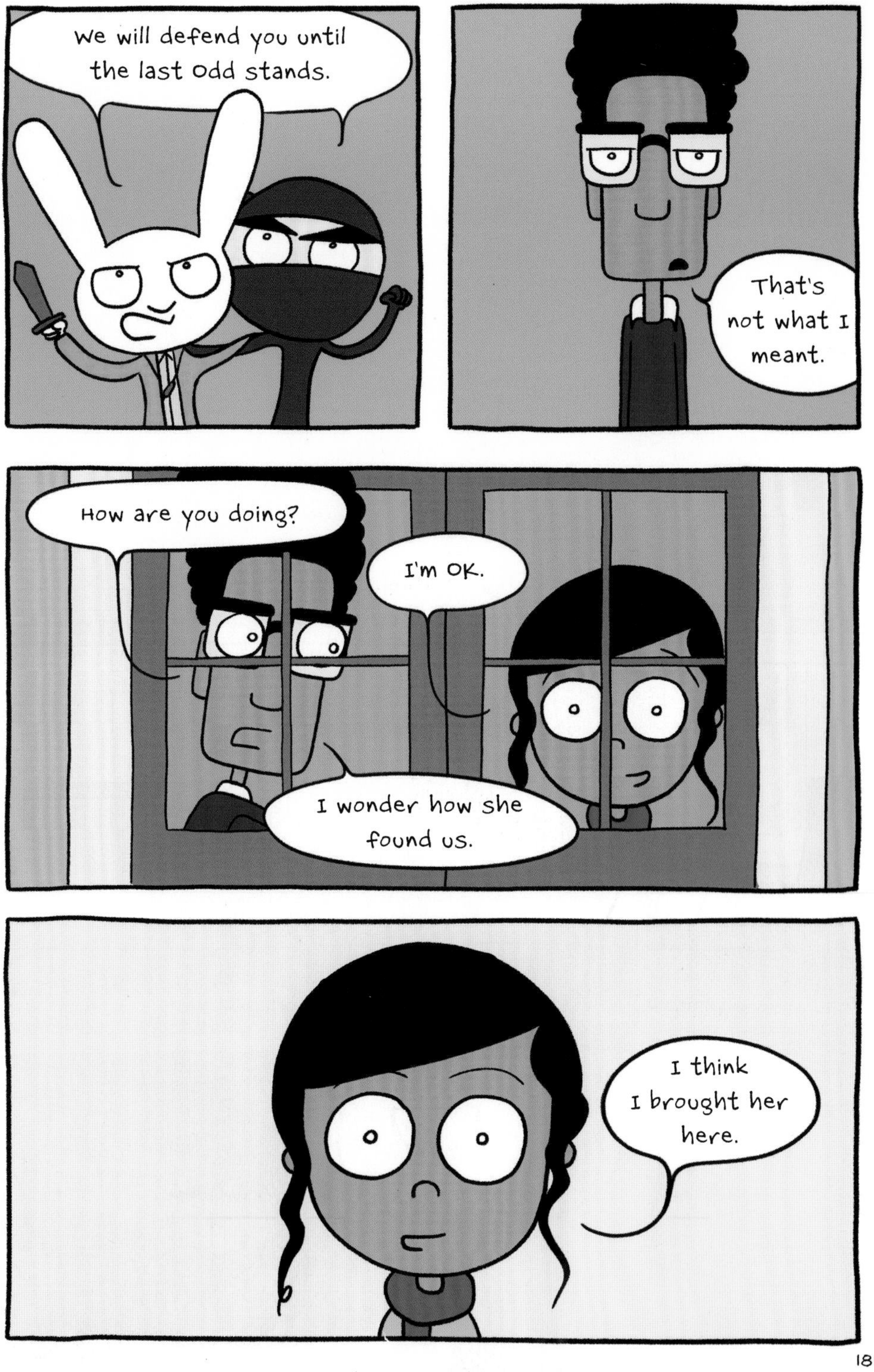
We will defend you until the last Odd stands.
That's not what I meant.
How are you doing?
I'm OK.
I wonder how she found us.
I think I brought her here.

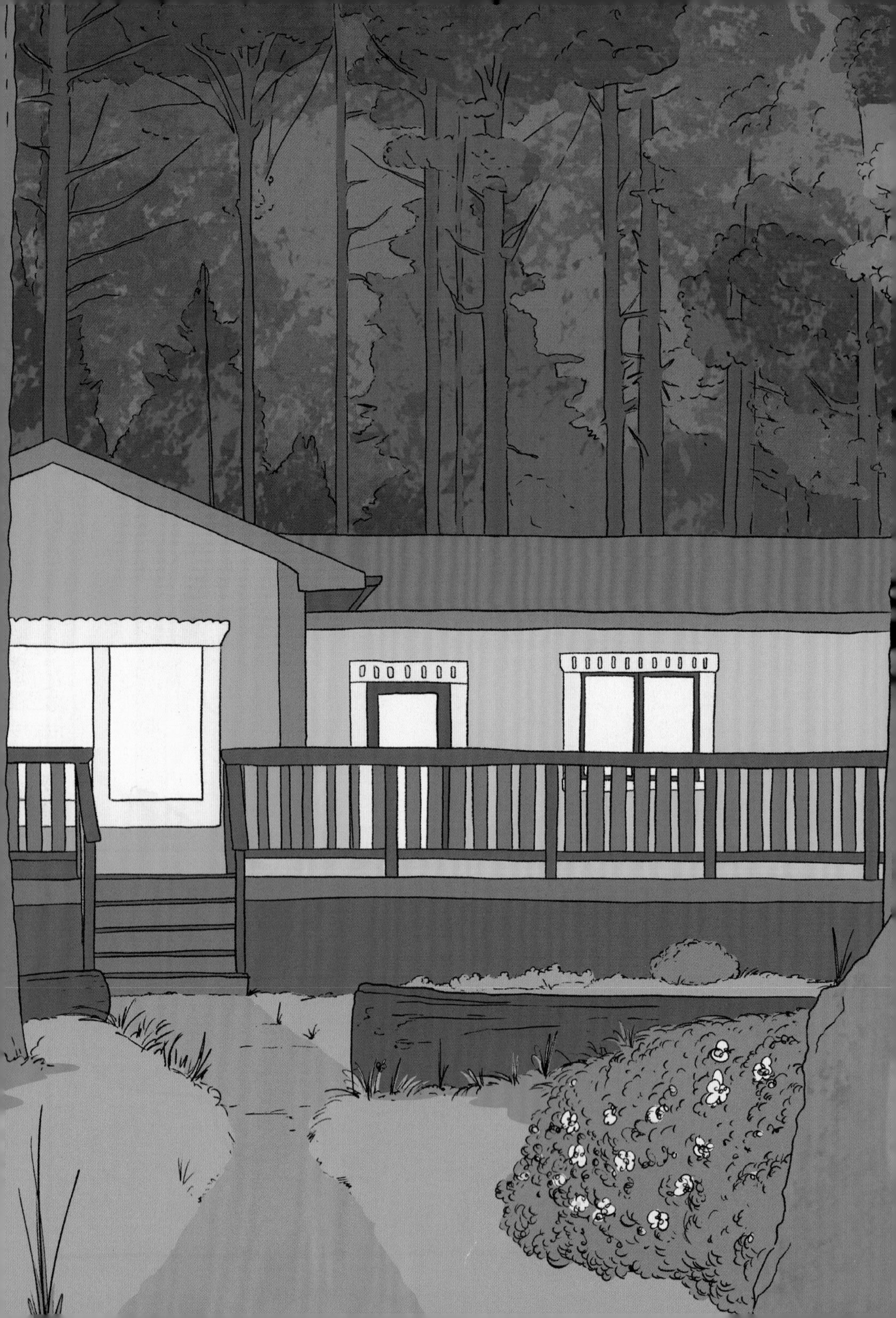

CHAPTER TWELVE
What are the odds?

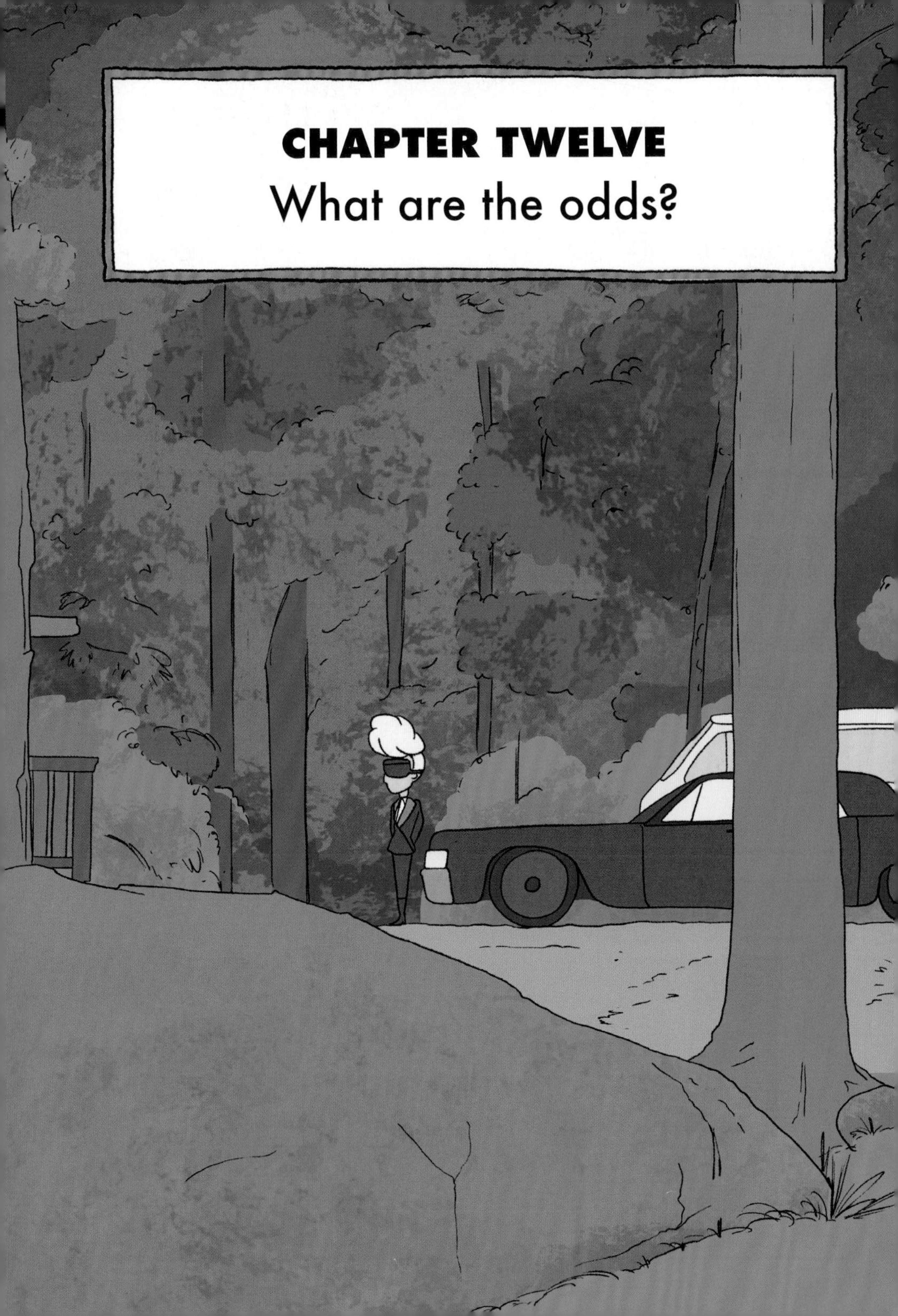

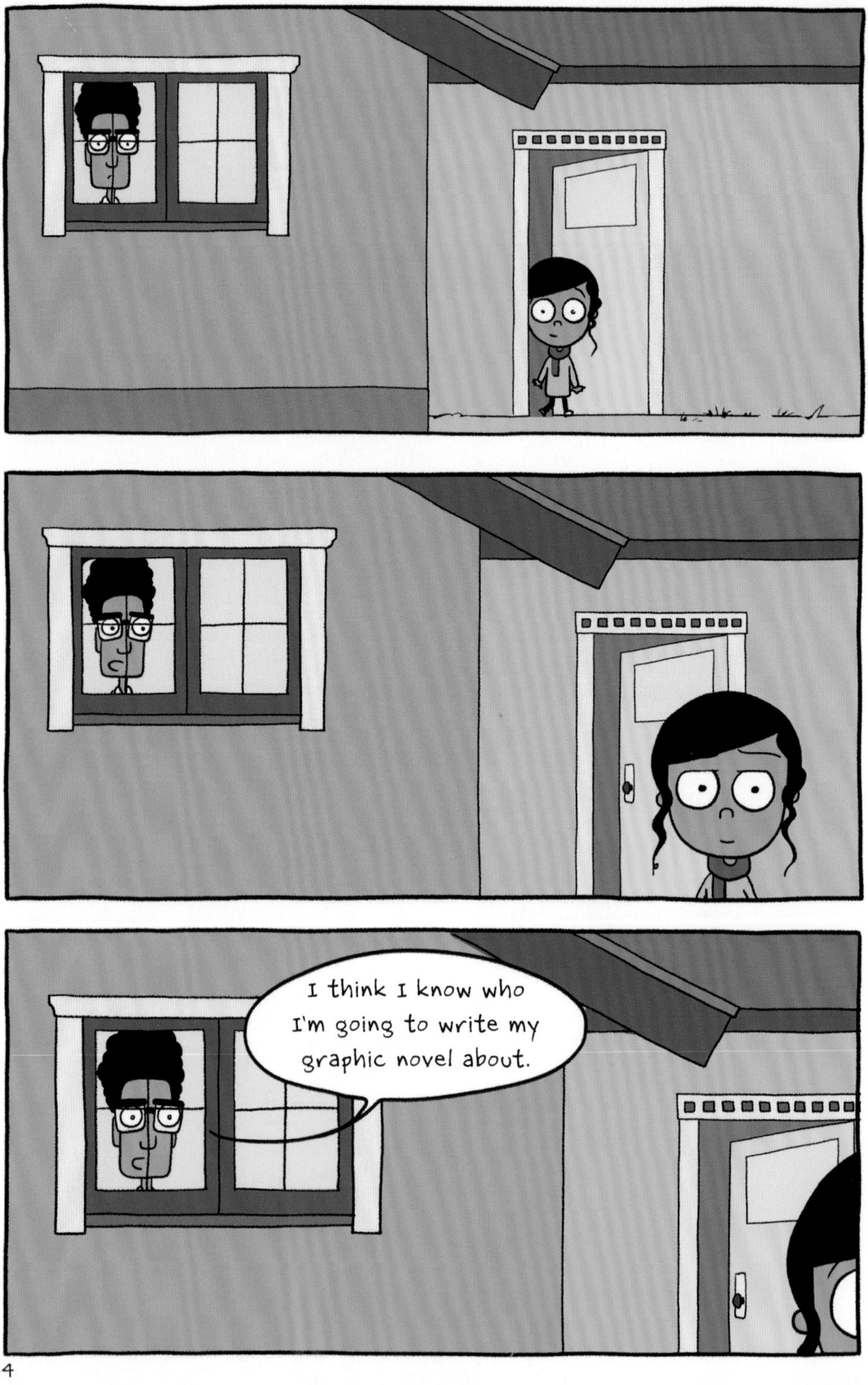
I think I know who I'm going to write my graphic novel about.

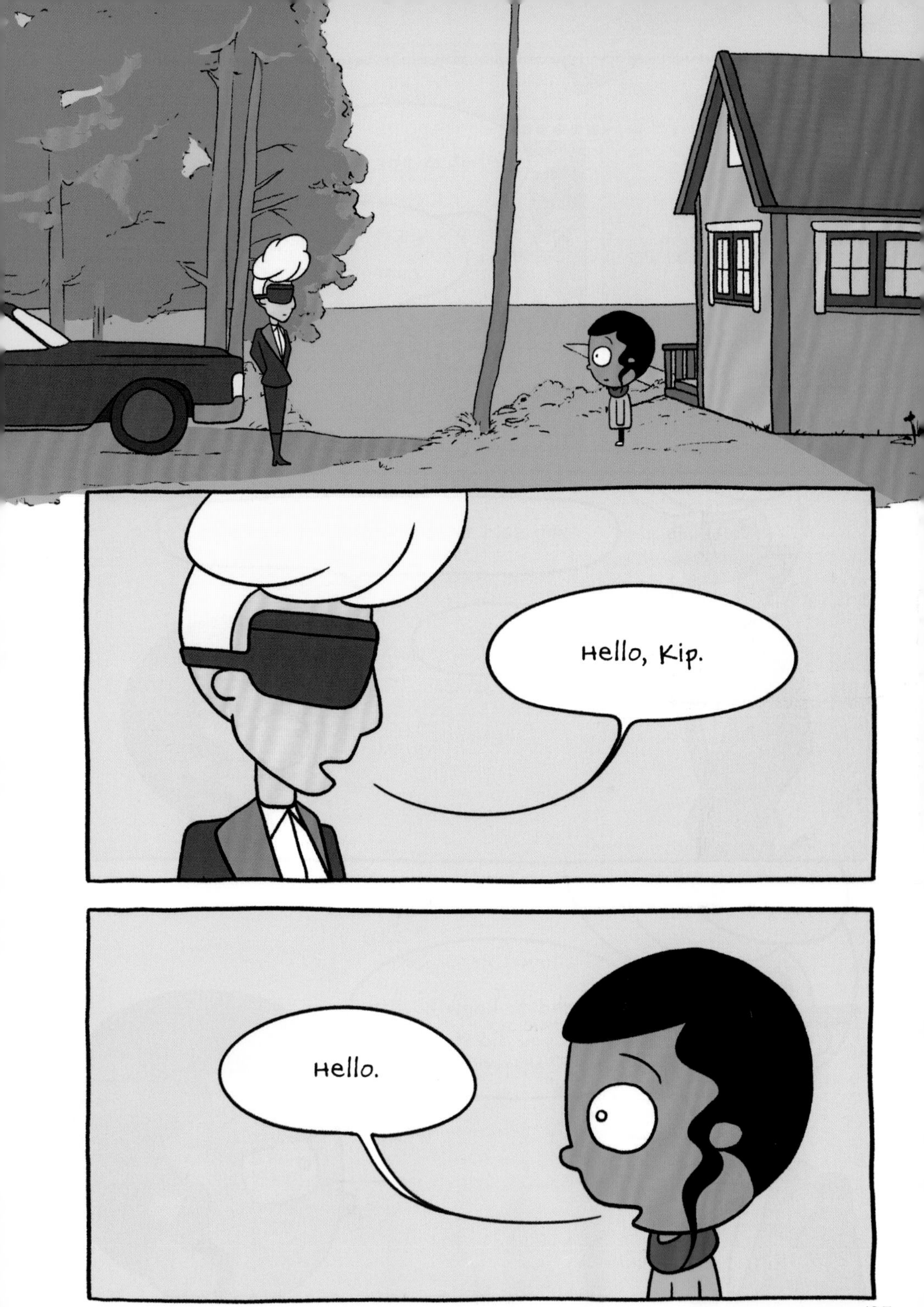
Hello, Kip.
Hello.

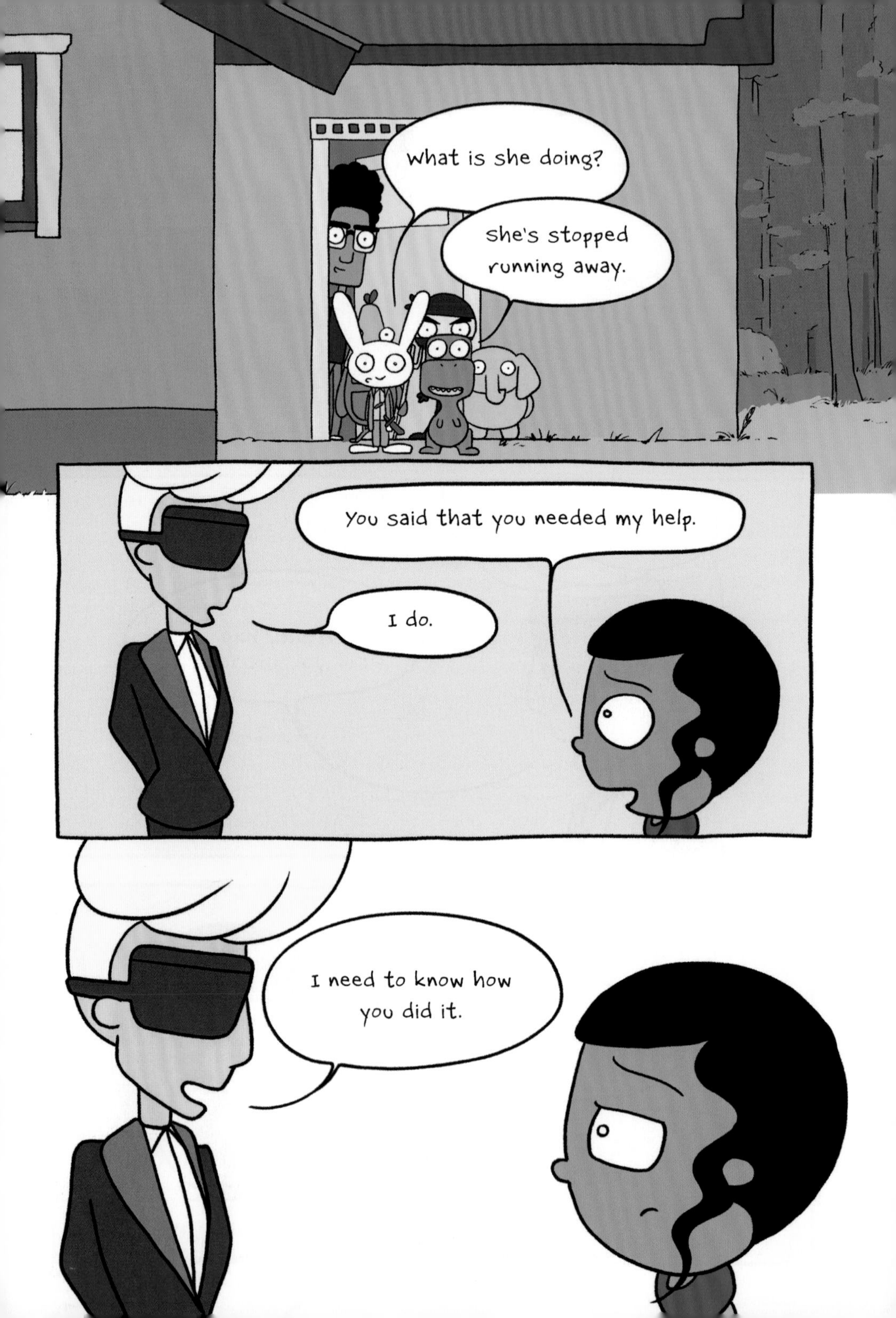
What is she doing?
she's stopped running away.
You said that you needed my help.
I do.
I need to know how you did it.

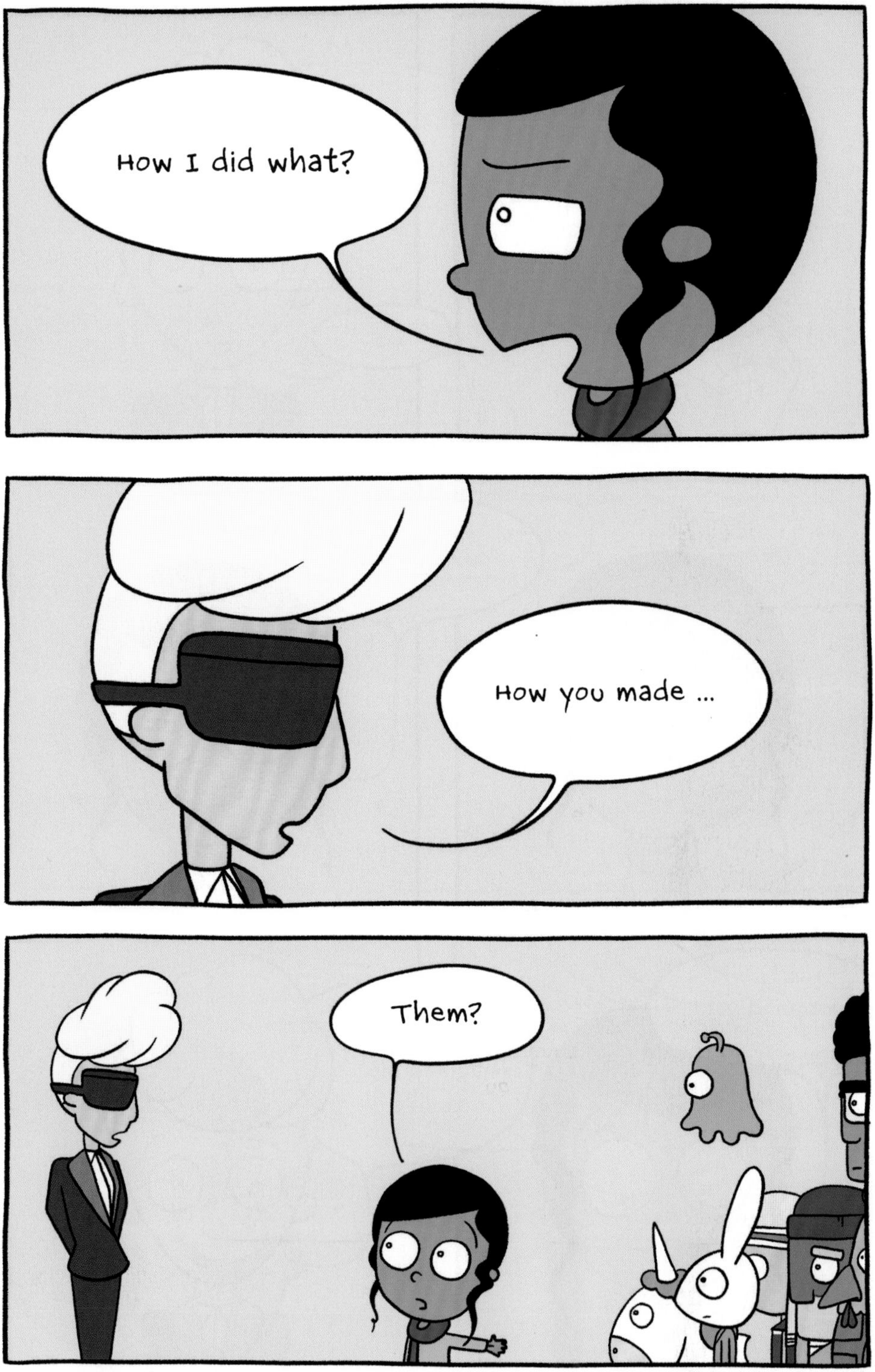
How I did what?
How you made ...
Them?

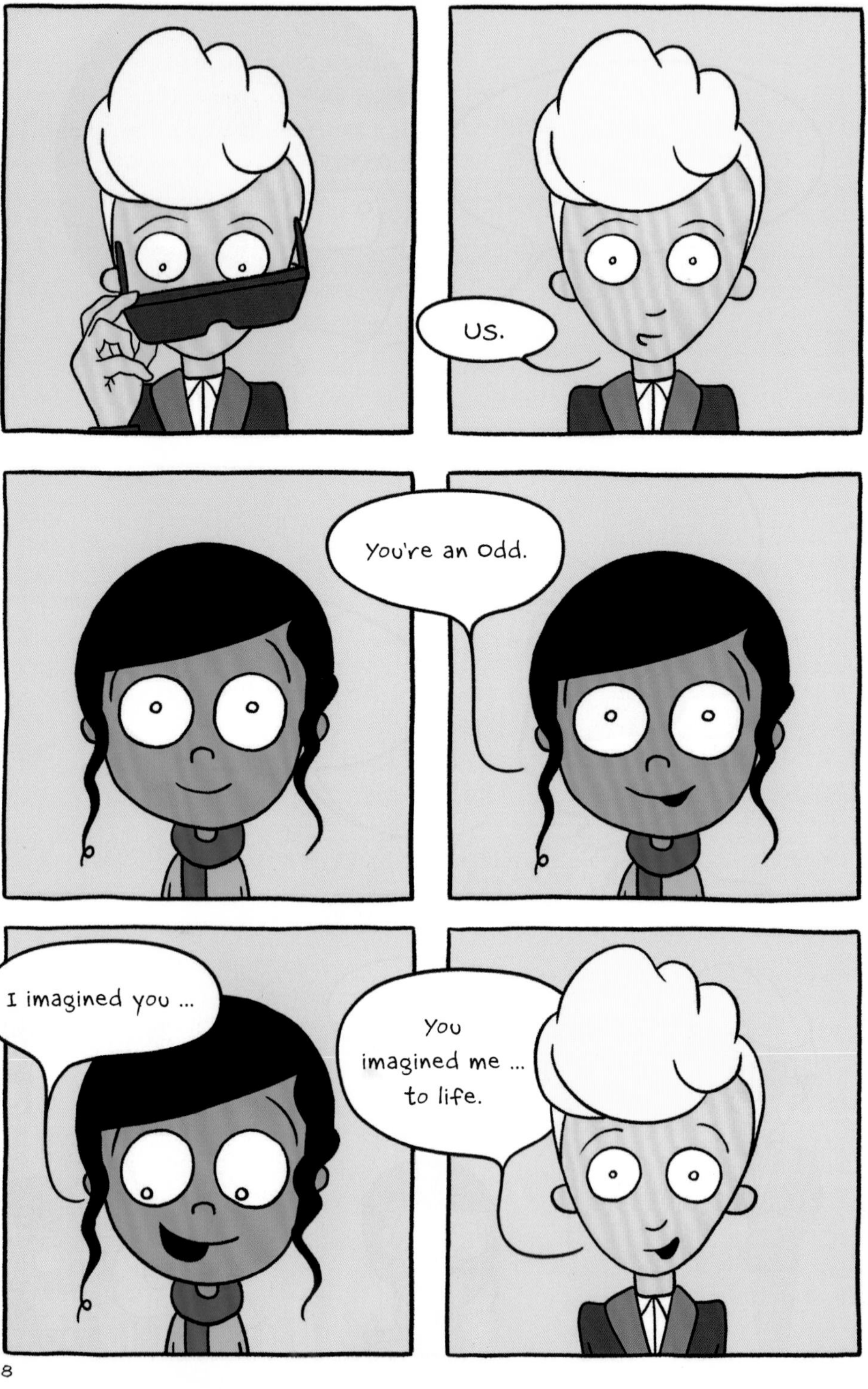
US.
You're an Odd.
I imagined you ...
You imagined me ... to life.

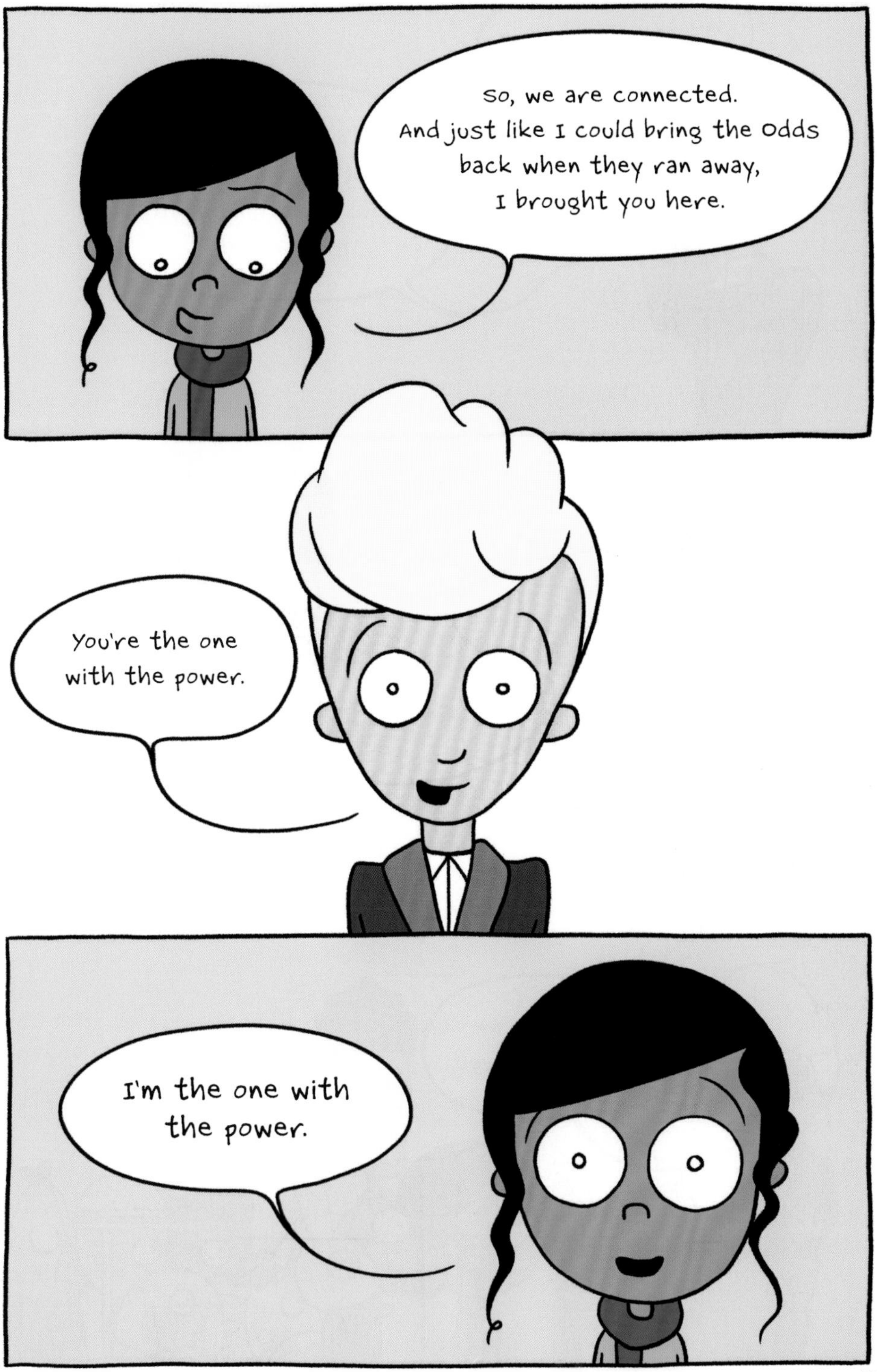
So, we are connected. And just like I could bring the Odds back when they ran away, I brought you here.
You're the one with the power.
I'm the one with the power.

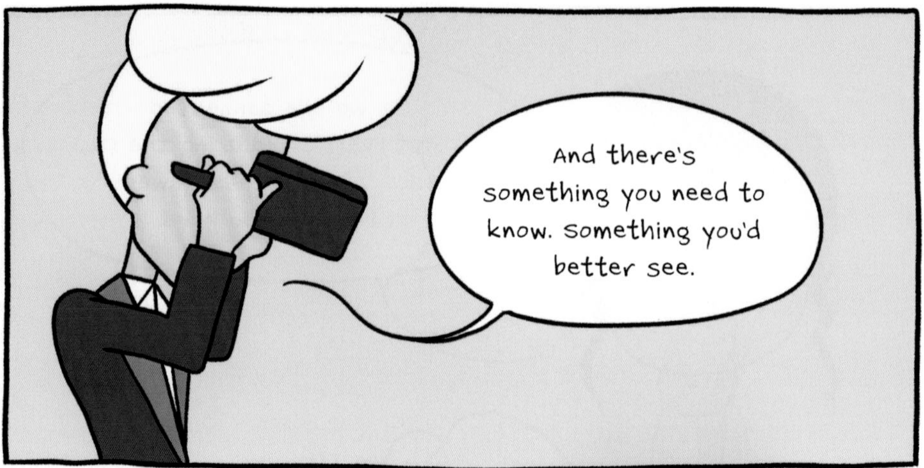
And there's something you need to know. Something you'd better see.

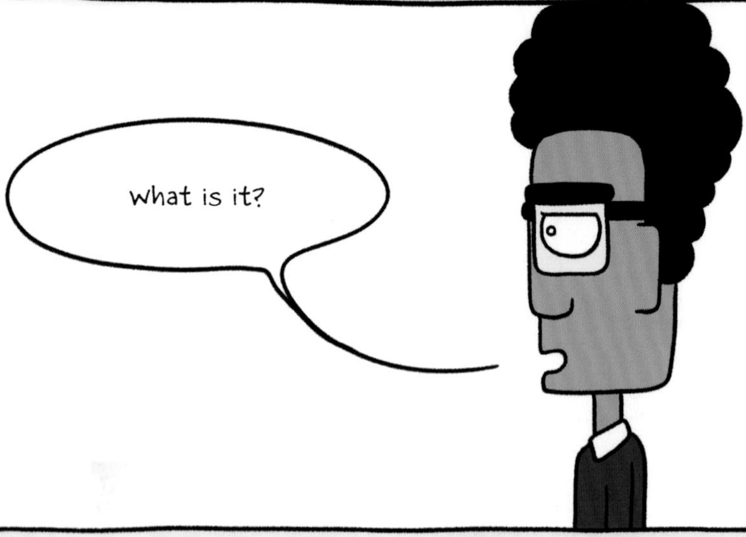
What is it?

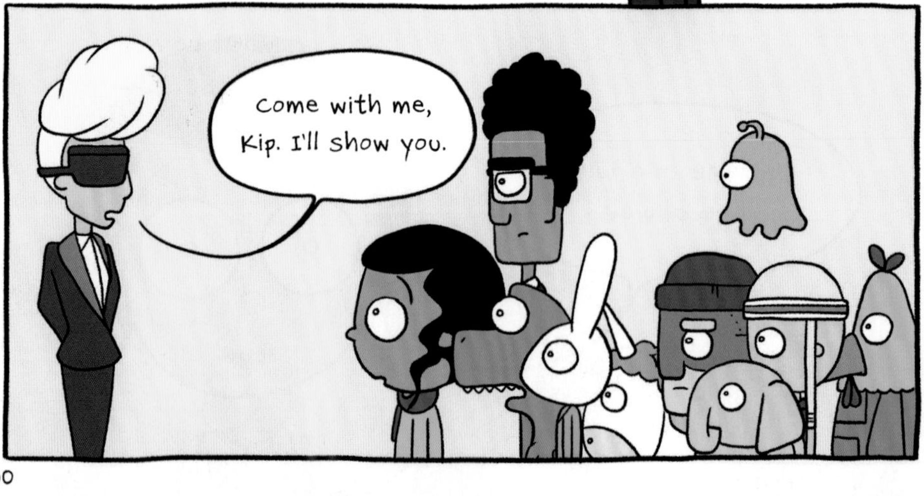
Come with me, Kip. I'll show you.

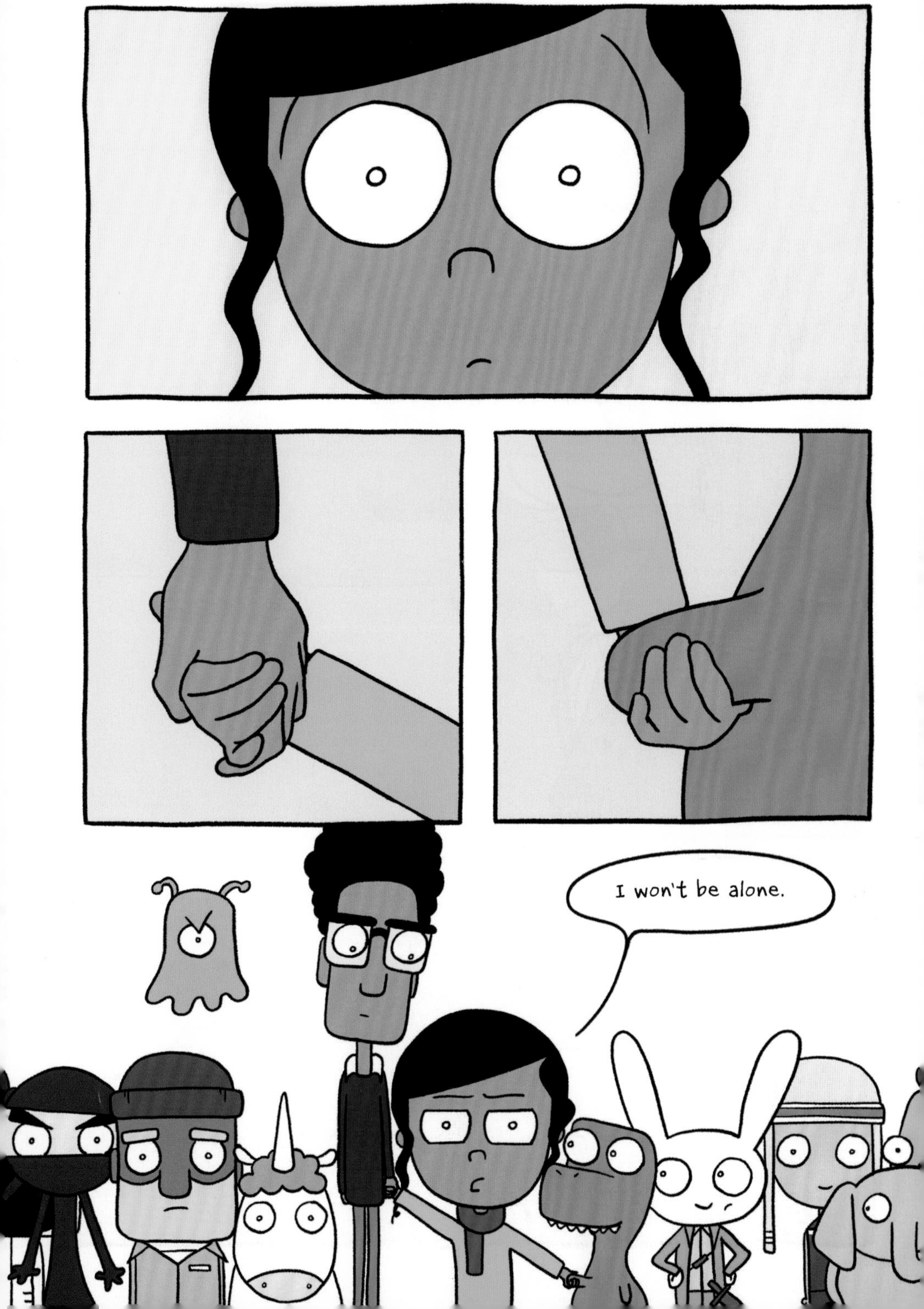
I won't be alone.

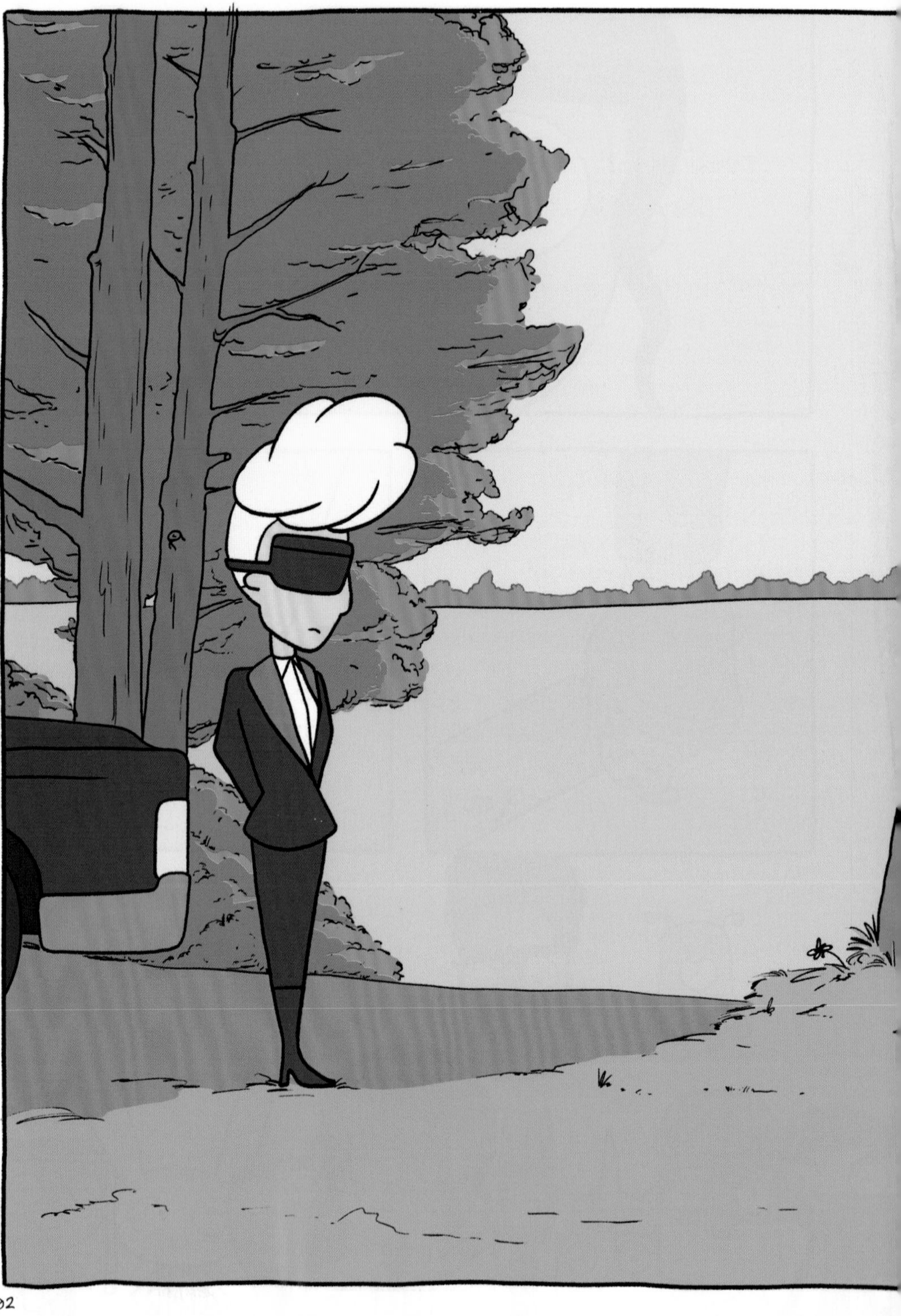

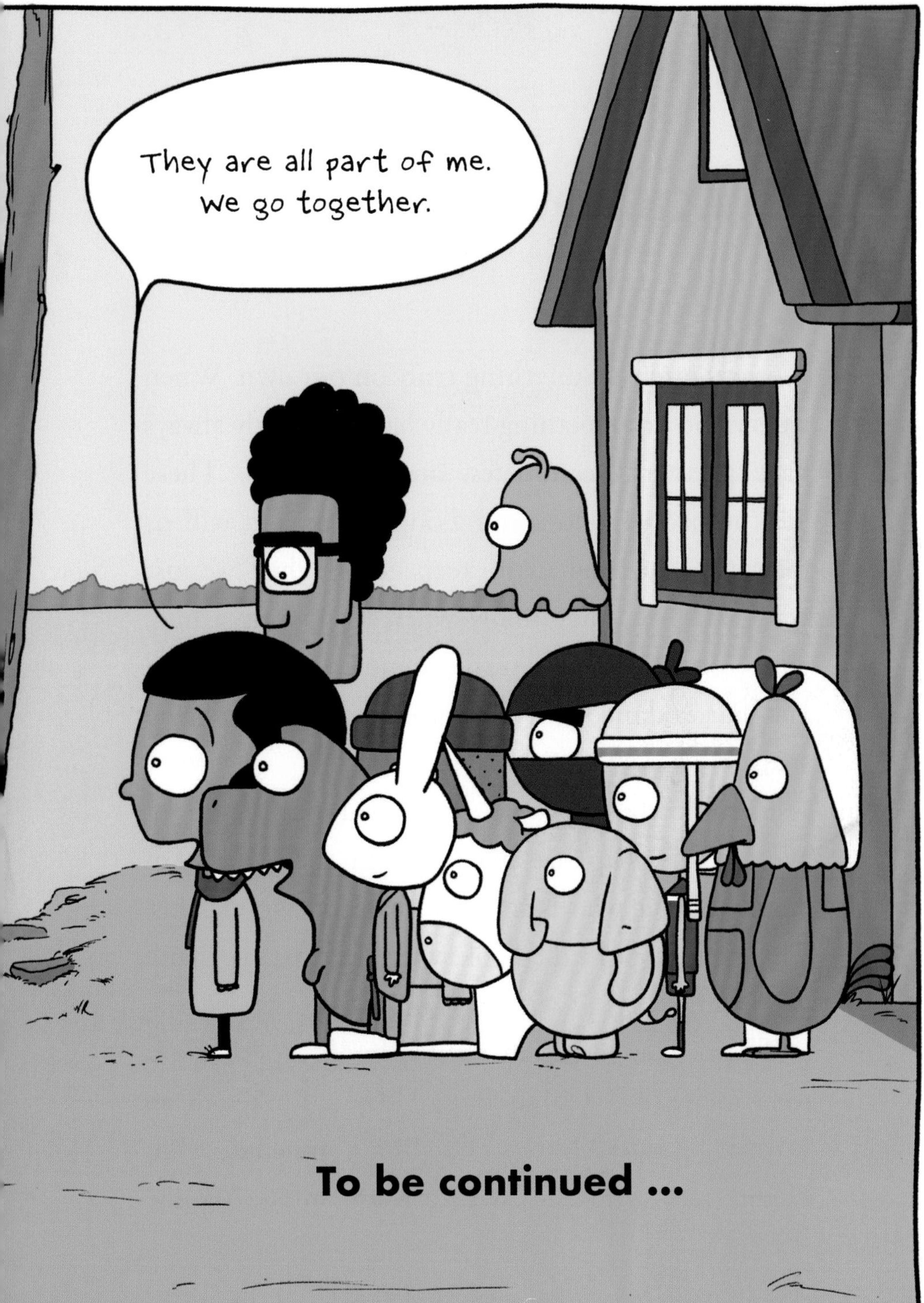
They are all part of me. We go together.
To be continued ...

ACKNOWLEDGMENTS

We very rarely do anything truly on our own. When we try and do something really hard we nearly always have partners, teammates, and supporters. These are the people who stand alongside us and will us forward. They tell us to keep going when we just want to stop. They know when to give us a hug, pat us on the back, or turn the music up really loud and start a dance party. Sometimes they even bring snacks.

I think these people are called our Team of Wonderfuls. Kip has her dad and the Odds. I'm curious about who is in your Team of Wonderfuls. This is the spot in the book where I get to say thank you to mine.

Thank you to the incredible book experts I get to work with – Chren Byng, David Linker, Kate Burnitt, Angie Masters, Cristina Cappelluto, Jim Demetriou, Michelle Weisz, Kady Gray, Yvonne

Sewankambo, Jemma Myors, Rachel Cramp, Kelli Lonergan, Fiona Luke, Janelle Garside, Amy Fox, Karen-Maree Griffiths, Pauline O'Carolan, Elizabeth O'Donnell, Brendon Redmond, Emily Mannon, Anna Bernard, Andrea Vandergrift, and Carolina Ortiz.

Thank you to all the people who work at the printers, drive the trucks, and unload the boxes. Thank you to those who work in bookshops and libraries, putting these books onto shelves and helping kids find them. Thank you to the teachers who read my stories in class and light a spark in young imaginations every day.

As always, a special thanks to Chren Byng. You have been with me every step and there's a part of you in each of my stories. I wouldn't want it any other way.

Thank you to Natalie Buckley-Cartwright for the hours you have poured into making *Run, Odds, Run* come to life.

Thank you to Beck Stanton – my love and all-of-life partner. I could write a hundred books marveling at who you are. Thank you to my favorite kids in all the world – Bonnie, Boston, Miller, and Sully. This book is for you.

I still can't believe it, but in my Team of Wonderfuls I also have thousands and thousands of kids who take the time out of their busy lives to send me emails. These are children from all around the world, most of whom I will never get to actually meet. But still, you send me encouraging letters and tell me how these stories have traveled from my imagination, through a book, and into your imagination. That means we have connected and that's such an honor for me. You tell me that the stories mean something to you, and that is the most inspiring thing of all.

Thank you for being in my Team of Wonderfuls. I really couldn't do hard things without you all.

Matt Stanton

**Kids all over the world
are emailing Matt!**

**Who's your favorite Odd?
Tell Matt!**

matt.stanton@gmail.com

Also available ...

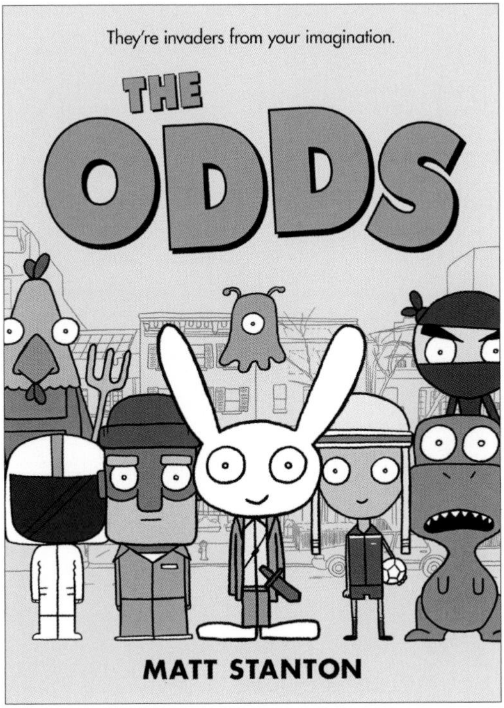

They're invaders from your imagination.
THE ODDS
MATT STANTON

Kip is a quiet kid in a loud city. She's easy to miss and that's the way she likes it.

Then, one day, Kip's life is interrupted when ten of her favorite characters step out of their worlds and into hers.

Meet the Odds ... because fitting in is overrated.

Look out for the incredible conclusion
to THE ODDS TRILOGY

Books by Matt Stanton

Funny Kid series

Funny Kid for President

Funny Kid Stand Up

Funny Kid Prank Wars

The Odds series

The Odds

The Odds: Run, Odds, Run

funny kid

You've read them all, right?

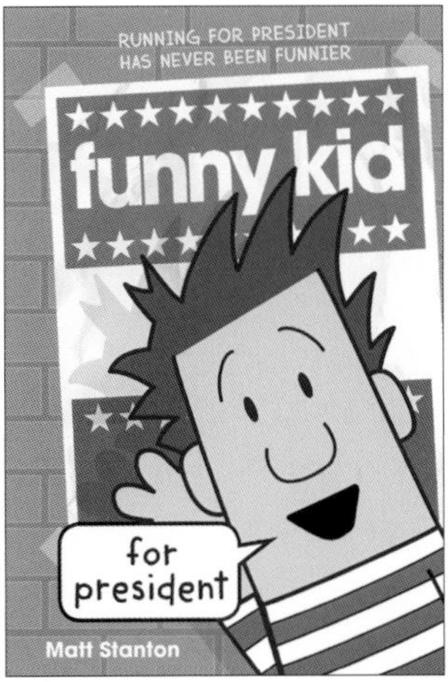
RUNNING FOR PRESIDENT
HAS NEVER BEEN FUNNIER
funny kid
for president
Matt Stanton

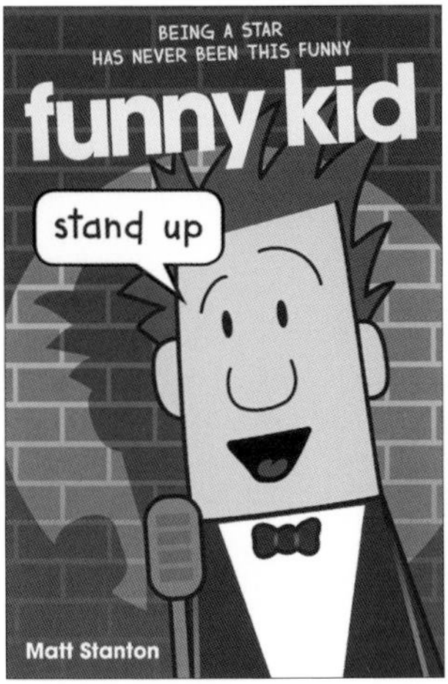
BEING A STAR
HAS NEVER BEEN THIS FUNNY
funny kid
stand up
Matt Stanton

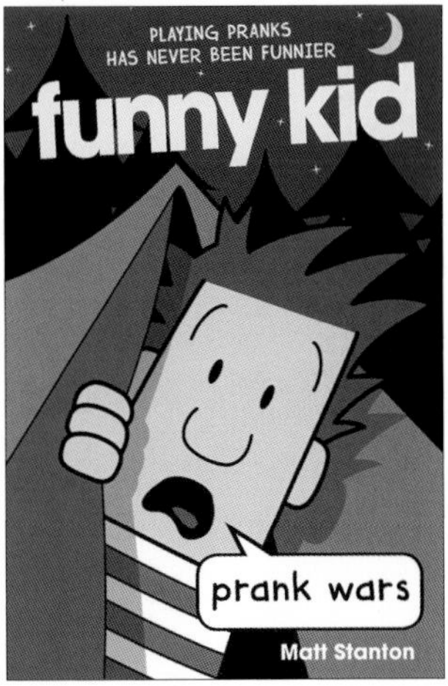
PLAYING PRANKS
HAS NEVER BEEN FUNNIER
funny kid
prank wars
Matt Stanton

Matt Stanton is a bestselling children's author and illustrator who has sold more than one million books worldwide. His middle grade series Funny Kid debuted as the #1 Australian kids' book and has legions of fans across the globe. He has published such bestselling picture books as *There Is a Monster Under My Bed Who Farts*, *This Is a Ball*, and *Pea + Nut!*, and he produces a daily YouTube show for kids. He lives and works in Sydney, Australia, with his wife, bestselling author Beck Stanton, and their children.

mattstanton.net

Come and subscribe to Matt's YouTube Channel!

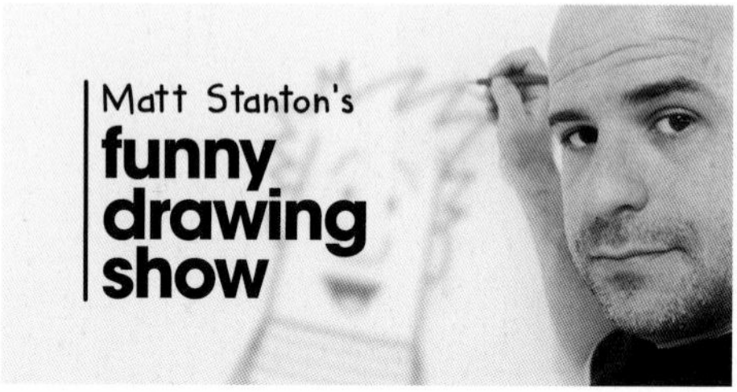
Matt Stanton's
funny drawing show

We learn to draw funny stuff!

Talk about how to write funny stories!

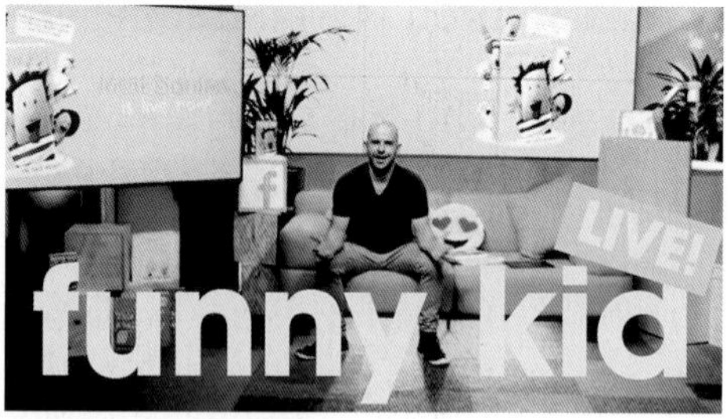
LIVE!
funny kid

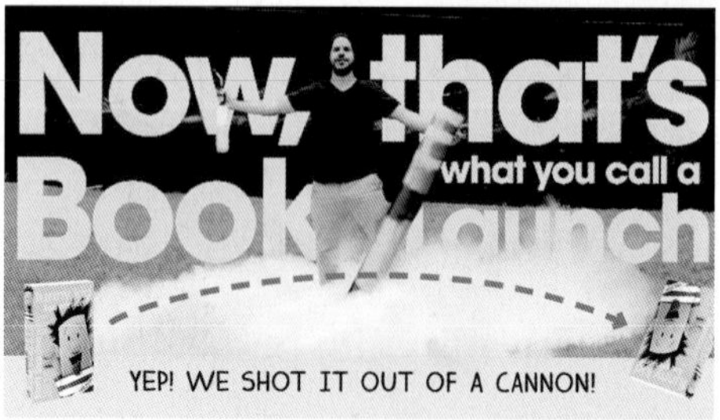
Now, that's Book Launch
what you call a
YEP! WE SHOT IT OUT OF A CANNON!

And sometimes we launch a book out of a cannon!

MattStantonTV

youtube.com/mattstanton